Finding Fa
the Rugged
Mountain Man's
Embrace

STAND-ALONE NOVEL

A Western Historical Romance Book

by

Sally M. Ross

Disclaimer & Copyright

Table of Contents

Letter from Sally M. Ross

"There are two kinds of people in the world those with guns and those that dig."

This iconic sentence from the *"Good the Bad and the Ugly"* was meant to change my life once and for all. I chose to be the one to hold the gun and, in my case...the pen!

I started writing as soon as I learned the alphabet. At first, it was some little fairytales, but I knew that this undimmed passion was my life's purpose.

I share the same love with my husband for the classic western movies, and we moved together to Texas to leave the dream on our little farm with Daisy, our lovely lab.

I'm a literary junkie reading everything that comes into my hands, with a bit of weakness on heartwarming romances and poetry.

If you choose to follow me on this journey, I can guarantee you characters that you would love to befriend, romances that will make your heart beat faster, and wholesome, genuine stories that will make you dream again!

Until next time,

Sally M. Ross

Prologue

Brooklyn, New York, Spring 1898

Thirty-year-old Emily McCoy closed the door to her classroom before she turned and walked down the hallway toward the stairs. As she walked, Emily was aware of the clap of her boots against the wooden floors. She descended the narrow staircase and stepped onto the ground floor landing. Emily paused for a moment. The school was silent, save for the cooing of the pigeons who had taken up residence in the steeply pitched roof of Briarwood House.

"Miss McCoy?"

Emily turned to find Camilla Lockhart, the school's headmistress, sitting at her desk. The door to her office was standing wide open.

"Have you got a minute?" she asked.

Emily nodded as she quickly reached up and smoothed her honey-blonde hair back. She walked across the entrance hall and into Headmistress Lockhart's office.

Even sitting behind her desk, it was easy to tell that the headmistress Lockhart was a tall woman with a long neck and unfaultable posture. She had auburn-colored hair, which she wore in a tight bun. She had dark green eyes and always wore a stiff, high-collared white blouse and navy skirt. She was only five years Emily's senior, but she seemed much older.

Emily stood before the headmistress's desk, shifting nervously on the heels of her black leather boots. As she did, she looked down at her hands, which were clasped in front of her, noticing that they were stained with ink. She quickly put them behind her back.

"I've been meaning to find a moment to talk with you," Headmistress Lockhart said. "To find out how you've settled in at Briarwood House."

"Oh," Emily said, her shoulders dropping. "Well..."

"You aren't finding the workload too strenuous?"

"No," Emily said without hesitation. "Not at all."

Headmistress Lockhart nodded as she sat forward in her chair. "Good," she said. "I know Briarwood is much bigger than your last school."

Emily nodded. She'd been teaching at Briarwood for only a month. When the position opened up, Emily jumped at the chance. Briarwood was the most progressive girls' school in Manhattan, open to young women from all walks of life, including girls of color. Since graduating from college, Emily had always hoped to work here, and recently, her dream had come true.

"The other teachers tell me you are an asset to this school," Headmistress Lockhart said. "And that you have quickly become the girls' favorite teacher."

Emily's face flushed, the color high in her cheeks. "Oh, I don't know about that," she said.

"They mentioned you were modest too," Headmistress Lockhart added, a twinkle in her green eyes.

"I am just grateful for the opportunity to teach here," Emily replied.

"Yes," Headmistress Lockhart agreed. "Well, at Briarwood, we pride ourselves on finding teachers who not only teach our students well, but who inspire them, too. Our job is to ensure that when our girls walk out of that door for the last time, they know they can achieve anything, even the seemingly impossible. Do you believe you are up to the task?"

"I do," Emily said. "I really do."

Headmistress Lockhart leaned forward in her seat. "I believe that you are, too," she said. "I see a lot of myself in you, Emily, and I hope you will continue to do well here at Briarwood."

"Thank you, Headmistress," Emily said.

Headmistress Lockhart nodded. "Good," she said, sitting back again. "Well, I will see you tomorrow, then."

Emily smiled as she turned and left the office. She walked back across the entrance hall and out the large double doors. As she descended the stone steps, she could not help but smile. She'd been so scared she'd do something to mess up her opportunity at Briarwood, so afraid that she wouldn't fit in with the students and staff, yet she was doing well; Headmistress Lockwood was happy with her and with the job she was doing.

Emily stepped out of the black wrought iron gates and turned, glancing back at the three-story Victorian building. She'd made it her business to know everything she could about the school. Briarwood had been founded almost fifteen years ago when Headmistress Lockhart's parents had passed away, leaving her the sole owner of the house.

At only twenty, she'd chosen to turn her home into a school for girls and had fought against the system to make it happen. Back then, girls had limited access to formal education and families would often prioritize the education of their sons over their daughters.

When girls were able to attend, the curriculums were geared towards their expected roles as homemakers, such as domestic science and needlework. This limited curriculum did not prepare them for any other roles than being wives and mothers. Headmistress Lockhart had overcome all of these barriers and in the years that followed, she'd worked tirelessly to cultivate a reputation as one of the finest schools in the whole of New York.

Emily could still remember how nervous she'd been on the day of her interview. Her stomach was tied in knots, and her throat was so dry she was certain she wouldn't be able to speak. Yet, she'd managed in the end, and the headmistress had offered her the position that very same day. From the moment Emily met Lockhart her, she'd admired her and hoped very much to one day be like her.

Although Emily had never gotten to attend a prestigious school, she had dreamed of being a teacher her whole life. After Emily's mother died, her father did everything he could to put food on the table. He worked from dawn to dusk and so Emily was responsible for caring for her younger sister. She was also the one who cooked the meals and did all the laundry.

There was never any time for schoolwork but Emily was born with an innate thirst for knowledge, and by ten, she'd taught herself to read fluently using discarded newspapers. In the years that followed, Emily read every resource she could get her hands on, borrowing books from neighbors and the local library. Then, when she was eighteen, the local church sponsored her application for a teacher's college and she was accepted.

Emily had graduated at the top of her class and since then, she'd dedicated her life to teaching and growing the minds of young women, helping them see that they are capable of so much more than society dictates.

Emily paused a moment longer before turning away from the school. The street where the school was situated was one of the prettiest in Brooklyn. It was lined with hundred-year-old oak trees, their dark leaves only partially obscuring the large houses. Some boasted the ornate gables of Victorian architecture, while others had large bay windows in the style of Queen Anne.

As she walked, Emily passed by beautifully dressed women with lace-rimmed parasols. Some were on an afternoon stroll, others returning from the high streets followed by their maids, hardly able to see over the piles of hat and dress boxes.

Emily walked all the way to the end of the street and crossed it. As she did, the large, fancy houses wilted in the late afternoon light, becoming narrower, duller versions of themselves in front of houses devoid of round towers or painted iron railings. It was like stepping across some invisible barrier into another world.

As she continued down the uneven cobbled road, carriages passed by, and the sweet, sharp scent of horse manure that littered the streets stung her nostrils. In the distance, she heard the ringing of the church bells.

She took another turn down a narrow alley between two houses and emerged onto her street and the cacophony of sound and color that came with the row of vendors who set up their stalls there every morning.

As Emily walked past them, the stench of horse manure was replaced by the saltiness of fresh fish and pungent rounds of bright yellow cheese. In the months that Emily had been living in this neighborhood, she'd gotten to know everyone. There was the grumpy Polish man who sold cured meats and the rowdy Irish family with fresh fruits and vegetables.

There was also the friendly but quiet German widow who sold loaves of bread and cakes and the Russian couple who were always arguing and sold household goods like linens, pots, pans, soaps, and candles. There were people from all walks of life, a patchwork quilt of characters and cultures.

"Miss Emily!" a voice called out.

Emily turned to find a tall, young man with olive skin and coal-black hair pushing through the crowds towards her. His name was Matteo Greco, and he moved to New York a few years earlier. He was the oldest of twelve brothers and sisters and worked as a fisherman to help support his family.

"What are you doing here?" Emily asked. "Tuesdays are your days off."

"Here," he said, handing her a package wrapped in newspaper.

Emily took it from him, unfolding it to find her favorite; fresh oysters.

"I went down to the Hudson," Matteo explained.

Emily folded the newspaper again, a small crease in her brow. This was not the first time Matteo had done something like this.

"Let me pay you for them at least," Emily said, reaching into her coat pocket.

"I don't want your money," Matteo said. "But if you want to repay me, you can come to dinner at my house tonight? My mamma keeps asking when she is going to meet you."

Emily sighed, shaking her head. While she was happy being friends, it had become abundantly clearer these past few weeks that Matteo wanted more. It wasn't that he wasn't handsome, thoughtful, and charming, but at twenty-three, he was much too young for her. Moreover, Emily didn't want to be someone's wife. She loved her independence and her job. She didn't want anything to get in the way of her career.

"Maybe another time," Emily said. "I have the girl's essays on *Wuthering Heights* to grade."

Matteo sighed, his bottom lip protruding slightly.

"Thank you for the oysters," Emily said. "It's very thoughtful."

"You're welcome," Matteo replied.

Emily gave him a tight-lipped smile. "Well, I'd better get going," she said. "You know what Mrs. Bird is like."

Mrs. Bird was the owner of the boarding house where Emily rented a room. She was a stiff, stern woman who kept a close eye on those who lived under her roof.

"I'll see you tomorrow?" Matteo said, his dark eyes fixed on hers.

Emily nodded as she turned. She walked past the rest of the vendors. Mrs. Bird's house was on the corner of the street and looked just like the others ; a tall, narrow, brown building made from wood. It had three stories and a gray slate roof.

"Good afternoon, Mrs. Bird," Emily greeted.

The older woman stood up, wincing as she did. On the ground around her feet were piles of weeds, clumps of soil still clutching to their exposed roots. Mrs. Bird was a short woman with thinning gray hair, a broad face, and a flat nose.

"I am not so sure good has anything to do with it," she grumbled.

"How's the gardening going?" Emily asked.

Mrs. Bird muttered something unintelligible as she wiped the back of her hands across her sweaty brow.

'A letter came for you," she announced.

Emily frowned. "A letter? Are you sure it's for me?"

"Apparently it was delivered to your old address," Mrs. Bird explained. "But a young woman brought it by this afternoon. Said her name was Mary O'Connerly, said she used to teach with you."

Emily had taught with Mary at her old school before coming to Briarwood. She had not seen Mary in ages but was grateful to her for bringing her the letter. She would have liked to have seen her old friend.

"Where is it?" Emily asked. "The letter."

"Do I look as if I have it on me?" Mrs. Bird replied, bristling with impatience. "I put it in your room."

"Thank you," Emily said as she turned and headed to the porch.

As she walked up the stairs, Emily wondered who the letter might be from. The only family she had left was her younger sister Marie, but they'd fallen out of touch after she married and moved to Texas. Before she'd gone, they'd had a huge fight and Emily had said things she regretted. It had been almost eight years since Emily had heard from her.

Mrs. Bird turned away, crouching down and reaching for another weed, which she mercilessly tugged from the soil. Emily watched her for a moment and then headed inside and up to her room on the second floor. As she entered the brightly lit room, she spotted the envelope propped up against a pile of books on the desk.

Emily walked across the room. She hesitated a moment before she picked up the envelope. It had come from Texas, but Emily did not recognize the handwriting. It wasn't her sister's. Emily pulled open the top drawer of the desk and retrieved a silver letter opener.

She carefully inserted the tip of the blade between the fold of the envelope and glided it along the sealed edge. She put down the opener and removed the single sheet of paper from inside, unfolding it as she did. Emily started to read, her lips silently tracing the words.

Dear Miss McCoy

We have not been acquainted, and I wish very much that I was writing this letter under happier circumstances, but I feel it is my duty to write and tell you that your sister, Marie, and your brother-in-law, Bill, are deceased.

Emily paused, staring at that word, deceased. Her mouth was dry.

A few days ago, your sister and her husband were traveling back from town and were attacked by a group of highwaymen. Their bodies were discovered a few miles from their ranch.

Bodies. Her baby sister was dead. A tear rolled down her cheek and onto the letter, smudging the ink. Emily wiped her cheek with the back of her hand.

I know that you and Marie had not spoken for some time. Your sister confided in me that she regretted your estrangement and wished to reach out. I hope she would approve of me doing so now, for we are all concerned about the children. The death of their parents has left them orphaned.

"Children?" Emily breathed. "Marie had children?"

Emily's hands were trembling as she stared down at the words. She never knew. She assumed as much, but part of her always believed that when they did, Marie would write to tell her the news.

As far as anyone knows, Bill had no other family save for Marie, their son and daughter. Your sister never mentioned any family other than you. We have made temporary arrangements for the children, but I am reaching out to you as their only living relative. I hope you will consider coming to Texas and taking charge of your nephew and niece.

I have enclosed a photograph of the children.

Yours faithfully.

Reverend Theodore Middleton

Emily blinked back tears, her throat raw with emotion. She'd always wanted to make things right with Marie. To tell her she was sorry for reacting to her departure the way that she had, for telling her that she was a bad sister, an ungrateful sister. She always thought there would be more time, but now she was gone and left behind her children.

Emily reached into the envelope and removed a black and white photograph of them. The girl was seated on a wooden stool; her brother standing on her right, his hand on her narrow shoulder. They looked so much like Marie at that age with their fair hair and heart-shaped faces. Emily turned over the photograph, and her breath caught in her chest as she recognized Marie's handwriting.

Seven-year-old Thomas and his three-year-old sister, Lily. Forest Hill, 1897

Emily put the photograph down on the desk and sat, exhaling shakily. The flood of tears that Emily had managed to hold back until that moment suddenly broke through, and a sob escaped her throat. She put her head down on her hands and cried, the tears wetting the sleeves of her blouse.

She wasn't sure how long she stayed like that; perhaps she'd fallen asleep. But when Emily eventually sat up, her neck and shoulders were stiff. Her eyes felt scratchy and swollen. She got up from the desk and walked over to the window. It was dark out now; the street outside her window was empty. Emily sighed softly to herself. She'd always loved the city, the smells, and the sounds, unlike Marie, who had longed for a quiet, simple life in the country.

While Emily had never wanted to get married, or have children, Marie dreamed of being a wife and mother and having a big family. Emily had been devastated when her sister left. It had broken her heart. She'd convinced herself she wasn't enough for Marie and resented her sister for abandoning her.

All these years, she'd been so stubborn, and now it was too late for her to make things right with her, but that didn't mean she couldn't make things right with her children.

Chapter One

Brooklyn, New York, Summer 1898

Headmistress Lockhart sat back in her chair, pressing her thin lips together tightly as Emily shifted uncomfortably in her seat. It was the last day of the semester, and all the staff and girls had gone home early. Emily had stayed to talk with the headmistress about her summer travel plans. She'd been dreading telling her that she was going to Texas to meet her nephew and niece and to settle the estate, but she felt it was dishonest not to.

"So, that is why you haven't volunteered to take any summer classes?" she asked.

Emily's heart sank. She'd been looking forward to the summer and teaching extra lessons. Still, four weeks had passed since she learned the news about her sister, and the Reverend's letter had said that her nephew and niece's situation was only temporary.

"I've been waiting for the summer break," she explained, "so that my trip wouldn't disrupt any of my usual classes."

The headmistress nodded as she sat forward in her chair. "And what about when you return to New York?" she asked. "Are you planning on bringing the children with you?"

"Yes," Emily confessed. "I am the only family they have left."

Headmistress Lockhart pursed her lips, a crease frowning between her dark brows. "And what are your plans after your return to New York with the children?"

Emily hesitated a moment before answering.

"And you plan to be back before the start of the fall semester?"

"Yes," Emily said with determination.

"Well," Headmistress Lockhart sighed. "I am sorry that you have found yourself in such a sad situation, and we will certainly miss your input in our summer sessions."

"I am sorry I won't be here," Emily said sincerely. "And if there was any other way, but the children are too young to make such a journey on their own—"

"Of course," Headmistress Lockhart said. "Family is family, after all, and you must do what you must."

Emily nodded, but her stomach was twisted in knots. She could tell by the headmistress's tone that she was disappointed and concerned about what the children might mean for Emily's future at the school.

"Headmistress Lockhart," Emily said, sitting forward in her chair. "I promise I won't let anything get in the way of my teaching here. This job is without question the most important thing in my life."

"I believe you mean that," Headmistress Lockhart replied. "And I appreciate it. But just remember, Emily, that promises, much like pie crusts, are easily broken."

"I intend to return," Emily said, her voice rising.

"I know you do," Headmistress Lockhart said. "But you are about to walk into something entirely new and unexpected, and you cannot know how you will feel or what you might have to do."

"I can make it work," Emily said, her tone firm. "Whatever happens."

The headmistress smiled kindly at her. "I know how much you love teaching here and how much you care about your students," she said. "And we will be glad to see you when you return, but do not feel bad if you find your path veering in another direction."

"There is only one direction I want my path to take," Emily insisted. "And that is back to this school."

Headmistress Lockhart nodded. "Very well, Emily," she said. "Then, I shall see you in the fall."

Yet something in her eyes made Emily feel like she did not quite believe she would.

"I'll be back in the fall," Emily repeated, clenching her jaw.

Emily left the school feeling determined that she could have it all if she just put her mind to it. She was not going to give up teaching at Briarwood. It was her dream job, and she planned to be back in a few weeks, no matter what.

Emily walked home quickly from the school and retrieved her small, threadbare bag. She said goodbye to Mrs. Bird and put on her bonnet, securely tying the two white ribbons under her chin. She left the boarding house and walked down to the corner of the street to catch a horse-drawn streetcar to the train station.

A short while later, she arrived at the large, gray brick train station, and as she climbed down from the streetcar, she clutched her bag tightly.

She walked around its side and towards the entrance, only to find Matteo standing there. As she approached him, he took off his newsboy cap, folding it in his hands. His dark curls were damp and clung to his neck.

"What are you doing here?" she asked in surprise.

"You didn't think I'd let you leave without saying goodbye," he said, smiling.

"You shouldn't have worried," Emily said. "I will be back before the start of fall."

"How can I be so sure you won't meet a handsome cowboy?" Matteo asked. "And fall hopelessly in love?"

Emily shook her head, smiling. "I promise you I have no intentions of falling in love, just meeting my nephew and niece."

Matteo nodded as he took a step toward her. "I am going to miss you," he said softly.

Emily said nothing; what could she say? She did not want to lead him on, but was now really the time to tell him she was only interested in being friends? Just then, the train whistled loudly.

"I'd better get going," Emily said. "I don't want to miss my train."

Matteo nodded, and Emily smiled at him. Then, without another word, she walked around him and into the train station. She was aware of Matteo's eyes on her, but she did not turn around. The station was busy with people rushing about, and for a moment, Emily was quite turned around.

"Do you need some help, Miss?" a voice asked.

Emily turned to find a thin, young man with a wispy mustache. He wore a dark double-breasted coat, matching vest, and round-brimmed cap. On his lapel was a shiny brass name tag that read, "Frederick."

Emily reached into the pocket of her coat and pulled out the ticket, and the porter took it from her with a gloved hand and examined it.

"Very good," Frederick said, handing her back the ticket. "And are you traveling alone?"

"Yes," Emily said.

Frederick nodded. "This way, please Miss," he said.

Emily had traveled on a train only once before with her sister and father. They'd been going to see their grandmother. Emily was no older than eleven or twelve, and they stayed in the third-class compartments.

"The first-class cars are just this way," Frederick said.

It was a little ostentatious, but with the salary she was earning from Briarwood and the length of her journey, she'd decided to book a first-class ticket.

"Here we are," Frederick announced.

"Thank you," Emily said.

Fredrick offered her a hand, and she stepped up into the car. As she did, she was greeted by the smell of polished wood and the cheerful gleam of brass fittings. The floor of the car was decorated by an intricate floral print Axminster carpet.

Frederick climbed up into the car behind her.

"Let me show you to your seat," he offered.

Emily followed him to the front of the car, where she found a row of plush, upholstered seats with high backs and ample leg room. The chairs were arranged in pairs, and each row had a large window.

"Here you are," Frederick said, showing Emily to an empty seat by the window.

Emily sat down, encased in the soft cushioning.

"The dining car is just through that door," Frederick explained. "Meals are served three times a day; however, refreshments are readily available whenever you require one."

"Thank you," Emily said, smiling up at him.

"If you need anything, don't hesitate to ask."

Emily smiled again as Frederick bowed his head and disappeared. She turned and looked out of the window. The station was quieter now, and more people were taking their seats in the first-class car. A family of four sat opposite her, including a pretty little girl with blonde ringlets and large blue eyes. She held a porcelain doll in her lap, its features identical to hers in almost every way.

"Sit up straight, Annabel," her mother chastised.

Little Annabel sat up straighter, and as she did, Emily caught her eye and smiled, but the little girl did not return it.

A short while later, the train whistled and began to move. Emily looked out the window again as the station disappeared behind them. They traveled through the city, buildings flashing passed in blurs of gray and brown, and then everything turned green all at once, and the city was left behind.

Emily sighed softly, her stomach feeling empty. She was doing the right thing, but doing the right thing meant leaving behind everything she knew and loved. It was terrifying, like stepping off the edge of a precipice and falling into the unknown.

Emily must have drifted off because she woke to a small bell announcing that it was time for dinner. She and the other first-class passengers got up and headed into the dining car.

As she stepped in, Emily was greeted by a mouthwatering array of aromas. There were rows of tables, each covered in crisp white linen with napkins to match. At the end of the dining car was a bar; various colored bottles of different shapes lined up on a glass shelf against the wall. A handsome young man stood behind the bar top, his hands folded behind his back, a smile plastered on his face.

Emily held back and watched as the first-class passengers chose their seats and the servers came forward with menus. When everyone else was seated, Emily walked over to an empty table at the front and sat down.

She picked up her crisp white napkin and unfolded it, placing it on her lap. A moment later, a waiter handed her a menu, and she looked up at him and smiled. He was a tall, balding man with a thin, black mustache.

"Thank you," she said.

The waiter nodded as he stepped back, and Emily bent her head, turning her attention to the menu. She suddenly felt ravenous and was amazed by the variety of food on offer. To start, there was Melon with Prosciutto, Chilled Consommé, and Waldorf Salad. Then, for mains, there was a Chicken à la Maryland, Filet Mignon, Lobster Newburg and Salmon Hollandaise, and for desserts, Chocolate Fondant, Fruit Tart, and Crème Brulé. There was also a selection of side dishes.

Emily had no idea what to choose; she wanted to try everything.

"Are you ready to order, Miss?" the waiter said.

"Yes," Emily said. "May I have the Chilled Consommé, the Lobster Newburg and the Crème Brulé?"

The waiter nodded. "Very good, Miss," he said. "And to drink? Champagne, perhaps?"

Emily had never tasted champagne before, but it seemed as good an occasion as any.

"Yes," she said, nodding. "Thank you."

The waiter nodded his head again as Emily handed him the menu, and he turned and walked away, leaving Emily alone.

As she sat, she looked around. The tables, which were all set for four, were full; Emily was the only passenger sitting alone. The family with the little girl, Annabel, were sitting across from her, and she was watching Emily with her bright blue eyes.

"Don't stare," her mother hissed. "It's rude."

"But why is she all by herself?" Annabel asked.

Emily bent her head and averted her gaze, pretending she could not hear what they were saying.

"Because she's a spinster," the older boy beside her said.

"Edward," his mother scolded. "It's not polite to make personal comments."

Edward shrugged, sinking back in his chair. "Well, it's true," he said.

"What's a spinster?" Annabel asked.

25

"Someone who isn't married," Edward said. "Like Aunt Margaret."

"Richard," the children's mother said, turning to her husband. "Speak to your children."

The children's father was a broad-shouldered man with a creased brow and a receding hairline. He was nursing a whiskey and made no effort to acknowledge his wife or his children.

Just then, the waiter arrived with the family's food, and the attention was taken off Emily, much to her relief. It was uncommon for a woman to travel alone, especially on a journey like this one. She was expected to have a chaperone, if not her husband, then a male relative. Women who traveled alone were often met with disapproval and suspicion as if they were suspects of some perceived impropriety.

Over the years, Emily often garnered disapproval simply because she was an unmarried woman, be it walking alone in the evening or eating alone at a restaurant. It was the price she had to pay for choosing her career over the traditional role of being a homemaker, and most of the time, Emily didn't mind, but sometimes she was lonely, and she wondered what it might be like to have someone to share dinner with.

The waiter returned with Emily's starter, and she ate hungrily. Every now and then, one of the tiny bubbles in the glass of champagne beside her plate broke off from the bottom and rose, popping as it reached the top.

When Emily was finished with her Chilled Consommé, she reached for the crystal flute and carefully lifted it to her lips, taking a tentative sip. The champagne was cold and crisp with a subtle hint of sweetness. The delicate tingling sensation on her tongue and palette lasted long after she'd swallowed. She'd never tasted anything quite like it, and as she placed the glass down beside her empty plate, she thought the French Benedictine monk Dom Pierre Pérignon was right; it was like drinking the stars.

A while later, Emily made her way back out of the dining cart and to her seat. It was late now, and the world outside was dark save for the bright moon hanging in the sky. Emily sat down, resting her head on the seat as she stared out into the night. As she did, her eyes grew heavy, and soon she was asleep.

Sometime later, Emily awoke, and for a moment, she looked around, confused not to find herself tucked into her bed in New York. She looked around, and suddenly, something caught her eye. In the seat beside her was the little porcelain doll with blonde ringlets and blue eyes she'd seen with the girl at dinner.

Emily reached over and picked her up, holding her in her hands as she glanced across at Annabel, but she was fast asleep, her head resting on her brother's shoulder. Emily looked down at the doll again, her frozen eyes staring into Emily's.

It was a kind gesture; Annabel hadn't wanted Emily to be all alone. Emily returned the doll to the seat beside her and looked out the window again.

When she woke again, the first glow of dawn was visible on the horizon, and Emily sighed softly. Over the years, she'd never allowed herself to imagine a reunion with her sister, but now she was just hours away from the place that Marie had called home, the place she'd raised her children.

Yet Marie wasn't there anymore; she was gone, and the reunion that Emily had never dared to dream about would never come true. All Emily could hope for now was to get all her affairs in order so that she could return home to New York as soon as possible.

Chapter Two

Forest Hill, Texas, Summer 1898

"Dagnabbit," Alec cried as he dropped the heavy cast-iron pan, falling to the floor with a loud bang.

Thirty-four-year-old Alec Kincaid sucked his burned thumb as he watched a sausage roll under the dresser while a fried egg landed face down, yellow yolk oozing out from under it. Alec turned to face the children, his thumb still in his mouth.

Seven-year-old Thomas and three-year-old Lily were seated at the round kitchen table; the plates of food in front of them sat almost untouched. They were both staring at the fried egg on the floor, their expressions unreadable.

"Sorry," Alec apologized as he bent over and picked up the pan.

He carried it over to the sink and put it down, his thumb still burning. He hadn't eaten yet, but he suddenly didn't have much of an appetite, so Alec walked over to the back door and whistled loudly between his two front teeth. A moment later, his Blue Heeler, Cobalt, Colby for short, came running in.

"Breakfast is up, buddy," Alec said, scratching his dog behind the ears.

Colby walked over to the egg and slurped it up into his mouth; licking up the spilled yolk before scratching the sausage out from under the drawer and eating that, too. Once he was done, he sniffed under the kitchen table for any scraps.

"You guys aren't hungry?" Alec asked.

Thomas and Lily shook their heads.

"Would you like me to make you something else?" he offered.

"May we please be excused?" Thomas asked.

Alec hesitated a moment and nodded. "Sure," he said. "But stick close to the house."

Thomas slid out of his seat, and Lily mirrored his movements, and the two children left the kitchen. Alec collected the plates and scraped the uneaten breakfast into the pail for the pigs. He washed up the dishes, and from the kitchen window, he could see Thomas and Lily standing by the chicken coop. Colby was with them, eyeing the newly hatched chicks pecking greedily at the ground.

It had been a month and a half since Thomas and Lily's parents were murdered. Alec would never forget that day for as long as he lived.

It was an unseasonably hot day for May, and as Alec hammered in a wooden fence post, he felt drips of perspiration running down his back. His dark hair was damp and clung to his neck and ears. He'd been unrolling a thick coil of barbed wire when he saw Thomas and Lily running towards the ranch, hand-in-hand.

He'd known from the expressions on their faces that something was very wrong, and besides, Marie would never let the children walk to the ranch on their own. Dropping his rubber mallet, Alec had raced over to meet them, kneeling on the hard ground before them.

Thomas hadn't been able to form the words at first, the tears rolling down his cheeks and onto his shirt, but eventually, he'd managed to tell Alec what had happened. They had been attacked by a band of highway men on their way back from town. The children had managed to get away and had run the two miles to get help.

Alec had sent the children inside and rode as fast as his horse would carry him, but Bill and Marie were already dead by the time he got to them. He'd gone to fetch the sheriff, and they'd organized a manhunt but never found the men responsible for their murders.

Since that fateful afternoon, Thomas and Lily had been staying with Alec. In all those weeks, Lily had not said a single word, and Thomas never left her side. Sometimes, it was like living with two little ghosts. Most of the time, Alec had no idea what he was doing. He'd never been a father and hardly knew what to say to them. Still, he'd offered to look after them because he knew that it was what Marie would have wanted.

But he wasn't sure how long they could go on like this. It was obvious that the children were struggling, and he didn't have the emotional tools to help them through their trauma. Reverend Middleton managed to get in touch with Marie's sister, who said she would come as soon as she could, but that was weeks ago.

Alec finished the breakfast dishes when Mrs. Tattlewell came bustling into the kitchen, her round face flushed from the walk from town.

"Mornin'," Alec said, turning to greet her.

"It's not even eight o'clock, and I'm already sweatin' like a sinner in church," Mrs. Tattlewell complained as she fetched her apron off the hook behind the door and fastened it around her broad waist.

Since Marie and Bill's murders, Mrs. Tattlewell had been helping at the house and keeping an eye on the children. Before, she'd come to the ranch a couple of times a week to help with the laundry and cleaning. She was heavily involved in the community and the church and was the first to know everyone's business. She was a good woman, born and raised off the land, and Alec was incredibly grateful for her help.

"The children hardly touched their breakfast again," Alec said in concern.

'They've had a terrible shock," Mrs. Tattlewell said. "But children are resilient by nature."

"They probably hate my cooking," Alec said. "Heck, I even hate my cooking."

Mrs. Tattlewell smiled. "You're doing a great job, Alec," she said. "No one would have expected you to take in two young children and care for them like your own. So, don't be so hard on yourself. The children will be alright; they just need time."

Alec nodded. Mrs. Tattlewell had raised five of her own, and she knew their ways much better than he did.

"Well, I'd best get to work," Alec said. "The children are out by the chicken coop."

Mrs. Tattlewell nodded. "I'll see you for lunch."

Alec headed out the backdoor and to the stables; as he did, Cobalt came running up behind him. Alec saddled up his horse while the dog waited patiently at the stable door, and together, they set out to check the fences.

As Alec rode along the boundary fence, he suddenly spotted a familiar figure riding up the road, and he sighed. It was his neighbor, Randall Caldwell. He was the biggest landowner in town and liked to brag about it to anyone who'd listen. His father had been a very successful rancher and had passed on his wealth and land to his son, but nothing was ever enough for Randall. He always wanted more and he wasn't afraid of taking it. He and Alec had their fair share of run-ins over the years, and he was certainly not a fan.

Colby barked loudly as Randall approached, his hackles raised.

"Mornin' Alec," Randall said as he brought his horse to a halt on the other side of the fence.

"Randall," Alec said coolly.

"How are things?" Randall asked.

"Fine," Alec said.

Randall nodded as he shifted in his saddle. He was a tall man with shoulder-length dirty blonde hair and dark eyes. His face was always clean-shaven, and he never had dirt under his fingernails.

"I was coming by to ask if you've heard any more about Bill's place?" Randall asked.

Alec sighed, shaking his head. Since the news of Bill and Marie's murders, Randall had been after their property. Riverbend Ranch was a good piece of land that had access to the river and plenty of grazing opportunities. The land bordered both Alec and Randall's property.

"There's been no news," Alec said.

Randall frowned, and Alec gritted his teeth. He knew Randall didn't believe him. He thought that Alec was after the Donnelly's place, which wasn't true. Alec was happy with what he had.

"So there has been no word from Marie's sister?" Randall confirmed.

"As I said, no news," Alex repeated. "She said she was coming but didn't say when."

Randall nodded. "Well, you'll let me know if that changes?"

"Sure," Alec replied.

Neither of the men spoke for a moment, and then Randall cleared his throat.

"Have a good day, Alec.".

Alec nodded as Randall turned his horse around and headed back in the direction that he'd come, and Alec finished checking the fences before returning back to the homestead. As he dismounted, Alec spotted Thomas and Lily playing on the old tire swing in the front yard. He watched them for a moment, Thomas pushing his little sister, but there was joy in their play. It was as if they were just going through the motions.

Alec turned away and led his horse into the stables. As he fetched his brush from the table, he thought how much better this all would be if Olivia were here. She and Marie had been close, best friends in fact, and she'd loved Thomas and Lily like her own. But Olivia had died almost four years ago now, in childbirth, along with their child and their deaths had broken Alec into a million pieces.

After they died, Alec retreated into himself, haunted by a life that could have been but now never would. He stopped eating, stopped living, and only got out of bed in the morning because he would not let the animals go hungry. Part of him died with Olivia and the baby, and he never thought he would find a reason to keep going until Marie stepped in and saved him.

It wasn't much to start with, a casserole left on the kitchen table or an invitation to dinner. Alec pushed back at first, refusing to accept her help, but Marie was a determined woman, and she would not let her best friend's husband fade into nothing.

So, eventually, she wore him down, little by little, and as fate would have it, they became friends. It was never anything romantic, besides, Marie was a married woman. Alec knew he would never feel that way about another woman. Still, what he grew to realize over the years was that although she never said anything, Marie had demons of her own, and she needed him as much as he needed her.

He'd felt Marie's loss deeply, and that was one reason he'd agreed to care for the children. He knew that it was what she would have wanted, and if things had been the other way around, he also knew it was what she would have done for him.

Alec brushed the horse's coat until it gleamed and then refilled the food and water troughs. As he stepped outside, he spotted the sheriff coming up the driveway. He was a big man with broad shoulders and a thick neck. He had dark hair, which he wore brushed back from his face, and he was a man who rarely smiled. Sheriff Wyatt Rourke was tough, but he was fair and protected the residents of Forest Hill.

"Sheriff," Alec said, tipping his hat to him. "What brings you out this way?"

The sheriff climbed down off his horse, sliding his two thumbs into the front pockets of his dark denim jeans.

"Just thought you'd want to know there's been some trouble at the Donnelly house," Sheriff Rouke said.

"What kind of trouble?" Alec asked, his brow furrowing.

"Someone broke in," the sheriff explained. "It doesn't look like anything was taken, so it's probably just a couple of youngsters stirrin' up trouble."

Alec nodded, but he was bothered by the news. Alec and the sheriff went by there every couple of days to check on the place, but the house had been sitting open for too long; it was only a matter of time before a group of bandits ransacked the place.

"Have you got any more news?" Alec asked.

Sheriff Rourke shook his head. "There have been no other reports of any other attacks in the neighboring towns," he said.

Alex pursed his lips. Since the Donnelly's murders, Sheriff Rourke had been keeping him updated on the investigation, but something about the attack felt off to Alec. In six weeks, there had been no others , which meant that the attack on the Donnelly's was an isolated incident.

To make matters even more suspicious, Bill, Marie, and the children hadn't been traveling with anything of value. They'd just been returning to their ranch from town with some farm supplies and groceries. Yet for some reason they'd been targeted. Why? Something about it didn't add up.

"Anyway, whoever got into the Donnelly's place broke in through the kitchen window," Sheriff Rourke said.

Alec sighed. "I'll go and board it up this afternoon," he said.

Sheriff Rourke nodded. "How are the children?" he asked.

Alec glanced over at the tire swing, but Thomas and Lily were gone.

"As well as can be expected," Alec said.

Sheriff Rourke sighed, shaking his head. "It's nasty business," he said. "Everyone in town loved Marie."

Alec nodded. Marie was well-liked, which was more than could be said for Bill.

"There's been no more news from the sister?" Sheriff Rourke asked.

"Not that I've heard," Alec said. "Although I haven't seen Reverend Middleton since last Sunday at church."

Sheriff Rourke nodded. "Well, hopefully, there is some response soon," he said. "For the children's sake."

Alec said nothing. Marie had not told him much about her sister. She didn't like to talk about it. All Alec knew was that they'd had some kind of falling out when Marie married Bill and moved to Texas and had not spoken in years. The Reverend Theodore Middleton had written to her after Marie and Bill were killed, and she'd written to say she was coming but no one knew exactly when.

"Well, I'd better get going," Sheriff Rourke said. "I'll be seeing you."

"Thanks for comin' by," Alec said.

The sheriff tipped his hat as he turned to leave. Alec waited until he'd mounted his horse and headed back to the gate before he headed inside for lunch.

Mrs. Tattlewell had made fried chicken, an old family recipe. Alec was relieved to see Thomas and Lily eating as he sat down at the table. Mrs. Tattlewell put a plate down in front of him piled with crispy chicken legs, fried potatoes, and slaw.

"You all need to put some meat on your bones," Mrs. Tattlewell said as she sat down.

Alec ate hungrily, having missed breakfast. Mrs. Tattlewell kept the conversation going without the help of anyone else. After Alec was finished, he sat back in his seat, his denim jeans suddenly feeling uncomfortably tight.

"The children and I are going on a walk after lunch," Mrs. Tattlewell said. "Do you wish to join us?"

"I would, but I have something I need to take care of," Alec said.

Mrs. Tattlewell nodded.

"Thank you for lunch," he said, pushing back his chair and standing up.

"Alec?"

He looked down at Thomas, his plate in his hands.

"What did the sheriff want?" he asked.

Alec said nothing for a moment. He had not realized that Thomas had seen him talking with the sheriff.

"Nothing important," Alec said.

"So, they haven't found them?" Thomas asked, his eyes intense.

Alec glanced at Lily and sighed.

"No," Alec said, shaking his head. "Not yet."

Thomas dropped his head in disappointment, pushing his plate away, and Alec's stomach sank.

"Enjoy your walk," he said.

He turned and carried his plate to the sink before heading out the back door and down the driveway towards the gate.

As he walked, Alec thought about the disappointment on Thomas's face, and he wished he could do something more. He'd given the children a place to stay and food to eat, but it wasn't enough. They wanted answers, but how could Alec even start to explain that the world didn't always make sense?

Bad things happened to good people, and there was nothing you could do about it but try to move on. It was hard enough for a man of his age to understand, so how could he even begin to help Thomas and Lily accept what had happened? How could he get them to accept that they were orphans and that the future they'd once imagined was lost to them now? The truth was that he couldn't. He didn't have it in him. What he needed was someone who could help the children in all the ways he couldn't.

Chapter Three

Emily stepped off of the train, smoothing her skirts as she did. It felt good to be on solid ground again. She looked around, spotting a porter talking to another couple a few feet away. He was an elderly man with gray hair bristling from both nostrils.

Carrying her suitcase in her left hand, Emily walked up to him. She stood patiently while he finished speaking with the young couple who appeared to have mislaid their luggage.

"Excuse me," Emily said.

The older man turned to her. He had soft blue-gray eyes but wasn't wearing a name tag.

"May I help you?" he asked.

"Yes, please," Emily said. "The porter on the train said that the tracks had been damaged, which was why we were getting off here instead of at Forest Hill?"

"That's right," he said, nodding. "Tornado came through a couple of weeks ago and uplifted the tracks from here to Forest Hill. We've been waiting for the repairs to be done, but between you and me, I think the company is stalling."

"Why's that?" Emily asked.

"Forest Hill ain't much of a town," he explained. "It's mainly ranchers, a small farming community."

Emily nodded. "My sister, she lives there; well, she used to," Emily corrected herself. "Is there someone, a carriage driver perhaps, who could give me a ride to Forest Hill?"

The porter nodded. "There's a man outside, a big chap in a straw hat, name's Leonard. He can take you."

"Thank you," Emily said.

She turned and headed out of the station. As she stepped out onto the street, she looked around for the man named Leonard. After a few moments, she spotted him a short distance away. He was resting in the shade of a large oak tree, his back pressed up against the trunk and his hat over his face.

She walked over to him, but as she approached, he did not move.

"Excuse me?" Emily said,

Still, the man remained motionless, and had it not been for the gentle rise and fall of his chest, Emily would have wondered if he was only sleeping.

"Excuse me?" she said again. "The porter at the train station said you might be able to help me?"

The man suddenly sat upright, his straw hat falling to the ground as he stared up at her.

"Sorry," Leonard apologized. "I was out like a lantern in a rainstorm."

Emily said nothing for a moment.

"What was it you needed?" Leonard asked, stifling a yawn.

"A ride to Forest Hill?" Emily repeated. "The porter said you would be able to give me a lift to Forest Hill?"

"Oh sure, sure," Leonard said, nodding. "Just give me a minute."

Leonard got up, dusting the sand off his pants. He walked around the thick trunk of the oak tree, emerging a moment later with a large, brown cart horse.

Emily stared at the horse for a long moment before she turned to Leonard.

"This is Mable," Leonard said. "Ain't she a beauty."

Leonard reached up and scratched the horse's nose, and she nuzzled into his neck.

"Where's the rest of it?" Emily asked.

Leonard frowned.

"I mean, where's the carriage?" Emily asked.

Leonard shook his head. "There ain't one," he replied.

"Then how do you propose we get to Forest Hill?" Emily asked.

"We ride," Leonard said.

Emily's eyes widened in surprise. She'd never ridden a horse in her entire life, and certainly, she'd never seen a horse as big as Mable.

Leonard chuckled. "Don't worry," he assured her. "She's as gentle as a lamb."

"Maybe it would be better if I walked," Emily said.

"Forest Hill's a good five miles from here," Leonard said. "It'll be dark by the time you arrive."

Emily sighed as she looked at the horse again. She did not want to find herself alone on a strange road in the dark, but she did not know this man or his horse.

"I promise I'll get you where you need to go," Leonard said.

Emily said nothing for a moment as she looked at Leonard, and despite her reservations he had kind eyes.

"Alright," she said. "I suppose there's a first time for everything."

"That's the spirit," Leonard said encouragingly.

With Leonard's help, Emily found herself on top of the large cart horse, with one leg on either side of the horse's narrow back. She shifted uncomfortably in her seat, as Leonard pulled himself up behind her, squeezing her suitcase between them.

"Ready?" he asked.

Before Emily could answer, Leonard took the reins in his two large hands, clicked his tongue, and Mable set off. Emily clutched tightly to the cantle; afraid she'd slide off at any minute.

"It helps if you relax," Leonard advised. "Move with the horse."

Emily said nothing as she took a deep breath, doing her best to follow Leonard's advice, but she couldn't seem to relax, no matter how hard she tried.

"I take it you aren't from Texas?" Leonard asked.

"What makes you say that?"

"Your accent, for one," Leonard said, chuckling. 'And you don't dress like a local."

Emily looked down at her attire and frowned.

"What I mean to say is you dress fancier," Leonard explained. "Where are you coming from?"

"New York," Emily said.

SALLY M. ROSS

Leonard whistled under his breath. "You've seen that big old statue then?" he asked.

"You mean the Statue of Liberty?" Emily asked.

Leonard nodded.

"Yes," Emily said. "I've seen it many times."

"Well, I'll be," Leonard said, chuckling. "You are the first person I've met who's seen it with their own eyes. What's it like?"

"It's wonderful," Emily said.

Leonard chuckled again. "So, what brings you south?" he asked.

"My sister," Emily said. "Well, no, not my sister, I suppose, but her children."

Leonard nodded. "Coming for a visit then?"

"Not exactly," Emily said.

For a few moments, they fell silent. Emily looked around at the wide-open space, where all you could see from your feet to the horizon was prairie. Forest Hill was located in the Texas Panhandle, known for its vast seas of grasslands. It was an ideal place for cattle farming with plenty of grazing.

Emily closed her eyes and took a deep breath; she could not ignore how much fresher the air was here and how quiet it was without the newsboys shouting the headlines and the rattle and rumble of the streetcars.

"You're getting the hang of it now," Leonard said.

Emily opened her eyes and realized Leonard was right; her back and shoulders were less tense now, and her body moved in rhythm with the horse.

"So, is this what you do?" Emily asked. "Ferry people from place to place?"

"It's not a bad job," Leonard reasoned. "Every day, I get to feel the sun on my back and the wind in my hair. I get to meet new people."

"But don't you ever want more?" Emily asked.

"More than all this?" Leonard said, letting go of the reins and gesturing to their surroundings where the tall grasses were now dancing in the breeze.

Emily said nothing for a moment. She'd never understood why her sister had wanted to leave New York for Texas. The city was just so exciting, and there were opportunities on every corner.

"You said you've come to see your sister's youngins?" Leonard asked.

"That's right," Emily confirmed.

"What's the name?" Leonard asked. "Maybe I know them?"

Emily hesitated a moment before answering. "Thomas and Lily Donnelly," she said.

Leonard said nothing, inhaling sharply. "Oh, heck," he said, his tone full of sympathy.

"So you know that happened to their parents?" Emily asked.

"Sure," Leonard said. "Well, I mean, everyone knows what happened."

"I don't," Emily said. "Well, not really."

"Are you sure you want to know?" Leonard asked.

"Yes," Emily said. "At least, I think so."

Leonard exhaled shakily. "I don't know all the details. I wasn't in Forest Hill when it happened, but from what I heard, it was a gang of highwaymen. They attacked your sister and her family on their way back from town."

"Family?" Emily repeated, frowning. "You mean that the children were with them?"

"That's what I heard," Leonard said. "The children managed to get away, but your sister and her husband, well, they weren't so lucky."

Emily's stomach was hollow as she thought of those poor children, how scared they must have been.

"Did they catch the men responsible?" Emily asked, her voice wavering.

"No," Leonard said. "At least not yet."

Emily chewed the inside of her cheek, trying not to imagine what it must have been like for her sister in those final moments.

Emily and Leonard fell silent again as the town of Forest Hill came into view at the end of the road. As the porter had said, there wasn't much to the place except for a few wooden buildings, most of which were worn and weathered looking with peeling paint and rotten porches. As they rode down the main street, a few people stopped to stare, and Leonard tipped his straw hat politely. They continued past the small church situated on the outskirts of the town and down another long, dusty road.

They passed several properties before they came to Riverbend, her sister's ranch. As she spotted the sign on the old wooden railing, her stomach sank further.

"You can leave me here," Emily said. "I'd like to walk the rest of the way."

"You sure?" Leonard asked.

Emily nodded. She wanted a few moments to think and to prepare herself to meet her nephew and niece.

Leonard pulled on the reins, bringing the horse to a halt. Leonard dismounted, his heavy boots landing on the ground with a thud. He helped Emily down. She then waited while he untied her suitcase.

"How much do I owe you?" Emily asked, reaching for her purse.

Leonard shook his head. "Nothing," he said.

"But I can't accept that," Emily said. "After all, you kept your word and delivered me here safely."

"Just promise that if I ever find my way to New York, you'll take me to the Statue of Liberty," Leonard said.

Emily smiled as she took her hand out of her pocket. "Alright," she agreed. "It's a deal."

Leonard tipped his hat to her as he handed Emily her suitcase.

"Goodbye," Emily said.

"Y'all take care now," Leonard said.

Emily smiled at him again as she turned and headed through the gate. She walked up the slope towards the ranch, and as she reached the top, she stopped and turned, but Leonard was far gone by then. She turned back and made her way towards the collection of buildings. As she got closer, she paused for a moment, her heart in her throat.

At the center of the property was a sizable double-story farmhouse with a wide porch in the front. Several shutters hung askew, and the steep roof was missing large portions of its shingles. On the left of the ranch house was a large barn; its red paint peeling in the sun.

Beside the barn was a chicken coop, but no chickens were inside, just the feathers they'd left behind. On the right of the ranch house was a stable; its doors were shut, and like the house and the barn, it sagged in places.

Emily exhaled deeply. Then she walked around a large puddle of water towards the ranch house. As she stepped onto the porch, the wooden boards sank slightly under her weight. She approached the front door, wondering for a moment if she should knock; then Emily reached for the door handle, but it was locked.

Just then, she heard hammering from the side of the house and walked back across the porch. She went around the corner and stopped. Standing with his back to her was a tall man with broad shoulders, the muscles in his arms and back tensing up as he worked. He wore denim jeans, a dark green shirt, and a beige Stetson.

Emily watched him for a moment before she took a step forward, but as she did, the man stopped hammering and turned to her. Emily noticed that his eyes were almost the exact same color as his shirt. He also had a dark, scraggly looking beard and brown curls which were clinging to his neck, damp with sweat. As Emily met his eye, a look of recognition crossed his face, but then he frowned.

"Who are you?" he asked, lowering his hammer.

"My name is Emily McCoy," she answered.

"Well, if you are here about the house, it's not for sale," he said, turning back to his work,

"No," Emily said, taking another step forward. "I am looking for my nephew and niece. I believe they used to live in this house?"

The man froze for a moment before he turned to her again.

"You're Marie's sister?" he asked.

"Yes," Emily said. "And you are?"

"I'm Alec Kincaid," he replied. "I live on the ranch next door."

Emily nodded. "Do you know where I can find my nephew and niece?"

Alec nodded. "They've been staying with me since, well, you know..."

Alec's voice trailed off, and Emily nodded.

"Let me just finish up here, and I'll take you to meet them," Alec said.

"That would be most appreciated."

Alec returned to his job while Emily found an old log and sat down, placing her suitcase at her feet. She looked around, but her attention kept coming back to Alec. As she watched him, her stomach fluttered, and she couldn't tell if she was nervous about meeting her nephew and niece or if he made her nervous, the handsome cowboy with the green eyes.

Chapter Four

Alec hammered in the last nail before he glanced over his shoulder at Emily McCoy. She was sitting on a log, her suitcase on the ground in front of her. When he'd first seen her standing behind him, he'd thought she was Marie, just slightly older.

They were alike in so many ways with their light blonde hair, hazel eyes, and high cheekbones. However, Emily was taller than Marie, and her face was slightly sharper. She was beautiful, though; there was no denying that.

Alec returned his hammer to his metal toolbox and picked it up. He turned around, and as he did, he caught Emily's eye.

"I just need to put this in the barn," he said, raising the toolbox. "And then we can go."

Emily nodded, getting up from her seat. She followed him to the barn, waiting outside as he returned the toolbox to its place on the shelf. He hesitated a moment, smoothing down his hair and wiping his forehead before turning around and heading back outside.

"I can carry that for you," Alec offered, gesturing to her suitcase.

"I can manage," Emily said. "I've got this far."

"Suit yourself," Alec said, shrugging.

They walked down the road together, and for a while, neither spoke. Alec had never seen a woman dressed the way that she was. Her olive-green dress had a high collar, ruffled trim, and long sleeves that were puffed at the shoulders and narrowed towards her wrists. Her black leather boots were pointed, and she wore black kid leather gloves. On her head she wore a bonnet with a green ribbon trim.

"We didn't know when you were coming," Alec said, casting her a sideways glance.

"I wasn't sure when I'd be able to get away." Emily replied.

Alec nodded, but he suddenly felt annoyed with this woman. Marie had been murdered over six weeks ago, and it had taken her sister this long to get here. Still, Alec shouldn't be surprised; the sisters hadn't spoken in over seven years.

"Did you know my sister well?" Emily asked.

"Yes," Alec said. "She and my wife were very good friends."

Emily nodded and then fell silent again.

A short while later, they arrived at Alec's gate and headed towards the house. In the distance, there was a rumble of thunder, and Alec turned to see large, black clouds gathering on the horizon. Cobalt, who was sitting in the shade of the barn suddenly spotted them and came running over, his tail wagging. He sniffed Emily's skirts as she leaned over and patted his head.

"Who's this?" she asked, scratching the dog behind his ears.

"Cobalt," Alec said. "Colby for short."

They continued towards the house with Colby at their heels but just as they approached the back door, Alec stopped and turned to Emily.

"The children have been through a lot," Alec said. "So I just need to ask what your plan is now that you are here?"

"I plan on taking them back to New York with me," Emily said plainly.

"What?" Alex said, frowning. "You can't do that; this is their home."

Emily frowned, tilting her head. "I am the only family the children have left," she said. "They should live with me; it's what Marie would have wanted."

"How do you know what Marie would have wanted," Alec argued. "You hadn't spoken in nearly eight years."

The color drained from Emily's face.

"You don't know anything about my relationship with my sister," she said, her voice low.

"Well, I probably know more than you think," Alec retorted. "And I also know this is the only home those two children have ever known; taking them away now would do more harm than good."

Emily exhaled sharply. "I am grateful you took my nephew and niece in," she said. "And I am sure you've done a good job, but this is a family matter."

Alec scoffed, shaking his head. "Are you really going to start preaching about family to me?"

"Are you going to introduce me to my niece and nephew or not? Emily countered.

Alex gritted his teeth and folded his arms. "I don't think I am," he said.

"What?" Emily replied, her mouth popping open in surprise.

"That's right," Alec said.

"B-but you can't just keep me away from them," Emily argued, her voice rising.

"I've known Thomas and Lily their whole lives," Alec said. "And I am certain I know what is best for them."

Emily opened her mouth to argue when suddenly the back door opened, and Mrs. Tattlewell stepped outside.

"Is everything alright?" she asked, looking between them.

"Fine," Alec said.

"And who is this?' Mrs. Tattlewell asked.

"I am Emily McCoy," Emily introduced herself, stepping forward. "Marie's sister."

Mrs. Tattlewell's dark eyes widened. "Well," she said, smiling. "This is wonderful. We were all hoping you would come soon after Reverend Middleton wrote. Why don't you come inside? I'll put the kettle on—"

"Miss McCoy was actually just about to leave," Alec said.

"Oh?" Mrs. Tattlewell said, frowning. "So soon?"

"Mr. Kincaid is mistaken," Emily said. "I'd love a cup of tea."

Emily shot Alec a hard glance before she followed Mrs. Tattlewell inside the house.

Alec stepped into the kitchen behind Emily and Mrs. Tattlewell. He expected to find the children at the kitchen table, reading or drawing, but the room was empty. Alec stood by the door as Mrs. Tattlewell pulled a chair out and invited Emily to sit. Then she walked over to the stove and put the copper kettle on to boil.

"How was your trip from New York?" Mrs. Tattlewell asked as she fetched the teapot from the dresser.

Alec, whose eyes had been fixed on Emily, saw her eyes widen.

"Oh, don't worry," Mrs. Tattlewell chuckled. "Everyone in this town knows everyone's business. Reverend Middleton's letter has been the talk of the town for weeks."

"Right," Emily said, grimacing slightly. "Well, the trip was fine, thank you. Long, but comfortable."

Mrs. Tattlewell nodded in satisfaction.

"Although it seems the railroad to Forest Hill was destroyed in a tornado," Emily continued. "So I had to make my way from Cattleman's Rest."

"That's right," Mrs. Tattlewell said, nodding. "So, how did you come to arrive in Forest Hill, Miss McCoy?"

"Please, call me Emily," she said. "I got a ride from a gentleman by the name of Leonard."

Alec chuckled dryly, and Emily looked at him, her brow furrowed.

"Ignore him," Mrs. Tattlewell said. "Leonard is a good man, albeit a bit of a rolling stone."

"Well, he was very kind to me," Emily said, throwing a hard glance at Alec. "And it takes all kinds of folk to make the world go round."

"Very well put," Mrs. Tattlewell said approvingly as she turned to Alec. "Are you staying for tea?"

Alec hesitated a moment. He was not inclined to sit down and make polite small talk with this woman, but he knew she wasn't just about to turn around and go back to New York.

"Sure," Alec said. "Why not."

He walked over to the table and sat down across from Emily. He caught her eye for a moment and then looked away.

"Here we are," Mrs. Tattlewell said brightly as she carried over the tea tray, placing it down in the middle of the table.

"Thank you," Emily said politely.

Mrs. Tattlewell sat down and served them all, and for a while, the room was silent.

"Where are the children?" Emily asked, looking at Mrs. Tattlewell.

"They are with young Jeremiah, the ranch hand," Mrs. Tattlewell said. "A pair of calves, twins, were born last night, but their poor mother didn't make it, so Thomas and Lily are helping Jeremiah to bottle feed them."

"Is that safe?" Emily asked. "For them to be out there alone?"

"They are not alone," Mrs. Tattlewell said, frowning slightly. "They are with young Jeremiah."

"Yes, of course," Emily agreed. "But Lily is only two? Surely she requires better supervision than a preoccupied ranch hand?"

Alec gritted his teeth as he turned to look at her. "We don't expect you to understand," he said dismissively. "But we do things differently here than in the city. Thomas and Lily have been raised off the land, and they're safer out there, bottle feeding calves, than in a disease-ridden city with trouble on every corner and sky's so polluted you can barely feel the sunshine on your face."

"I take it you are not a fan of New York?" Emily said dryly.

"Never been," Alec said, taking a sip of tea. "But your sister told me a lot about it; it seems she wasn't a fan either."

Emily pressed her lips into a hard line. "Yes, well, my sister always preferred country life."

"Which is why we got along so well," Alec said.

Emily glared at him as Mrs. Tattlewell cleared her throat.

"So, Emily," she said, changing the subject. "Where are you planning on staying while you're here in Forest Hill?"

Emily frowned. "I'm not entirely sure," she confessed. "I had planned to take a room at a hotel or boarding house, but I see that Forest Hill has neither."

"No," Mrs. Tattlewell confirmed. "But I am sure we can find someone in town to put you up. I know Reverend Middleton would be happy to do so if his wife hadn't suddenly taken so ill."

"I do not wish to be any trouble—"

Alec scoffed loudly, and Emily glared at him again.

"I thought perhaps I might stay in my sister's house," Emily said.

"That's not a good idea," Alec replied, shaking his head.

"Why not?' Emily asked.

"Because a woman shouldn't stay alone," Alec said. "It's too dangerous."

Emily frowned, shaking her head. "I live on my own in New York," she said. "I am perfectly capable of looking after myself."

"It's not the same," Alec argued. "Forest Hill is a whole different breed of place."

"Well, why do you care?" Emily challenged. "You don't want me here anyway."

"Alec is right," Mrs. Tattlewell said, cutting in. "Life out here is different. It lacks the comforts and order of the city. For a newcomer, it can be a tough and unforgiving place. Look what happened to Bill and your sister; Bill had lived here his whole life."

"Yes, well, that being said, I think I will take my chances," Emily said.

Alec shook his head but said nothing. If this big city girl thought she knew better, then who was he to argue?

Just then, there was another rumble of thunder, loud enough to rattle the glass in its panes.

"You should be getting home, Mrs. Tattlewell," Alec said, turning to look at her. "Before the rain comes."

"You're probably right," Mrs. Tattlewell agreed. "We've had such terrible storms this summer."

Mrs. Tattlewell got up from the table and removed her apron, hanging it on the hook behind the door.

"I've left supper on the stove," Mrs. Tattlewell said.

"Thank you," Alec replied gratefully.

Mrs. Tattlewell turned to Emily. "I am sure I will be seeing you again soon," she said.

"Thank you for the tea," Emily said.

Mrs. Tattlewell smiled at them before she turned and exited the kitchen, leaving Emily and Alec alone. For a long moment, neither of them said anything.

"I'd better go and finish up the chores before the rain comes," Alec said.

Without another word, Alec got up from the table and left the kitchen via the back door.

The first drops of rain were starting to fall as Alec secured the stable doors. A flash of lightning struck a tree a few feet away, and a sharp crack pierced the air. Alec turned to see young Jeremiah hurrying toward him. He was carrying Lily in his arms, with Thomas running by his side.

"Cutting it a bit close, Jeremiah," Alec said, taking Lily from him.

"Sorry, Alec," Jeremiah apologized. "But the kids didn't want to leave, and the storm blew in so quick."

Alec nodded. "No harm done," he said. "Now go and get yourself home."

Jeremiah nodded as he ruffled Thomas's damp hair and took off.

"Come on," Alec said. "Let's get inside."

By the time they stepped in through the back door, they were soaked through. Emily was still sitting at the kitchen table, just as he'd left her.

"Goodness," she said, getting up from the table. "You two are soaked to the bone."

"Go and stand by the fire," Alec said.

Thomas and Lily walked over to the fire, their teeth chattering while Emily fussed over them, beginning to strip them of their wet clothes, but Thomas took a step back, putting his arm around Lily's shoulders protectively.

"Who is she?" Thomas asked seriously as he looked at Alec. "She looks familiar."

"That's your Aunt Emily," Alec said. "Your mother's sister."

Both Thomas and Lily's eyes widened, but neither of them spoke. Alec knelt down beside the children and began to strip them of their wet clothes. There were puddles of water at their feet and they were shivering.

"Can you get a towel?" Alec asked, barely turning to look at Emily. "There are some in the basket by the door."

A moment later, Emily handed Alec two towels and he wrapped the children up in them, securing the towels tightly under their chins. Then he fetched two kitchen chairs and placed them in front of the fire.

"You two stay put," Alec instructed. "I'll go and fetch you some dry clothes."

Alec turned and left the kitchen with Emily on his heels. She followed him upstairs to the children's bedroom. It was small with only two beds and a narrow wooden dresser between them. Emily hesitated in the doorway, her brow creased as Alec walked over to the dresser and knelt down, pulling open the first drawer and removing the children's night clothes.

"Are these the only things they have?" Emily asked, frowning as she eyed the garments in Alec's hands. "There aren't any others?"

Alec said nothing. He'd noticed recently that the children's clothes were rather threadbare and that most were getting too small for them now. He'd been meaning to talk to Mrs. Tattlewell about it, but he hadn't found a moment with everything that had been going on.

"That's what was brought over from the house," Alec said.

Emily pursed her lips. "Well, I suppose they will have to do," she said.

Without another word, Alec closed the dresser drawer. Carrying the clothes, he walked back out of the room past Emily and downstairs.

Emily stood in the doorway as Alec dressed Lily and then Thomas. He was kneeling between them, talking softly. The children kept their curious eyes fixed on Emily.

"There,' Alec said, smiling at them. "Nice and warm."

"Are you really our aunt?" Thomas asked, tilting his head slightly as he looked at Emily.

"Of course I am," Emily said. "Did your mother never mention me?"

"She said you lived in New York," Thomas said.

"I do," Emily confirmed. "But I took a train all the way to Texas so that I could come and meet you."

"Our ma and pa are dead," Thomas said matter-of-factly.

"I know," Emly said sadly. "And I am very sorry for that."

Without another word, Emily reached across, pulling Thomas and Lily into a tight hug but it was awkward and the children squirmed uncomfortably in her arms.

As Alec watched their interaction, he felt a mixture of relief and concern. In all these weeks since Marie and Bill had been gone, he had wanted someone to come along and help him with the children. Now Emily was here, but she didn't want to be. He wanted what was best for Thomas and Lily, but the idea that Emily was here to take them away was not something that Alec could get on board with.

He understood she was their only living relative, but he knew the children better. They'd lost so much already, and Alec could not agree that moving to a strange city would do them any good. They were country children who needed to walk barefoot in the soil and ride bareback through the fields.

Marie knew this. It's why she never officially named her sister as the children's guardian. She knew that Thomas and Lily would never thrive in the city. They belonged here in Forest Hill, and Alec would fight for them to stay.

While he had no idea how to be a full-time parent, the possibility of losing Thomas and Lily was scarier, and although he did not know how, he needed to convince Emily to let the children remain in Texas.

Chapter Five

"How about some dinner?" Emily asked, looking from Thomas to Lily. "I am sure you are hungry."

Thomas nodded, and Emily got up. She returned the two chairs to the table and steered Thomas and Lily into their seats. As she did, she could feel Alec's eyes on her, but she did her best to ignore him and focus on the children instead.

"Shall we see what's for dinner then?" Emily asked.

She turned and walked to the stove where Mrs. Tattlewell had left their dinner. She lifted the dish towel and frowned, wrinkling her nose.

"What is this?" she asked, turning to Alec.

"It's Cowboy Casserole," Alec said. "It's one of the children's favorites."

Emily frowned as she turned back to examine the dish, which appeared to be made up of beans, ground beef, and biscuit dough.

"Where are the vegetables?" she asked.

"There are beans," Thomas said, shrugging.

Emily frowned again.

"It's a Texas staple," Alec said, fetching plates from the dresser. "But if it's not up to your high standards, you can always leave it."

Emily bristled. "No," she said. "Cowboy Casserole sounds fine."

Alec smirked as Emily threw him a withering look before she turned to Thomas and Lily, smiling brightly. She picked up the casserole and put it into the Dutch oven to heat up. While Alec set the table, Emily sat with her nephew and niece. It was surreal to be sitting here with them; they looked so much more like Marie in person.

"So what else did your ma tell you about me?" Emily asked.

Thomas shrugged and Lily said nothing. Emily's smile faltered.

"Well I am a teacher," Emily said. "I teach at a school called Briarwood House."

"Do you like being a teacher?" Thomas asked.

"I do," Emily said. "Very much."

"I wish I could go to school," Thomas said. "But there isn't one in Forest Hill."

"Oh?" Emily said, turning to look at Alec.

"There used to be," he explained. "But a smallpox epidemic wiped out half the town about ten years ago, including the teacher, and a replacement was never found."

"What a tragedy," Emily said. "There is no better opportunity in this life than an education. Still, don't lose heart, Thomas; you may be able to attend school before too long."

"Really? —"

"Dinner's ready," Alec said, cutting Thomas off. "Let's eat."

Emily pursed her lips as Alec carried the casserole to the table and put it down in the center. Then he served Thomas and Lily each a spoonful.

"Eat up," Alec said. "Before it gets cold."

Thomas and Lily both picked up their forks and began to eat. Emily looked down at the food for a long moment before she reached for the spoon and served herself up a small portion.

They all ate in silence as the rain continued falling on the tin roof. Emily really wanted to get to know the children but they were so much more reserved than she expected.

"Lily," Emily said suddenly, turning to the little girl. "How old are you?"

The little girl kept her head down and said nothing.

'Lily—"

"She's two, turning three," Thomas replied.

"Can Lily not answer for herself?" Emily asked.

"She doesn't talk," Thomas explained.

Emily frowned slightly, turning to look at Alec, but he had his head bent over his supper. The table fell silent again.

A short while later, the children had finished eating.

"Why don't you go and get ready for bed?" Alec said.

"Maybe I could come up and tuck you in?" Emily suggested.

'No, thank you," Thomas said. "Alec tucks us in."

Emily's face fell but she quickly recovered herself. "Of course," she said. "There will be plenty of time for us to get to know one another."

Both Thomas and Lily looked unsure.

"I'll be up shortly," Alec said.

'Will you finish telling us the story about the Old Prospector's Gold?" Thomas asked.

"Yes," Alec agreed. "Now off you go."

'Goodnight, children," Emily said. "I'll see you both in the morning."

Without another word, Thomas took Lily's hand and led her out the kitchen door. Once they were gone, Emily turned to Alec, frowning.

"Lily doesn't talk?" she said accusingly.

"She did before," Alec said. "But since her parents were killed, she's not said a word."

"Well, don't you think that's a bit concerning?" Emily said, her voice rising. "Why haven't you done anything about it?"

"What was I supposed to do?" Alec said, the muscles in his jaw tightening.

"Talk to a doctor?" Emily said, her eyes flashing.

"I did," Alex explained. "And there is nothing physically wrong with her."

Emily exhaled deeply, shaking her head. "This is exactly why the children must return to New York with me. There are proper doctors there, people who can help."

"Dr. Hastings is a proper doctor," Alec argued. "And Thomas and Lily like him; they trust him."

"Yes, well, that may be so, but I still believe the doctors in New York have a better chance of helping Lily."

Alec sighed, shaking his head.

65

"You don't agree?" Emily asked.

"I think you rode in here on your high horse, thinking that you know Thomas and Lily better than anyone else," Alec said, glowering at her. "But you are wrong. You don't know them at all, and you don't know what they've been through."

Emily opened her mouth and shut it again, her cheeks growing warm.

"Now, if you'll excuse me, I am going to tuck the children into bed," he said.

Without another word, Alec got up from the table and turned to go, leaving Emily all alone. She sat back in her chair and sighed. She had not known what to expect coming to Forest Hill, but it certainly hadn't been Alec Kincaid. While she appreciated that he cared for Thomas and Lily, and she was grateful he'd taken them in; he was going to be a problem.

Emily got up from the table and cleared the plates and cutlery, carrying them to the sink. She scraped her leftover casserole into Cobalt's bowl and the dog wagged his tail gratefully as he bent his head to eat.

As Emily washed the dishes, her mind was on the children. Alec was not wrong when he said that she didn't know her nephew and niece; that was true. But she wanted to get to know them; that was why she wanted them to come and live with her, so that they could get to know one another and be a family.

After washing the dishes, Emily put the leftover food away and wiped the table clean. She'd just finished when Alec stepped back into the kitchen.

"Are the children asleep?" she asked.

Alec nodded, and they fell silent for a moment.

"Well, the rain has stopped," Emily said. "So I think I'll get going. Do you have the keys to the house?"

Alec turned and disappeared, reemerging a minute later with the keys which he handed to Emily.

"Thank you," she said.

"I really think it's better if you slept here," Alec said. "You shouldn't stay at the house alone."

"I will be perfectly fine," Emily insisted.

"Miss McCoy—"

But Emily was not listening to him as she turned to go, fetching her suitcase from the floor beside the sink. She pulled open the door and stepped outside. It was still light out, and the rain clouds began to part, revealing an orange and blue sky behind them.

Without turning around, Emily made her way down the muddy driveway and out of the gate. She walked along the road the same way she'd come with Alec earlier that day.

She inserted the key into the lock on the front door and turned it. The damp had gotten into the wood, causing it to swell, and it took all of Emily's effort to push the front door open. As she stepped inside, all she could smell was mold.

Emily put her suitcase on the floor by the door and slowly made her way down the narrow passage. She had no idea where anything was, and her only guide was the fading daylight that pressed against the grimy windows.

At the end of the hallway was the kitchen, and Emily found a small paraffin lamp hanging from a nail by the sink. She lit its wick, and the room was cast into a warm glow. Emily then lit the fire in the small coal stove and looked around. In just six weeks, cobwebs were forming in the corners, and all the surfaces were covered in a thick layer of dust. There was also the sharp, unmistakable smell of mouse droppings.

As Emily stared into the flames, the house creaked softly, and somewhere in the distance, a coyote howled. For the first time in a long time, Emily was completely alone. In the previous weeks, she had her work, but now, she had nothing to distract her from the knowledge that she was seated in her sister's kitchen, but her sister was not there.

Emily fetched the paraffin lamp and left the kitchen, walking down towards the front door where she'd left her bag. As she did, she passed by the dining and the sitting rooms, as well as a small study.

She picked up her bag and headed upstairs. There were two bedrooms and a large nursery. Emily walked to the furthest room and pushed open the door. She recognized the quilt on the bed; it had been their parents, and Emily had forgotten all about it until that moment. There was a small table beside the bed and a washstand on the opposite side beside a large wooden dresser.

Emily willed her legs to move, but even as exhausted as she was, she could not bring herself to go into her sister's bedroom or to sleep in Marie's bed. She could not hang her things in the dresser beside her sister's as they'd done as girls.

Emily turned and walked across the hallway and into the nursery. She placed her suitcase down on the small bed and opened it, removing a thin shawl that she pulled around her shoulders.

She then headed back downstairs and into the kitchen, walking over to the kitchen table and sitting down. The flames in the kitchen stove crackled in the cold silence as Emily sighed. She should have taken Mrs. Tattlewell up on her offer to find somewhere else for her to stay the night, but it was too late now.

Emily wasn't sure how long she sat at the table, but she must have dozed off because she awoke to the sound of glass shattering and jumped up. The doorway was dark save for the smoldering coals in the stove. The lamp must have run out of paraffin and gone out.

"Is somebody there?" Emily called out, her voice shaking.

But there was no response, and Emily felt a shiver run up her spine. Then there was a loud thump, thump, thump above her head followed by a scratching sound, and without hesitating a moment longer, Emily threw open the back door and rushed outside, running down the road and out the gate, not looking back. A wind blew from the east, but the sky above her was cloudless, and the full moon guided her as she hurried up to Alec's house and banged on the front door.

Alec pulled the door open, squinting, sleeping in the darkness. He was dressed in a pair of cotton pants and nothing else.

"What is going on?" he said, his eyes widening. "What are you doing here?"

"Someone's in the house," Emily said, trying to catch her breath.

Alec sighed as Cobalt pushed past him, sniffing Emily's skirts, and wagging his tail.

"I fell asleep downstairs, and I woke up to a crashing sound, and then there was a thump."

"Are you sure it wasn't just a rat?" Alec asked, stifling a yawn.

"I'm sure," Emily insisted. "I live in New York, I know rats."

"Alright," Alec sighed. "Stay here with the children, and I'll go and have a look."

Emily nodded gratefully as Alec turned and headed back upstairs. Emily stepped into the house and waited on the landing for a minute or so before Alec came back downstairs, this time wearing a shirt and boots. He was also gripping his shotgun tightly in his right hand.

He left through the open door, and Emily waited until he was gone before she headed into the kitchen. As her heart rate finally returned to normal, Emily filled the copper kettle on the stove and put it on to boil.

A short while later, Alec returned, and Emily turned to him expectantly as he stepped into the kitchen.

"It was a branch," he said.

"A branch?" Emily repeated, frowning.

"It must have been hit during the last storm and broke loose in the wind," Alec explained. "It broke through the nursery window.

"Oh," Emily said, feeling both relieved and embarrassed. "Well, I am sorry I woke you."

"It's fine," Alec said. "Truthfully, we've had some trouble over at the house."

"What kind of trouble?" Emily asked, frowning.

"We think a couple of kids broke in the other night," Alex explained. "Probably just lookin' for a hideout from their folks, a place to wet their non-existent whiskers."

Emily folded her hands across her chest as she glared at Alex.

"And you let me stay there?" she accused. "Knowing that it had been broken into?"

Alec shrugged. "You insisted," he said.

Emily gritted her teeth. "Well, I am not going back there," she said.

Alec sighed. "Fine," he said. "You can stay here."

"Really?" Emily asked, not bothering to hide her surprise.

Alec shrugged. "There's a spare room downstairs."

"Thank you," she said gratefully.

Alec nodded.

"Oh, I left my bag at the house," Emily realized suddenly.

"I brought it," Alec said. "It's by the front door."

Emily frowned. "How did you know I would agree to stay?" she asked.

"Let me show you to your room," Alec offered, ignoring her question.

Emily followed him out of the kitchen and down the hallway into a small bedroom. Beside the door was a table with an oil lamp atop it. Alec reached over and lit the lamp, casting the room into a warm glow. Emily looked around the bedroom. Its walls were decorated in floral paper, and a large bay window was directly opposite the door. A single bed was pressed against the far wall, and beside it was a large oak dresser. There was also a washstand beside a narrow bookshelf.

Emily stepped into the room and turned back to Alec.

"There is an extra quilt in the bottom drawer of the dresser," he said. "In case you get cold."

"Thank you," Emily said.

Alec nodded. "Well, if there is nothing else, I'll see you in the morning."

"Wait," Emily said as Alec turned back to face her. "Where is your wife? You said earlier that my sister and your wife were close friends."

Alec hesitated, a shadow moving across his face.

"My wife is dead," Alec said, his voice low.

"Oh," Emily said, her stomach sinking. "I am sorry, I didn't mean to pry—"

"It's late," Alec said. "Goodnight."

Without another word, Alec turned, leaving Emily alone, standing in the middle of the room. She wished she hadn't asked about his wife, but it was too late now. Emily sighed to herself as she carried the oil lamp from the table by the door to the one beside the bed. She sat down, taking off her boots before she blew out the light and lay down.

As Emily stared up at the ceiling, she felt overwhelmed by everything. She hadn't expected to meet such strong opposition, rather, she'd hoped her arrival would bring only relief and gratitude. The children did not seem particularly thrilled by her arrival either and it was obvious they were attached to Alec.

Still, it was her first night here, and she was determined to make Alec see things her way. After all, the children would have a better life in New York. They'd receive proper schooling and have a world of opportunities at their fingertips. She was sure taking them back with her was the right thing to do, and she needed to make everyone see that too.

The children had already experienced enough trauma and she did not want to take them back with her kicking and screaming. So, she would spend the next week or so getting to know them and once she had, she was sure they'd agree to come back to New York with her.

Chapter Six

Alec woke up early the following day. He had not slept well; between the unexpected visitor and the midnight runarounds, he'd had too much on his mind to get much shuteye.

Alec got up and dressed. He pulled open the bedroom door and headed downstairs.

In the kitchen, he found Thomas and Lily waiting for him. Cobalt was lying under the table at their feet. He smiled at them both. "What's on the menu today?"

"Boiled eggs and soldiers, please," Thomas said, while Lily nodded enthusiastically.

"Did you two collect the eggs this morning?" he asked.

They both nodded, and Alec smiled again. "Boiled eggs and soldiers it is, then," Alec agreed.

Alec fetched three eggs from the basket in the pantry; they were still warm. Then he filled a pot of water and put it on to boil.

"Have you seen your aunt this morning?" he asked as he uncovered a loaf of bread and began slicing it into pieces.

Thomas and Lily both shook their heads.

Alec nodded; she probably wasn't up yet. He walked over to where the water was boiling and put the three eggs into the pot. Then he filled the copper kettle and put it on to boil beside the eggs.

"What is she doing here?" Thomas asked.

Alec sighed as he turned to face the children. He wasn't prepared to lie to them; they deserved better.

"She's come to take you back to New York with her," Alec said.

The color drained from Thomas's face, and Lily's bottom lip began to quiver.

"But we don't want to leave," Thomas said. "Please don't let her take us."

Alec sighed as he walked to the table and sat opposite the children. "I am going to do everything I can, okay?"

Thomas and Lily nodded, but their eyes were wide with worry. Just then, Emily came into the kitchen smiling. Her fancy dress from the day before was wrinkled, and she had dark circles under her eyes, suggesting to Alec that she had not slept very well either.

"Good morning, children," Emily said brightly.

"We won't go with you," Thomas shouted, his eyes flashing. "We like it here!"

Before anyone could say anything else, Thomas grabbed Lily's hand, and they slid out of their seats and ran from the room.

Emily turned sharply to Alec, her lips pressed into a hard line.

"What did you tell them?" she shouted.

"The truth," Alec said, turning back to the stove and removing the pot from the heat.

Emily exhaled deeply. "I wished you had let me explain," she said.

"Why?" Alec challenged, turning to her again. "So that you could spin some fairytale about life in the city?"

"No," Emily said, frowning. "I don't plan on spinning anything. I plan on telling them the truth."

Alec raised his eyebrows skeptically, and Emily sighed.

"I know you aren't pleased that I am here," she said. "But I am not going anywhere. Thomas and Lily are my family."

"Well, they are my family, too," Alec argued.

Emily crossed her arms but said nothing as Alec fetched the coffee tin from the pantry.

"Would you like some?" he offered.

Emily nodded as she walked over to the table and sat down. Neither spoke while Alec made two cups of coffee and handed one to Emily.

"So what now?' Emily asked, taking the cup from him.

"I don't know," Alec sighed, taking a sip of his own.

The kitchen fell silent for a few moments, and as Alec looked down at his coffee mug, he could sense Emily watching him.

"Look," Alec sighed. "I think it's pretty clear that the only thing we have in common is Thomas and Lily. So you should stay, get to know them, and then let them decide."

Emily pursed her lips and nodded. "Alright," she agreed.

Alec drained the last of the coffee from his cup, placing it down on the side of the sink. As he did, Mrs. Tattlewell arrived, stepping into the kitchen, and smiling at them both.

"Oh," she said in surprise. "I didn't expect to see you here so early, Emily."

"She was excited to spend time with the children," Alec said.

"How nice," Mrs. Tattlewell said, fetching her apron from the hook behind the door. "I am sure they are excited to get to know you and hear all about the big city."

Alec turned to Emily to see her biting her lip apprehensively.

"Don't worry, dear," Mrs. Tattlewell said sympathetically. "It will take some time for familiarity to grow, but they are kind children with generous hearts; just look how much they love Alec."

Emily looked across at Alec, who cleared his throat.

"I'd best get to work," he said.

"Where are the children?" Mrs. Tattlewell enquired. "Did they eat breakfast already?"

"No," Alec said, shaking his head. "But I'll send them in as soon as I find them."

Mrs. Tattlewell nodded, and Alec left the kitchen, his head down. He headed outside, past the washing line and vegetable patch, towards the stables. As he reached the doors, he hesitated a moment before he stepped inside to find Thomas and Lily standing on upside-down pails, feeding his horse carrots.

"And where did you get those?" he asked, his lips twitching in amusement.

"From the vegetable patch," Thomas confessed. "But they are the old ones Mrs. Tattlewell turned over from last season."

Alec nodded as he walked across the stables, reaching over and scratching his horse behind the ears.

"Do you two want to go inside and have your breakfast?" Alec asked. "Mrs. Tattlewell is here."

"And Aunt Emily?" Thomas asked, not meeting Alec's eyes.

"Yes," Alec said. "Your Aunt Emily has come a long way to get to know you and Lily."

Thomas said nothing as Alec reached over, putting a hand on his shoulder.

"It's going to be okay, Thomas," he said. "I promise."

"But how do you know?" Thomas insisted. "What if Aunty Emily takes us away to New York, and we never get to see you again."

Alec glanced over at Lily, her hazel eyes wide with concern, and his stomach sank.

"Promise that you won't let her take us," Thomas said, his face full of determination.

"Thomas—"

"Promise," Thomas repeated.

"It's not that simple," Alec sighed. "She's your family."

"But ma would never have wanted us to go and live in the city," Thomas said. "She hated the city, so did pa."

Lily nodded in agreement.

"I know," Alec agreed. "But legally, your aunt gets to decide."

Thomas frowned. 'But you could fight her," he said. "You could tell everyone that we are better off here with you."

Alec said nothing for a moment. He couldn't help but think how much Thomas had matured these past weeks since his parents died. He was only seven years old, but he was so much wiser than his years. In many ways, his parents' murders had robbed him of his innocence, and Alec would always be sorry for that.

"Listen," Alec said, meeting Thomas's eye. "I think your aunt is here to get to know you both, and I think you should give her that chance. If for no reason other than that, it is what your mother would have wanted."

Thomas pressed his lips into a hard line.

"Do you think you can at least try?" Alec asked.

Thomas hesitated a moment and nodded. Alec looked over at Lily, and she nodded, too.

"Alright," Alec said. "Well, why don't you two go inside and get some breakfast."

Without another word, Thomas and Lily climbed off the pails and left the stables. Alec watched them go, hoping that he was doing the right thing. Part of him wanted to tell Emily to leave and to keep the children as far from her reach as possible, but the more sensible part told him that was the wrong decision to make. Emily was their only relative, and if she took this in front of a judge, chances are he'd side with her. However, if Alec played along and let her get to know the children, he was confident she'd see they were better off with him.

Chapter Seven

Emily sat in a straight-backed wooden chair across the table from the children eating their soldiers and eggs. Her pale hands sat twisted together in her lap, and every now and again, she picked nervously at the skin on the side of her left thumb. Emily did not know what was happening. Usually, she was so good with kids. Her students loved her; she was always the favorite, and yet she couldn't think of the right thing to say to her nephew and niece. Every time she opened her mouth, she put her foot in it.

"Why don't you take your Aunt Emily around the ranch after breakfast?" Mrs. Tattlewell suggested, breaking the silence that hung over the table. 'I'm sure she'd love to see all of your favorite spots."

Emily threw a grateful glance at the older woman, who smiled sympathetically.

"Do you like snakes?" Thomas asked as he dipped a finger of bread into his egg yolk.

"I can't say I've ever seen one," Emily confessed.

"There are lots of rattlers on the ranch," Thomas continued. "Especially in the summer. You have to be really careful where you walk in case you accidentally step on one."

Emily paled at the thought.

"Thomas," Mrs. Tattlewell said disapprovingly. "Don't frighten your aunt."

"It's fine, Mrs. Tattlewell," Emily assured her. "Thomas is only making sure I watch where I walk."

"Our pa once shot a rattler right between the eyes," Thomas said.

Emily raised her eyebrows.

"The children's father, Bill, was a very protective man," she explained.

"He was also the best shot in the whole of Forest Hill," Thomas interjected.

"That he was," Mrs. Tattlewell agreed.

Emily nodded, but there was something about Mrs. Tattlewell's tone that suggested to her that there was more to the story.

"Are you all done with your breakfast?" Mrs. Tattlewell asked.

The children nodded.

"Good, well then, clear your plates and go upstairs and fetch your hats. When you get back, you can take your aunt for a walk."

Without argument, Thomas and Lily picked their plates up off the table and carried them to the sink. Then, hand-in-hand, they left the kitchen and headed upstairs. Mrs. Tattlewell watched them go, smiling.

"Thomas takes such good care of his little sister," she said in admiration.

"Thomas said that Lily doesn't talk?" Emily said.

"That's right," Mrs. Tattlewell replied, a frown on her face.

"Alec said that she's seen a doctor?"

Mrs. Tattlewell nodded. "Poor lamb's been through quite an ordeal," she said. "Some folks in town judged Alec for not taking her to see more doctors, but Alec decided against it."

"Why?" Emily asked.

"He felt she had been poked and prodded enough," Mrs. Tattlewell explained. "Alec believes that all Lily needs is time to grieve and adjust. Alec should know after all; he is no stranger to loss."

"He told me that he lost his wife," Emily said.

"Did he now?" Mrs. Tattlewell replied, her eyebrows raised. "Alec doesn't like to talk about it much."

"I didn't really give him a choice," Emily confessed.

Mrs. Tattlewell nodded. "Olivia was a special woman, kind and full of grace," she said. "Most people said it was cruel that she was taken so young, and the baby along with her, but we are not privy to God's plans. All we can do is have faith."

"They had a baby?" Emily asked, her eyes wide.

"She died in Oliva's arms," Mrs. Tattlewell said. "And well, being the person Olivia was, she wasn't going to let her baby girl make the trip up to heaven alone, so she closed her eyes and went with her."

Despite the sticky heat of the morning, a shiver ran up Emily's spine. "How terrible," she said, shaking her head.

"I suppose it's part of the reason Alec is so close to the children," Mrs. Tattlewell said. "After all, Lily was born only weeks after he lost his own daughter, and most would argue that Alec was more of a father to her than her own pa."

Emily frowned. "What do you mean?" she asked.

Mrs. Tattlewell opened her mouth to reply, but as she did, the children reappeared in the kitchen doorway, and she closed it again.

"Off you all go now," Mrs. Tattlewell said, shooing them out of the kitchen. "I've got a lot of cleaning to do."

Emily got up from her chair and followed the children outside. The air was heavy, and the mountains in the distance were hazy from the heat.

In silence, Emily followed Thomas and Lily across the ranch. As they walked, she thought about what Mrs. Tattlewell had just said about Alec being more of a father to Lily than Bill. Alec has said he and Marie were only friends, but what if they were more? What if Emily had walked into something else entirely? She knew nothing about Bill and Marie's marriage. Had they been unhappy? Had her sister sought solace somewhere else?

Despite all these thoughts now plaguing Emily's mind, she could not ignore the beads of perspiration running down her back or how her throat was so dry it was like sandpaper.

"Maybe we should head back?" Emily said.

"We're almost there," Thomas called over his shoulder.

"Where?" Emily asked.

But the children did not answer, so Emily followed them through the tall prairie grasses, muttering under her breath. Just then, she spotted a wide, slow-moving stream, its water glinting as it caught the sun's rays. Along the banks of the stream were tall willow trees, their branches dancing delicately in the breeze.

"Come on, Aunty Emily," Thomas shouted, racing over to her and taking her hand.

Emily was so surprised at the warmness of the gesture that she forgot all about how hot and bothered she felt.

As they reached the bank, the children sat down and began to remove their shoes and socks.

"Take off your boots," Thomas encouraged.

Emily hesitated.

"It's okay," Thomas assured her. "We do it all the time."

Emily had not once in her life waded in a stream, and although she had no desire to do so now, she did not want to let her nephew and niece down.

"Alright," Emily agreed, sitting down on the soft sand.

She removed her black leather boots, placing them beside her. Then she removed one stocking and the other, folding them together before slipping them into one of her boots for safekeeping.

Emily stood up and walked to the edge of the water. The children were already in the stream, splashing one another. Emily dipped one toe in gingerly, but the water was deliciously cool, so she took a step forward and then another, closing her eyes as the water soothed her hot and swollen feet.

"Look out, Aunty Emily," Thomas cried.

Emily opened her eyes, but before she had a chance to do anything, Thomas swept his arm over the surface of the water, sending a large splash of water her way.

Emily gasped as the water soaked her dress and face. She reached up and wiped the water from her eyes as Thomas giggled mischievously.

Another wave of water sent Emily wading at speed to the other side of the steam, where the water was darker, and she could feel the mud squelching between her toes as she walked. Here, at least she was out of Thomas's reach.

"I'm sorry, Aunty Emily," Thomas called. "I promise I won't splash you again.

Emily was not unfamiliar with the mischievous nature of children, which is why she felt foolish at getting caught out this way.

"I think I am going to get out now," Emily said.

Emily waded back across the stream and climbed out onto the sand, her skirts in her hands. However, as she looked down, she caught sight of the dark brown, slimy creatures that were now attached to her feet, ankles, and shins, and without thinking, Emily let out a piercing scream.

"Get them off!" she cried, throwing her left leg out and shaking it around like a mad woman.

From the stream, Thomas could be seen laughing so hard that he had tears running down his cheeks while poor Lily watched Emily with wide eyes.

Emily continued to shake her legs about, but the creatures would not budge. Then, Email caught sight of Alec rushing towards them and Thomas stopped laughing at once.

"What is going on?" he asked, trying to catch his breath. "I heard someone scream."

Emily looked down at her legs, her face pale. "What are they?" she cried, her voice trembling.

Alec's lips twitched as he did his best not to smile. "They're just leeches," he said.

85

"It's not funny," Emily warned, her pale face suddenly flushing.

"No," Alec agreed. "But you're going to do yourself more harm by flinging your legs around like that."

"Well, then, help me," Emily insisted.

Alec walked over to her and knelt down on one knee. He reached into his back pocket and removed a small knife from its holster. Emily flinched.

"Don't worry," he said. "I won't hurt you."

Emily exhaled shakily as Alec pressed the flat side of the knife against her skin and slid it under each leech. He then raised the blade slowly and steadily, careful not to jerk or twist it, and a second later, the leech let go of its grip on her skin and fell to the floor.

Alec repeated the process with the others, each of them popping off and landing on the sand. Despite how revolted Emily was by the whole ordeal, she couldn't ignore the feeling of Alec's warm fingers on her skin.

"There," Alec said. "That's all of them."

He got up, putting the knife back into its holster. Emily dropped her skirts, which fell to her ankles, and stepped back.

"Thank you," Emily said.

"It's no problem. What were you doing on that side of the steam anyway? Didn't the children tell you not to go there?"

"No," Emily said. "They must have forgotten."

Alec raised an eyebrow as he turned to Thomas, looking less pleased with himself than he had a few minutes earlier.

"Take your sister and get home," Alec said. "See if Mrs. Tattlewell has anything for you to do that'll keep you out of mischief."

Without a word, the children quickly put their socks and shoes back on, and Thomas took Lily's hand and led her back to the house. When they were out of earshot, Alec turned back to Emily.

"I am sorry," he said. "I promise I did ask the children to be nice."

"Maybe they did genuinely forget," Emily said unconvincingly.

Alec raised an eyebrow, and Emily sighed again. "No, you're right," she said. "Although I am not sure I'd put any of the blame on poor Lily."

"No," Alec agreed.

They fell silent for a moment.

"I am sorry too..." Emily said. "For pulling you away from your work."

"It's fine," Alec said.

Emily pressed her lips together,

"Well, I'd better get back," he said. "Do you think you can make it back to the house without getting into any more danger?"

"I am sure I'll be fine," Emily assured him.

"Well, look out for snakes," Alec grinned.

Emily grimaced as he turned and headed back in the direction that he had come from, leaving Emily alone with her thoughts. She watched him go; his shirt, damp with perspiration, clinging to the muscles in his back, and Emily felt an unfamiliar stirring in the pit of her stomach.

"Pull it together, Emily," she muttered to herself as she sat back on the sand, pulling on her stockings and boots.

A short while later, Emily was back at the ranch house. She headed into the kitchen to find Mrs. Tattlewell seated at the table; however, she was not alone. Seated beside her was a tall man with dirty-blonde hair and dark eyes. She guessed he must be about Alec's age, maybe a little older and he was also handsome.

The tall man got up from his seat and walked across the room to where Emily stood. He reached for her hand and brought it to his lips. Emily took a step back, startled by the familiarity of his gesture.

"I apologize," he said, bowing his head. "I thought that was how it was done in the city."

"Emily, this is Mr. Randall Caldwell," Mrs. Tattlewell said. "He lives on the neighboring ranch."

Emily nodded, feeling quite uncomfortable under Mr. Caldwell's intense gaze.

"I've been hoping to meet you for a long time, Miss McCoy," he said.

"Oh?" Emily said. "Why so?"

Randall opened his mouth and let out a throaty chuckle, and Emily frowned.

"Why don't we sit down?" Mrs. Tattlewell said. "Emily, you look like you could use a cup of tea."

"Thank you, Mrs. Tattlewell, but no," Emily said. "I think I am going to lie down for a bit. I am quite unused to this Texas heat."

Mrs. Tattlewell nodded, but Mr. Caldwell's eyes flashed dangerously.

"Are you sure you won't have a cup of tea?" Randall said. "After all, it would be rude to refuse some southern hospitality."

Emily frowned, looking at Mrs. Tattlewell, who would not meet her eye.

"Fine," Emily said. "A cup of tea would be most welcome, Mrs. Tattlewell."

"Excellent," Randall said, clapping his hands together. "Shall we all take a seat."

Emily walked over to the table and sat down. Randall sat beside her while Mrs. Tattlewell picked the teapot up and served the tea while Randall kept his eyes firmly fixed on Emily.

"So, Miss McCoy, how are you finding our little town?" Randall asked, taking a sip.

"I haven't been here long enough to form much of an opinion, Mr. Caldwell," Emily said. "I only arrived from New York yesterday."

"Is that so?" Randall said .

Emily frowned but said nothing as she brought her cup to her lips.

"And how long are you planning to stay?" Randall questioned her further.

"I need to be back in New York by the end of the summer," Emily said. "For the start of the fall semester."

Randall nodded as the corners of his lips turned up.

"So, have you thought about what you will do with your sister's property?" he asked. "Seeing as you don't plan on staying in Forest Hill."

Emily hesitated, taking a sip of her tea. "No," she said truthfully. "I haven't decided what will happen to the ranch."

Randall put his cup down, leaning forward in his chair. "I would like to buy Riverbend from you," he said, holding her gaze. "Money is no object."

Emily echoed Randall's movements, placing her cup down on its saucer. "That is very generous, Mr. Caldwell," Emily said. "But as I said, I do not know what the future of the property will be. As far as I am aware, the last will and testament of my brother-in-law has not been found."

Mr. Caldwell sat back in his chair, sucking his teeth.

"Do you intend to look for it?" he asked. "While you are here."

"I do," Emily said. "However if the will is not discovered then I believe the ownership of the ranch will be determined by the laws of intestate succession."

Randall raised an eyebrow. "You are familiar with the law then?" he asked.

"I've read up on some things," Emily replied.

Randall nodded. "This of course means that Riverbend will belong to their son."

"Thomas, yes," Emily confirmed.

"How old is the boy?" Randall asked.

"Seven," Mrs. Tattlewell said. "Turning eight in September."

Mr. Randall smiled, his shoulders relaxing. "Well, that settles it then," he said. "The boy is much too young to handle so much responsibility, which means as his guardian, Miss McCoy, the decision will fall to you."

Emily shook her head. "It's not that simple, Mr. Caldwell. Thomas may very well wish to run the ranch one day."

"But you plan to take the children back to New York, do you not?"

Emily glanced at Mrs. Tattlewell whose cheeks turned pink.

"That's right," Emily confirmed. "But if Thomas wishes to return one day, that will be his choice."

"And what do you think is going to happen to the property in the meanwhile?" Mr. Caldwell challenged. "Ten years is a lifetime out here."

"I suppose we would get a foreman," Emily said. "Someone to manage the property until Thomas is old enough to himself."

"And who would you choose as this foreman?" Randall asked, a glint in his eyes. "Alec Kincaid, I assume?"

Emily frowned, glancing briefly at Mrs. Tattlewell.

"To be frank with you, Mr. Calwell, I hadn't thought that far. Right now, my main priority is the children."

Randall exhaled deeply as he folded his hands across his chest.

"I understand how difficult this must be for all of you," he said, his eyes burning into hers. "And I did not come here to place any undue pressure on you. However, I am set on acquiring your late brother-in-law's ranch, no matter the price."

"As of now, Riverbend is unfortunately not for sale," Emily announced firmly.

Randall dropped his arms, sitting forward in his chair.

"Name your price," he pressed.

"I am sorry to disappoint you, Mr. Caldwell," Emily insisted.

Without warning, Randall brought a fist down on the table, causing the teacups as well as Mrs. Tattlewell to jump.

Emily held his gaze for a moment, not saying a word. She was not unaccustomed to men like this one; as a working woman, she'd encountered his type more often than she cared to; men who thought the world owed them some kind of favor

"I am sorry," Randall apologized, doing his best to recover his composure. "I forgot myself for a moment—"

"Well," Emily interjected, getting up from her seat. "Thank you for coming to introduce yourself, Mr. Caldwell, but if you'll excuse me, I think I will go and check on the children."

Without waiting for a reply, Emily turned and left the kitchen. She walked up the stairs to the children's bedroom. The door was slightly ajar, and she stopped to peek inside. Thomas and Lily were sitting on the bed by the open window; warm sunlight streaming into the room. Thomas had a book open on his lap that he was reading to Lily.

92

As she watched the two, Emily thought back to when she and Marie were just girls and how she'd read to her younger sister every night. Their mother died from consumption when Marie was just three, and their father was always working, trying to give them the best life he could, so most of the time, they were all each other had. Seeing young Thomas and Lily now, Emily saw the same kind of bond she and Marie had, and it made her heart ache.

She watched them for a little while longer before turning and heading back downstairs. As she stepped into the kitchen, she found Mrs. Tattlewell standing at the sink washing the teacups. Randall was thankfully gone.

"How are the children?" Mrs. Tattlewell said, turning to look at Emily.

"Fine," Emily said. "They were reading, so I didn't want to disturb them."

Mrs. Tattlewell nodded. "I am sorry about Mr. Caldwell," she said. "He just showed up and is not a man who likes to be told no."

"What is his story?" Emily asked.

"He's the wealthiest man in Forest Hill," Mrs. Tattlewell explained. "His father left him everything when he died, and Randall has made it his business to buy up as much land as he can to expand his empire."

"Surely there are other properties?" Emily said. "Why is he so interested in my brother-in-law's ranch?"

"It's good land," Mrs. Tattlewell replied. "There's access to the river and ample grazing. The Caldwell family have been after the place for generations."

"Generations?" Emily said, her eyes widening.

Mrs. Tattlewell nodded. "When my great-grandmother was a young woman, the property was auctioned off by the bank. People came from all over to bid on the place, but there were only two real contenders, Brain Donnelly, Bill's great-grandfather, and Alexander Caldwell—"

"Randall's great-grandfather," Emily deduced.

"That's right," Mrs. Tattlewell said.

"So what happened?' Emily asked.

"Well, on the morning that the property was to be sold, Alexander Caldwell's youngest son drowned in the river, and as a result, he never made it to the auction. Brian Donnelly was the highest bidder and walked away with the deed to the property."

"That's terrible," Emily exclaimed.

"Yes," Mrs. Tattlewell agreed. "And the Caldwell's blamed the Donnelly's, claiming that they'd put an old Irish curse on them."

"Surely they didn't truly believe that?" Emily said, shaking her head in disbelief.

"They sure did," Mrs. Tattlewell said. "Alexander Caldwell truly believed that Brian Donnelly had made a deal with the devil, and from that day on, a bitter rivalry was forged between the two families, a rivalry that's been passed from one generation to the next."

"So that's why Randall wants the property?" Emily asked. "Because of some foolish family rivalry?"

"It may seem foolish to you," Mrs. Tattlewell said. "But the rivalry between the families has been around as long as the town itself."

Emily said nothing for a moment, thinking about Randall's earlier outburst. It was obvious he wanted Bill and Marie's land, but as Emily had told him, she was not in a position to sell it. At least not until she found Bill's will.

"Ever since Bill and Marie's murders, Randall has been by every second day," Mrs. Tattlewell explained. "I think he believed that when you finally made an appearance, you'd be more than willing to sell the property to him so that you could get back to New York and on with your life as soon as possible."

"But surely he can understand my position?" Emily said.

"Mr. Caldwell is not a particularly understanding man," Mrs. Tattlewell said.

Emily sighed. She'd hoped her trip to Forest Hill would not be so fraught with complications, but everywhere she turned, there was another one.

"Try not to worry about it, dear" Mrs. Tattlewell said, smiling. "Things have a way of working themselves out."

Emily pressed her lips together. She hoped that Mrs. Tattlewell was right. After her morning activities with the leeches and the unexpected tea with Mr. Caldwell, she was feeling rather forlorn.

Chapter Eight

"Colby?" Alec yelled from the top of his horse. "Let's go."

The blue-gray dog, who'd been sniffing at a molehill for the last five minutes, turned and ran up to Alec, falling in line beside the horse. Alec clicked softly under his breath, and they set off back towards the homestead.

As he rode, Alec thought about the trick Thomas had played on his aunt. From the outside, it looked like harmless fun, a childish joke, but Alec knew that Thomas was acting out, looking for a way to drive his aunt away.

The house and barn came into view, and as they approached the stable, Alec dismounted, his boots hitting the ground with a heavy thud. Instead of leading his horse into the stables, Alec led him to a grassy patch at the back and left him alone to graze. Then he walked back around the building and towards the house; and as he did, he spotted Mrs. Tattlewell harvesting baby tomatoes from the vegetable garden.

"You should get the children to do that," Alec shouted.

Mrs. Tattlewell looked up, smiling. "You're probably right," she said. "But they've been so quiet this morning I thought perhaps they weren't feeling well."

"More like they are laying low after this morning's shenanigans," Alec said as he approached, grimacing slightly.

"What happened?" Mrs. Tattlewell asked, shifting the small basket to her left hand.

"Emily didn't tell you?" Alec asked in surprise.

"No," Mrs. Tattlewell said. "But she was probably distracted by our unexpected visitor."

Alec raised a questioning eyebrow, and Mrs. Tattlewell sighed.

"Randall Caldwell stopped by," she said.

Alec gritted his teeth, although he should not have been too surprised. The way that gossip spread around town, everyone would know by now that Emily had arrived.

"What did he say?" Alec asked.

"He made an offer on the Donnelly property," Mrs. Tattlewell explained. "But Emily told him that she is not planning on selling it."

Alec raised his eyebrows.

"You're surprised?" Mrs. Tattlewell asked.

"I just figured she'd want to tie up any loose ends before heading back home," Alec said.

"Yes, well, Randall assumed the same, and he wasn't happy when Emily told him otherwise."

"What did he do?" Alec asked, his tone concerned.

"He lost his temper," Mrs. Tattlewell said. "Slammed his hand down on the table."

Alec shook his head in disbelief.

"He apologized after," Mrs. Tattlewell continued. "But he's not going to give up until he gets what he wants; I saw it written on his face, as plain as day."

Alec sighed. Mrs. Tattlewell was right. Everyone knew the story of the Donnelly's and the Caldwell's. It was a rivalry as old as time, and at the heart of that rivalry was Riverbend Ranch.

"Where is Emily?" Alec asked.

"She went over to Riverbend," Mrs. Tattlewell explained. "But she said that she'll be back by lunchtime."

Alec nodded.

"Are you coming inside?" Mrs. Tattlewell asked.

Alec hesitated a moment. He'd planned on having a conversation with the children, but that could wait.

"Actually, there is something I need to do," he said. "I'll be back for lunch."

Without waiting for Mrs. Tattlewell to respond, Alec turned and headed down the driveway and out of the gates.

"Emily?" Alec called as he stepped into the house. "Are you here?"

"In here," Emily called back.

Alec walked down the narrow hallway and into the small study. Emily was seated at the desk, sorting through a mound of paperwork. As he stepped inside, she looked up at him, surprised.

"What are you doing here?" Emily asked.

"I could ask you the same thing," Alec said. "I never thought you'd step foot into this house again."

Emily sighed. "Did Marie ever say anything to you about a will?" she asked. "Or what was to happen to the property if they died?"

Alec shook his head. "No," he said.

"I've searched every drawer, but I haven't found anything," Emily said, sitting back in the chair.

Alec said nothing, but the truth was that Bill wasn't the type of man to leave a will because he wasn't the type of man who thought much about the future.

"What is it?" Emily asked, reading Alec's expression.

Alec sighed. "You didn't know Bill very well," he said. "But he was a bit of a featherbedder."

Emily frowned, not understanding the terminology.

"He liked the easy life," Alec explained. "He didn't like to deal with anything too challenging, so most of the responsibilities fell on your sister."

"But it just doesn't make sense," Emily said. "Mrs. Tattlewell told me about the rivalry between the two families. Surely Bill would have wanted to leave a will, to have the inheritance of the property in writing so that there were no doubts."

Alec pressed his lips together. "Everyone in town knew that Bill Donnelly wasn't like his father or his grandfather," Alec said. "Everything he ever had was handed to him, and he took it for granted."

Emily sighed, shaking her head. "So what do I do now?" she asked.

"I suggest you talk to a lawyer," Alec said. "Figure out how it all works without a will."

Emily nodded. "Is there one in town?' she asked.

"No," Alec said. "But there is a lawyer in Rosewood. I can take you tomorrow."

"Thank you," Emily said.

"We should get back," Alec said. "Mrs. Tattlewell will have lunch waiting."

Emily nodded as she got up from the chair, and they left the study together.

"How well did you know my brother-in-law?" Emily asked as they made their way down the road.

"We grew up together," Alec said.

"So you were friends?" Emily asked.

Alec hesitated a moment and then shook his head. "No," he said. "We were never friends, not really."

Emily nodded slowly. "Did something happen between you?" she asked, her tone curious.

"No," Alec shrugged. "But the Donnelly's, much like the Caldwell's, always acted like they were better than the other families in town. Bill Donnelly was no different."

"And Marie?" Emily asked.

"Your sister never pretended to be anyone other than who she was," Alec said. "She had a heart as big as the prairie, and she was as dependable as a mesquite post."

Emily said nothing for a long moment, but Alec could tell by the way she pressed her lips together that there was something on her mind.

"What is it?" Alec asked.

"It's nothing," Emily said.

"It's not nothing," Alec insisted. "Tell me."

Emily stopped walking and turned to him. "Was there something going on between you and Marie?" she asked.

"No," Alec said firmly. "We were just friends."

Emily frowned, and it was obvious she thought he was being dishonest.

"Why don't you believe me?" he asked, a hint of irritation to his voice.

"Because my sister was married," Emily said. "She loved Bill, so why would she spend so much time with another man unless there was something going on?"

Alec sighed, shaking his head. "You hadn't seen your sister in a long time," he said. "And her marriage was complicated."

"How so?" Emily asked.

Alec hesitated a moment. He'd made Marie a promise a long time ago that he would never tell her secret. And even now when she was dead and buried, it still didn't feel right to break that promise.

"It's in the past now," Alec said. "Best to leave it there."

Emily opened her mouth, but Alec turned and carried on walking, his pace quicker now as he made his way up the drive toward the ranch.

"Alec!" Emily called after him.

But Alec didn't slow down; making his way into the kitchen, where Mrs. Tattlewell and the children were already seated for lunch. Cobalt was lying under the table.

"Good, you're here," Mrs. Tattlewell said. "We were just about to start."

Alec walked across the kitchen and took his seat at the table. As he did, Emily appeared in the doorway. Her cheeks were flushed, and she was out of breath.

"Goodness, Emily," Mrs. Tattlewell said, her eyes widening. "Come and sit down and catch your breath."

Emily sat down at the table opposite Alec. He could sense her watching him, but he refused to meet her eyes.

"Are you not staying at Riverbend then?" Mrs. Tattlewell asked, eyeing her suitcase still sitting by the door.

Emily hesitated.

"No," Alec stepped in. "With Emily only staying a few weeks, we thought it best that she stay here, so that she can spend more time with the children."

"Oh, how wonderful," Mrs. Tattlewell said approvingly. "I am sure the children are very grateful to be able to spend more time with their aunt."

Alec looked across at Thomas and Lily, catching Thomas's eye.

"We are," Thomas said, nodding.

Mrs. Tattlewell smiled as Alec bent his head over his plate.

A short while later, they'd finished lunch, and Alec headed outside with Cobalt on his heels. As he crossed the garden, he suddenly felt a hand on his arm, and he turned.

"Alec," Emily said, not removing it. "Why did you rush off like that?"

Alec was aware of the warmth of her skin, the softness of her touch, and for a moment, that was all he could think about.

"Alec?" Emily pressed. 'Did you hear me?"

Alec cleared his throat as he took a step back. "I have to get back to work," he said.

Without another word, he turned and headed to the stables.

For the rest of the afternoon, Alec was busy out on the ranch. It was time to start weaning the calves from their mothers and of all the ranch tasks this was Alec's least favorite. He hated having to tear the youngsters away and then listen to them cry all night. As necessary as it was, he hated doing it.

When Alec returned to the ranch at dusk; Mrs. Tattlewell had already gone home, leaving supper on the stove. The kitchen was empty, and Alec walked over to the sink to wash up. Just as he was drying his face, Thomas and Lily appeared in the kitchen doorway.

"Where's your aunt?" Alec asked as he dabbed at his beard with a towel.

"In her room," Thomas said. "She's been there most of the afternoon."

Alec nodded. "Come and sit down," he said. "I want to talk to you both about what happened this morning."

Thomas and Lily walked over to the table and sat, their heads bent. Alec sat across from them, his hands folded on the table.

"What you did to your aunt at the stream wasn't kind," Alec said. "You frightened her."

"It wasn't Lily's fault," Thomas said. "She didn't know."

Alec pursed his lips. "You're the oldest, Thomas," Alec said. "Which means it's your responsibility to set a good example for your sister."

Thomas nodded, not meeting Alec's eye.

"I know this isn't easy," Alec sighed.

The room fell silent for a moment as Alec looked from Thomas to Lily, wishing he knew the right thing to say. Just then, however, Emily appeared in the doorway.

"Right, well, let's eat, shall we?" Alec said.

They all sat down to dinner together, but no one spoke. Emily looked lost in her thoughts, hardly touching the beef stew before her. Thomas and Lily kept their heads bent, pushing the food around their plates.

"If you two are finished, why don't you go upstairs and get ready for bed?" Alec finally said.

Thomas took Lily's hand, and they slid out of their seats.

"Thomas," Alec said. "Isn't there something you want to say to your aunt?"

Thomas sighed. "I'm sorry for what happened at the stream today," he apologized.

"That's alright," Emily said kindly.

Without another word, the children exited the kitchen, leaving Alec and Emily alone.

"Why don't you go and get some rest too?" Alec said. "We'll set off for the lawyers right after breakfast tomorrow."

Emily nodded and got up from the table. She hesitated a moment, and Alec thought she was going to say something, but then she turned to leave.

"Goodnight," she said.

"Goodnight," Alec echoed.

Alec waited for the soft click of her bedroom door before he got up and cleared the table. He carried the dirty dishes to the sink, scraping the leftover food into the pail for the pigs. As he washed up, he thought about the day Marie had told him her secret, how afraid she'd been to open up to him, and how she'd made him swear never to utter a word to anyone. He'd promised to take her secret to the grave, not knowing then that this decision would become one of the greatest regrets of his life.

Chapter Nine

"Please, take a seat."

"Thank you," Emily said, sitting in the dark wooden Captain's Chair and crossing her ankles.

Alec sat down in the matching chair beside her as the lawyer, Oliver Blackwood, took his seat behind the desk. He was a petite man with brown hair neatly combed and slicked down with pomade. His mustache and beard were immaculately groomed, and he wore a well-fitted dark suit.

"So, how can I help you today?" Oliver asked, looking between them.

"My sister and brother-in-law recently passed away," Emily said.

"I am sorry to hear that," Oliver said sympathetically.

"Thank you," Emily said. "I had not seen my sister in some time, nor had we spoken."

"I see," Oliver said. "Did your sister and her husband have children?"

"Yes," Emily said. "Two, a boy and a girl."

"They've been staying with me," Alec said. "I own the property next door."

Oliver Blackwood nodded.

"The thing is, Mr. Blackwood, is that we cannot find a will," Emily said. "Mr. Kincaid and I have both searched the study but to no avail."

Oliver Blackwood leaned forward in his seat, forming a steeple with his thin fingers.

"Well, if your brother-in-law did not leave one, then we will enter a process called probate, which deals with the distribution of the deceased's property and assets."

"And what does probate entail?" Emily asked.

"Well, a judge will supervise the process," Mr. Blackwood explained. "But before anything can be distributed to the appropriate heirs, all of the deceased person's debts and taxes must be paid. This money is usually taken from the estate's assets."

Emily nodded as she glanced at Alec.

"Do you have any knowledge of your brother-in-law's finances?" Oliver asked.

"No," Emily admitted. "There was a ledger in the study, but I didn't open it."

Oliver nodded. "Well, my advice would be to first visit the bank which handled your late brother-in-law's assets. From there, we can get an idea of what is owed."

"I don't know what bank it is." Emily noted.

"Chances are it's the one in town," Alec said. "It's the closest to Forest Hill; most ranchers bank there."

Emily nodded. "Thank you for your time, Mr. Blackwood," she said. "We shall be in touch once we've spoken to the bank."

Oliver Blackwood stood up as Emily and Alec exited the room. They headed out of the small office and onto the dusty street.

"The bank's this way," Alec said.

Emily followed Alec to the end of the street where a large three-story red brick building stood. As they got to the door Emily hesitated. She liked doing things herself but she was not very familiar with property taxes and ranch finances. She did not want to misunderstand anything and so, despite not wanting to ask for help, she needed to.

"Will you come in with me to talk with the banker?' Emily asked.

"Sure," Alec agreed.

Emily smiled gratefully as they headed inside where two pretty receptionists were seated at a broad wooden counter.

Emily and Alec crossed the room.

"Welcome to Rosewood National Bank," the receptionist on the right said. "How can we help you today?"

"My name is Emily McCoy," she said. "I was wondering if there was someone I could speak to about my late brother-in-law's accounts."

"And what is his name?"

"Bill Donnelly," Emily said.

The two secretaries shared a look that suggested they knew about the tragedy.

"Certainly," she said. "Just a moment."

The woman got up and disappeared upstairs.

"We were so sorry to hear about Mr. and Mrs. Donnelly," the remaining secretary said, tilting her head sympathetically.

"Thank you," Emily replied.

A few minutes later, the first secretary reemerged.

"Mr. Pembrooke will see you now," she said brightly. "If you'd like to follow me."

Emily and Alec followed the woman up the stairs and down the hallway. They came to a stop at the last door. There was a nameplate attached: Mr. Walter Pembrooke, Bank Manager."

The secretary wrapped lightly on the door with her knuckles.

"Come in," a deep voice said from inside.

"You can go in," the woman said, pushing the door open.

Emily smiled at her as she stepped inside. The office was large and spacious, and it smelt like cigars and money. Seated behind the mahogany desk was a large man with gray hair and a mustache to match. His crisp white shirt stretched over his significant stomach.

"Thank you for seeing us, Mr. Pembrooke," Emily said, crossing the room. "This is Mr. Kincaid. He owns the ranch next to my late brother-in-law's property and has been taking care of the children."

"It's nice to meet you Mr. Kincaid," Mr. Pembrooke said politely before turning to look at Emily again. "And we're very relieved to see you, Miss McCoy."

"Oh?" Emily said, not hiding her surprise.

"Why don't you both take a seat?" he offered.

Emily and Alec sat down as Mr. Pembrooke leaned forward in his seat, the leather over his chair squeaking.

"I was sorry to hear about your brother-in-law and your sister," Mr. Pembrooke said. "The Donnelly family have been loyal customers for years."

"Thank you," Emily said.

The room fell silent for a moment as Mr. Pembrooke opened the ledger on his desk. After a few moments, he closed it again, sitting back in his chair.

"Did your brother-in-law or sister ever talk to you about the ranch's finances?" he asked.

"No," Emily said. "We weren't close."

Mr. Pembrooke nodded. "Well, it's not uncommon for big ranches to go through periods of growth and loss. We, as a financial institution, understand that farming is not an exact science. Over the many years, we've been in charge of the Donnelly's finances, we've seen them through some hard times, but the family always managed to keep a profit. However, I am afraid to tell you that over the past couple of years, things have become quite desperate."

"How so?" Emily asked, leaning forward in her chair.

"Well, over the past year, profits have been poor and expenses high," Mr. Pembrooke said. "In early February, Mr. Donnelly took out a second mortgage on the ranch but since the spring he's defaulted on every payment."

Emily glanced at Alec, whose brow was creased in concern.

"So, what does this mean?" Emily asked.

"Well, there are several taxes that need to be paid, including a tax on the estate's total value," Mr. Pembrooke explained. "There is also the question of inheritance tax, which the heirs will be required to settle before they receive any of the assets from the estate. And, of course, there are the death duties that must be paid."

As Mr. Pembrooke spoke, Emily's stomach continued to sink. If the ranch was in so much financial trouble, how would they be able to pay back all of these amounts? And the mortgage?

"So what do you advise we do?' Emily asked.

"Well, you have two possible options," Mr. Pembrooke said. "Miss McCoy, are you planning on taking over the ranch?"

"Not personally, no," Emily said. "I plan to take the children back to New York with me at the end of the summer."

'Well then, your first option is to sell," Mr. Pembrooke said. "Riverbend Ranch is a valuable property. If you should choose to sell, you would certainly be able to repay the mortgage as well as the taxes and death duties while still retaining a sizable amount for the children's future."

Emily nodded thoughtfully.

"And what is the other option?' Alec asked.

"You stay and work the ranch," Mr. Pembrooke said. "Until recent years, Riverbend was profitable, and there is no reason that it shouldn't be again with the right management."

Emily bit her bottom lip but said nothing.

"We would be willing to negotiate a payment plan should you decide not to sell," Mr. Pembrooke added.

Alec turned and looked at Emily, whose mind was racing. What was she going to do? There was no way she could stay and get the ranch up and running again.

Mr. Pembrooke exhaled as he leaned forward in his seat. "There is quite a lot to consider," he said. "So why don't you take a few days and think it over?"

"Thank you, Mr. Pembrooke," Emily said gratefully.

He nodded. "I am sure you will make the right decision," he said.

Emily and Alec left the office and headed back downstairs. They left the bank and walked up the road in silence.

"Did you know that the ranch was in trouble?" she asked, turning to Alec.

"No," Alec said. "Marie never mentioned anything."

Emily nodded, chewing the inside of her cheek as they approached the small wagon parked under a tree. Emily and Alec climbed up onto the seat, and Alec clicked his tongue, and the horse started forward back towards Forest Hill.

For a long while, neither of them spoke as the gravel crunched under the wagon wheels.

"Do you know what you are going to do?" Alec asked, casting a sideways glance at her.

Emily sighed. "I need to be back in New York by the end of the summer," she said. "And who knows how long it would take to get the ranch up and running again."

"You could hire someone?" Alec suggested. "A foreman."

"With what?" Emily challenged. "You heard Mr. Pembrooke, there is no money."

They both fell silent for a moment.

"I know that the ranch is the children's inheritance," Emily said. "But maybe it would be better to sell and make a clean break."

Alec said nothing, but the muscles in his jaw tightened.

"Mr. Pembrooke also said there would be a sizeable amount left over for Thomas and Lily, which we could invest and which one day could give them both a comfortable life—"

"There is more to life than just money," Alec said sharply.

"I know that," Emily frowned. "But I am just trying to do what is best for the children."

"What is best for the children is for you not to sell their home," Alec argued.

Emily exhaled sharply. "It's not that simple, Alec."

"It is that simple. The bank is giving you a chance to get the ranch back on its feet."

"I don't have the time," Emily said.

"Oh right," Alec replied, shaking his head. "Because you need to be back in New York."

"Yes," Emily said, her eyes flashing. "I need to get back to my life, my job—"

"Which is obviously more important than Thomas and Lily's happiness."

"Stop the cart," Emily commanded.

"What?" Alec said, frowning.

'I said stop the wagon," Emily cried.

Alec pulled on the reins, and the wagon came to a sudden stop; Emily climbed down.

"What are you doing?" Alec asked in exasperation.

"I am walking," Emily said, her jaw locked in determination.

"Don't be foolish," Alec insisted. "It's an eight-mile walk. Besides, it's hotter than a branding iron in a bonfire."

"I don't care," Emily said, not bothering to turn around.

She started walking, aware of Alec's eyes on her, but she kept going. Suddenly, she stepped into a hole in the road, and her ankle rolled.

"Ow," Emily cried, almost losing her balance.

A moment later, Alec was by her side.

"Are you alright?" he asked, his tone full of concern.

"I hurt my ankle," Emily said, wincing.

"Here," Alec said. "Put your arm around my shoulder."

Emily did as instructed, and Alec helped her back to the wagon. He smelt like sweat and dust, and Emily was very aware of the heat of his skin pressing against her.

"Here," Alec said.

He led her around the rear of the wagon and helped her up.

"Can I take a look?" he asked.

Emily nodded as Alec carefully removed her boot. He then gently pressed down on the skin around the ankle.

"It's just a sprain," he said.

Emily nodded as Alec carefully put on her boot again. He then sat down beside her on the back of the wagon, and for a while, neither of them spoke.

"Why can't you just stay?" Alec asked.

"Because if I do, then it will have all been for nothing," Emily said, shaking her head.

"What do you mean?' Alec asked.

Emily sighed. "For these past eight years, I've done nothing but focus on my teaching. I used it to fill the hole inside of me that appeared after Marie left. So if I give it all up now, what will I have?"

"Thomas and Lily," Alec said. "You'd have Thomas and Lily."

"I never wanted to be a mother," Emily confessed.

"Then leave them with me," Alec said. "I'll take care of them."

Emily said nothing for a long moment. In many ways, it would be easier just to do what Alec asked. To visit them in the summer holidays and at Christmas, but she knew she couldn't. The children were the last she had of her sister, and caring for them was the only way she could make up for what had happened between them. She'd never wanted to be a mother, but she would raise them for Marie.

"I know you love them, Alec," she said. "But the plan was always for us to return to New York. So we'll stay till the end of the summer, pack up the house and get the ranch ready to sell."

Alec said nothing, his expression hard.

"I thought we had a deal," he said. "That the children would get to decide where they lived."

Emily sighed. "It was a nice idea, Alec," she said. "But that's all it was."

"They want to stay," Alec insisted.

"I know they do," Emily agreed. "Because it's all they know, but with time, they'll see that the world is a very big place."

"Riverbend is their home," Alec said. "It's where they belong. It's where Marie wanted them to grow up, to raise families of their own."

"If that's what my sister wanted, then why didn't she name you the children's guardian?" she asked.

"I don't know," Alec said.

Emily sighed. "I wish things were different, Alec," she said. "But they're not. Thomas and Lily should be with me, their family."

Alec hesitated a moment and then got up, not looking at Emily.

"We should get back," he said.

Emily nodded as she pushed herself back, leaning against the wooden side of the wagon while Alec walked around to the front and climbed into the seat.

They set off again towards home, and as they did, neither talked. Emily knew Alec was disappointed, hurt even, but this was how it had to be. She'd give him a few more weeks with the children, a chance to make some memories, and then when the summer was over, they'd pack up and leave Texas.

Chapter Ten

"Goodness me," Mrs. Tattlewell said as they entered through the backdoor. "What happened?"

"It's nothing," Emily said. "I just hurt my ankle."

Alec helped her across the kitchen and into a chair before he turned to Mrs. Tattlewell.

"It needs to be iced," he said.

Mrs. Tattlewell nodded, and without another word, Alec turned and left the kitchen. He walked briskly across the back yard and around the stables, out of sight. There, out of sight, he began to pace, his mind racing. So, she was just going to take the children? After making him believe that she was really going to get to know them and respect their choice, she'd just decided otherwise.

"Alec?"

Alec whirled around to find Mrs. Tattlewell watching him, a concerned look in her eye.

"Are you alright?" she asked.

"No," Alec said, still pacing.

"Do you want to tell me what happened?" she asked.

Alec stopped. "Emily is going to sell the ranch and take the children back to New York at the end of the summer," he said.

Mrs. Tattlewell frowned. "Did you think there was going to be another outcome?" she asked.

"I hoped she was going to let the children decide where they wanted to live," Alec said, his voice rising. "That she'd respect their decision."

Mrs. Tattlewell sighed. "Alec—"

"She hadn't seen her sister in eight years," Alec said, pacing again. "And now she thinks she knows what is best? The children don't want to leave; this is their home, and now she wants to just uproot their lives."

"Alec," Mrs. Tattlewell said again, her voice gentle.

Alec stopped pacing and looked at her.

"The children's lives were uprooted the moment their parents were murdered," she said. "And I know you don't want them to go, but maybe it would be for the best. Here, in Forest Hill, they will always be their parents' story, but somewhere else, they could finally be free to move on from this tragedy."

"No," Alec said, shaking his head. "I am not just going to let her take them. This is their home."

Mrs. Tattlewell sighed.

"There is nothing you can do," she said.

"I could go to a lawyer," Alec said. "Take the matter to court."

"You know that no judge is going to side with you," Mrs. Tattlewell said. "Not when the children have a natural aunt."

"I could tell the judge that the children are mine," Alec said, grasping at straws.

"And we both know that would be a lie," Mrs. Tattlewell said.

Alec sighed, running his hands through his hair.

"It's not fair," he said.

"I know," Mrs. Tattlewell agreed. "But the children have been through enough already. They don't need to be in the middle of a fight for guardianship."

Alec sighed, shaking his head. He knew that Mrs. Tattlewell was right. The children had been through so much trauma.

"So why not just try and enjoy these last few weeks?" Mrs. Tattlewell suggested.

Alec said nothing.

"I was just making some tea," Mrs. Tattlewell said. "Why don't you come inside—"

"No," Alec said shortly. "No, thank you. I'm gonna take a walk and clear my head."

Mrs. Tattlewell nodded, and without another word, Alec turned and walked away.

Twenty minutes later, he found himself on the edge of the property at the family cemetery. He walked over to where his wife and baby were buried. He had not been here for close on two months now, not since the children had come to stay with him.

"Hey, Livi," he said quietly as he ran his fingers over the stone.

Alec sat down on the soft grass, his heartbeat slowing as he leaned back, the warm gravestone pressed into his back. Alec sighed, tilting his head so it rested on the top of the hard stone. He closed his eyes for a moment and then opened them again, sighing. He'd lost so many people; his mother, his father, Olivia, the baby, and now Marie. Grief had fed on him for years, leaving him full of holes, and he'd been so lonely. Then Thomas and Lily came to stay with him, and for the first time in years, the house didn't feel like a crypt full of ghosts. The whole time, he'd been so scared of failing them, of not knowing the right things to say or do, that he'd hardly given any thought to what life would be like without them.

"I wish you were here," Alec said. "You always knew what to do."

In the tree above his head, a mourning dove cooed softly, and Alec looked up, but he couldn't see it through the thick leaves.

Alec wasn't sure how long he sat there, but eventually, he got up, his back and buttocks stiff from sitting on the hard ground. He turned and headed back to the homestead to get started on the afternoon chores. As he arrived back at the house, he bumped into Mrs. Tattlewell.

"I was just on my way home," she said.

Alec nodded. "Where are the children?" he asked.

"Up in their room," Mrs. Tattlewell said. "Playing cards."

"Are you alright?" she asked.

"I'm fine," Alec answered.

Mrs. Tattlewell nodded. "Well, I'll see you tomorrow," she said.

"See you in the morning," Alec replied.

Mrs. Tattlewell walked past him, stopping momentarily to pat him on the arm.

"It will all work out," she said quietly. "Things always have a way of working themselves out."

Alec said nothing as Mrs. Tattlewell continued towards the ranch gate. He wished he could believe her, but experience had taught him otherwise.

Alec finished up his chores and headed into the house. It was quiet, and there was no sign of Emily, so Alec headed through the kitchen and down the hallway. The spare bedroom door was closed, and Alec hesitated a moment, but there was no sound from inside.

He proceeded up the stairs to the children's bedroom, where he found Thomas and Lily lying on their stomachs on the floor, a pile of cards between them.

"Alec," Thomas cried, pushing himself into a sitting position. "Come and play with us."

Alec hesitated.

"Please," Thomas pleaded.

Alec looked at Lily, who was nodding enthusiastically, and he smiled.

"Alright," he agreed. "One game."

Alec walked over to the children and sat down on the floor between Lily and Thomas.

"What are we playing?" Alec asked.

"Old Maid," Thomas replied.

"Alright," Alec said. "Deal me in."

Three rounds later, Thomas was on his feet, doing a victory lap of the room, his arms outstretched as if he were some great winged bird. Alec watched him chuckling as he shook his head. He glanced over at Lily; she was smiling brightly. However, suddenly, Thomas stopped, his shoulders falling. Alec followed his line of sight to find Emily standing in the doorway.

"Sorry," she apologized. "I didn't mean to spoil the fun."

No one said anything for a moment.

"What are you playing?" she asked, eyeing the cards.

"Old Maid," Alec said.

"I used to love that game as a girl," Emily said. "In fact, your mother used to beat me every time we played."

"It was ma who taught us," Thomas said.

"No one could beat your ma," Alec said, smiling fondly.

"And what about your father?" Emily asked. "Did he like to play too?"

"No," Thomas said shortly. "He didn't like to lose."

"Oh," Emily said, a small crease forming between her brows.

The room fell silent again.

"Maybe we could all play a game?" Emily said, taking a step into the small bedroom. "Although I can't guarantee I'll be as good a player as your mother."

"No, thanks," Thomas said, shaking his head. "We're tired of playing cards."

Alec glanced at Lily, who nodded solemnly.

"Oh, okay," Emily said, unable to hide her disappointment. "Well, maybe another time then—"

"May we go out and help Jeremiah feed the calves?" Thomas asked, looking at Alec.

"You may," Alec said. "But don't stay out there too long; we'll be havin' supper soon."

"Okay," Thomas said, reaching for Lily's hand.

The children exited the room, leaving Alec and Emily alone. Alec got up from the floor and dusted his denim jeans with his hands.

"Well, I'd better go and warm up the supper," he said.

"Do you need any help?" Emily volunteered.

"I think I can manage," Alec said. "But thanks."

Alec walked past Emily and down the stairs. He went into the kitchen and uncovered the pork chops, potato salad, and slaw Mrs. Tattlewell had prepared. He fetched the heavy-bottomed saucepan from its hook on the wall and placed it down on the top of the coal stove. As he did, he was suddenly aware of a pair of eyes on him, and he turned to Emily standing in the doorway, her arms folded across her chest.

"How's your ankle?" Alec asked.

"Better," Emily said.

They fell silent.

"I was thinking I could take the children into town tomorrow," Emily said. "Get them some new things to wear."

Alec nodded but said nothing as he fetched the salt from the pantry.

"Although I didn't see a tailor or seamstress in town," Emily said. "Is there one in Rosewood?"

"The general store in town has clothes," Alec said, glancing at her.

"If it's all the same, I'd rather take them to Rosewood," Emily said, dropping her arms. "Get the clothes properly fitted."

Alec sighed, turning to her. "The general store was always good enough for Marie," he remarked.

"What is that supposed to mean?" Emily asked, frowning.

"Thomas and Lily are simple country children," he said. "They need clothes that they can play in, that they can get dirty without having to worry."

"Well, forgive me for trying to do something nice," Emily said.

Alec sighed. "I know you are trying to get to know the children," he said. "But you will not win them over with brass buttons and cream-colored lace."

"There is nothing wrong with taking pride in your appearance," Emily insisted.

"No," Alec agreed. "But on a ranch, children need to dress practically. There is no point spending money on fancy clothes that will just get ruined."

"The children won't be here much longer," Emily reminded him. "They'll need proper clothes for New York."

The knots in Alec's stomach tightened as he turned back to the stove and sprinkle salt over the pork chops.

"I'll ask Jeremiah to take you to Rosewood in the morning," Alec said stiffly.

"Thank you," Emily said. "That would be much appreciated."

Alec said nothing more as he placed the salted chops into the hot pan. When he paused to look again, the doorway was empty.

Alec turned back to the stove and sighed. For the briefest moment that afternoon when he was playing cards with the children, he'd forgotten about Emily and her plan to take them back to New York. But now, as he stood frying the pork chops, he thought about the conversation they'd had on the way back from Rosewood.

Why had Marie not named him the children's guardian? Was it because she did not believe that he, a lonely widower, was up to the task? Or maybe she felt the children would be better off with her sister, that Emily was better equipped to take care of them? Alec didn't know the answer and Marie wasn't around to say.

Yet, he had to know. If Marie wanted Emily to be their guardian then he would respect her decision, but he had to know for sure. So, he would return to their house and look for the will again; after all, he had nothing to lose and everything to gain.

Chapter Eleven

Emily hesitated in the hallway for a moment; the smell of bacon and eggs drifted from the kitchen.

"Why can't you come with us?" Thomas whined.

"Because it will do you and your sister good to spend some time with your aunt," Alec said.

"But why do we have to go all the way to Rosewood?" Thomas asked. "Ma always used to get our clothes from the store in Forest Hill."

"Well, your Aunt Emily wants to go to Rosewood," Alec said.

"She wants to dress us up like dolls," Thomas grumbled. "I bet the clothes will be all stiff and scratchy."

"Thomas," Alec said sharply. "Promise me you'll be on your best behavior today. No tricks."

"I promise," Thomas said sulkily.

Emily took a deep breath and stepped into the kitchen, smiling as she looked around the room.

"Good morning, everyone," she said brightly.

"Mornin'," Alec replied. "There's coffee on the table."

Emily walked over and sat down, reaching for a mug.

"How did you all sleep?" she asked.

"Fine," Thomas said, shrugging.

"And you, Lily?" Emily asked, smiling at the little girl. "Did you sleep well?"

Lily said nothing, but she nodded.

"Jeremiah is getting the cart hitched up now," Alec said. "He'll take you straight after breakfast."

Emily nodded as Alec carried over the frying pan and began to serve the eggs and bacon. He was wearing the same white apron that Mrs. Tattlewell had and it fitted snugly over his broad chest.

"No Mrs. Tattlewell, this morning?" Emily asked.

"No," Alec said. "She helps out at the church on a Saturday, preparing it for the Sunday service."

Emily nodded as Alec served her an egg and two rashers of bacon.

"Thank you," she said.

They all ate breakfast together and as they did, Emily looked over at Alec. She could not help but notice how the rust-colored cotton shirt he was wearing made his eyes look even greener. He caught her eye and she quickly bowed her head, her cheeks flushing.

A short while later they were done eating and Alec sent the children upstairs to fetch their hats.

"You are welcome to join us," Emily said, looking across the table at Alec.

Alec shook his head as he reached for the children's empty breakfast plates and stacked them on top of his own.

"I appreciate the invitation," Alec said. "But no, thanks. There is work to be gettin' on with here."

"Do ranchers ever rest?" she asked.

"Sundays," Alec said as he got up from the table.

Emily nodded as Alec walked over to the sink and began to wash the dishes. Just then, the children reappeared in the doorway wearing their wide-brimmed straw hats.

"Shall we get going?" Emily asked, getting up from the table.

The children nodded, both looking less than enthusiastic.

"Alright then," Emily said. "Let's go."

She walked around the table and to the back door. She stood waiting as the children walked across the kitchen, dragging their feet.

"Have a nice time," Alec said, turning to them. "And be good."

Without a word, the children left the kitchen. Emily caught Alec's eye for a moment before she stepped outside and followed them to the cart where Jeremiah was waiting, his cap in his hand.

"We haven't met," he said, smiling nervously. "But I'm Jeremiah."

"Emily McCoy," Emily said, returning his smile. "Thank you for taking time out of your day to drive us to Rosewood."

"It's no problem," Jeremiah said.

Emily smiled at him again as he turned and helped the children up onto the back of the cart. Emily climbed up onto the front seat, her injured ankle twinging slightly as she did. Jeremiah climbed up onto the seat beside her and took the reins.

As they bumped down the driveway towards the road, Emily glanced over her shoulder at the children, who were quiet.

"How are you liking it here in Forest Hill?" Jeremiah asked, casting her a sideways glance.

"It's hot," Emily said.

Jeremiah grinned. "Takes some getting used to," he agreed.

"What about you?" Emily asked. "Have you lived here your whole life?"

Jeremiah nodded. "Born and raised," he said, a hint of pride in his voice.

"Do your family live in town?" Emily asked.

Jeremiah's face fell slightly. "My sister does," he said. "We stay together."

Emily nodded. "And how long have you worked for Mr. Kincaid?"

"Four years," Jeremiah said. "It was actually your sister who got me the job."

"Really?" Emily said curiously.

Jeremiah nodded, smiling. "We were living through hard times," he explained. "My sister and me, we lost our folks to the smallpox when we were just youngins. We did our best, working odd jobs here and there, enough to scrape by. But then my sister, well, she was in an accident, stepped into the road in front of a buggy, and was crushed by a horse."

"How awful," Emily said sympathetically.

Jeremiah nodded sadly. "It was," he agreed. "But she survived, although she's crippled."

Emily listened to Jeremiah's sad story, her heart going out to him, having suffered so much tragedy so young.

"With my sister to care for, I couldn't work no more," Jeremiah continued. "And we were starving. So I swallowed my pride and went out onto the streets to beg. Then I met your sister. She came right up to me and asked me for my story. I told her, and she promised to help. A few days later, she got me a job as a ranch hand here on Mr. Kincaid's ranch and found a neighbor willing to care for my sister during the day while I was at work."

Emily smiled. Marie had always had a generous spirit. Their father used to say she'd inherited her compassion from their mother.

"I don't know what I would have done if it hadn't been for her," Jeremiah said. "She was the kindest person I ever met, and it was a great tragedy that God decided to call her home so soon."

Emily said nothing, thinking about Marie. For years, she had done her best not to think about her sister. She'd believed if she did not allow herself to think about their estrangement, then it wouldn't hurt so much. Yet all the time she'd been not thinking about her sister, she'd been carving out an entire life for herself here. Now Emily was here too, at the center of her sister's world, hearing stories about her from strangers, and Emily wished she'd not fought so hard to forget her.

"Are we almost there?" Thomas asked.

"Still a few miles to go, little man," Jeremiah replied.

"It's hot," Thomas whined. "I'd rather be back at the ranch, swimming in the stream."

Emily grimaced, thinking back to the stream. The bites on her legs from the leeches still hadn't quite healed, and they felt hot and scratchy under her stockings.

The cart fell silent for a while. Emily watched the long road stretching out before them with the seas of prairie on either side swaying in the wind, the grass rippling out like a golden tide.

A few miles later, the town of Rosewood arose before them, shimmering like a mirage in the heat of the morning. Jeremiah rode down the main street, bringing the cart to a stop in front of the seamstress's shop.

"Thank you, Jeremiah," Emily said, climbing down.

Jeremiah helped the children and turned to Emily. "Mr. Kincaid asked if I'd get some things for the ranch while we're here," he said. "But I won't be long."

"Take your time," Emily said.

Jeremiah tipped his cap to her as he climbed back on the cart. He clicked his tongue softly, and the horse started back down the road.

"Come on, children," Emily said.

She herded the children towards the shop. As she did, Emily glanced into the large window, which had several sample garments on display as well as fabric swatches.

A small bell tinkled prettily as Emily and the children entered the modest shop. The air was cooler inside and a welcome respite from the heat of the day.

"Hello," a bright voice called. "I'll be with you in a mo'."

Emily looked over to see a pretty young woman with light hair and blue eyes smiling at her. She was sitting at the back of the room behind a sewing machine. She was working away, her foot pedaling fiercely as she fed the fabric through the machine. Behind her was a sign which read: Miss Evangeline Tailor - Seamstress. Below her name was a list of services available.

"Thank you," Emily said as she looked around the room.

Several finished garments were hung over chairs and other surfaces; in fact, one could barely see anything beneath all the cotton, silk, and lace.

Suddenly, the whirling of the sewing machine stopped, and the seamstress got up from her seat and walked over to them.

"I am so sorry for keeping you waiting," she apologized. "A customer of mine is having their baby's baptism tomorrow, and I am behind on her dress."

"You seem to be very busy, Emily agreed, looking around.

"Rosewood has grown so much these past few months," the seamstress explained. "Hardly a day goes by when I don't have a new customer walking through the door."

Emily smiled.

"Although, I'm not complaining," she said.

"Of course not," Emily agreed. "I am Emily McCoy, and this is my nephew, Thomas and my niece, Lily."

"It's a pleasure to make your acquaintance," the seamstress said. "My name is Evangeline Taylor."

"You are very talented, Miss Taylor," Emily said, admiring the dark crimson dress hanging to her left.

"You are too kind," she said, smiling. "My ma put a needle in my hand when I was five-year-old and I haven't put it down since."

"It shows," Emily said, approvingly.

Evangeline smiled, looking down at the children. "So, how may I be of service to you today?" she asked.

"I'd like to have some new things made for the children," Emily said. "Three pairs of knee-high pants for Thomas and three shirts and for Lily, two new dresses and two new pinafores. Perhaps also a flat cap for Thomas and a new bonnet for Lily."

Evangeline nodded. "Of course," she said, nodding as she looked at Thomas. "What is your favorite color, young man?"

Thomas shrugged; his head bent forward.

"Thomas," Emily pressed. "Miss Taylor asked you a question."

"Green," Thomas said quietly, folding his arms over his chest.

Emily smiled apologetically at the seamstress.

"And you?" Evangeline said, smiling down at Lily.

Lily looked up at her with her big hazel eyes but said nothing.

"Something in the warmer tones," Emily said. "Browns and reds."

Evangeline nodded. "That will suit her coloring well," she agreed. "Have you thought about the type of material you'd like? I personally prefer to use cotton for children's clothes and maybe calico for the pinafores?"

"Yes," Emily agreed, nodding her head. "And I suppose the children will also need wool coats. By the time we arrive in New York the weather will be turning."

"New York?" Evangeline said, her blue eyes widening. "I had a feeling you weren't from around here."

Emily smiled, but out of the corner of her eye Thomas was frowning, his lower lip pushed forward in a pout.

Why don't you both come with me so we can do your measurements?" Evangeline said, looking down at the children again.

Thomas and Lily hesitated, but Emily put a hand on each of their shoulders.

"Go on," she said.

Evangeline led them across the room to where the sewing machine was, and she picked up the measuring tape which hung over the back of the chair. She measured Thomas first, wrapping the tape around his chest, waist, and hips. She made a note of all of the measurements in a small notebook.

"We just need to measure your height, and then we will be done," she said.

Evangeline stretched the measuring tape from Thomas's head to his toes and then made another note.

"You're tall," she said. "Is your pa tall too?"

"My pa is dead," Thomas said curtly.

The color drained from Evangeline's face as she looked across at Emily.

"Thomas," Emily scolded.

"What?" Thomas said, turning to her, his eyes flashing. "It's true."

"There is a time and a place—"

"You didn't even like my father," Thomas shouted. "I bet you are glad that he's dead."

Before Emily had a chance to say anything, Thomas pushed past Evangeline and ran, throwing the door open and disappearing to the street outside.

"I am so sorry," Emily apologized, turning to Evangeline. "The children lost both of their parents a couple of months ago, and it's been an adjustment."

"That's awful," Evangeline said sympathetically.

Emily sighed. "I'd better go and find him before he gets lost."

Evangeline nodded.

"I'll be back in a moment, Lily," Emily said, looking down at the little girl.

Lily nodded, and Emily turned and left the shop. She looked up and down the street, but there was no sign of Thomas. Emily sighed as she turned left and began to walk down the road. She'd only gone a few hundred feet when she heard sobbing. She turned to see Thomas crouched between two buildings, his head in his hands.

"Thomas," Emily said, walking up to him. "Are you alright?"

Thomas said nothing as Emily put a hand on his shoulder, and he shook it off, standing up.

"Thomas," Emily said. "Why do you think I didn't like your father?"

Thomas shrugged. "I heard ma and pa arguing about it once," he said. "Ma wanted to invite you for Christmas, but pa didn't want you to come."

Emily's stomach sank.

"Why didn't you like him?" Thomas asked.

Emily sighed. "It's complicated," she said.

"I didn't like him either," Thomas said.

"What?" Emily said, frowning. "Why would you say that, Thomas?"

Thomas shrugged again, his head bent low, and Emily waited for him to answer her, but after a few moments, it became clear Thomas was not going to say anything more.

"We should get back," Emily said.

Thomas nodded as he turned and walked back out onto the street. They headed to the seamstress without another word, and Thomas kept his head down.

As they stepped back into the shop, Evangeline smiled at them, and Lily ran up to Thomas and took his hand.

"I have all the measurements I need," Evangeline said. "I'll get started on the children's clothes as soon as I've finished the Christening dress."

"Thank you," Emily said gratefully. "Would you be able to send a telegram to Forest Hill when the garments are finished?"

"Certainly," Evangeline agreed. "To whom should I address the telegram?'

"Mr. Alec Kincaid," Emily said.

Evangeline picked up her small notebook and scribbled Alec's name down before she looked up and smiled again.

"Well, it was a pleasure meeting you," Emily said.

"And you," Evangeline said.

"Come on, children," Emily said, herding them back across the shop and out the front door.

Just as they stepped onto the street, Emily spotted Jeremiah. He was parked a short way up the road in the shade of a cedar elm tree.

Emily took Lily by the hand and led her across the road with Thomas trailing behind.

"How did it go?" Jeremiah asked, climbing down off the cart.

"Fine," Emily said, nodding. "Did you get everything you needed?"

"I did," Jeremiah said.

The back of the cart was now loaded with bags of grain and seed. There were also a couple of rolls of wire and a can of linseed oil.

"Shall we get back on the road then?" he said.

"Actually, I thought we might stop at the bakery," Emily said. "I saw the sign for it; it's just down the road."

Jeremiah hesitated a moment.

"Unless you have to get back," she said. "I don't want to get you into any trouble."

"It's fine," Jeremiah said.

"How about it, children?" Emily said, smiling at them.

Lily nodded enthusiastically, but Thomas just shrugged, not meeting her eye.

They headed down the road, past the seamstress, stopping a short while later in front of the bakery. They found a table at the back of the room, and Emily ordered four lemonades.

"All the cakes are on display over there," Emily said. "Why don't you choose which one you'd like?"

Without a word, Thomas and Lily got up and walked over to the display cabinet, pressing their noses against the glass. As Emily watched them, she could not help but wonder what Thomas had meant earlier, in the alleyway, when he'd said that he didn't like his father. It wasn't just what he'd said but the way he'd said it.

"Jeremiah, may I ask you something?" Emily said, turning to look at him.

Jeremiah nodded as he swallowed a mouthful of lemonade.

"How well did you know my brother-in-law?" Emily asked.

"Not well," Jeremiah said, not meeting her eye.

"Really?" Emily said. "I thought being neighbors, you'd have spent time together."

"Mr. Kincaid and Mr. Donnelly didn't get on," Jeremiah said. "Mr. Kincaid once told me Mr. Donnelly wasn't a good man."

Emily frowned. "Why would he say that?"

Jeremiah shook his head. "I don't know, Miss Emily," he said.

Just then, the children returned and took their seats, and the waitress brought over the slices of cakes they had chosen. Thomas had chosen a piece of Battenberg, a checkered cake made of almond sponge and apricot jam and covered in marzipan. While Lily had chosen a slice of pound cake decorated in a delicate layer of icing sugar.

As the children tucked in, Emily watched them, her mind troubled. She'd never liked Bill Donnelly but over the years she'd come to wonder if her prejudice against him was just because he'd taken her sister from her. Now she wondered if she hadn't been right all along about him. If Alec had told Jeremiah that Bill was a bad person then she needed to know why.

Chapter Twelve

Alec slammed the desk drawer shut, burying his head in his hands. He'd been in the Donnelly's study all morning searching for the will and found nothing. All around him, papers littered the desk and floor. It looked like a tornado had torn through the room, leaving nothing but chaos in its wake.

"What are you doing, Alec?" he mumbled to himself.

Cobalt, who was sitting at the door to the study, whined quietly.

"I know," Alec agreed. "It's time to go."

Alec got up from the chair and began to pick up the papers off the floor of the study. He'd been so hopeful he'd find the will. That somehow, in their previous attempts to find it, they'd overlooked it, and he'd find it now and discover that he was the children's rightful guardian, and everything would be fine. But there was no will; Bill Donnelly couldn't even be bothered to make sure his children were looked after.

A short while later, Alec had collected all the papers, leaving them in a pile on the desk. He got his hat off the small side table near the window and left the room, proceeding down the hallway and the staircase to the front door with Cobalt on his heels.

Alec stepped out onto the porch; as he did, almost bumping right into Randall Caldwell. Cobalt growled, and Alec put a firm hand on his head.

"Mr. Kincaid," Randall said in surprise. "I didn't expect to find you here."

"I could say the same," Alec said.

Randall smiled, but there was no warmth in it. "I was actually looking for Miss McCoy," he said. "Is she in?"

"No," Alec said. "She went to Rosewood with the children."

A flicker of annoyance passed over Randall's face. "Do you know when she is expected back?" he asked.

Alec shook his head. "I do not, I'm afraid."

Randall nodded as he ran his tongue over his front teeth. "Has Miss McCoy come to a decision about Riverbend?" he asked. "Is she going to sell?"

"You'll have to ask her," Alec said.

"Oh, don't play coy with me, Alec," Randall said, his mouth twisting into a sneer. "I know that you have Miss McCoy's ear."

Alec frowned. "I have no such thing," he said. "And if I have learned anything from my acquaintance with Miss McCoy, it's that she doesn't need any help making up her mind."

Randall said nothing for a moment, his eyes fixed on Alec.

"I mean to buy Riverbend," he said. "And I am willing to do whatever it takes to convince Miss McCoy to sell."

Alec frowned, not liking the threatening edge to Randall's tone.

"I should be going," Alec said.

As he walked past Randall, the man suddenly reached out and grabbed Alec's arm, and he tensed.

"I mean it, Alec," Randall said, his voice dangerously low. "Don't get in my way."

Alec pulled himself roughly from Randall's grasp, his teeth clenched. He glowered at him for a moment and then turned.

"Tell Miss McCoy I stopped by, won't you?" Randall called after him.

Alec did not turn around as he marched across the front yard and down towards the gate. He didn't slow down until he was back on his property. Randall Caldwell was a real piece of work, but Alec was not willing to give him the satisfaction of knowing Emily's plans to sell the ranch. He'd know soon enough; word spread in Forest Hill quicker than wildfire.

Alec headed into the house, which was empty and quiet. Mrs. Tattlewell didn't come in over the weekends. He made himself a cup of coffee and sat on the step at the backdoor with Cobalt at his feet. The late morning sun was shining through the leafy trees that surrounded the house.

It had been weeks since he'd had a moment like this without the children. At one time, after Olivia and the baby died, Alec thought he'd always be alone and that he'd prefer it that way. If he got close to anyone, there was always the risk of getting hurt, and he'd been hurt enough for one lifetime. But now, he couldn't imagine his life without the children here.

Alec drained the last sip of coffee from his cup and got up. He left it on the step and headed out to the barn with Cobalt trailing behind him. The summer rains had been heavy that year, heavier than usual, and rot had set in on the south wall of the wooden barn. Alec had been meaning to get it fixed before the cooler weather set in but hadn't found a chance to do it until now.

Alec fetched a hammer and began to remove the rotten sections of the wood, using the back of the hammer to pry the boards loose. Most came away without much effort, and Alec stacked the rotten planks to the side.

Removing it took the rest of the morning, and by the time noon came around, Alec's shirt was wet with perspiration. He chucked the final piece of wood on the pile and walked over to the large barrel of water near the door. He cupped his hands and scooped up the water, splashing his face and neck before taking a long drink. Cobalt watched him, his tail wagging.

"You thirsty, boy?" Alec asked.

He fetched a pail and filled it with water, putting it on the ground beside the barrel, and Cobalt walked over and began to drink. Alec watched him for a moment before he turned back to the task at hand. Just then, however, he heard the sound of cart wheels, and he headed out to find Jeremiah, Emily, and the children coming up the road.

"Afternoon, Mr. Kincaid," Jeremiah said, smiling brightly.

"Everything go alright?" he asked.

Jeremiah nodded as Alec walked around the side of the cart where the children were sitting.

"Did you two have a good time?" he asked.

Lily nodded, but Thomas just shrugged.

"Well, why don't you two go on inside?" Alec said. "I'll help Jeremiah unload and then make you something for lunch."

"I can make lunch," Emily said. "Come on, children."

Alec helped Lily and Thomas down, and they followed Emily to the house. Jeremiah was already starting to unload the bags of grain. Alec grabbed one, lifting it onto his shoulder as he followed Jeremiah into the barn.

"Were the children alright?" Alec asked as he dumped the bag against the barn wall.

"Fine," Jeremiah said. "Although Thomas was quieter than usual."

Alec nodded but said nothing as Jeremiah walked back out to the cart, and he followed him.

A while later, they'd finished unloading the cart and Alec turned to the young man.

"Would you like to come in for some lunch?" Alec offered.

"If it's alright, Mr. Kincaid, I promised my sister I'd have lunch with her today," Jeremiah said.

"Of course, I'll see you on Monday."

Jeremiah tipped his cap and smiled before he turned and headed off down the road, whistling under his breath. Alec headed to the house and found the children sitting at the table. Emily was standing at the coal stove.

"Something smells good," Alec said, walking over to the sink.

"Biscuits and gravy," Emily said.

Alec nodded, as he dried his hands on the dish towel.

"Why don't you sit down," Emily said, looking over her shoulder at him. 'It's almost ready."

Alec dried his hands on the dish towel and walked over to the table and took his seat. Emily carried over the meal and served everyone a portion.

"Well, dig in, everyone," she said.

Alec picked up his knife and fork, but the children did not move.

"What is the matter?" he asked. "Are you two not hungry again?"

Thomas and Lily both shook their heads.

"Oh, dear," Emily said. "I am afraid this is my fault. We stopped in at the bakery in Rosewood and it must have spoiled their appetites."

"Can we go outside and play?' Thomas asked.

Alec looked at Emily and nodded.

"You can have your lunch for dinner," he said.

Thomas and Lily slid out of their seats and headed out the back door hand-in-hand, leaving Alec and Emily alone.

"This is good," Alec said, indicating the food on his plate with his fork.

"I don't cook much now," Emily admitted. "But when we were growing up, I used to make this meal often for Marie and our father."

Alec nodded, taking another bite of the soft, buttery biscuit.

"How did things go with the seamstress?" he asked.

Emily sighed as she put down her fork.

"Thomas ran out," she said. "I mentioned New York, and it upset him. He shouted at me in the shop."

"What did he say?" Alec asked, frowning.

"That I did not like his father," Emily said. "Which was true enough, but what was strange was that when I went to find him, he told me that he didn't like him either."

Alec's shoulders stiffened as he glanced down at his plate.

"Do you know why he would say that?" Emily asked.

"No," Alec lied.

He could feel Emily's eyes on him, but he kept his eyes on his plate.

"How did you feel about my brother-in-law?" Emily asked.

Alec said nothing for a moment. What could he say? He couldn't tell her the truth. He promised Marie that he would never tell anyone.

"Bill and I didn't see eye-to-eye on most things," Alec said. "It's like I told you the other day; he and Randall Caldwell always thought that they were better than everyone else."

Emily frowned. "But you didn't think Bill was a bad person, did you?" she asked.

Alec said nothing for a moment and then shook his head, but as he met Emily's eyes, he could sense that she didn't believe him.

"Why didn't you like him?" Alec asked, deflecting.

Emily sighed, shaking her head. "I don't know," she confessed. "I hardly knew him when he swept my sister off to Texas. But my father always said I had a good sense of people, of what they were made of, and I never got a good feeling about Bill Donnelly."

Alec nodded, saying nothing about how right Emily had been about her brother-in-law.

"Well, I'd better get back to work," Alec said. "Thank you for lunch."

Alec got up, but as he did, so did Emily.

"Alec, wait..."

Emily's voice trailed off as the color drained from her face, and she swayed slightly.

"Are you alright?" Alec asked in concern.

"I don't know," Emily admitted, putting her hands on the table to steady herself. "I am suddenly feeling quite light-headed."

"Why don't you go and lie down?" Alec suggested.

"I might just do that," Emily said, exhaling shakily.

"Do you need some help?" Alec offered.

"I can manage," Emily said.

She turned and walked slowly across the room as Alec watched. He waited until he heard the soft click of her bedroom door before he headed outside to the barn.

It was late afternoon by the time Alec returned to the house, and the sun was setting in the distance, turning the world gold. As he approached the backdoor, he found Thomas and Lily in the garden, waiting for fireflies.

"Where's your aunt?" Alec asked.

Thomas shrugged. "We haven't seen her since lunchtime," he said.

Alec frowned as he headed into the house. He walked through the kitchen and down the hallway, stopping outside

Emily's bedroom door. He listened for a moment, but there was no sound from within.

"Emily?" Alec said, knocking on the wood.

Still, there was no reply. Perhaps she was just sleeping? However, Alec had a bad feeling in his gut, so he knocked again, but still, there was no answer.

Alec reached for the brass doorknob and turned it. He stepped inside to find Emily lying on the bed. Her eyes were closed, but she was shivering so severely that her teeth were chattering, and she was damp with sweat.

"Thomas!" Alec yelled.

Thomas appeared in the doorway a moment later with Lily at his heels.

"Run over to the neighbors and tell them to fetch the doctor," Alec said. "Your aunt is unwell."

Thomas hesitated a moment, his eyes wide.

"Now!" Alec insisted.

Thomas turned and ran as Alec sat down on the bed and put a hand on Emily's forehead. She was burning up. Lily was still standing in the doorway, her hazel eyes as wide as saucers.

"Lily," Alec said, turning to look at her. 'Why don't you go up to your room and play?"

Without a word, Lily turned and headed upstairs, and Alec got up from the bed; as he did, he noticed that Emily had removed her shoes and stockings. He frowned, leaning in. Alec had almost forgotten about the leech bites on her legs, but now it was impossible not to notice them. The bites were bright red and swollen, and as Alec reached over and gently felt the wounds with his fingers, they were hot to the touch.

Emily groaned, her head rolling on her shoulders as Alec stepped back. He turned and quickly left the room, returning a short while later with a bowl of tepid water and a clean towel. He placed them down on the bedside table and sat down on the edge of the bed again. Then he dipped the towel in the bowl and wrung it out before placing it on Emily's forehead. She groaned softly.

Alec sat with her, replacing the towel every few minutes. When he heard hurried footsteps in the hallway, he turned.

"Mr. Caldwell said he'd go for the doctor," Thomas said, panting.

"Good boy," Alec said. "Now, I need you to sit with your aunt while I fetch some herbs from the garden."

"Do I have to?' Thomas said.

"Yes," Alec said plainly.

Thomas stepped into the room, and Alec explained to him how to soak the towel and how to ring it out.

"I won't be long," he said.

Without another word, Alec turned and left the room. He hurried down the passage and into the back yard. Thick bushes of comfrey grew around the stables; Alec's father had planted them. They used comfrey to treat horse wounds by making a poultice. Alec grabbed handfuls of it, hardly noticing the fine, bristle-like hair scratching his fingers and palms. He turned and headed back to the house.

In the kitchen, he put the water on to boil on the stove. While he waited, he chopped the comfrey leaves into pieces. Then he fetched a mixing bowl from the kitchen dresser and a

149

tin of cornmeal from the pantry. Alec added the chopped-up comfrey to the cornmeal, and then, using the hot water from the kettle, he slowly added it, mixing the ingredients together to form a thick paste.

Alec entered the bedroom to find Thomas still seated on the side of the bed, his hands holding the towel over his aunt's face.

"What is that?" Thomas asked as Alec approached the bed.

"A poultice," he explained.

Thomas watched as Alec knelt down and began to apply the thick paste to Emily's wounds with his fingers. When he'd covered each, he stood up again.

"There are some bandages in the dresser in my bedroom," Alec said. "Will you fetch them, please?"

Thomas nodded, getting up from the bed and disappearing, reappearing a minute later with the roll of fresh bandage. Alec took it from him and began to dress Emily's wounds, careful not to disturb the poultice.

"Alec?" Thomas said.

"Hmm?" Alec said, not looking up from the task at hand.

"It's my fault," Thomas said. "That Aunt Emily is sick."

Alec stopped for a moment and looked up at Thomas; the boy's face was pale.

"Thomas—"

"I was the one who tricked her into going into the shady part of the stream," Thomas said, his voice wavering. "It's my fault."

"You couldn't have known this would happen," Alec said. "No one could have."

"But what if she dies?" Thomas said, his voice barely above a whisper now.

"She's not going to die," Alec said, his voice determined.

Thomas said nothing as Emily groaned again, and Alec reached over and touched her forehead. He looked over at Thomas, doing his best to hide his concern. Despite their attempts to break the fever, she was hotter than she'd been when Alec had first found her. They needed the doctor and soon.

Chapter Thirteen

Emily could hear muffled voices, but she couldn't make out what they were saying. It was as if she were trapped in some thick fog, a disjointed reality that made no sense to her. All she could think about was how cold she was, how her body felt as if it were being pricked by a thousand tiny needles.

She tried to sit up, to speak, but she had no control; she was at the mercy of this feverish delirium. All she wanted was a sip of water, something to ease her dry throat.

Then, as if by some miracle, she felt a gentle hand on the back of her head lifting her up. The glass clinked against her teeth as she drank thirstily. Then, all too soon, the glass was gone, and the hand too, and she was slipping back into a restless sleep.

Marie was there, standing at the front room window of their old house. She had her back to Emily but as she stepped closer, she turned and smiled. How many years had they spent at that window watching the world go by, dreaming of the future?

Emily walked over to her and put a gentle hand on her sister's back, but as she did, Emily frowned. She pulled her hand away and looked down at the dark red blood staining her palms and fingers. Her heart began to race as a metallic smell stung her nose, and when she looked up again, Marie had turned to face her.

Her cream dress was stained with blood, and her face was as white as a sheet. Marie put out a hand to Emily, and as Emily reached out for her sister, she began to turn gray, first her fingers, then her hand, her arm, her neck, and her face, and then her body began to crumble, and she was gone, carried away by a breeze through the open window.

Emily's eyes popped open as she looked around the room, her heart racing. She stared at the ceiling for a moment, disorientated.

"Emily?"

She did not recognize the voice as she turned her head; her vision was blurry. The dawn light from the window cast a warm glow around his head and broad shoulders.

"Emily?" Alec repeated.

Emily squinted as Alec's strong features started to come into focus.

"Alec?" she said, her voice hoarse. "What happened?"

Emily tried to pull herself into a sitting position, but Alec stopped her, putting a gentle hand on her shoulder.

"Don't," he said. "You need to rest. Would you like some water?"

Emily nodded, sitting back as Alec fetched the glass. He placed a gentle hand behind her head and helped her to drink. Emily was certain she'd never tasted anything so good in her life.

"What happened?" Emily asked again.

"The leech bites on your ankles got infected," Alec explained. "And you caught a bad fever."

Emily nodded slowly, her head still feeling thick with fog.

"But its broken," Alec said, reaching over and putting a hand on her forehead. "So now you just need to get some rest."

Emily closed her eyes and nodded, feeling comforted by Alec's touch, and before she knew it she was asleep again.

Emily did not know how long it had been, but when she opened her eyes again, the room was dim.

"Aunt Emily?" Thomas said. "Are you awake?"

Emily looked down to see Thomas sitting on the bed; he was holding her hand.

"Thomas?" Emily frowned. "What time is it?"

"The sun's about to set," Thomas said. "How are you feeling?"

Emily did not answer right away. Her body was sore, but otherwise, she felt fine.

"I am feeling much better," she answered.

Thomas's shoulders dropped in relief, but before he could reply, Alec stepped into the room with a tray in his hands.

"Thomas," he chided, frowning in disapproval. "I thought I told you to let your aunt rest."

"Sorry," Thomas apologized.

"Your sister's in the kitchen," Alec said. "And dinner's on the table. Go and eat."

Thomas smiled at Emily before he let go of her hand and exited the bedroom. Alec waited until Thomas was gone before he walked over to the bed, putting the tray down on the bedside table. Cobalt was right behind him.

"How are you feeling?" he asked.

"Better," Emily said, managing to sit up.

"I brought you some soup," Alec said. "I wasn't sure if you would be hungry."

Emily was suddenly aware of the nagging sensation in her stomach. "I am, actually," she said.

"Well, that's good," Alec replied, smiling. "Here."

He handed Emily the tray, helping her to position it on her lap. As she ate, Alec sat, watching her.

"You gave us all a bit of a scare," Alec said. "Thomas hardly left your side all night."

"Did the doctor come?" Emily asked.

"No," Alec said grimly.

"So you were the one who cared for me?" Emily asked, meeting his eye.

"Well, I couldn't just let you die," Alec said. "It would be bad manners; you are a guest, after all."

Emily smiled. "Well, you have my gratitude," she said.

Alec smiled as he looked down at the empty bowl. "Would you like some more?"

"Maybe later," Emily said, sitting back.

Alec reached over for the tray just as Emily handed it to him, and as they did, their fingers brushed, and Emily felt her heart skip a beat. Their eyes met for a moment, but Alec looked away, placing the tray back on the bedside table.

"So, how did you come to know how to care for someone with a fever?" Emily asked with interest.

"Your sister taught me," Alec said. "A few years ago, both Thomas and Lily came down with terrible fevers. Bill was away on a cattle drive, and I helped Marie to care for them. She taught me what to do."

Emily nodded, suddenly thinking back to the dream she had about Marie.

"Are you alright?" Alec asked, reading her expression.

"Fine," Emily said. "I was just thinking of a dream I had."

"A fever dream?" Alec said. "What was it about?"

"It was about Marie," Emily said.

She explained the dream to Alec, and, for a fever dream, she remembered the details with startling clarity.

"Do you think the dream was trying to tell you something?" Alec asked.

"What do you mean?" Emily asked.

"Well, cowboys believe that dreams convey messages," he explained. "Dreams about storms, rain, or sunshine tell us what weather is on the way. While finding gold or silver is a sign of upcoming prosperity or good fortune."

"And dreaming about your deceased sister?" Emily asked. "What would a cowboy say about that?"

"That maybe you came to Texas for more than just the children," Alec said. "That maybe this is the place to lay the past to rest and start movin' on down the trail."

"But how?" Emily asked.

"I don't know," Alec admitted. "But chances are you are going to have to stick around a while to figure it out."

Emily said nothing, and the room fell silent.

156

"Well, I'll let you rest," Alec said, getting up. "Raise a ruckus if you need anything."

Emily smiled as Alec picked up the tray and turned to go.

"Alec," she said.

He turned around and looked at her.

"Thank you," she said. "For taking care of me."

His green eyes softened. "Get some rest," he said.

He turned and left the room, and Emily sank down in the bed, feeling tired again.

Emily woke the following day to bird song as the sunlight poured in through the open curtains. She heard scratching at the door.

"Aunt Emily?" a voice said.

She turned to see Thomas and Lily peering apprehensively around the corner.

"Come in," Emily said, smiling.

The children stepped into the room and Cobalt jumped onto the bottom of the bed, his tail wagging.

"Where's Alec?" Emily asked.

"Still sleeping," Thomas replied.

Emily nodded. "Are you two hungry?"

Thomas and Lily nodded.

"How about pancakes?" Emily asked.

"Our ma used to make us pancakes," Thomas said, his tone bright.

"Well, who do you think taught her? Emily said, throwing the covers off. "I'll get dressed and meet you in the kitchen. You can gather up the ingredients from the pantry."

The children left, and Emily got out of bed, a little shakily. She got dressed slowly and left the bedroom, making her way down the hallway and into the kitchen. Thomas and Lily had placed all the ingredients on the table and were waiting patiently.

"Good work," Emily said approvingly. "Thomas, can you please fetch me an apron?"

Thomas fetched one and handed it to Emily, who secured it around her narrow waist.

"Alright," she said. "Let's get to work."

The first batch of pancakes were beginning to bubble in the pan when Alec stepped into the kitchen, his eyes widening in surprise. The children were both kneeling on chairs by the stove, watching their creations take shape.

"What are you doing up?" he asked, frowning slightly. "You should be resting."

"I am fine," Emily said. "And besides, the children were hungry, so we made pancakes."

"I can see that," Alec said, the corners of his mouth twitching.

Emily turned away from the stove to see the mess they'd left. There were broken eggshells scattered across the table, small puddles of milk, and sprinklings of flour.

"So, we might have got a little carried away," Emily admitted, smiling sheepishly.

"Are they ready to turn, Aunt Emily?" Thomas said, turning his head to face her.

Emily peered into the pan and nodded.

"Yes," she said. "But be mindful that you turn them carefully."

"I will," Thomas promised, poising his spatula underneath the first one.

Emily watched as he carefully turned all of them, revealing their perfectly golden sides.

"I think we will make a master pancake maker out of you, yet," Emily said, nodding in approval.

Thomas smiled as Emily turned to Alec, who was staring at her.

"What is it?" Emily asked.

"You've got flour on your nose," Alec said.

Emily reached up and dusted her nose with the sleeve of her blouse.

"It's still there," Alec said, smiling. "Here, let me."

Before Emily could say anything, Alec reached over and ran his thumb over the bridge of her nose. As he did, their eyes met, and Emily felt her heart catch in her throat.

A loud clatter caused Emily to jump, and she looked down to see the metal spatula lying on the floor at her feet.

"Sorry," Thomas apologized, scrambling to retrieve it.

"I'd better get on with the chores," Alec said, clearing his throat.

"You're not staying for breakfast?" Emily asked.

"Save me some," Alec said as he turned and headed out the back door.

Emily helped the children cook the rest of the pancakes, and they sat down to eat. As they did, Emily could not help but feel strangely grateful for the events of the past twenty-four hours. The children were finally warming to her, and it had only taken her almost dying.

"Aunt Emily?" Thomas said.

"Mm?" Emily murmured, looking across the table at him.

"Why did you never come and visit us before?" he asked.

Emily said nothing for a long moment, wondering what the best answer would be to give her nephew and niece. Both Thomas and Lily were looking at her expectantly, and if she'd learned one thing in all her years of teaching, it was that to teach honesty, you must be honest yourself.

"Well," Emily said. "Your mother and I had a fight before she left New York."

"What about?" Thomas asked.

"I didn't want her to leave," Emily said. "I was afraid of being alone."

Thomas said nothing for a moment.

"But I was wrong," Emily continued. "To be so selfish. I should have supported her choices, and I should have been happy that she was happy."

"She wasn't always happy," Thomas said. "She used to cry a lot."

Lily nodded, her thin face solemn, and Emily frowned.

"She did?" Emily asked. "Do you know what made her sad?"

"Pa, mostly," Thomas said.

Emily's stomach sank.

"I wish you had come to visit," Thomas said. "It would have made ma smile."

Emily's throat was raw as she looked between the two children.

"I wished I had come to visit too," Emily said.

The room fell silent for a moment, and the whole world was resting on Emily's shoulders. What had Bill done to her sister?

"Can we go out and play?" Thomas asked.

"Of course you can," Emily said, doing her best to smile.

The children left the kitchen, and Emily set about washing the breakfast dishes. As she did, she thought about the first time she met Bill Donnelly. He'd been charming, handsome, and rich, and it was easy to see why Marie had fallen head over heels for him. But there was also something dark about him, something dangerous.

It was hard to see, like a stain that had been scrubbed again and again until it was barely noticeable. Marie had barely known Bill for two weeks when he asked her to marry him. Marie hadn't seen it, how possessive he was, how authoritarian.

Emily had brought it up with her sister on more than one occasion, but she'd brushed it off, claiming that Emily had always looked down on the traditional roles of a woman, of a wife looking after her husband.

Then, the morning that Marie was due to leave for Texas, Emily had begged her to stay, and when begging didn't work, she yelled. She called Marie a fool to believe a man like Bill was capable of loving anyone but himself. She called her selfish for leaving after everything that Emily had sacrificed, her childhood and her freedom. Yet nothing Emily said made the slightest difference, Marie still left, and Emily hated her for it. She'd fought but she hadn't fought hard enough. She should have visited; she should have checked in on her sister. But she didn't. Instead she let her wounded pride keep her away and how could she ever begin to forgive herself for that?

Chapter Fourteen

Alec was carrying a pail of warm milk across the back garden when he spotted Randall Caldwell coming up the road. Cobalt whined as Alec put down the milk pail, the liquid sloshing against the sides.

"He's like a burr on a saddle blanket," Alec muttered.

A few moments later, Randall brought his horse to a stop and dismounted, taking his hat off.

"Mornin' Kincaid," Randall said.

"What can I do for you, Caldwell?" Alec sighed. "I thought you'd be in church?"

"I just came to check in on poor Miss McCoy," Randall said. "I figured God would understand."

Alec nodded, exhaling through his nose.

"How is she?" he asked.

"Better," Alec said. "Although we'd have all been much less worried if you'd fetched the doctor like you said you would."

"I tried," Randall said. "But he'd gone out of town to deliver a baby."

Alec said nothing. He had no idea if that was true, but what could Randall gain by lying?

"Is she inside?" Randall asked. "May I see her?"

"She's resting," Alec said.

Just then, the back door opened, and Emily stepped outside. Randall threw Alec a hard glance before walking past him towards her. Alec followed on his heels.

"Miss McCoy," Randall said brightly. "How pleased I am to see you looking so well."

"Mr. Caldwell," Emily said, a slight crease forming between her brows. "What are you doing here?"

"I came to see if you were alright," he said. "As I told Mr. Kincaid, I rode into town yesterday evening to fetch the doctor, but unfortunately, he was away."

"Oh," Emily said. "I didn't know you'd done that for me."

Randall glanced at Alec and then back at Emily, smiling.

"Of course," he said. "We look out for one another in this community."

Alec snorted softly, but Randall ignored him.

"I actually came by Riverbend yesterday looking for you," Randall continued. "I was hoping to have a word."

Emily glanced at Alec. With everything that had happened, he'd forgotten to tell her about running into Randall.

"I was wondering if you'd made a decision about what you plan to do with Riverbend?" Randall asked.

"I have," Emily said.

"And?"

"I plan to sell it," she said.

"Excellent," Randall said, clapping his hands. "What wonderful news. I shall have the papers drawn up first thing tomorrow."

Emily pressed her lips together, not meeting Alec's eye.

"You've made the right choice, Miss McCoy," Randall said. "You won't regret it; I can promise you that."

Without another word, Randall turned and headed back to his horse, pulling himself up into the saddle.

"I'll be back with the papers," he said, grinning.

Randall pressed his heels into the sides of his horse as he turned and rode back down towards the gate. As he did, Alec rounded on Emily.

"What?" she said, frowning. "You knew that I was planning on selling."

"I just thought that after yesterday, you might have changed your mind," Alec said.

"Why?" Emily asked. "Because of the fever dream?"

"You said you wanted to saddle up the past," Alec insisted. "Find a way to ride on from it."

"I do, Emily said. "I will raise my sister's children, and that is how I will make it up to her."

Alec shook his head, sighing in frustration.

"You don't get it," he said. "Marie would never have wanted Thomas and Lily raised in New York."

"Well, if you knew my sister so well, why don't you tell me what was happening with her and Bill?" Emily insisted. "And don't tell me there wasn't anything going on."

Alec opened his mouth and closed it again.

"You claim to have known Marie better than me," Emily pressed on. "Then tell me, why did Bill make my sister cry?"

165

Alec opened his mouth, but just then, he heard voices and turned to see Mrs. Tattlewell coming up the road accompanied by a man, a woman, and two children.

"I hope we are not interrupting," Mrs. Tattlewell said cheerfully.

"No," Alec said, doing his best to smile. "We just weren't expecting you."

"Well, we had to come," Mrs. Tattlewell said. "Once we heard that Emily had taken ill. It was all anyone could talk about at church. How are you, dear?"

"Much better, thank you," Emily said.

"I am so relieved to hear it," Mrs. Tattlewell said. "Those poor children have lost enough."

Mrs. Tattlewell's companions were standing quietly a few steps behind her. They were a handsome couple, both dark haired and tall.

"Who are your friends? Alec asked.

"Oh, how rude of me," Mrs. Tattlewell said. "This is my great niece, Mrs. Kara Jones, her husband, Mr. Mark Jones, and their children, Sarah, and Benjamin. This is Mr. Alec Kincaid and Miss Emily McCoy."

"It's nice to meet you," Alec said, tipping his hat. "I recall your aunt mentioning that you were from Chicago. What's brought you all the way out here?" Alec asked.

"We've actually just moved here," Mark said.

"And how are you finding it?"

"Quiet," Mark joked.

Kara rolled her eyes, smiling. "I always wanted to come back to the country so it was my idea to move out here," she said. "I was raised on a ranch you see, and while the city has its conveniences, it's not the right place to raise children. They need wide open spaces to run and play and learn about the world."

Alec glanced at Emily, but she did not meet his eye.

"I couldn't agree more," Alec said.

"Miss McCoy is from the big city," Mrs. Tattlewell said.

"Really?" Mark said, turning to look at Emily. "Which one, Miss McCoy?"

"New York," she said. "And please, call me Emily."

Just then, Thomas and Lily came running around the side of the house.

"Thomas, Lily, come meet Sarah and Ben," Alec said.

The children walked over and introduced themselves. They were all of similar ages.

"Why don't you go and show them the chicken coop?" Alec suggested.

"Come on," Thomas said.

They watched the children walk over to the coop, and Alec turned back to their parents.

"How about some coffee?" he offered.

"We don't want to intrude," Kara said.

"You're not," Alec said. "Mrs. Tattlewell has been so good to us these past months, a cup of coffee is the least we can do."

"A cup of coffee would be welcome," Mark said. "I can't say I am too keen on the coffee served at church."

Mrs. Tattlewell swatted him playfully with her fan.

"That stuff wouldn't rouse a rooster at dawn," Alec said, in agreement.

Mark chuckled.

"Come on, kitchen's this way."

Alec picked up the pail of milk and led the way, with everyone following behind. As they stepped into the brightly lit room, he turned to them.

"Please, take a seat," he said. "I'll put the water on."

Everyone sat down at the kitchen table as Alec filled the large copper kettle and set it on over the heat on the coal stove. From outside, they could hear the children laughing.

"I am so glad the children have met others their own age," Kara said, smiling in relief. "They were so devastated to leave their friends behind."

"Well, they should enjoy it while it lasts," Alec said.

Kara frowned.

"Emily plans to take the children back to New York at the end of the summer," Mrs. Tattlewell explained.

"Oh," Kara said. "What a pity."

Alec glanced at Emily.

"I am unsure if your aunt told you why I am here?" Emily asked.

"She did," Mark said sympathetically. "Dreadful business."

"We are so sorry for your loss," Kara added. "It must have been such a shock."

"Yes," Emily agreed. "It's been rather difficult knowing the right thing to do."

"Of course," Kara agreed. "It's never easy to know if you are making the right choices for your children. All you can do is follow your gut."

Emily nodded. "So, I have decided to sell my sister's ranch, although I have no idea how I am going to get it packed up in time."

"Well, perhaps Mark and I can help," Kara suggested. "We haven't found a house yet and so we have some time on our hands. I am sure my aunt would be grateful to have us out from under her feet."

"Really?" Emily said. "That would be wonderful."

"Perhaps after coffee, you can all take a walk down to the house," Mrs. Tattlewell suggested. "Assess what needs to be done."

"What do you plan on doing with all of Bill and Marie's things?" Alec piped in.

Emily turned her head toward him and frowned.

"Sell them, I suppose," Emily said. "Although I have no idea what state anything is in. The house is full of mold from all the rain."

"And what about Thomas and Lily?" Alec asked. "Are they going to be able to keep anything of their parents for them or will you just sell it all?"

"Of course," she said, frowning slightly. "Although we will be going back to New York by train so the children won't be

169

able to take all their things. What we leave behind perhaps can be stored."

"Stored where?" Alec asked.

Emily exhaled in frustration. "What do you want me to do, Alec?" she asked. "I am trying my best."

"I want you not to sell the ranch to Randall Caldwell," Alec said. "Bill would be rolling in his grave if he knew who you were selling the ranch to."

"I don't see any other buyers lining up outside the gates," Emily said, her voice rising.

Mrs. Tattlewell cleared her throat, and Alec suddenly realized that in their quarreling, they'd forgotten they weren't alone.

"Sorry," Alec apologized.

Emily looked around the table apologetically.

"How are the children looking forward to the move?" Kara asked, changing the subject. "Are they excited?"

Emily glanced at Alec for a moment.

"I think they'll come around to the idea," she said. "It's a big change for them."

"And what is it you do in New York?" Mark asked.

"I am a teacher," Emily said.

Just then, the children came running in through the back door.

"May we please have something to eat?' Thomas asked.

"There are still pancakes leftover from this morning," Emily said.

The children helped themselves.

"Go on and eat outside," Mrs. Tattlewell said. "There's enough work to be done without having to clean up after you lot."

"Can we show Sarah and Ben the stream?" Thomas asked.

"I think it's best if you stick closer to the house," Alec said. "You can show them the stream another day."

Thomas nodded, and the children filed out of the kitchen and back outside.

The kettle was boiling, so Alec made the coffee, placing the cups on the kitchen table. As everyone drank, they talked about the Jones's move and what they planned to do now that they were here.

"So, you're looking for work?" Alec asked, taking a sip of coffee.

"That's right," Mark said. "I am an accountant by trade but I always wanted to be a good ol' fashioned cowboy."

Mark chuckled, shaking his head. "You're not looking for an extra ranch hand are you?" he asked.

"Unfortunately not," Alec said. "I can barely afford young Jeremiah. But I am sure you'll find something."

The table fell silent for a few moments.

"Forest Hill has no school," Emily said, looking at Kara. "What do you plan to do with the children?"

"Teach them myself," Kara said. "I am not a teacher like yourself, but I can teach them to read, write, and do basic arithmetic."

"Kara is being modest," Mark said, smiling at his wife. "She went to one of the best schools in Chicago and would have continued into college if she hadn't met me."

"Well, what can I say?" Kara said, smiling back at him. "I fell in love."

Alec watched them, and something about the look they shared struck a chord in him.

"I think I'll go and check on the children," he said, getting up.

Without a word, Alec left the kitchen. As he stepped outside, he took a deep breath. He couldn't understand why he was so affected by a simple look shared between husband and wife. After Olivia and the baby died, Alec swore he would never want someone to look at him that way again. That look meant pain and heartbreak, but now, as much as he didn't want to, he realized he missed it.

"Alec?"

Alec turned around to find Emily, Kara, and Mark exiting through the kitchen doorway.

"We are going to Riverbend," Emily said. "Will you come with us? You know the house better than I do."

Alec hesitated. The truth was he didn't want to be involved in packing up Marie's house or the sale. He'd much prefer it if Emily just left him out of it.

"Mrs. Tattlewell said she would stay and keep an eye on the children," Emily added.

"Alright," Alec said. "I'll fetch the keys."

A short while later, they arrived at Riverbend. The large stone house with its gabled roof stood out against the landscape.

"It's a beautiful spot," Mark said, looking up at the great loblolly pines surrounding the house and barn. "What's its history?"

"The Donnelly family were one of the first families in the area," Alec explained. "They arrived at the same time as my ancestors and the Caldwell's. Between the three families, they built most of the town."

"So, your family was here right from the beginning?" Kara said.

"That's right," Alec confirmed. "My great-grandfather was a veteran of the Revolutionary War and was compensated for his services with a land warrant. He and my great-grandmother traveled south from Oklahoma with only a handful of seeds in their pockets and claimed their land right here."

"And the other families?" Mark asked. "The Donnelly's and the Caldwell's."

"They were already settled here in Forest Hill when my ancestors arrived," Alec explained. "The Donnelly's came over from Ireland and had made their fortune in trade, while the Caldwell's like to call themselves true-blue American cowboys, born and bred here. When in truth, their ancestors had arrived in Jamestown two hundred years earlier, just like everyone else."

"I'd give an arm and a leg for a place like this," Mark said enviously.

"Well, I don't know if you've heard, but it's for sale," Emily joked.

"We could never afford it," Kara said, smiling sadly.

"Do you mind if we take a walk around the property?" Mark asked.

"Please do," Emily said. "We'll meet you in the house."

Mark and Kara walked off, hand in hand, and as Alec watched them go, he suddenly had a brilliant idea.

Chapter Fifteen

"Emily," Alec said, catching her hand.

"What is it?" Emily asked, turning to face him.

"Remember we spoke about finding a foreman for the ranch?" Alec said. 'To manage it until Thomas is old enough."

Emily nodded, frowning.

"What about Mark?" he said.

Emily said nothing as she looked into Alec's green eyes, which were alight with excitement.

"Mark?" she said.

"You heard what he said back in the kitchen. He's always wanted to work on a ranch, and they haven't found a house to buy in Forest Hill yet."

"Yes, but he's an accountant, Alec," Emily argued. "He doesn't know the first thing about running a ranch."

"I can help him," Alec said. "I can teach him what he needs to know about growing crops and raising cattle."

"How will you find the time?" Emily asked. "You have your own ranch to run."

"I'll make the time," Alec promised. "And we don't have to worry about the finances because as you just said, Mark was an accountant. He'll know better than anyone how to manage the money."

Emily said nothing as she bit her bottom lip, her mind racing.

"You have to admit that they are a good couple," Alec said. "Solid."

Alec wasn't wrong. The Jones's were those rare breed of people who you liked right away. There was something about them, a goodness, that couldn't really be explained, but felt.

Emily sighed, shaking her head. "It's a nice idea," she said. "But I just don't know—"

"Will you not at least think about it?" Alec said, gritting his teeth in frustration.

"Selling the place will give the children security," Emily said.

"Seling Riverbend would mean that at the end of the summer, you can put all this behind you and never look back. It's the easier choice for you."

Emily sighed. "I know that you think I am selfish," she said. "But I am doing this for the children."

"You can convince yourself of anything if you want it badly enough," Alec said.

"And what's that supposed to mean?" Emily challenged.

"If you truly wanted what was best for the children, then you would keep this place so that if they choose to come home one day, they have a home to return to."

Emily turned, looking at the house with its wide porch. Was Alec right? When she'd first arrived in Forest Hill, she had contemplated keeping the house for the children; in fact, she had wanted to, but the idea of finding a foreman and getting the place back up and running had seemed like too big a task. Yet, the Jones's timing couldn't be better, and if Alec were willing to teach Mark and make the ranch profitable again, then maybe they wouldn't have to sell after all.

"The ranch would have to make enough for the family to live on and to pay what is owed to the bank," Emily said.

"It's doable," Alec said confidently. "It will take some time to get everything up and running again, but in the meantime, we can lease out grazing land to bring in an income."

Emily nodded.

"And I suppose in the long term, if Thomas and Lily do decide to return to Riverbend then the Jones's can build a house on the property, so that they won't be cast out of their home."

"So, are you really considering this?" Alec said, his green eyes twinkling.

"We still need to propose the idea to them," Emily reminded him. "They may not want to take on such a task when they learn all of the details."

"They will," Alec said. "I can feel it in my britches."

Emily met Alec's eye, and there was a warmth and a tenderness in them that she had not seen before and it took her quite by surprise.

A short while later, they were all seated in the Riverbend kitchen. Emily and Alec had opened the doors and the windows to bring in as much fresh air and sunlight as possible.

"I know this is sudden," Emily said. "But we have a proposal that we would like to discuss with you."

Mark and Kara exchanged a surprised look as they waited for Emily to continue.

"Riverbend belongs to my nephew," Emily explained. "And when I first arrived in Forest Hill, I hoped to keep the property for him to inherit one day when he was old enough. However, in order to keep the ranch, we need to find a custodian to oversee the running of it."

Emily glanced at Alec, and he smiled encouragingly.

"Until a short while ago, we did not think I'd be able to find that person in time, which was why I was prepared to sell," Emily said. "But then, you two came walking up the driveway."

"Us?" Mark said, his brown eyes widening in surprise.

"We want you to take over the running of Riverbend," Emily said. "And to live here, in this house. To make it your home until Thomas comes of age, after which we will build a place for you on the property if that's what you would like."

Mark and Kara were lost for words.

"I can't believe this," Kara said after a few moments. "We'd never have imagined walking around a place like this, let alone living here."

"Are you really offering us this life?" Mark asked, his eyes full of apprehension and excitement.

"It's not all good news, I'm afraid," Emily continued. "The property is in quite substantial debt. But the bank has agreed to a payment plan should the decision be made not to sell the ranch."

"So, the ranch would need to make enough money to pay off the debts and pay your wages," Alec explained. "We'd need to put in place some money-making measures right away."

"I may not be much of a cowboy yet," Mark said. "But I do know a few things about money."

"So what do you say?" Emily asked. "Will you take over the running of Riverbend?"

Mark turned to Kara, who smiled back at him.

"Yes," Mark said, smiling. "Yes, we sure will."

"Wonderful," Emily said, suddenly feeling a great weight had been lifted off her shoulders.

For the next while, they all sat together, discussing plans for the near future. Emily had not realized up until then just how much she didn't want to sell the place. Now, it would have a family to look after it until the children were older.

"We'd better get back," Emily said, "before your aunt thinks we've run away for good."

They got up, and Alec closed the windows before they left through the back door.

As they made their way back towards the road, Alec and Mark walked ahead, discussing plans on how to get the ranch making money again, while Emily and Kara walked behind.

"Are you sure about all of this?" Kara asked.

"I am," Emily said. "Truthfully, I never wanted to sell my sister's house. It belongs to the children."

"Do you think they will want to come back one day?" Kara asked.

"I do," Emily confessed.

The two women fell silent for a few moments.

"We'll spend the next couple of weeks packing up the house," Emily said. "I am sure you will be able to make use of the furniture; and what you cannot use, we can store in the barn."

"I am sure we can make use of it all," Kara said. "We did not bring much with us from Chicago."

"It will take a bit of work to get the place livable again," Emily said. "But if we all work together, I am certain we can prepare it for you to move into by the end of the summer."

"I still can't believe this is happening," Kara said.

Emily smiled.

"Can I be truthful with you, Emily," Kara said, turning to look at her.

"Of course," Emily said.

"We found ourselves in a bit of trouble in Chicago," Kara said, lowering her voice. "You see, Mark worked as an accountant for a firm embroiled in illicit financial dealings. Of course, Mark had no idea."

"How terrible," Emily said, shaking her head.

"Mark was devastated," Kara said. "And no other firm would take him on after they learned who he'd worked for."

"So is that why you moved to Forest Hill?" Emily asked.

"When the money ran out, we didn't have much choice," Kara said. "I wrote to my aunt, who kindly offered us a place in her home, and we spent the last of what we had getting here."

"I am so sorry for your hardships," Emily said.

"Thank you, Emily," Kara replied. "But when God closes a door, he opens a window."

They arrived back at Alec's ranch to find Mrs. Tattlewell sitting on a chair on the porch while the children played in the front yard.

"We're back, aunty," Kara said, walking up the porch and kissing her aunt on the cheek. "And we have some good news."

They told Mrs. Tattlewell the plan they'd devised, and she was so pleased that she was brought to tears.

"Oh, how wonderful," she said, beaming. "It's like I was saying to you after church this morning: God always provides."

Emily smiled as she looked up and caught Alec's eye. He'd been right to push her on this one, she could see that now.

"Well, we've intruded on your Sunday for long enough," Mrs. Tattlewell said, getting up from her seat. "I'll see you both in the morning."

"You could never be an intrusion," Alec said, smiling at her.

Mrs. Tattlewell reached up and patted Alec's cheek before she turned to Emily.

"You've done my niece and her family a great kindness," she said. "I won't forget it."

Emily smiled. "I am just relieved it's all worked out for the best," she said.

Mrs. Tattlewell nodded as she turned to Kara.

"Let's get going," she said. "Where are the children?"

"I'll go and round them up," Mark said, turning to Emily and Alec. "I don't know how to thank you for this opportunity. Words seem to fall short."

"You don't need to thank us," Emily said. "Just take care of the place."

"We will," Kara promised.

"We'll see you both in the morning?" Alec said. "We can get started on the house and get to work on turning you into a real cowboy."

Mark chuckled, and Kara smiled. Then, together with Mrs. Tattlewell, they set off across the porch and down the steps. Emily leaned on the railing, watching them go, calling for the children.

Emily sighed contently, feeling for the first time since getting to Forest Hill that she had actually done something right.

"You've given that family a second chance," Alec said, stepping up beside her.

"Well, it was your idea," Emily reminded him.

Alec smiled. 'Who thought we'd make a good team?" he said, poking her playfully in the ribs with his elbow.

Emily laughed, and as their eyes met, her stomach did a somersault, but then, Alec frowned.

"What is it?" Emily asked.

"I know one person who isn't going to be pleased about our newly acquired foreman," he said, grimacing.

Up until that moment, Emily had forgotten all about Mr. Caldwell.

"I'd better go and tell him," Emily said. "Before he goes to all the trouble of drawing up those papers."

"I'll go," Alec offered.

"I can do it," Emily said. "I am not afraid of him."

"It's better if I go," Alec insisted. "Can you just trust me on this, please?"

Emily said nothing for a moment and nodded.

Alec and Emily both turned to see Mrs. Tattlewell and the Jones family disappearing down the road. Thomas and Lily were there too, standing with their backs to the house as they waved their new friends goodbye. Emily glanced at Alec, feeling both relieved and grateful. She did not know precisely how Randall would react when he learned that she was not going to sell him the ranch, but he did not strike her as a man who handled disappointment gracefully.

Chapter Sixteen

"He ain't here," the young ranch hand said, lazily leaning on his pitchfork.

"Do you know where he is?" Alec asked. "When will he be back?"

The boy shrugged. "He went into Rosewood," He said. "Never said what time he'd be back."

Alec sighed. He'd left to speak with Randall right after he'd finished the morning chores, but he should have come earlier. He missed him, and by all accounts, he was on his way to see a lawyer in Rosewood about the transfer deeds.

"When he returns, will you give him a message for me?" Alec asked.

The young ranch hand spat out the tobacco he'd been chewing on, and brown spit ran down his chin as he nodded.

"Tell him that Miss McCoy has decided not to sell Riverbend after all," Alec said, speaking slowly.

The ranch hand nodded again, looking bored.

"You think you can remember all that?" Alec asked dryly.

"I ain't thick," he said.

"Just make sure Mr. Caldwell gets the message."

Without another word, Alec turned and headed back to his horse, pulling himself up into the saddle. He had not wanted Emily to be the one to tell Randall she wasn't going to sell because the man was going to explode when he learned the truth. This way, it worked out best for all of them.

Alec took a left onto the road, but instead of heading back to the ranch, Alec went on to Riverbend. As he approached the house, he found Mark and Kara were already there; they were drinking coffee with Emily in the kitchen. They had left the four children in the care of Mrs. Tattlewell, deciding they'd get more done without them under their feet all day.

"So?" she asked tentatively. "How did it go?"

"He wasn't there," Alec said. "But I left a message with one of his ranch hands."

Emily nodded, pursing her lips.

"Do you want some coffee?" she offered.

"Please," Alec said gratefully as he turned and sat down at the table with Mark and Kara.

"We hope there isn't any trouble?" Mark asked.

"Nothing that can't be sorted," Alec said. "If Mr. Caldwell is going to take the news as badly as I expect, then it's best coming from someone other than myself or Emily."

"But the poor ranch hand," Emily said, putting a cup on the table before Alec. "No man delights in being the bearer of bad news."

"Well, there is a good chance that he'll entirely forget to deliver the message," Alec said, sipping coffee.

Emily sat down, and after a few moments, Randall Caldwell was forgotten as they discussed how best to move forward with getting Riverbend back to its former glory.

"I think firstly we should go around and note any repairs needed to the buildings or fences," Alec said. "Once we know everything is secure and safe, we can bring the horses and cows back here from my place."

"Then Kara and I will handle the house," Emily suggested.

"Are you sure?" Alec asked. "It's quite a job."

"We can manage," Emily said.

Alec nodded. Though he had known Emily for only a short time, he had learned better not to argue with her about the smaller things.

"Alright," Alec said, slapping the table. "Then let's get to work."

Alec and Mark spent most of the morning walking around the ranch. They started in the barn, which needed some repairs done to the roof. They then went to the stables, which required a good mucking out but was otherwise fine. The door on the woodshed had lost its bottom hinge, and the water pump had rusted shut, but all of these could be fixed without much effort.

By the time they'd finished walking around the barn, stable and woodshed it was mid-morning and beads of perspiration were running down Alec's back.

"We should start checking the fences," Alec said. "I am thinking we started on the east boundary."

Mark nodded in agreement.

"I'll just go and let Emily know not to expect us for lunch," Alec said.

As Alec stepped into the kitchen, he found Kara wiping down the shelves in the pantry. He looked around expectantly.

"Emily's upstairs," Kara said, smiling.

"Thanks," Alec said.

He walked through the kitchen and then headed upstairs. He checked the children's bedroom first, but the room was empty. He then headed down the hallway to Marie and Bill's bedroom, where he found Emily sitting on the floor, her cream skirts fanned out around her. The wardrobe door was wide open.

"Emily?" Alec said, stepping into the room.

Emily turned to him, her face pale. On the floor in front of her was a small metal box, and she was holding a single piece of paper in her hand, which was trembling.

"What happened?" Alec asked, stepping into the room. "Are you alright?"

Emily shook her head as she turned back to the box. "They're letters," she said, her voice barely above a whisper.

Alec walked over to her and knelt down, frowning as he looked at the metal box stuffed full of unopened envelopes.

"They're letters," Emily repeated. "Marie wrote me letters nearly every month."

Alec reached over and picked up one of the envelopes, turning it over in his hands.

"But I don't understand," Emily said, looking up at him. "Why did she never send any of them?"

Alec said nothing for a moment, but he could guess why Marie hadn't sent them.

"I don't know," Alec said, putting the envelope back in the box.

Emily frowned. "Did you know about these?" she asked.

"No," Alec said. "Marie never told me she had written you letters."

Emily sighed. "It just doesn't make sense," she said, shaking her head. "Why would she write them and then hide them at the back of her wardrobe?"

"Maybe she found it cathartic?" Alec said. "Like writing in a journal."

"No," Emily said, shaking her head. "I know my sister, and she wrote these if she wanted them to be read. Here, listen to this—"

Emily picked up a letter off the floor and began to read.

The more time passes, the more I feel like I am living in the past, longing for it. For the girl I once was, for the happiness and hope I used to feel for the future. I don't feel like myself anymore; I don't know myself. I am living under a shadow that no amount of light can chase away. Long to speak with you again, sister, to hear your voice. I know in my heart that if you were here, I could step out into the sun again.

As Emily read, the knots in Alec's stomach tightened.

"What can she mean?" Emily asked. "What is the shadow she is referring to?"

Alec said nothing.

"Please, Alec," Emily begged. "You knew my sister; you two were friends. If you know what she is talking about here, please tell me."

Alec sighed as he walked across the room and sat down on the bottom of the bed. Emily got up, still carrying the letter, and sat down beside him.

"I knew about the shadow," Alec said, looking down at his hands.

Emily exhaled shakily. "It was Bill, wasn't it?"

Alec nodded; he could feel Emily's eyes on him.

"And you knew?" Emily asked, her eyes full of anger and disappointment. "You knew the whole time?"

"No," Alec said. "Not the whole time. Marie only told me when she learned she was pregnant with Lily, but she asked me not to say anything. She made me swear."

"And so you did nothing?" Emily asked, getting off the bed and turning to face him.

"She knew Bill would take the children," Alec said, looking up at her. "That he'd leave her with nothing."

"Did she tell anyone else?" Emily asked, her voice dropping.

"I don't know," Alec admitted. "But she was scared, Emily. She knew Bill could destroy her if he wanted to, and she would never let that happen. She could not risk losing Thomas or Lily."

"I can't believe this," Emily said, shaking her head.

"I know," Alec said. "And I'm sorry."

"Did he ever hurt the children?" Emily asked.

"He was hard on Thomas," Alec said. "But Marie shielded them both the best she could and I looked out for them as best I could. I tried to protect them, Emily."

Emily walked over and sat back down next to Alec. Her fingers brushed against his as she did, but he did not pull away.

"I wouldn't blame you for being disappointed in me," Alec said. "For not doing more for Marie and the children. I thought I was doing the right thing, keeping Marie's secret."

Emily sighed. "I don't blame you, Alec," she said. "It was an impossible situation and you did the best you could."

The room fell silent for a moment.

"I think you were right," Alec said.

"About what?" Emily said, turning to look at him.

"Marie wanted you to read those letters," Alec said. "That's why she kept them."

"But why didn't she send them?" Emily asked.

"Maybe she was afraid," Alec said. "Afraid that you'd come here to rescue her only to find out that she couldn't be rescued, at least not without losing the children."

"I'd have come," Emily said. "Even if my sister had only sent one letter, I'd have boarded the first train to Texas."

"And Marie knew that," Alec said. "That is why she never sent them, but that didn't mean she never thought of you."

The room fell silent for a few moments.

"I know you and Marie were friends," Emily said. "But I've never asked how you became friends?"

Alec smiled. "It's a good story," he said. "And I will tell you, but can it wait? Mark is waiting downstairs for me—"

"Of course," Emily said. "You should go."

Alec got up from the bed and walked over to the door.

"Alec?"

He turned around and looked at her.

"Thank you for telling me the truth," Emily said.

Alec nodded as he turned and left the room. When he reached the top of the stairs, he paused. For all these years, Alec had never spoken about Marie's secret and always regretted it.

He could not help but wish he had convinced her to stand up for herself and promised to stand by her side. If he had, then maybe she wouldn't have been with Bill on the road that day, and she'd be alive; the children would have their mother, Emily, her sister, and he'd still have his best friend.

The whinny of a horse drew Alec from his thoughts. He looked out the second-landing window to see Randall Caldwell coming to a blinding halt in front of the house and jumping from his horse. A moment later, Alec heard pounding at the front door, and Emily emerged from the bedroom.

"What is that?" she asked, frowning.

"I think Randall got the message," Alec said, grimacing.

The pounding grew louder as Alec sighed and descended the stairs. Emily hesitated a moment and then followed him downstairs. As they stepped onto the landing, Alec glanced down the hall to the kitchen where Mark and Kara were standing in the doorway.

"It's okay," Alec said, turning back to Emily. "I can talk to him."

Emily exhaled shakily. "We're a team, remember?" she said.

Despite the irate man banging on the other side of the door, Alec smiled.

"Right," he agreed, reaching for the doorknob as he pulled open the door.

Chapter Seventeen

Randall Caldwell stared at Emily for a long moment; his eyes were hard and cold.

"Mr. Caldwell—"

"I warned you, Kincaid," Randall said between gritted teeth. "I warned you that if you got in the way, there would be consequences."

"It's not Alec's fault," Emily said, stepping forward. "It was my decision to hire a foreman. I never wanted to sell Riverbend, but I didn't think I'd be able to find the right person in time—"

"We had a verbal contract," Randall spat, cutting her off. "And In Texas, that's as good as a written one."

"I am sorry, Mr. Caldwell," Emily apologized.

"Save your apologies," Randall said dismissively. "I will give you one chance to honor your agreement to sell Riverbend to me."

Emily sighed, shaking her head. "I am sorry, but the property is not for sale."

Randall Caldwell said nothing for a moment as he locked his jaw. Emily could sense Alec standing right behind her, and knowing he was there made her feel safer.

"Then you will be hearing from my lawyer," he said.

Without another word, Randall turned and marched away. Neither Emily nor Alec spoke until he had disappeared down the road. Then Emily turned and looked up at Alec.

"Is what he said true?" she asked. "About verbal contracts."

"I am not sure," Alec admitted. "Ranchers often make verbal agreements, but I am not familiar with all the law behind it."

Emily frowned, but Mark and Kara appeared in the kitchen doorway before she could ask any more questions.

"I assume that it was Mr. Caldwell?" Mark grimaced.

"Lovely chap, isn't he?" Alec said dryly.

"We hope you offering us this job isn't going to cause any trouble," Kara said, her eyes full of concern.

Emily glanced at Alec, who smiled reassuringly.

"It will all be fine," he said. "Shall we get back to work? The fences aren't going to repair themselves."

Alec walked down the hallway toward the kitchen and disappeared outside with Mark. Emily followed Kara into the kitchen.

"You look like you could use a cup of tea," she said.

"That would be appreciated," Emily said, sitting down at the table. "It's been an eventful morning."

While Kara made the tea, Emily thought about the letters in their tin box upstairs. She'd only read a few, but her heart ached knowing that Marie had been living with such a secret for all these years, protecting the monster that she married. Emily couldn't help but feel that she could have saved Marie from so much hurt and sorrow if she'd just swallowed her pride and come to visit. She could have snuck them all away in the night, and they could have run far, far away. It wouldn't have mattered where they would have been together.

"There we go," Kara said, placing the cup down.

"Thank you," Emily said, picking up the cup and cradling it in her hands.

Kara sat down opposite her, and Emily could tell she was still worried about the conversation they'd had with Mr. Caldwell.

"Do you think he really will get a lawyer involved?" Kara asked.

"I am afraid he will," Emily sighed.

"What will you do?" Kara asked.

"I don't know," Emily admitted. "But if there is one thing that I am certain of, it's that I will not sell the ranch."

Kara nodded as she sipped her tea, and the kitchen fell silent for a moment. Emily did not know Kara well, but she could see by the way she was twisting her fingers together that the scene she'd witnessed between them and Randall was weighing heavily on her mind.

"Are you alright, Kara?" Emily asked.

Kara said nothing for a moment and then exhaled shakily.

"Mark and I are just so grateful for this opportunity," Kara said.

Emily leaned forward and put her hand over Kara's. "It will all work out," she said. "I promise."

Kara smiled, and Emily sat back, hoping her words would stay true.

Just then, they heard voices, and Mrs. Tattlewell appeared in the doorway with the children.

"We brought lunch," she said, lifting the large wicker basket onto the table.

"How kind," Emily said, smiling.

"I thought you might be hungry," she said. "And the children were keen to come and see the place."

"Why don't you go and show Sarah and Ben upstairs?" Emily suggested.

The children left the kitchen and headed down the hallway, and Emily turned her attention back to the basket.

A short while later, Just as they were finished setting the table, they heard shouts from upstairs followed by a loud thud, and Emily, Kara, and Mrs. Tattlewell dropped what they were doing and hurried upstairs. When they got to the second floor, they found the children in Marie and Bill's bedroom. Ben was sitting on the floor, his cheeks pin and his eyes brimming with tears while Thomas stood over him, shaking in anger. Sarah and Lily were standing by the window, their eyes as big as saucers.

"What is the meaning of this?" Emily asked. "Thomas?

Thomas said nothing, his head bowed.

"Benjamin?" Kara prompted. "Do you want to tell us what happened?"

"I don't know," Ben shrugged, his bottom lip already swelling. "He just hit me."

"He called this his ma and pa's bedroom," Thomas said, blinking back tears. "But it's not. This is not their house; it's ours."

"Oh dear," Mrs. Tattlewell said. "Maybe bringing the children here wasn't such a good idea."

Emily sighed. "It's not your fault, Mrs. Tattlewell," she said. "If anything, it's mine."

Emily should have spoken to Thomas and Lily about their plans with the Joneses and explained that they were moving in to take care of the place until they were old enough to take it over. It was her mistake.

"Why don't we all go downstairs and get something to eat?" she suggested.

"I am not hungry," Thomas said, folding his arms across his chest.

"Why don't you all go back downstairs?" Emily suggested. "I'd like to speak with Thomas and Lily."

"Of course," Mrs. Tattlewell agreed. "Come along, dears."

Mrs. Tattlewell, Kara, Sarah, and Benjamin left the bedroom. Emily waited until their footsteps had faded away before she turned back to the children.

"Lily," she said. "Come here."

Lily walked across the bedroom and stood beside her brother, and Emily knelt in front of them.

"Children," Emily said. "I am sorry I didn't speak with you yet about the Joneses moving onto the ranch."

A tear rolled down Thomas's cheek and onto his shoe, and the corners of Lily's mouth were turned downwards.

"As you know, I don't have any children of my own," Emily continued. "So I am going to ask you both to try and be patient with me while I learn. Do you think you can do that?"

Lily nodded but Thomas kept his head bent.

SALLY M. ROSS

"Thomas?" Emily said, tilting her head.

"But this is our home," Thomas said, his voice breaking.

"And it will always be your home," Emily said. "The Joneses are just going to look after it for you, and then one day, when you are old enough, you can move back."

'But why do we have to leave?" Thomas asked.

Emily sighed. "Because I am a teacher," Emily said. "And I have a job in New York."

"Forest Hill needs a teacher," Thomas said. "So why can't we all just stay here?"

Emily reached over and wiped a tear from Thomas's cheek.

"I know it's going to be hard to leave Forest Hill," Emily said. "But how about I make you both a promise?"

"What?' Thomas asked.

"We will return to Forest Hill every summer," Emily said.

"You promise?" Thomas asked.

"Cross my heart," Emily said.

Thomas nodded, and Lily's expression brightened.

"Now, I think we should get down to the kitchen," Emily said. "And get something to eat."

Emily got up, and the children followed her out of the bedroom and down the stairs. As they entered the kitchen, Thomas walked over to Ben.

"I am sorry I hit you," Thomas apologized.

"That's okay," Ben said.

198

Emily caught Kara's eye, and she smiled. Then she took her seat at the table.

After lunch, Mrs. Tattlewell took the children home, and Kara and Emily returned to work. While Kara cleaned the kitchen, Emily continued upstairs. She packed all of her sister's dresses away in a large trunk she found in the basement. She was in a mind to burn Bill's things but thought it wasteful, so instead, she packed them with Marie's.

She would give them all to Jeremiah and his sister. In fact, she'd ask Alec to take the trunk that evening when they returned to the ranch. As Emily worked, she stopped now and then to read another of her sister's letters. Some were happier than others, more hopeful, and as hard as it was to read them, she felt as if each letter was a small piece of her sister.

"How is it going?" Alec asked.

Emily turned to find Alec standing in the doorway, leaning against the wooden frame. His hair was damp with perspiration, as was his shirt. He'd rolled the sleeves of his shirt up to reveal his tanned, muscular arms, and for a moment, Emily caught herself staring.

"You alright?" Alec asked, tilting his head.

"Hmm? No, I'm fine," Emily said, quickly turning away so he wouldn't see her blush. "Did you manage to start accessing the fences?"

"Yes," Alec said. "There is quite a lot of work to be done, but Mark seems capable and he's not afraid of hard work."

"Good," Emily said, getting up from the floor where she'd been kneeling. "I want to give these things to Jeremiah and his sister."

Alec nodded. "Are you ready to head back?" he asked.

Emily hesitated. "Actually, I was wondering if you'd take me to see the place where my sister is buried."

Alec nodded. "I was wondering when you'd ask," he said.

Emily said nothing for a moment. The truth was that she hadn't been sure she wanted to but finding the letters had made her feel closer to her sister again.

"It's a bit of a walk," Alec said. "About three miles from here as the crow flies."

"That's okay," Emily said.

Alec nodded, and Emily followed him out of the bedroom and downstairs. They left the house together and walked past the barn tables and the woodshed. The sun sank behind the trees, casting long shadows across the ground. For a while, Emily and Alec walked in silence.

"Thomas got into a fight today," Emily said.

"What?" Alec said, turning to her, frowning. "With who?"

"Ben," Emily said.

She explained what had happened between the two boys that afternoon while Alec listened.

"But I promised that we'd return to Forest Hill every summer," Emily said. "And I think that cheered them both up some."

"Did you mean it?" Alec asked, his green eyes suddenly full of hope.

"Of course I did," Emily said.

Alec smiled and it was a smile that reached his eyes and set Emily's heart racing.

"Why are you so surprised?" Emily asked.

"Because I thought you hated it here," Alec shrugged.

"I don't hate it here," Emily said.

"Besides the heat, the leeches and snakes and the things that go bump in the night," Alec teased.

"Yes, besides all those things," Emily agreed, smiling. "Did my sister love it here?"

"She did," Alec said. "She once told me that if she'd been born a man she would have been a cowboy and slept under the stars every night."

Alec glanced at Emily who was smiling.

"Marie always loved the stars, even as a girl," Emily said. "Some nights I used to wake up and find she'd climbed out of the window and onto the roof."

Email shook her head, smiling and Alec chuckled softly.

"Tell me more about, Marie," he asked. "When you were girls?"

"Well, I was only six when our mother died," Emily said. "Marie used to have these terrible nightmares, and the only way I could get her to sleep was by reading to her. Every Christmas, our father used what little money he had to buy us a book, and one year, he bought us *Little Women* by Louisa May Alcott."

Emily paused, still remembering how excited they were that morning.

"I read that book to Marie so often that she learned it off by heart," Emily said. "One day, I came into the bedroom and heard her reading. I couldn't believe it. A five-year-old reading a novel."

Emily smiled, shaking her head, and Alec mirrored her smile.

"Of course, I soon discovered that she was just pretending," Emily said. "But she loved that book, we both did, and I think that's what made her want to live out in the country. She wanted that humble, cozy life in the country, to fill a house with children and live a life wanting nothing more than the joy of each other's company."

Emily sighed sadly as she thought of what Marie's life had become.

"It wasn't all bad, you know," Alec said. "She was happy too."

"Really?" Emily asked, her voice hopeful.

"You asked me earlier to tell you how Marie and I became friends?" Alec said. "Well, Marie and Olivia, my wife, were always good friends, but I hardly knew Marie. I was always working. Then my wife died, and Marie came barging into my life."

Emily smiled at the smile in Alec's voice.

"At first, I resisted; I didn't want a friend; I didn't want to feel. All I wanted to do was give up," Alec said. "But Marie wouldn't let me. She once told me that Olivia came to her in a dream and asked her to keep an eye on me."

"Did you believe her?" Emily asked.

"I did, actually," Alec said. "So every day, come rain or shine, Marie would come to check on me, and soon we became friends. I didn't realize at the time how much I needed her; how much I needed an escape from my pain and grief. Only years later, when Marie told me the truth about Bill, I realized she needed me to. I was her escape from him."

"Did Bill ever find out you two were friends?" Emily asked.

"No," Alec said. "He would've stopped it if he'd ever found out."

"But how did you keep your friendship a secret?

"Bill liked to drink at lunch and then sleep it off in the afternoon," Alec explained. "Marie used to tell him she was taking the children on walks or to tea with Mrs. Tattlewell or the Minister's wife, and Bill didn't question it; he liked the house quiet."

Emily nodded. "I am glad she had you," she said.

Alec smiled sadly. "Despite everything she was going through at home, Marie was always so much stronger than I was," he said. "She laughed so easily and never lost her sense of wonder. Sometimes, I'd find myself watching her, especially with the children, and I'd think to myself, This girl is as pure as prairie sunlight."

"Did you love her?" Emily asked.

"Yes," Alec said without hesitating. "But I was never in love with her. Not because she wasn't loveable, but after Olive, well I didn't believe I would feel like that again.

They fell silent, and Emily could not help but envy Alec for knowing her sister the way he did. She'd lost so much of her over the years. Sometimes, when she thought of her sister, it felt like sand slipping through her fingers.

"Do you think you'll ever get married again?" Emily asked.

"I don't know," Alec admitted. "'After my wife died, I wanted to be alone, but after everything that's happened and having the children around…"

Alec's voice trailed off as Emily nodded.

"And what about you?" Alec asked. "Do you want to get married?"

"I am happy as I am," Emily smiled.

"So, no male suitors back home in New York?" Alec asked, his voice curious. "No beau's pining away, longing for your return?"

Emily shook her head and laughed. "Not unless you count Dickens, Hardy, and Stevenson."

"I find that hard to believe," Alec said.

"Fine," Emily sighed. "There is one, a fishmonger in fact, but he's much too young for me. Besides, I have no intention of getting married.

"Why not?" Alec asked.

"Because I like my work," Emily said. "And I've always worried that marriage would get in the way of that."

"So does this fish monger know you plan on breaking his heart?" Alec asked.

"I am, in fact, saving him," Emily said. "What man wants to take on a thirty-year-old woman with two children?"

"I wouldn't sell yourself so short," Alec said.

Emily caught Alec's eye then and felt her heart skip a beat. However, Alec looked away.

"The grave is just up head," Alec said.

Emily turned to see a black, wrought iron fence surrounding several gravestones. As they got closer, she saw that some were covered in moss and lichen, their engravings almost worn entirely away over years of sun, wind, rain, and snow. But two, on the end, were new, and as Emily approached them, her mouth silently traced the letters of her sister's name.

"I'll give you a moment," Alec said.

But as he turned to go, Emily caught his arm. "Stay," she said. "Please."

Alec nodded as Emily walked over to Marie's gravestone and knelt down. Under Marie's name was a scripture.

"He will wipe away every tear from their eyes, and death shall be no more, neither shall there be mourning, nor crying, nor pain anymore, for the former things have passed away." - *Revelation 21:4*

Emily read the words, her throat swelling with emotion as she blinked back tears. She was so full of regret and remorse that she thought it might tear her open. After all this time, this was their reunion.

Emily bent her head, a sob escaping from her chest as her shoulders began to shake. She wasn't aware of Alec until she was encased in his arms, her forehead pressed against his chest as she sobbed and sobbed. She wasn't sure how long she cried, but it felt as if she'd released an ocean, and her throat ached. Alec's shirt was stained with tears, and her eyes were red and swollen.

"I am sorry," Emily sniffed. "I've soaked your shirt."

"I have others," Alec said.

Emily wiped her cheek with the back of her hand, and Alec let her go, leaning back.

"We should probably get home," Emily said, clearing her throat. "The sun's already setting."

"We can stay a while longer if you want to," Alec said.

Emily nodded as she turned back to the gravestone. "It's okay," she said. "I can come back; I know where she is now."

Alec got up and then offered his hand to Emily. She took it, getting to her feet, and they turned around and headed back home.

"My ma used to say that crying was how your heart speaks," Alec said as they walked.

"Your mother sounds like a wise woman," Emily said.

"She was," Alec said, smiling. "You remind me of her a bit. She was also strong-willed and stubborn."

Emily smiled as she playfully swatted him with her hand, and they fell silent. She'd always known that going to see Marie's grave would break her heart, and it had. It was as if she'd been carrying around all that grief, it sloshing inside her with every step, but now she'd finally released it into the world, and she felt lighter.

Chapter Eighteen

"Thank you," Alec said to Oliver Blackwood's secretary as he stepped into the small, brightly lit office. The lawyer, who was seated behind his desk, a book open in front of him got up, closing the book as he did.

"Mr. Kincaid," Oliver Blackwood said. "I wasn't expecting you."

"Thanks for taking the time to see me," Alec said. "At such short notice."

Is Miss McCoy with you today?" Mr. Blackwood asked.

"No," Alec said, shaking his head.

He had not told Emily that he was coming to Rosewood to meet with the lawyer. With everything going on, first with the letters and then with Emily finding out about Bill, Alec did not want to give her anything else to worry about. He'd told her he was coming for farm supplies, which was not entirely a lie. He planned to stop at the farm store on his way back home.

"Please take a seat," Mr. Blackwood said as he sat down again.

"Thank you," Alec said, sitting down as he rested his hat in his lap.

"So what can I do for you, Mr. Kincaid?" Mr. Blackwood asked. "Is it related to your last visit?"

"To some degree," Alec said.

"Is it not better than Miss McCoy is with you then?" he asked.

Alec sighed, leaning forward in his chair. "To be frank with you, Mr. Blackwood, Miss McCoy doesn't know I am here. I wanted to get some legal advice, find out if there was anything worth worrying about."

"Alright," Mr. Blackwood said, frowning slightly. "For what matter do you need legal advice?"

"Miss McCoy planned to sell her late brother-in-law's ranch," Alec explained. "But then she changed her mind. Trouble is she spoke with a rancher and offered to sell him the place."

Mr. Blackwood nodded, sitting back in his chair.

"I assume this other rancher was unhappy to learn that Miss McCoy had changed her mind?"

"No," Alec said, grimacing slightly. "If it were another rancher, they'd have understood Miss McCoy's indecisiveness, but Randall Caldwell is not most gracious man."

"The rancher was Randall Caldwell?" Oliver asked, a crease between his brows.

"So you've heard of him then?" Alec said, not entirely surprised.

"I have," Mr. Blackwood said. "He's no stranger to the courthouse here in Rosewood."

"Well, he's threatened to take legal action against Miss McCoy," Alec explained. "And I just wanted to know if it's something we should be concerned about."

Mr. Blackwood leaned forward in his chair. "Well, as I am sure you are away, Mr. Kincaid, in the state of Texas, verbal contracts are generally considered legally binding provided that they meet certain criteria."

"What are the criteria?" Alec asked.

"Well, firstly, in order for there to be a valid contract, three essential elements have to be present. The first is offer and acceptance. Was any other party present when Miss McCoy made her offer to sell the ranch to Mr. Caldwell?"

"I was there," Alec said.

"And did you hear him accept the offer?" Mr. Blackwood asked.

"I did," Alec said.

"Right, well then, the first of the three elements is present. Now, the second essential element is what we refer to as the intention to create legal relations, which means that both parties, Miss McCoy, and Mr. Caldwell, must have intend for the agreement made to create legal obligations."

"Meaning?"

"Meaning that when Miss McCoy made the offer to sell she knew that she was making a legally binding agreement," Mr. Blackwood clarified.

"I do believe that Miss McCoy wanted to sell the ranch to Mr. Caldwell," Alec said. "But I do not believe she understood the seriousness of her offer or that a verbal agreement would mean she was now legally obligated to sell."

"Alright," Mr. Blackwood said, nodding. "And the third element is what we call consideration. This means that something of value, be it money, goods, or services, must be exchanged between the parties."

"Nothing was exchanged other than words," Alec said. "I am certain of that."

"Good," Mr. Blackwood said. "Well, should Mr. Caldwell take this matter before a judge, I don't think he would rule in his favor. Miss McCoy is not a native of Texas. As such, she cannot be expected to understand the seriousness of verbal contracts. What is more, consideration was not met between the two parties.

Alec nodded, feeling a wave of relief wash over him.

"That is my professional opinion," Mr. Blackwood said. "However, I would not underestimate Randall Caldwell."

"No," Alec agreed. "I do not plan to."

Mr. Blackwood sat back in his chair. "Good," he said. "Because even men who have sworn to uphold the law have their price."

Alec nodded. He's often wondered how many palms Randall Caldwell had greased over the years.

"Theoretically speaking, if Caldwell did win against Miss MCoy what outcome could follow?"

'Well, if Mr. Caldwell was to win there could be a number of outcomes. Miss Mc Coy might have to pay damages. This can include compensation for any financial losses suffered due to the breach of the verbal contract."

Mr. Blackwell paused for a moment.

"But it is also possible that the judge might order a specific performance," he said.

"What does that mean?" Alec asked.

"This means that the defendant, Miss McCoy, would be required to fulfill the terms of the verbal agreement as originally promised," Mr. Blackwood explained.

"So she would have to sell him the ranch?" Alec asked.

Mr. Blackwood nodded. "It's the outcome Mr. Caldwell would be fighting for," he said.

The two men fell silent for a moment.

"Well, thank you for your time, Mr. Blackwood," Alec said. "I appreciate it."

"Of course," Oliver said, smiling. "And you'll come and see me should Mr. Caldwell choose to take this matter further?"

"You'll be the first door we knock on," Alec said.

"I am sure Miss McCoy is grateful to have someone looking out for her," Oliver said.

Alec smiled as he got up, and Oliver stood up and walked over to the door to show him out.

"Thanks again," Alec said.

Alec arrived back on the ranch shortly after midday. On the ride home, he'd felt quite relieved knowing that Randall didn't have much of a legal case against Emily. Still, he would heed Mr. Blackwood's words and not underestimate him, which was good because just as he rode up the driveway, he spotted Sheriff Rourke leaning up against the barn.

Alec brought his horse to a stop and climbed down.

"Sheriff," he said, tipping his hat. "I wasn't expecting to see you."

"Mornin' Kincaid," Sheriff Rourke said.

"So, what brings you all the way out here?" Alec asked.

"I am looking for Miss McCoy," he said.

"Oh?" Alec said.

Sheriff Rourke sighed. "You know, Alec, I have better things to be doing than chasing after greenhorns who don't know the laws of the land."

Alec sighed. "She changed her mind, Sheriff, that's all."

"You know as well as I do that no one goes back on their word, especially when that word was given to Randall Caldwell."

"She wants to keep the ranch for the kids," Alec said.

"And that's good and well," Sheriff Wyatt agreed. "But the complaint has already been filed, and it's my duty to inform Miss McCoy."

Alec sighed. "There is nothing you can do?"

"I don't like Randall Caldwell any more than you do," Sheriff Wyatt sighed. "But this is the law, Alec."

Alec nodded. Wyatt Rourke was nothing if not a lawful man, a dutiful man. He may not agree with it, but he'd make sure the law was served without exception.

"She'll be at Riverbend," Alec said. "They are getting the place fixed up for the new foreman and his family."

Sheriff Rourke nodded.

"I'll walk you over," Alec said. "Just give me a moment to find young Jeremiah."

Alec turned and headed first to the stables, where Jeremiah was mucking out the stalls.

"Can you unpack the cart?" Alec asked. "I am going over to Riverbend with the Sheriff."

"Everything alright?" Jeremiah asked.

Alec grimaced but said nothing as he turned and returned to where the sheriff was waiting. Together, they walked the short distance to Riverbend. They found Emily out in the front garden, beating a carpet as plumes of dust rose into the air. Her cheeks were pink, and strands of long blonde hair had shaken loose and now hung over her back and shoulders.

She stopped beating the carpet when she spotted Alec and the Sheriff approaching.

"Emily," Alec said. "This is Sheriff Rourke."

"Miss McCoy," Sheriff Rourke said. "I wish we were meeting under better circumstances, but a petition of complaint has been filed against you by Mr. Randall Caldwell."

Emily said nothing as she looked at Alec.

"You have until the end of the week to travel to Rosewood and enter your plea at the court," Sheriff Rourke explained.

Emily opened her mouth and closed it again, lost for words.

"What will happen after she makes her plea?" Alec asked.

"Will I have to go to trial?" Emily asked.

"Not necessarily," Sheriff Rourke said. "The judge will look at the case and determine if the matter cannot be settled out of court."

Alec nodded and for a moment no one spoke.

"Well,, I'd better be getting back," Sheriff Rourke said, looking at Emily. "I am sorry for all your troubles, Miss McCoy, truly."

"Thank you," Emily said.

Sheriff Rourke tipped his hat and then turned to go.

"Alec," Emily said, her shoulders dropping. "What am I going to do?"

"It'll be fine," Alec said. "I spoke with Oliver Blackwood this morning."

"You did?" Emily said, frowning. "Why didn't you tell me?"

"I was going to," Alec said.

"So what did he say?" Emily asked, her voice urgent.

"Come inside," Alec said.

Emily followed Alec into the kitchen, and they sat at the table. He told her everything Mr. Blackwood had told him, and he could see the growing relief in Emily's eyes as he spoke.

"So he doesn't think that Mr. Caldwell can win?" Emily asked.

"He says it's very unlikely," Alec confirmed.

Without warning, Emily threw her arms around him and hugged him tightly. Alec hesitated a moment and then hugged her back, and as he did, he closed his eyes for a moment and breathed her in. She smelt sweet, like sweat, but also like dust and soap.

"Oh," a voice said.

Alec and Emily pulled away to see Kara standing in the doorway.

"Sorry," she apologized.

"It's fine," Alec said, getting up from his seat. "I'd better go and find Mark; make sure he's got his saddle on the right side of the horse."

Alec glanced at Emily before he headed out the backdoor.

Alec did not see Emily again until later that afternoon when he and Mark returned from fixing more boundary fences.

Emily was in the kitchen when Alec and Mark came in. She was sitting at the table, mending a curtain that hung off her knees and draped around her feet.

"Kara took the children home," Emily said. "Sarah wasn't feeling well."

Mark nodded. "I'd best be getting home then, too," he said. "I'll see you both tomorrow."

"See you," Alec said.

"Bye," Emily said, smiling.

Mark turned and exited the kitchen, leaving Alec and Emily alone. Alec walked over and sat down.

"You ready to head home?" Alec said.

"Almost," Emily said.

Alec watched her working for a moment, noticing the way she chewed the inside of her cheek when she was concentrating and the little crease that formed between her brows.

"You're staring," Emily said, smiling as she looked across at him.

"Sorry," Alec apologized, suddenly feeling embarrassed.

He got up and went to the sink, but as he did, he could feel Emily's eyes on him.

"You're staring," he said, turning to smile at her.

"Sorry," Emily apologized, looking down.

Alec smiled. He could not pinpoint the exact moment when things had started to change between him and Emily, when they went from being enemies to friends. The best thing he could compare it to was falling asleep, not at all, and then all at once. Perhaps it was Emily's decision not to sell the ranch that had brought them closer or that she'd promised to bring the children back to Forest Hills every summer.

When Emily arrived on the ranch just over two weeks ago her presence had been so threatening that Alec was always on the defensive, but it didn't feel that way anymore. Yes, Emily was still planning on moving the children to New York but she was trying hard to make everyone happy and Alec appreciated that, more than he could say.

"Okay," Emily said, putting down the curtain. "I am ready to go."

Alec and Emily left the house together and headed back to the ranch. Every now and again Alec glanced over at Emily who was quiet and thoughtful.

"I thought we could send Jeremiah into Rosewood tomorrow with a letter for Mr. Blackwood."

Emily nodded. "Alright," she agreed.

They fell silent again as the sun sank behind a distant hill.

"Did you ask Mr. Blackwood what would happen if the judge did rule in Randall's favor?" Emily asked.

"No," Alec lied. "We didn't discuss that."

He felt bad for lying but what good would it do to tell her the truth?

Emily nodded and they fell silent again. He knew she was worried; he was worried too. If Randall did somehow win this case, Emily would most probably have to sell the ranch and the Joneses would be out of a job. Not only that but the children would lose their inheritance and their home. He did not want to think about the possibility of that happening but he could not ignore the voice in the back of his mind reminding him that, in this world, money was king and if there was one person who had plenty of money, it was Randall Caldwell.

Chapter Nineteen

As he'd promised, Alec sent Jeremiah with a letter the next morning to Oliver Blackwood's office in Rosewood. He returned at midday with a reply from the lawyer who would be traveling through Forest Hill the next day and promised to stop in.

"You see?" Alec said brightly. "We've got luck on our side."

Emily smiled, wishing she felt the way that Alec did, but ever since the Sheriff's visit, her stomach had been in knots.

So, the next day, Mrs. Tattlewell had the tea all prepared when Oliver Blackwood's buggy came bumping up the road to the house.

"I hope you didn't have any trouble finding us," Alec said, walking up to greet him.

"I admit I did ask a man for directions," Oliver Blackwood said, climbing down from the buggy.

Emily held back; she'd been feeling so extraordinarily foolish for getting herself into this situation, and my Blackwood's arrival.

"Miss McCoy," Mr. Blackwood said, walking up to her. "It is good to see you again."

"And you, Mr. Blackwood," Emily said. "Thank you for taking the time to come here today."

"Of course," Mr. Blackwood said, smiling kindly. "And I don't want you to worry; we will get this messy business cleaned up."

Emily smiled gratefully. "Now, won't you come in for some tea or perhaps a glass of lemonade?"

"That would be most welcome," Oliver said. "I am quite parched from the journey."

They made their way inside, where Mrs. Tattlewell had laid everything out on the table and had taken the children into town to help out in the church gardens. According to Mrs. Tattlewell, all the late rain followed by the hot days had sent the weeds into a frenzy and now the church gardens had more weeds than the prairie had wildflowers. She was determined to get the gardens back in order before the service on Sunday.

"Please sit," Emily invited.

Oliver Blackwood sat down, and Emily poured him a glass of lemonade. She and Alec then sat down opposite him.

"I went to the court as soon as I received your letter yesterday," Oliver said. "And I entered your response. I was also able to talk with Judge Hiram Kane, who is the presiding judge in this area, and he's set a meeting for Monday."

"A meeting?" Emily asked.

"Yes," Mr. Blackwood confirmed. "It is an opportunity to discuss the case and potentially encourage settlement."

"I don't think Mr. Caldwell will settle," Emily said. "Not for anything but the ranch."

"Yes," Mr. Blackwood said. "I do believe that you are right."

"Not that we'd have anything else to offer him," Emily added, sighing.

"Do you know this Judge Kane well?" Alec asked.

"I don't," Mr. Blackwood admitted. "He's a local who grew up not far from here but has only just moved back west from Louisiana."

Emily nodded as she glanced at Alec and he smiled encouragingly.

"I assume Mr. Kincaid told you about our meeting?" Mr. Blackwood asked.

"I've told her some," Alec said. "But I thought I'd leave the details to you; you tell it so much better."

Mr. Blackwood chuckled. "Well, I've had some practice," he said.

As they drank their lemonade, Oliver Blackwood went over all of the things he'd told Alec including the necessary elements for a case based on a broken verbal agreement. He also explained what would happen if they did go to trial and Randall won.

"So I would have to sell him the ranch?" Emily confirmed.

"It is one of the potential outcomes, yes," Mr. Blackwood confirmed.

Emily nodded, the knots in her stomach tightening. She'd known this was possible; why else would Randall be dragging her to court? Yet hearing it out loud made it worse somehow.

"And what can I do to prepare?" she asked.

"There isn't anything you can do," Mr. Blackwood said. "I will be there for the legal parts, and all you need to do is turn up and be yourself."

"You think that will be enough?" Emily asked wryly.

"I do," Mr. Blackwood said confidently. "In a case such as this the judge will be closely considering the character of the defendant. I am of the mind that he will see you and see what I see."

"Which is?" Emily asked.

"A woman trying to do the best in an impossibly difficult situation," Mr. Blackwood said.

A lump rose in Emily's throat. "Thank you for saying that, Mr. Blackwood."

A little while later, Emily and Alec were standing beside the barn while Mr. Blackwood's buggy disappeared down the road. As it did Alec turned to her.

"How are you feeling?" Alec asked.

Emily sighed, turning to him. "Like I wish I had listened to you in the first place."

"Emily," Alec said. "Mr. Blackwood was right; you've only been trying your best—"

"Maybe," Emily said, blinking back tears. "But if the children lose the ranch, it will be my fault."

"They are not going to lose the ranch," Alec said firmly.

Emily said nothing. She'd always been so stubborn, a trait she'd inherited from her father, and so many times in her life, it had led her to moments like this, moments of regret. When she'd arrived in Texas, she was so set about doing things her way. She had refused to listen to Alec, and now they might lose the ranch. It had also been her stubbornness that had kept her from making things right with Marie.

"How about we do something?" Alec suggested. "Take your mind off of everything."

"What did you have in mind?" Emily asked.

Alec looked thoughtful for a moment. "Well, I do keep promising the children that I'll take them camping upstream, on the river."

Emily hesitated. She wasn't sure she was the camping type.

"Come on," Alec encouraged. "Cowboys have been sleeping under the stars for as long as they've hung in the sky. It'll do you good."

Emily smiled. "Alright," she agreed. "Let's go camping."

Together Emily and Alec set about getting together all the things they would need for their spontaneous camping trip, and by the time Mrs. Tattlewell arrived back with the children, they'd packed almost everything they needed including their bedrolls, food, a pot for boiling water, a pan from frying breakfast, Alec's rifle, and his fishing rod.

"We're going camping?" Thomas said, his eyes widening in excitement.

"I promised you that we'd go before the end of the summer, didn't I?" Alec said, reaching over and ruffling his hair. "Before you head to New York"

"Thomas," Emily said. "Take your sister upstairs and pack some clothes. I left your bedrolls upstairs for you."

Thomas grabbed Lily's hand, and they raced off upstairs.

"I'll just go and check again that we have everything we need," Alec said, turning to go.

"Camping?" Mrs. Tattlewell said, smiling at Emily, a twinkle in her eye.

"I know," Emily said. "But Alec is convinced it will take my mind off everything, and he promised the children and summer is almost over."

Mrs. Tattlewell nodded, still smiling.

"You know, Alec hasn't been camping upstream since before Olivia and the baby died," Mrs. Tattlewell said. "They used to go at the end of every summer."

"Oh?" Emily said.

Just then, she turned to see Alec. He was loading everything into the back of the cart, singing cheerfully to himself.

"It's nice to see him happy," Mrs. Tattlewell said. "It's been much too long since I've heard him sing."

Emily said nothing as she glanced at Alec again, and she couldn't help but wonder if this camping trip was a good idea. She and Alec were getting on so much better now, and it had happened so suddenly that she hadn't really stopped to consider what it might mean.

"Maybe I should stay behind," Emily said. "After all there is still so much packing to be done at the house."

"Nonsense," Mrs. Tattlewell said. "Kara and Mark can handle the packing."

Emily pursed her lips, but before she had a chance to come up with another excuse, Thomas and Lily came racing into the kitchen, their blanket rolls slung over their shoulders.

"Well, you'd better get going," Mrs. Tattlewell said.

Emily hesitated a moment.

"Emily," Mrs. Tattlewell said. "You said it yourself, the summer is nearly over, and in a couple of weeks you and the children will be gone."

Emily knew what Mrs. Tattlewell was trying to say. That come the end of August they would be on a train bound for New York, leaving Alec alone with nothing but his happy memories.

"We will be back on Sunday evening," Emily said.

"Have a nice time," Mrs. Tattlewell said.

Emily smiled as she turned and headed out of the back door. Alec, Thomas, and Lily were all already seated on the cart.

"Come on, slowpoke," Alec teased.

"I'm coming," Emily called.

As she walked over to the cart, Alec, Thomas, and Lily smiled down at her, and for a moment, it was as if she were looking up at some alternative reality, where this was her home and they were a family.

Chapter Twenty

It was late afternoon when they arrived at the camping site beside the river. Alec had been coming to this spot since he was a boy. It was a small, flat area nestled in the crook of a river bend. There were no trees save for a large weeping willow on the bank of the river. It was an old tree, sixty years or more, and its long branches arched elegantly downwards toward the water.

"The river is flowing heavily," Emily noted as they climbed down from the cart.

"It is," Alec agreed. "I don't think I've seen it this full before, but with all the rain this summer, it's no surprise."

Emily nodded as she glanced back at the children, and Alec knew what she was thinking.

"Thomas, Lily," he said firmly. "You two stay away from the water's edge, you hear?"

"But I thought you said we could swim?" Thomas pouted.

"There's a spot half a mile back where we can swim," Alec said.

Thomas nodded, looking satisfied.

"Come on," Alec said. 'Let's get the cart unpacked and set up camp."

Together, they unpacked the bedrolls and baskets of food.

"Where's the tent?" Emily asked, peering into the back of the cart.

"No tent," Alec said.

"So you literally meant we were sleeping under the stars?" Emily said, her eyes widening in disbelief. "What if it rains?"

"It won't rain," Alec said.

Emily raised her eyebrows but said nothing.

"Come on," Alec said. "I'll show you how to unroll your bed."

"I am sure I can manage."

"It's trickier than it looks," Alec remarked, poking her playfully in the ribs with his elbow. "Come on."

By the time they'd finished setting up, the sun was beginning to drop into the west. Despite the lateness of the afternoon, the cicadas were still buzzing noisily and Alec's neck and shirt were damp with perspiration.

"How about that swim?" Alec suggested.

"Yeah," Thomas said as Lily nodded enthusiastically.

"Emily?" Alec said.

"No, thanks," she replied, shaking her head. "If it's all the same, I think I'll stay here."

Alec chuckled. It was clear she had not forgotten about the leech incident.

"Alright," he said. "Suit yourself."

It was dusk by the time they got back to camp. Emily was crouched over a pile of sticks, attempting to start a fire as she grumbled under her breath.

"Need a hand?" Alec offered.

"You're back," Emily said, not hiding the relief in her voice. "How was the swim?"

"Leech free," Alec said, his lips twitching.

Emily threw him a withering look as he walked over to where she was standing. He knelt down and picked up one of the sticks.

"It's wet," he said. "All this wood is wet, where did you find it?"

Emily bit her bottom lip. "From over there, somewhere," she said, gesturing vaguely to a spot near the river.

"Thomas, Lily, go and find some dry wood and leaves please. We passed by that clump of birch trees not far from here."

The children turned and walked back towards them while Alec glanced down at the ground littered with matches.

"Are there any left?" he smiled.

"I told you I wouldn't be good at this stuff," Emily sighed.

"What would your students say if they saw you giving up so easily?" Alec asked. "Come here, I'll show you."

Emily walked over to him as he crouched down on his haunches. She crouched down next to him, and he was very aware of the warmth of her skin.

"Now, here's the secret," Alec said, digging a shallow pit with his hands in the soft river sand as he began to arrange some of the drier sticks in the shape of a teepee.

"You can't just dump a pile of sticks on top of one another," he continued. "You gotta let it breathe, like a newborn foal taking its first gulp of air."

Alec glanced at Emily.

"You try," he said, handing her a stick.

Emily took it from him, fumbling as she almost collapsed the structure. Alec reached over and took her hand, gently guiding it.

"There," he said. "You're a natural."

Emily turned to him, smiling, and she was so close that he could count each of her long, dark eyelashes and feel the warmth of her breath as his heart pounded in his chest. He leaned in, but as he did, Thomas dumped a pile of sticks and leaves beside them, and they both jumped.

"We're hungry," he said. "Is supper almost ready?"

"Not quite," Alec said, as he reached for them and tucked some under the teepee. Then he took a match out of the box and struck it, placing it on top of the leaves. As the flames grew they licked hungrily at the sticks.

"I packed some biscuits and jerky," Emily said as she got up.

Alec watched her go, feeling a mixture of regret and relief. At that moment, he'd wanted to kiss her; every nerve in his body was screaming at him to press his lips against hers, to taste her. But now that his brain was in charge again, Alec wondered if it wouldn't have been a very bad idea.

After all, she was leaving Texas in less than two weeks, and anyway, was he ready to move on? Was he passed grieving Olivia and the baby? But as he gazed across at Emily handing out biscuits and jerky to the children, he realized he already knew. But admitting that would mean the beginning of something that would soon be over.

Everyone gathered around the fire, as the stars began to twinkle in the sky above them. It was Thomas who spotted the first one, squeezing his eyes shut as he made a wish.

For dinner, Emily had packed beans and salted pork which Alec fried in the pan over the fire. There was also fresh cornbread and biscuits as well as homemade lemonade to wash it all down with.

"We can go fishing in the morning," Alec said. "Eat what we catch for lunch."

"And what if you don't catch anything?" Emily asked, smiling at him across the campfire.

Alec put his hand on his heart, wincing dramatically as the children giggled.

"You wound me," Alec said. "I've never once been fishing, not once, and not caught something."

"Well, I sincerely apologize for underestimating you then."

"Apology accepted," Alec said, his eyes twinkling.

Once they were finished eating, the children lay down on their bedrolls, and Alec removed the small harmonica from his back pocket.

"I didn't know you played."

"I haven't," Alec said. "Not for a long time, anyway."

Alec brought the warm metal to his lips and began to play, and although he hadn't in years, it felt effortless, as simple as breathing. As the notes lifted higher and higher into the air, they disappeared into the darkness.

After a few songs, Alec slipped the harmonica back into his pocket. Thomas and Lily were now asleep, the flames from the campfire still dancing across their soft faces. A full moon was rising behind the weeping willow tree, bathing it in silvery light like something out of a dream.

Alec got up from where he was sitting and fetched a flask from his saddlebag and sat down next to Emily.

"Nightcap?" he offered.

Emily hesitated a moment and took the flask from him, unscrewing the lid. She brought it to her lips and took a sip, wincing slightly as she did.

"When I was a boy, my grandfather told me a story about the weeping willow," Alec said as he took the flask from Emily.

"It was an old Native American legend," Alec continued. "According to it, the first weeping willow was formed when a beautiful woman sacrificed herself to save her people. As her soul left her body, it transformed into this tree, and her tears transformed into its branches, drooping down toward the earth."

"How beautiful," Emily said softly. "And sad."

"My grandpa also used to say that the weeping willow tree grew on the river bank so that her tears would fall into the water and become part of the flowing river, returning her to the earth from which she rose."

"It must have been wonderful," Emily said. "Coming here as a boy with your grandfather."

"It was," Alec agreed. "He could tell a good story."

"Growing up, I always wished Marie and I had grandparents to tell us stories," Emily confessed. "But our parents were both orphaned."

"Were you lonely growing up?" Alec asked.

"I had Marie," Emily said. "After our mother died, our father worked all the time. But it didn't matter because we had each other."

They fell silent for a while, listening to the crackle of the fire and the distant screech of an owl. As they sat, Alec glanced at Emily, and he thought to himself in that moment that she'd never looked prettier, bathed in fire and moon light.

"You wouldn't consider staying," Alec asked. "Would you?"

Emily turned to him in surprise and although he had not intended to say it, it was too late.

"Alec—"

"No, you're right," Alec said. "You have to get back."

Emily opened her mouth and then closed it again.

"We should probably get some sleep," he said.

Emily nodded as Alec got up and walked over to his bedroll. He lay down on the blanket and rolled over on his side, his back to the flames. After a while, he rolled onto his back, staring up at the stars, knowing what he would have wished for if he'd been lucky enough to see the first one.

***

Alec was awake first in the morning, getting up and walking down to the river. Before going to sleep the night before, he'd decided to forget the near-kiss and his question. He and Emily were finally in a good place, which was important for the children. He did not want things to be uncomfortable between them.

Alec sat on the river bank as the sun rose, just as he had done for so many summers growing up. He'd stopped coming here after Olivia and the baby died; he was afraid of the memories, but as the dawn sun warmed his face, he was glad he'd come back.

"Coffee?" Emily asked.

Alec turned to see her holding a tin cup out to him.

"You lit the fire?" Alec asked, raising his eyebrows.

"You don't have to sound so surprised," Emily smiled. "You're a good teacher."

"High praise coming from you," Alec said, as he took the cup. "Thanks."

Emily took a seat beside him. Her long, blonde hair was loose and hung down her back and over her shoulders. She wore a cream shawl.

"How did you sleep?" Alec asked, sipping the strong, bitter coffee.

"Surprisingly well," Emily replied.

Alec nodded, and they fell silent for a moment.

"Alec, about last night..."

"It's okay," Alec said, smiling at her. "I blame the moonlight and the nightcap."

Emily smiled softly at his attempt at humor.

"I am so glad we are friends," he said.

"So am I," Emily agreed.

Just then, they heard Thomas and Lily rifling through the food basket.

"Do you think they ever stop eating?" Emily asked.

"Only when they're asleep," Alec said, smiling.

Emily got up, and as she did, she put a hand on Alec's shoulder. "Do you want to show me how to cook eggs over a fire?" she asked.

"Ahh," Alec said, nodding sagely. "That skill takes years of practice."

"Good," Emily said. "So, you're making breakfast then?"

Alec laughed as Emily helped him up, and they walked back to the campsite.

After breakfast, they walked a couple of miles down the river to Alec's favorite fishing spot.

"So, are you ready to learn how to fish?" he asked.

Emily, who was already seated on the riverbank, shook her head. She'd brought a book with her, which was resting in her lap.

"I don't think I am going to be needing that particular skill when I return to New York," Emily said.

"It could come in handy if you marry a fishmonger," Alec teased.

"You're marrying a fishmonger, aunty Emily?" Thomas asked.

"Ignore Alec, Thomas," Emily said, her cheeks pink. "Now, why don't you show us all these impressive fishing techniques you've been bragging about?"

It was just shy of midday when Alex chucked his fishing rod onto the riverbank and sat down beside Emily. Thomas and Lily, who had long since given up on Alec actually catching anything, had walked down the river a bit to find interesting pebbles.

"I can't believe it," he said, shaking his head. "I've never been an unlucky fisherman, never."

"Don't be so hard on yourself," Emily said. "Maybe the fish have just gotten smarter while you've been gone."

"Ha-ha," Alec said dryly. "If you suddenly know so much about fish, why don't you give it a go?"

He picked up the rod and offered it to Emily, who, to his surprise, took it.

"What?" she said, getting up. "I can't in good conscience let you all starve."

Alec chuckled as he got up and followed Emily down to the water's edge.

"Okay," he said, standing behind her. "Put your one hand here."

Alec put his hand over Emily's, guiding her right hand up the handle. As he did, his heart skipped a beat. "Right there," he said. "Good, and your other hand goes here."

Alec then guided her left hand down a bit.

"Like that?" Emily asked.

"Good," Alec said.

Just then, a gentle breeze blew across the water, catching a few strands of Emily's hair, which brushed against Alec's cheek. Alec closed his eyes for the briefest moment; he'd forgotten how that felt. But, suddenly, Emily yelped, and Alec opened his eyes.

"I felt a tug," she said.

"That's impossible—"

But the words had barely left his mouth when there was another hard tug on the line, and Alec laughed.

"You've got one," he said. "Bring it in."

"How?" Emily asked.

Before Alec could explain, Lily suddenly appeared, her face as white as a sheet.

"Lily?" Emily said, dropping the rod. "What's the matter?"

"T-t-thomas," Lily stuttered.

It had been over two months since Alec had heard Lily's voice, and how often had he longed for this moment? But there was no relief, no joy, only fear.

"Show me," Alec said.

Lily turned and ran with Alec and Emily on her heels. As they got closer, Alec could hear Thomas screaming and looked across the river to see him clutching tightly to a fallen log wedged between two rocks. Before their eyes, the log began to loosen and wobble under the boy's weight.

"Thomas!" Emily cried.

Without hesitation, Alec rushed down the bank and plunged into the water, fighting against the current as he made his way across the river.

When he reached the opposite side of the bank, he raced towards the log, his chest burning and his breath ragged.

"Hold on, Thomas," Alec cried. "I'm coming."

Carefully, he stepped onto the log, which was full of rot. He put his arms out on either side to keep his balance and when he got close enough, he slowly crouched down onto his knees and stretched out his hand.

'Thomas," Alec called out over the rushing water. "Give me your hand."

But the little boy did not move, clutching tightly to the log.

"Thomas—"

There was a dull crack, hardly audible above the rush of the water, and the log that Thomas was grappling onto began breaking free from its anchoring.

"Thomas!" Alec yelled, leaning further forward. "Take my hand, now!"

Alec met Thomas's eyes, which were wild and fearful.

"It's okay, Thomas," Alec said. "I won't let you go."

Thomas let go of the branch with his right hand and reached for Alec, who grabbed him tightly around the forearm. Using all his strength, he pulled the little boy out of the water and into his arms.

Alec hugged Thomas tightly as he sobbed into Alec's sodden shirt. A moment later, the log broke free from its lodging and sailed down the river. Alec watched it go, shocked and relieved he'd managed to get Thomas out just in time.

"It's alright," Alec soothed. "I've got you. You're alright."

He picked up Thomas and carried him carefully onto the bank. He could see Emily and Lily watching from the other side, their faces alight with relief.

"He's okay," Alec called to them. "We'll walk upstream and cross where it's safer."

Alec walked upstream about half a mile before he found a section narrow enough to cross. As he did, Thomas clung tightly to him, as tight as a barnacle to the bottom of a boat. When they reached the other side, Alec put him down, and Emily rushed up to them, pulling the shawl off her shoulders and wrapping Thomas up tightly before hugging him. Lily was small enough to press herself in between them and held tightly onto her older brother's waist.

After a few moments, Emily let go of Thomas. Despite the heat of the day, the little boy was still shivering so hard his teeth were chattering.

"What did I say about going in the river?" Alec said, a flicker of anger in his voice. "If your sister hadn't come to find us, you could have drowned."

"I- I- I didn't mean to," Thomas stuttered. "I saw something in the water, and I wanted to get a closer look."

"What was it?" Emily asked. "That you saw?"

Thomas frowned. "It was silver," he said. "I thought it might be treasure."

Alec frowned. "It was probably just a fish, Thomas," he said.

Thomas said nothing, but Alec had a feeling he did not entirely agree.

"Let's get back to camp," Emily said, putting her hands on Thomas's shoulders. "Get you changed into some dry clothes."

They all walked back to the camp, and Alec and Thomas changed. Emily lit a fire to warm them and made sandwiches for lunch. They took a blanket down to the riverbank and sat underneath the shade of the weeping willow tree.

Lily had not said another word since that morning, but as Alec watched her eating her sandwich, he could sense that something had changed, that her silence was now broken.

"How are you feeling, Thomas?" Emily asked.

"Alright," Thomas said.

He had a few scrapes from the tree branch, but otherwise, he was fine.

"Lily?" Thomas said after finishing his sandwich. "Do you want to play with my rubber ball?"

Lily nodded as she got up and took Thomas's hand, leaving Alec and Emily alone again.

"I wonder what Thomas saw in the water," Emily said thoughtfully.

Alec shook his head. "I don't know," he admitted. "But nature has a way of inspiring a child's imagination, and Thomas has always had an adventurous spirit. It's not the first time it's landed him in trouble."

"Oh?" Emily asked.

Alec smiled, shaking his head. "Last year, we were going through a drought," Alec explained. "And when it finally broke, Thomas disappeared during the thunderstorm. Marie was sick with worry. I found him stuck at the very top of an oak tree with one of Mrs. Tattlewell's jam jars. Lightning was flashing in the sky, just above his head."

"What did you do?" Emily asked, her eyes widening.

"I climbed up and got him," Alec said. "And when I asked him what he'd been thinking, climbing a tree in a thunderstorm, you know what he told me?"

"What?" Emily asked.

"He was trying to bottle some of the rain clouds in case there was ever another drought."

Emily said nothing as Alec smiled, remembering Marie's reaction when he brought Thomas safely home and told her the story. She didn't know whether to send him to his room or to hug him.

"I don't suppose there will be much opportunity for adventures like that in New York," Emily said.

"Perhaps not," Alec agreed. "But there will always be the summer."

"There will always be the summer," Emily agreed.

They fell silent for a moment, and Alec glanced over his shoulder where Thomas and Lily were kicking the ball to one another.

"How about a game?" Alec asked. "Boys vs. girls?"

Emily hesitated a moment and nodded. "You're on," she said.

Alec got up and offered Emily his hand, and they walked over to the children together.

***

"You're back," Mrs. Tattlewell said, stepping through the kitchen doorway.

It was Sunday afternoon, and they'd just got back to the ranch.

"We didn't expect to find you here,' Alec said as he walked around the side of the cart.

"I thought you could all use a warm cooked meal," Mrs. Tattlewell explained.

"That's very thoughtful of you, Mrs. Tattlewell," Emily said. "Especially since all we've been living on is bread, biscuits, and jerky."

"No fish?" Mrs. Tattlewell asked in surprise.

Emily caught Alec's eye but said nothing.

"Children, why don't you take your things upstairs and then wash up for dinner?" Emily said, changing the subject.

"How have things been here?" Alec asked as he unloaded the empty food baskets.

"All fine," Mrs. Tattlewell said. "Kara and Mark have been working hard at the house and have made some good progress."

"I hope they haven't been working too hard," Emily said.

"Don't worry about them," Mrs. Tattlewell said. "They are just enjoying being out on the ranch."

"Will you stay for dinner?" Alec offered.

"Thank you, but no," Mrs. Tattlewell said. "Kara made dinner, and I am already late setting off."

"Well, we'll see you in the morning then," Alec said.

"Yes," Mrs. Tattlewell replied. "What time are you setting off for Rosewood?"

Alec caught Emily's eye, and her shoulders stiffened.

"Just after breakfast," Alec said.

"Well, I'll come early then," she said. "Make sure you don't go on the road without a proper breakfast."

"It's really not necessary, Mrs. Tattlewell," Emily said.

"I can't do much to help you, dear," she said. "But let me at least see that you are properly fed."

"Thank you, Mrs. Tattlewell," Alec said.

The older woman smiled at them as she turned and headed inside, emerging a few moments later with her bonnet.

"Goodnight, then," she said.

"Goodnight," Alec and Emily responded in union.

Mrs. Tattlewell set off down the road, and Alec and Emily watched her go.

"You okay?" he asked, turning to her.

Emily sighed. "I wish we could have stayed down by the river," she said. "It was so easy to forget the world existed there."

Alec smiled.

"We can go back?" he asked.

"Shall I go get the children?" Emily answered.

Alec chuckled, and for a long moment, neither of them spoke. Then Alec turned and smiled at her.

"You know, I reckon' if Marie could see you now, she would be pretty proud of you," he remarked.

Emily sighed softly as she leaned her head on Alec's arm, and he put a hand around her shoulder.

"It will all work out," he said. "You'll see."

Emily stood silent as they watched the sun setting behind the trees. Everything could be very different this time tomorrow.

Chapter Twenty-One

The next morning, Emily awoke to the sounds of pots and pans clattering in the kitchen. She lay in bed for a moment, wishing she could roll over and go back to sleep. However, as much as she wanted to bury her head under the pillow, it wouldn't make her problems disappear.

So, Emily swung her legs over the edge of the bed and got up. She dressed, choosing a long, midnight blue skirt and a white blouse. She also made careful efforts to make sure the bun at the back of her head was knotted just right and fastened the buttons at the cuffs of her white blouse securely.

Once dressed, she took her cream shawl from the back of the chair and her hat with the matching cream ribbon from the closet and left the bedroom.

As Emily stepped into the kitchen, she was greeted by the smell of bacon, eggs, beans, and biscuits. While she usually loved breakfast, Emily's stomach was tied up in knots, leaving her with no appetite at all.

"Good morning, Mrs. Tattlewell," Emily greeted, stepping into the kitchen.

The older woman turned to her, her cheeks pink from the heat of the stove. "Good morning, dear," she said brightly. "Don't you look nice today."

Emily smiled.

"Would you like some coffee?" Mrs. Tattlewell offered. "I've just made a fresh pot."

"Please," Emily said.

Mrs. Tattlewell poured a cup of coffee and handed it to Emily before she walked back over to the stove.

"Thank you," she said gratefully. "Is no one else up?"

"Alec is out doing the chores," Mrs. Tattlewell said. "But the children are still sleeping; I think the camping trip tired them out."

Emily smiled. "Did Alec tell you that Lily spoke?"

Mrs. Tattlewell was so surprised she almost dropped the frying pan she was holding.

"It was only one word," Emily said. "But it's something."

Emily went on to tell Mrs. Tattlewell the whole story of Thomas's fall into the river, Lily's coming to find them, and Alec's daring rescue.

"Well," Mrs. Tattlewell said, shaking her head. "You did have quite an adventure."

"Alec is so good with the children," Emily said, walking over to the table and sitting down.

"He is," Mrs. Tattlewell agreed. "And he was so looking forward to being a father before that whole awful business."

"Did he ever think of remarrying?" Emily asked.

"No," Mrs. Tattlewell said. "I don't think anyone believed he'd ever get over losing Olivia and the baby."

Emily nodded.

"But then Marie came along, and she gave Alec a chance to be a father to those children, at least in all the ways that really count."

"Mrs. Tattlewell," Emily said, lowering her voice. Did you know what was happening between Bill and my sister?"

Mrs. Tattlewell sighed, turning to her.

"No one really knew anything," she said. "But some of us suspected."

"I know I have no right to ask this," Emily said, "because I wasn't here either, but why didn't someone do something? Try to stop him, I mean?"

Mrs. Tattlewell sighed as she walked over to the table and sat down opposite her.

"Things are different here, Emily," Mrs. Tattlewell said. "Women do not have as many rights as in New York. In Forest Hill, women don't take to the streets and demand to be treated as equals. What goes on between a husband and his wife is a private matter."

"But how can it be private if everyone knows?" Emily argued.

"Emily," Mrs. Tattlewell said. "In a small community like this one, where everyone knows each other's business, there are consequences for speaking out, especially against a man like Bill Donnelly who was not only well-connected but who had a temper hotter than a branding iron. Who would you have asked to risk their families? Their livelihoods?"

Emily said nothing for a moment. As hard as it was to accept, things were different here; the south was conservative, and abuse laws were virtually non-existent. She could not blame anyone for not coming forward; it just wasn't how it was done here.

"You're right," Emily sighed. "I'm sorry. There is no one person to blame."

Mrs. Tattlewell leaned over and put her hand on Emily's. "Being a woman in this world is a hard card to be dealt," she said. "But we prayed for your Marie every Sunday in church."

Emily put her other hand over Mrs. Tattlewell's, and they sat together in silence for a moment.

"Goodness," Mrs. Tattlewell said suddenly. "The bacon is burning."

The older woman hopped up and rushed to the stove, pulling the pan off the heat. Just then, Alec came in through the back door. He was dressed in a green shirt and a pair of dark denim jeans. He's polished his brown boots which gleamed in the morning light.

"Mornin'," he said, smiling at Emily. "You look nice."

"Thank you," Emily said.

"Breakfast is ready if you two want to eat," Mrs. Tattlewell said. "I'll put the children's breakfast aside."

"Thanks, Mrs. Tattlewell," Alec said, walking over to the sink.

Alec washed up and then sat down next to Emily. Mrs. Tattlewell carried over the pan and began to serve rashers of bacon, eggs, beans, and biscuits.

Alec tucked into his food, but Emily ate very little, pushing her food around on the plate. When she looked up, she saw Mrs. Tattlewell watching her, and she smiled kindly at her.

"You two should be getting going," she said. "You don't want to be late."

"Thank you for the breakfast," Emily said.

She and Alec got up and headed towards the back door.

"We'll be waiting for you when you get home," Mrs. Tattlewell said.

Emily turned around and smiled at her before she followed Alec outside. He was heading to the barn.

"I'll bring the buggy around," Alec said.

Emily nodded as she stood and waited. Just then, Jeremiah came out of the stables, and as he approached Emily, he took off his cap.

"Good morning, Miss Emily," he said, his head bent as he wrung his cap in his hands.

Emily frowned, sensing there was something wrong.

"Good morning, Jeremiah," Emily said. "Is everything alright?"

Jeremiah reached into his pocket and pulled out an envelope, and Emily immediately recognized Marie's stationery.

"My sister found this in the pocket of one of the coats you gave us," Jeremiah said, handing Emily the letter.

Emily took it without a word and glanced down at the envelope, wondering if it was another letter from Marie.

"I hope I've not upset you," Jeremiah said. "Reminders of those who have passed, well, they can be painful.

"No, you haven't," Emily said, trying her best to smile. "Thank you, Jeremiah, and thank your sister for me."

Jeremiah nodded.

"Are you ready to go?" Alec called from the buggy.

Emily nodded as she slipped the envelope into her pocket.

They didn't talk much on the ride to Rosewood; Emily's thoughts were swirling. She did not want to sit in a room with Randall Caldwell all morning, but if they could resolve matters, then there wouldn't be a trial.

They arrived in Rosewood around midmorning. As they passed by the bakery, she thought about that first morning they'd come to town, how desperate she'd been to win over the children and now she was on trial for a crime she had not intended to commit.

"You okay?' Alec asked as he brought the buggy to a stop outside the courthouse.

Emily nodded, her mouth dry.

Alec climbed down and came around the front, offering Emily his hand. She took it, stepping down onto the street outside the courthouse.

"Shall we go inside?" Alec asked.

Emily nodded. Together, they walked up to the courthouse and through the open doors. The entrance hall was large with wooden flooring and a high ceiling. Bright morning light streamed in through the windows.

"Miss McCoy, Mr. Kincaid," Oliver Blackwood said, walking over to them.

He was dressed in a dark green suit, and his leather shoes squeaked against the polished wood as he walked.

"How was your trip?" he asked.

"Fine," Alec said. "Is Caldwell here yet?"

"Not yet," Oliver said.

Emily looked at Mr. Blackwood, but he would not meet her eye.

"What is it?" Emily asked.

Oliver sighed. "Mr. Caldwell and the judge have some connections," he said.

"What kind of connections?" Alec asked, frowning.

"I'm not exactly sure," he admitted. "As you know, Judge Kane used to live around here, and apparently, he and Caldwell's father had some interactions before he moved east."

"What kind?" Emily asked.

"I don't know," Oliver admitted. "And it may mean nothing."

"Or it might mean that Caldwell's father and the judge were old friends," Alec said.

"Let's try not to jump to conclusions," Oliver said. "It may be nothing."

Emily turned to the window, her heart in her stomach. If the judge was old friends with Mr. Caldwell's father, what chance did they have?

"Emily," Alec said, putting his hand on her arm.

But just as he did, Randall Caldwell stepped in through the doors and turned to look at them, his eye lingering on Alec's hand.

Alec dropped it as Randall approached.

Randall kept his eyes fixed on Emily, but he did not say a word as he walked past them and disappeared down the hallway.

"We should probably go," Oliver said. "We don't want to be late."

"I'll be right here," Alec said. "When you are done."

Emily nodded, wishing Alec could come with her but Mr. Blackwood had said that there were no spectators in these kinds of meetings.

"This way, Miss. McCoy," Oliver directed.

Emily glanced at Alec once last time before she turned and followed Mr. Blackwood down the same hallway that Mr. Caldwell had walked down only moments before. They got to a door on the end and Oliver knocked.

"Come in," a deep voice said.

Oliver turned the brass knob and pushed open the door. He stepped aside so that Emily could enter first. As she did, she removed her hat, holding it tightly between her hands.

The room was a modest size but well-lit. A large mahogany desk took up most of the space. Behind the desk sat a tall man with broad shoulders and graying hair. He had a large nose and a pair of coarse, wiry eyebrows dense with hairs that stuck out in different directions.

Oliver stepped in after Emily and closed the door behind them. Randall was standing by the window, his back turned. There was no one else in the room besides the two men. Where was Randall's lawyer?

"Miss McCoy," Judge Kane said. "Please take a seat."

Emily approached the two leather chairs in front of the judge's desk, sitting down while Oliver stayed standing on her right.

"Mr. Caldwell?" Judge Kane said.

Randall turned from the window and walked over to the second chair, sitting down without glancing at Emily.

"Right," Judge Kane said. "I've been able to review the case, and before I say anything, I wish to ask Miss McCoy a question."

Emily sat up a little straighter in her chair, her heart racing.

"When you offered to sell Riverbend Ranch to Mr. Caldwell, did you realize you were making a legally binding contract?"

"No," Emily said, honestly. "When Mr. Caldwell learned of my arrival in Forest Hill, he came to see me straight away and made it clear he was interested in buying the ranch. However, when I made the verbal offer, I was completely unaware it was equivalent to signing a contract."

"So, you had no intention of creating legal relations at that point?" Judge Kane queried.

"No," Emily said. "At the time, I did not understand the seriousness of my offer or what a verbal agreement would mean regarding my legal obligations."

"And no money, goods, or services were exchanged between the two of you?" Judge Kane continued.

"No," Emily said without hesitation.

"Mr. Caldwell?" Judge Kane prompted.

"No," Randall said, shaking his head.

The judge nodded, sitting back in his chair. "Well, based on the depositions that Mr. Blackwood has gathered, the lack of intention and consideration, and Miss McCoy's rather extenuating circumstances, I have decided to end this matter here."

"What?" Randall said, jumping from his chair in outrage.

Emily could hardly breathe; had she heard Judge Kane, right? Was he dropping the case? Emily looked up at Oliver, and he looked as stunned as she felt.

"You can't just drop the case—"

"Sit down, Mr. Caldwell," Judge Kane said.

Randall hesitated a moment and then did as he was told.

"This case has no standing," Judge Kane said. "You have not suffered any injuries or losses, Mr. Caldwell, and from the evidence submitted, not more than twenty-four hours passed between Miss McCoy making the offer and rescinding it."

"I traveled here to Rosewood to have my lawyer draw up the transfer deeds," Randall said. "Does that not count as a loss? A loss of my time and my money?"

"You are drawing at straws, Mr. Caldwell."

"Judge Kane," Randall said, trying to keep his voice level. "You are making a mistake—"

"And what gives you the authority to say that?" Judge Kane asked, his voice dangerously low. "I know your reputation, Mr. Caldwell. I know how many men you've brought into my courthouse and ruined all for your own ill-gotten gains. Did you think that coming here today without a lawyer was wise? Did you think you had some special advantage because I knew your father?"

Emily glanced over at Randall, whose neck and ears were puce.

"No, Mr. Caldwell," Judge Kane continued. "It is clear to me that you are nothing more than a bully. Who else would bring a case against a woman whose sister and brother-in-law were just recently murdered and who is now doing her best to save the ranch for her sister's children."

"It's just business," Randall argued.

Judge Kane shook his head. "It's astonishing to me how many men regard compassion as a weakness when it is, in fact, a person's greatest strength."

"Without a word, Randall got up from his chair. He turned to Emily, his eyes glimmering dangerously as he leaned towards her.

"This isn't over," he hissed.

Emily's heart was pounding as Randall stood over her. He threw a hard glance at Judge Kane before he turned and left the room, throwing the door open as he did.

"Well, he certainly knows how to make a dramatic exit," Judge Kane said dryly.

Emily turned to him. "Thank you, Judge Kane."

"Men like Mr. Caldwell are used to getting what they want," he said. "So, if I may offer you one piece of advice, it would be not to make any more deals with men like him."

"I certainly won't be," Emily agreed.

Judge Kane nodded. "Good," he said. "Now that is resolved, I am off home. My wife's making her famous southern fried chicken for lunch."

Oliver cleared his throat, and Emily stood up.

"Thank you again," Emily said.

Judge Kane nodded, and Emily and Oliver turned and left the judge's office. As they stepped out the hallway, Emily turned to Oliver, who shook his head in amazement.

Alec was pacing the floor when they arrived back in the entrance hall.

"What happened?" he asked. "Randall looked as mad as a snake."

"The judge threw out the case," Emily said, hardly believing the words coming out of her mouth.

"And he gave Mr. Caldwell a stern dressing down," Oliver added.

"I wish I'd been a fly on the wall," Alec said.

Emily looked up at him, relief washing over her, and without thinking, she threw her arms around him and hugged him tight.

"It's over," she said.

"It's over," Alec echoed.

A short while later, after having thanked Oliver Blackwood profusely, they set off back home to Forest Hill.

"Tell me everything," Alec said, as he held the buggy reins. "And don't leave out any of the details."

Emily told Alec every single word that had been said in Judge Kane's office and when she finished, Alec was grinning ear to ear.

"I've always wanted to see Randall Caldwell taken down a peg or two," Alec remarked.

Emily smiled. She had decided not to tell Alec what Randall had whispered to her before he left. It seemed a pity to destroy this moment and in truth, what could he do to her now?

Chapter Twenty-Two

"I think we should throw a party," Mrs. Tattlewell said. "To celebrate."

They were all standing in the ranch house kitchen, having just given Mrs. Tattlewell a full breakdown of what happened at the courthouse.

"Something small," Mrs. Tattlewell said thoughtfully to herself more than anyone else. "Just us, Kara, Mark, and the children."

Alec glanced at Emily, a twinkle in his eye. When Mrs. Tattlewell got it in her mind to do something, there was no stopping her.

"And maybe Jeremiah and his sister?" Emily suggested.

"Yes," Mrs. Tattlewell agreed. "Alec, you'll invite him?"

Alec nodded. "I will leave you ladies to figure out the details," he said.

Without another word, Alec turned and headed to the barn to find Jeremiah, who was checking on the calves. Thomas and Lily were with him, sitting on the wooden post and rail fencing that enclosed the east pasture.

"How they lookin'?" Alec asked.

Jeremiah sighed. "Grounds too wet here," he observed. "And the rains last night didn't help none."

Alec sucked his teeth as he looked around. It had rained all night, and even now, he could see the patches of sunken ground still filled with water.

"Alright," Alec said. "Let's move them before it damages their hooves."

Jeremiah nodded as Thomas turned to Alec. "Can we help?" he asked.

"I'd like nothing more than two new ranch hands," Alec said. "But neither of you can ride a horse."

"Then teach us," Thomas said.

Alec said nothing for a moment. He wanted to teach them, but first, he'd have to get them a starter horse with a good and gentle nature.

"There isn't a suitable horse for you to learn on yet," Alec said.

Thomas pouted.

"How about this? Next summer, when you and your sister come to visit, I'll teach you to ride on a smaller one."

"But that's forever away," Thomas complained.

"It may feel like that now—"

"I wish we weren't going to New York," Thomas complained. "I wish we could just stay here with you."

Lily nodded, folding her arms across her chest.

Alec sighed. He didn't want them to go either, but it was no use saying so out loud.

"Things will be different there," he said. "But you'll get to go to school and make new friends; I bet your aunty will even take you to the Statue of Liberty."

"Really?" Thomas asked.

Alec nodded. "And when you are in New York, you can ride a carriage all the way across the Brooklyn Bridge and take a boat ride in Central Park. There is even a place called Longacre Square, which is full of theaters and restaurants."

"Will you come and visit us too?" Thomas asked.

Alec hesitated a moment and then nodded. "Sure," he said. "And we can go to Coney Island and ride the rollercoasters there until we're just about ready to throw up," he laughed.

Thomas and Lily nodded enthusiastically, and Alec smiled.

"Come on," he said. "Let's get you back up to the house for lunch."

Alec turned to go but then remembered the party and turned back to where Jeremiah was herding the calves.

"Jeremiah?" he called.

The young man stopped, looking across at Alec.

"Mrs. Tattlewell is having a dinner party this evening," he said. "Would you and your sister like to come?"

"We'd be honored," Jeremiah smiled.

"Good," Alec said. "Take the buggy later to fetch your sister."

Alec turned, and together, he and the children walked back up to the house. As they did, Thomas asked him more questions about New York, but in truth, Alec only knew what Marie had told him, which wasn't all that much.

"You should ask your aunty," Alec said as they stepped into the kitchen.

"Ask me what?" Emily said, suddenly appearing out of the pantry.

"Alec said you will take us to see a play in Longacre Square," Thomas said excitedly.

"And ride a boat," Lily chipped in softly.

"And when Alec comes to visit us, he is going to take us to Coney Island to ride rollercoasters."

"Is he now?' Emily said, raising her eyebrows.

Alec grinned sheepishly.

"Lunch is almost ready,' Emily announced. "So why don't you two go and wash up."

Thomas took Lily's hand and led her out of the kitchen, talking excitedly about roller coasters and popcorn.

"I had no idea you were such an expert on New York," Emily said.

Alec shrugged. "I only know what Marie told me," he said. "She used to talk about taking the kids there for a visit when they were older."

"She did?" Emily said, her expression softening.

Alec nodded. "She didn't talk about New York often," Alec said. "It used to bring her down, but I think part of her heart was always there with you."

Emily smiled sadly. "I appreciate you saying all that to the children," she said. "For the first time, they seemed excited about moving to New York."

"If you told them that Death Valley had a carousel and popcorn, they'd already have their bags packed."

Emily chuckled.

"Where's Mrs. Tattlewell?" Alec asked, suddenly noticing her absence.

"She went over to Riverbend to invite Kara and Mark to the dinner party this evening," Emily explained.

Alec nodded as he met Emily's eye.

"Did I hear correctly just then?" she asked. "Did Thomas say you were coming to New York to visit?"

Alec shrugged. "I thought I might," he said. "If it's okay with you?"

"Of course," Emily agreed. "Perhaps you could come around Christmas? I'll have a few days off from school to show you and the children around the city."

Alec had never wanted to visit New York City, not even a little, and yet the possibility of spending Christmas there with Emily and the children was exciting.

Just then, the children returned with clean hands and faces and sat down at the table.

They all ate lunch together, and as they did, they talked more about New York and all the things they could do when Alec visited over Christmas. As they did, Alec caught Emily's eye, and she smiled at him, and it was the kind of smile that set his heart skipping.

The aroma from the kitchen was drifting upstairs as Alec changed his clothes that evening. He could hardly keep his mouth from watering as he buttoned up his sage-green cotton shirt. Just as Alec fastened the last button, there was a crunch of stone beneath buggy wheels, and Alec looked out the bedroom window to see Jeremiah returning with his sister. He brought the buggy to a stop outside the barn and then hopped down. Alec watched as he walked around the front of the vehicle and removed his sister's wheelchair before he lifted her down into it.

Alec turned away from the window and walked over to the dresser. He picked up his comb and pulled it through his dark curls. On the floor at his feet lay bits of scraggly hair that had fallen when he trimmed his beard.

Alec had not cared much for his appearance these past few years, not since Oliva had passed; what was the point? But that evening, he'd wanted to make more of an effort, telling himself it was because they were having guests, but deep down, there was only one person he really cared about impressing.

"Alec?" Mrs. Tattlewell called from downstairs. "The guests are arriving."

Alec put down the comb and turned. He left his bedroom and headed downstairs, and as he reached the landing, he almost bumped right into Emily as she came out of her bedroom into the hall.

"Sorry..."

Alec's voice trailed off as he stared at Emily. She wore an emerald green bodice and matching skirt, the color setting off the blue of her eyes. Her shiny blonde hair was pulled into an elegant updo, held in place by a velvet ribbon hairpin.

"Are you alright?" Emily asked, a crease appearing between her brows.

"Fine," Alec said, clearing his throat. "Shall we go into the dining room?"

Emily nodded as she turned and headed in with Alec. As they stepped into the room, their eyes met the dark oak table set for seven, and in the middle were long candles, their pretty light reflecting in the shining silverware. Alec could not remember the last time he'd eaten in this room. Mrs. Tattlewell and Emily have spent the better part of the afternoon getting it dust-free, and even now, the large windows were wide open, letting in the cool summer evening breeze.

"Are the children not joining us?" Alec asked.

"No," Emily said. "Mrs. Tattlewell is feeding them in the kitchen now and has given them strict instructions to stay upstairs in their room after."

Just then, Jeremiah came in pushing his sister in her wheelchair. She was pretty as a picture with reddish-brown hair and a heart-shaped face.

"Mr. Kincaid, Miss Emily, this is my lovely sister, Martha," Jeremiah introduced.

"It's a pleasure to meet you both," Martha said. "I knew your sister, Miss Emily, and she was the kindest woman I've ever met."

"It's wonderful to make your acquaintance," Emily said. "Please come and sit."

Alec walked over to the table and pulled out a chair and Jeremiah carefully lifted his sister down onto it. Just as he did, Kara and Mark appeared in the doorway.

"Sorry we are late," Mark apologized.

"You're not," Alec said, "Welcome."

A short while later, they were all seated around the dining room table, holding hands with their heads bent down as Alec said grace.

"Amen."

"Amen," everyone echoed.

Everyone looked around the table, which was laden with platters of food.

"You've outdone yourself, Mrs. Tattlewell," Emily remarked.

Mrs. Tattlewell had made roast beef as well as chicken fried steak. There was a large bowl of potato salad with sliced hard-boiled eggs, mayonnaise, and mustard. The braised collard greens were seasoned with bacon and black pepper. There were also two loaves of freshly baked cornbread and a basket of soft, flaky biscuits served with butter.

"Well, dig in," Mrs. Tattlewell said. "Before it gets cold."

Alec and Mark reached for dishes, passing them around the table, and soon, everyone's plates were piled high.

They all ate and talked, and Emily was asked to recount the meeting with Judge Kane that morning. Every now and then, Alec caught Emily's eye, and she smiled back at him. Alec had been so sure for the longest time that he would never feel like his old self again, that he'd forever be altered by his grief, and perhaps part of him would be, but at that moment, he felt more like himself than he had in years.

"I hope you've all saved some room for dessert," Mrs. Tattlewell announced.

Alec sat back in his chair, unsure he could manage another mouthful, but just then came in the peach cobbler, the treacle tart, and a large jug of sweet tea.

"I am not sure the last time I ate so well," Mark said, placing his dessert fork down on his empty plate. "Or if I've ever eaten so much."

"No," Kara agreed. "But it's a good thing we are moving out to Riverbend Ranch because I fear if we stayed with my aunt much longer, we'd find ourselves unable to fit through the front door."

"Nonsense," Mrs. Tattlewell said, chuckling.

"It's true," Mark said. "I can't fit into any of the pants I brought from Chicago."

There were giggles of laughter around the table as Alec caught Emily's eye.

"Well, I think a toast is in order," he said, raising his glass.

Everyone reached for theirs and raised them in unison.

"To Mrs. Tattlewell for this extraordinary meal," Alec said. "And to the future of Riverbend Ranch."

"To Mrs. Tattlewell and the future of Riverbend Ranch," everyone echoed.

It was late by the time the party ended, and all the children were fast asleep upstairs.

"Leave them," Alec said. "They can stay the night, and we will bring them over to Riverbend in the morning."

"Are you sure?" Kara asked. "We don't want to impose."

"It's no imposition," Alec assured them.

Kara smiled gratefully as Mark draped her shawl across her shoulders. That evening, they'd agreed that the Jones's would move into the house at Riverbend the following day. There was still a lot of work to be done, but the place was livable, and it made sense to stay rather than travel from town any longer.

"Goodnight, Emily," Kara said.

"Good night," Emily smiled.

"I'll walk you out," Alec volunteered.

Alec walked with Mark and Kara to their buggy which was parked a short distance from the house. Mrs. Tattlewell was already seated beside Martha. The Jones's had kindly offered to give Jeremiah and his sister a lift back into town.

"Thank you for dinner, Mr. Kincaid," Jeremiah said.

He was standing beside the vehicle, his hands folded behind his back.

"We are glad you could make it," Alec said, clapping him on the shoulder.

Jeremiah hesitated, and Alec frowned.

"What is it?" he asked.

"I just hope Miss. Emily wasn't too upset about the envelope," he said. 'I know when our folks passed, it was hard to be reminded of them."

"Envelope?' Alec asked.

Jeremiah nodded. "Martha found it in one of Marie's coats," he explained. "I gave it to Miss Emily this morning before you left for Rosewood."

Alec had not heard about the envelope; Emily had not mentioned it to him.

"I wouldn't worry about it," Alec said.

Jeremiah nodded, looking relieved. "Good night, sir," he said.

"Good night," Alec replied.

He waited while Jeremiah climbed up into the buggy and sat down beside his sister. Mark and Kara were sitting up front.

"It was a wonderful evening, Mrs. Tattlewell," Alec said. "Thank you."

Mrs. Tattlewell smiled at him as Mark clicked his tongue, and the buggy set off down the road, disappearing into the night.

Alec turned and walked back to the house; Emily was standing on the porch, a thin shawl wrapped around her shoulders. Alec climbed the porch steps and walked over to where she was leaning on the wooden railing.

"You okay?' he asked.

Emily turned her head and nodded. "Did everyone get off alright?" she asked.

"Fine," Alec said. "How are the children?"

'Sound asleep."

Alec nodded. "Jeremiah said he was worried he'd upset you, something about an envelope?"

"Oh," Emily breathed. "I'd forgotten about that. He gave it to me this morning, and my mind was so preoccupied with everything else going on. Let me fetch it."

Emily turned and headed into the house, remerging moments later with it in her hands.

Emily carefully broke the seal using her pinky finger and pulled out the single sheet of white paper. She unfolded it and frowned, looking up at Alec.

"What is it?" Alec asked.

"It's addressed to you," Emily said, handing him the page.

Alec took it, suspiciously, but Emily was right. There was his name, as plain as day.

"Dear Alec," the letter began.

I had a terrible nightmare last night, and when I woke up, a feeling of dread crept into my bones. I can't quite explain it, and I know that you would laugh at me and call me superstitious, but I have the strongest sensation that something terrible is going to happen. This is why I am writing you this letter and intend to deliver it to you tomorrow afternoon.

Alec, If something should happen to me or Bill, soon or one day in the near future, I want you to take care of Thomas and Lily for me, to be their guardian. I came to Texas because I wanted a different life for my children than the one I had growing up, and I want them to grow up in Forest Hill so that they can ride bareback across the prairie at sunset and fall asleep on hot summer evenings to the sound of the crickets chirping in the long grass. I want them to grow up with neighbors who are like family to them and to know how to sow seeds and harvest crops so they never need to wonder where their next meal is coming from.

I love my sister, but she has another life in New York. I could never ask her to give that up to raise my children here, not after all she gave up for me.

I hope I will always be around, but in case I am not, please care for them, Alec, and raise them as your own.

I am putting this all in writing so that, should anyone ever contest your claim for guardianship, you can show them this letter and they will stand as my will.

Your dearest friend,

Marie.

Alec looked up from the letter.

"What does it say?" she asked.

He opened his mouth but no words came out. What was he going to do?

Chapter Twenty-Three

"Alec?" Emily repeated. 'What does the letter say?"

Alec stared at her for a long moment and then looked back down at the page.

"Here," he said.

Emily took it from him and read, her mouth moving wordlessly over each sentence. As she did, her heart sank further and further, and by the time she'd finished, it was at her feet.

"She chose you," Emily said, her voice wavering.

"Emily—"

"You were right," Emily said, looking down at the words again. "All this time, you were right. Marie did not want me to take the children back to New York. She wanted them raised here, with you."

"Emily."

"Here," Emily said, her hand trembling as she handed him back the letter. "It's yours. I don't even know what I am doing here."

"You came for Thomas and Lily," Alec reminded her.

"But they don't need me," Emily said. "They have you."

"That's not true," Alec argued. "You are there aunt."

"So?" Emily said, her voice rising. "What does that matter?"

At that moment, everything that Emily had done since arriving in Forest Hill felt pointless.

"I should never have come," she said.

"No," Alec argued. "How can you say that?"

Emily sighed, shaking her head.

"Emily," Alec said, taking a step forward and reaching for her hand. "Don't go back to New York. Stay here in Forest Hill."

Emily frowned. "I know I said it was the moonlight and the nightcap," Alec continued. "But I wasn't being truthful with you, Emily. I want you to stay."

"I can't stay, Alec," Emily said.

"You can," Alec insisted.

"No," Emily said firmly. "I can't."

Alec dropped her hand and took a step backward. "So, all this time you've spent in Forest Hill, has it meant nothing to you?"

"Of course it has," Emily said. "But I came here to get to know the children, to take them back home with me. I don't belong here; you know that as well as I do. My home is in New York, so is the job that I love."

"Marie wasn't from here either," Alec said. "But she made it her home."

"Because she wanted this life," Emily said.

"And you don't?" Alec challenged.

Emily hesitated and then sighed. "It's more complicated than that, Alec," she said. "You know how important my job is to me, how many years I've wanted to work at Briarwood where I can make a difference—"

"You can make a difference here, too," Alec insisted. "Forest Hill needs a teacher."

"No, Alec," Emily said, shaking her head.

"Why?" Alec insisted. "Is one teaching position better than another? Or is Forest Hill just not good enough for a fancy teacher from New York?"

Emily winced. "That's not fair, Alec," she said.

"Maybe not," Alec agreed. "But you talk a lot about how much you love being a teacher, and here you have a community of children who are desperate for one."

Emily said nothing. What could she say? Alec was right. The Forest Hill children needed a teacher, but that person wasn't her. She didn't belong in a place like this; her home and her job were in New York. She loved the city life. She couldn't just give it all up.

"It's been a long day, Alec—"

"Why can't you admit to yourself that you could be happy here?" Alec asked. "That you've been happy here."

"I have been happy," Emily agreed.

"So?" Alec said, stepping forward again. "Stay."

"With you?" Emily asked.

"With us," Alec said.

Emily said nothing for a moment. These past few days, she and Alec had grown closer; there was no denying that. She found herself drawn to him, and it terrified her because if she admitted the truth to herself, she wouldn't know what to do about it.

For all these years, Emily had dedicated her life to her career. She'd given up her relationship with her only sister, she'd given up on the possibility of love, of marriage, all so she could be the best teacher she could be. So, if she chose to stay, and give up her position at Briarwood, wouldn't everything she'd sacrificed all been for nothing?

"I can't, Alec," Emily said. "I'm sorry."

Alec's green eyes were full of disappointment as he stared at her, but before either of them had a chance to say anything else, Emily spotted Thomas and Lily standing in the doorway.

"What are you two doing up?" Emily asked.

"We're thirsty," Thomas said.

"I'll fetch you some water," Alec said, turning and disappearing inside the house.

"Come on," Emily said. "Let's get you back to bed."

Emily took each of their hands and led them back upstairs. Sarah and Benjamin were asleep in Lily's bed, so she guided them to Thomas's and tucked them in side by side. Alec arrived a few moments later with two glasses of water.

"There you go," he whispered.

Thomas and Lily took the glasses from him and drank thirstily. When they were done, Emily put them down on the bedside table.

"All right," she said. "Snuggle down now and close your eyes."

Thomas and Lily did as she asked, and Emily sat with them until they'd fallen back asleep. Then she left the bedroom, pulling the door shut behind her. As she did, Emily glanced down the hallway to see Alec's bedroom door was already shut.

***

Emily sat with the children at the breakfast table as Mrs. Tattlewell made a pot of tea. She had not seen Alec that morning, in fact, she'd not seen him at breakfast since Monday, the day they went to Rosewood. Ever since the discovery of Marie's letter and their argument, a rift had formed between them that was only growing wider with each passing day. But maybe it was for the best; after all, Emily was going Back to New York the following week.

"Mrs. Tattlewell," Emily said. "May I ask you to watch the children this morning?"

"Of course," Mrs. Tattlewell agreed.

"Where are you going aunty Emily?" Thomas asked, looking up from his bowl of oats.

"To town," Emily said. "I want to see if there is any word from the seamstress, Miss Taylor."

'Do we still need the clothes?" Thomas asked, "If we're not going to New York anymore?"

Emily had told the children about their mother's letter and her wish for them to stay in Forest Hill with Alec. They'd taken the news rather well once Emily had promised they could still come and visit at Christmas, with or without their guardian.

"You are still coming to visit at Christmas," Emily reminded him.

Thomas nodded.

"Well, I think I'll get going," Emily said, getting up from the table.

"If you don't mind picking up a few things for the house, I have a list," Mrs. Tattlewell said.

"Of course," Emily agreed.

The older woman, who was wearing a light pink dress and a crisp white apron, fetched the list and handed it to Emily who glanced down at it before folding it in half and slipping it into the pocket of her blouse.

Emily fetched her hat and basket and set off towards the gate. As she did, she could sense someone watching her, but when she turned around there was no one there.

Emily was hot and sticky by the time she arrived in town. She'd gone early hoping to avoid the heat of the day but with no such luck.

She made her way down the one road towards the general store. Emily had not been in town much since coming to Forest Hill but she knew the post office was at the back.

Emily entered the store; and as she did, the little bell above the door tinkled, alerting everyone inside to her arrival.

Emily looked around, aware that people were staring at her. She bent her head and made a beeline for the little alcove in the back.

Behind a broad wooden counter sat a girl, about fifteen or sixteen years old. She had a large stack of letters in front of her, which she was sorting into smaller piles. To her left sat a heavy scale used for weighing parcels, and a collection of stamps, while on the wall behind the girl, were a collection of wooden pigeon holes. On either side of them were posters displaying the various postal rates. There were also some advertisements and several announcements from the U.S. Postal Service.

"Good morning," the girl said politely, getting up from the small wooden stool.

"Good morning," Emily replied, smiling.

As the girl looked up at Emily, her brown eyes suddenly widened.

"I was wondering if any letters had come for me?" Emily asked. "I am staying—"

"At the Kincaid property," she said, nodding while the corner of her lips turned up.

"Yes," Emily said, frowning slightly. "That's right."

"Let me check," the girl said.

She turned away for a moment, and Emily watched as she reached up and removed a single envelope from one of the pigeonholes.

"Here we are," she said. "It arrived from New York just this morning."

"New York?" Emily said, frowning.

She took the envelope from the girl and stared down at it. The girl was right; it was from New York, from the Headmistress of Briarwood, to be exact.

"Thank you," Emily said, turning away.

She walked back across the shop, hardly noticing the stares or the whispers, as she pulled open the door and stepped outside. She walked across the road to a small park and sat down on a bench under a tree. She slid a finger under the lip of the envelope and carefully tore open the flap. Then she removed the single sheet of paper and unfolded it. As she silently read the letter, knots formed in her stomach and by the time she was finished, she could scarcely breathe.

"Emily?"

She turned to see Kara standing a few feet away, but her throat was swollen, and she couldn't speak.

"Are you alright?" Kara asked, walking over, and sitting down beside her. "You're as white as a sheet."

Emily opened her mouth and closed it again, still unable to reply. Her hands were trembling.

"Tell me?" Kara insisted. "What is wrong?"

Emily passed Kara the piece of paper, and she took it and began to read.

"But this is a terrible lie!" Kara exclaimed, frowning in outrage.

"I know," Emily whispered.

"Was it Mr. Caldwell?" Kara asked, looking down at the letter again.

Emily nodded. It made perfect sense. He was the only person who would be motivated enough to do something like this.

"Come on," Kara said, getting up. "Let's get you home."

Emily let Kara help her up from the bench. As they walked back up to the ranch, Emily thought only of the letter and of the disappointment in Headmistress Lockhart's words.

"What's happened?" Mrs. Tattlewell said, turning from the stove.

Kara guided Emily through the back door.

"She's had a shock," Kara explained, helping Emily into a seat.

"I'll make some tea," Mrs. Tattlewell said, hurrying to fill the kettle.

Just then, Alec came into the kitchen and he looked at Emily and frowned. Cobalt, who was at his side, ran over to her and licked her hand, whining softly.

"What's happened?" Alec asked in concern as he crossed the kitchen and knelt down beside her. "Are you alright? Are you hurt?"

Emily looked down at him and shook her head.

"No, I'm not hurt," she replied.

"Then what is it?" Alec insisted. "Tell me."

Emily exhaled shakily, a lump still in her throat.

"I went to the post office to see if there was a letter from the seamstress," Emily explained. "But instead, there was one from the Headmistress at Briarwood."

"The school where you teach in New York?" Alec confirmed.

Emily nodded. "She wrote to say that she had received a letter from a concerned citizen in Forest Hill," Emily explained. "In the letter, they questioned the appropriateness of my situation here, living with a widowed gentleman, and worried that a teacher, such as myself, in a position of influence, should find herself in such an unconventional situation."

Emily paused, shaking her head in disbelief.

"I can't believe it," Alec replied, shaking his head. "That snake."

Emily bit her bottom lip trying not to cry.

"What else did she say?" Alec prompted.

"That they claimed to have witnessed inappropriate behavior between us, in public," Emily continued. 'And as the headmistress of an institution such as Briarwood, Mrs. Lockhart should be aware of how all of this could be perceived by the school's parents, fellow teachers, and the broader community, should they hear of this."

"So, what does that mean?" Alec asked.

Emily exhaled shakily, her eyes brimming with tears.

"She's considering whether or not I should return to the school in the fall," Emily said.

Alec shook his head. "No," he said. "That can't be right. You've told me about her; she doesn't sound like someone who would believe idle gossip."

"She built Briarwood from nothing," Emily said, her voice raw. "And even now, she still struggles against the frameworks of society. She can't risk tarnishing the school's reputation, and I would never ask her to do that."

Alec stood up, running a hand through his dark hair.

"But it's not right," he insisted. "We haven't done anything wrong."

Emily said nothing. What was there to say? After everything, she might lose her job at Briarwood.

"What's Randall Caldwell playing at," Alec said, his voice hard. "I am in a mind to go over there right now—"

"No," Emily said, shaking her head. "It's what he wants. To know that he's shaken us."

Alec looked at her, frowning.

"Emily's right," Mrs. Tattlewell said. "And everyone in town is already talking about the two of you."

"What?" Alec said. "Why didn't you tell us?"

"I didn't want to burden you any further," Mrs. Tattlewell said. "We know that none of it is true."

Alec exhaled deeply. "So what are we supposed to do?"

"I've been telling everyone who will listen that it's all nonsense," Mrs. Tattlewell said. "And I am sure it will blow over soon. After all, the prairie's plenty big enough for rumors to get lost in."

Emily suddenly got up from the table and walked across the kitchen.

"Emily?" Alec asked. "Where are you going?"

Emily paused in the doorway and turned her head, meeting Alec's eye.

"To pack," she said. "It's time I went home."

Chapter Twenty-Four

Alec stood in the doorway as Emily crouched down and pulled her suitcase out from under the bed.

"Emily."

"Mm?" Emily said, not turning to look at him as she opened the case up.

"You can't just go," Alec insisted.

"Why not?" Emily asked as she walked across the dresser and pulled open the top drawers.

"Because there is still a whole week of summer left," Alec reasoned, clutching at straws. "And Mrs. Tattlewell wants to plan a birthday party for Lily."

"I need to get back," Emily insisted. "I need to talk with Headmistress Lockhart."

"Will a week really make any difference?" Alec asked.

Emily said nothing as she carried an armful of clothes and placed them in the suitcase. Alec took a step into the bedroom, wishing he knew the right thing to say, the thing that would get her to stay. He knew why she felt she had to go, that she had to address the issue as soon as possible, but he didn't want her to leave.

"Emily," Alec sighed. "I know you are upset—"

Emily stopped packing and looked up at him, her eyes cold. "Of course I'm upset, Alec," she said. "This is my job."

"I know," Alec agreed. "And I am sorry."

"Why did you touch my arm?" Emily asked suddenly.

"What?" Alec said, frowning.

"That day we went to Rosewood to meet with Judge Kane. You touched my arm, and Randall saw it."

Alec was speechless for a moment. "Are you truly blaming me for this?" he asked in disbelief.

"You shouldn't have touched my arm," Emily said.

Alec shook his head. "It's not like I planned to," he insisted.

Emily said nothing as she walked over to the wardrobe and began to remove the dresses from their hangers.

"So that's it then?" Alec asked. "You're just leaving?"

"The children are still welcome to come for Christmas," Emily said.

Alec stared at Emily, hoping that she'd say something else, but after a few moments, it became obvious that she had nothing else she wanted to say.

"Well, if you've made up your mind, then that's that, I guess," Alec said.

"That's that," Emily agreed, not looking back at him.

Alec hesitated a moment longer and turned and left the room. What had he expected? Now that she might have lost her job, she'd have no reason to return to New York and she'd stay with them in Texas? That they'd start to build a life together?

Instead of turning to the kitchen, Alec left via the front door. He walked until he found himself at the edge of the property at the family graveyard, in front of Olivia's tombstone and he crouched down on his haunches.

"Hey, Liv," he said softly, reaching over and brushing her name in the stone with the tips of his fingers.

The morning he'd married Olivia had been the best day of his life, and the afternoon she'd died the worst. From their relationship, he'd known great joy but an even greater sorrow, a sorrow so great that he'd been almost crushed under its weight. Even now, after having swallowed so much of that pain and heartache, grief still had an aftertaste; it lingered on the underside of his tongue. He did not know if it would ever go away entirely, and over the years, he'd learned to live with it, to understand it as a part of him.

"I miss you," Alec said. 'I miss you both so much."

A light breeze blew across from the east, and Alec closed his eyes for a moment as the leaves, like tiny dancers, swayed above him, tethered to the world by nothing but a narrow stem.

Alec opened his eyes again and sighed. Sometimes, he thought himself a better man from the pain he'd suffered, a more compassionate man, and others, he thought his grief had hardened him, turning his heart to stone to protect itself.

On the afternoon that Olivia had their baby, Alec was with her in the bedroom holding her hand. He'd seen the look on the doctor's face as he pulled their daughter into the world, still and silent. At the time, he did not think he'd ever know gratitude again, but days later, when it was all over, he was grateful that Olivia was not awake to see the baby born, glad she'd never had to know. Olivia knew she was going to die; she'd said it to Alec, pushing the words out in her agony. She'd made him promise to love their baby enough for them both, and she had made him promise that he would not do it alone.

"Mourn me," she whispered, "but when the time comes, move on and be happy again."

Alec had refused to listen, refused to accept what she was saying, and the next day when he buried Olivia and the baby, he'd vowed never to love like that again. Choosing to forsake Olivia's dying words, Alec stuck by his word until the day Emily McCoy walked into his life and turned everything upside down.

"Of course, you got what you wanted, Liv" Alec whispered, shaking his head as he smiled. "You always did."

Without meaning to, Alec had lowered his guard, and somehow, love had crept back into his heart. Yet Emily was leaving, and he hadn't stopped her, and he couldn't decide if he'd made the biggest mistake of his life or if it was better that he'd let her go, after all, she did not seem to want to stay.

Alec did not return to the house, instead walking the boundary of the ranch trying to clear his mind. It was late afternoon by the time he returned home and found the children outside with sticks, drawing pictures in the sand. Cobalt was lying lazily in the shade, his one eye opening as Alec approached.

"Aunt Emily's gone," Thomas said, the corners of his mouth turned down.

Alec nodded as he reached over and put a hand on his shoulder. "You alright?" he asked gently.

Thomas shrugged. "She said we can come and visit at Christmas," Thomas replied.

Alec nodded as he looked over at Lily. "You alright, Lil?" he asked.

Lily nodded.

"Have you both had dinner?" he asked.

The children nodded. "Mrs. Tattlewell left your supper on the table," Thomas said.

Alec smiled at the children before he turned and headed inside. The kitchen was empty and he walked over to the table to sit down. He removed the fly cloth from his plate and reached for a pickle, but as he did, he realized he had no appetite.

"Oh," Mrs. Tattlewell said, stepping into the kitchen from the hallway. "We were wondering where you'd gotten to."

"Sorry I missed supper," Alec apologized. "I was checking the fences and lost track of time."

Mrs. Tattlewell nodded as she bustled over to the sink, which was full of dirty dishes.

"Thomas said Emily's gone?" Alec asked.

"That's right," Mrs. Tattlewell said, nodding. "Leonard came by about an hour ago to fetch her. She is taking the last train to the city this evening."

Alec nodded, looking down at his plate of food.

"You know," Mrs. Tattlewell said, turning to face him. "I've known you for a long time, Alec Kincaid, and I would have taken you for a lot of things, but never a fool."

Alec's mouth popped open in surprise.

Mrs. Tattlewell stood with her hands on her hips. "You heard me right. You are a damn fool to let that woman leave."

"I didn't let her leave," Alec argued. "She chose to go."

284

Mrs. Tattlewell sighed, dropping her arms as she walked across the room and sat opposite him at the table.

"You know as well as I do that if you let Emily McCoy leave, you'll regret it for the rest of your life," she said.

Alec sighed, sitting back in his chair.

"I don't know what to say to her to make her stay," Alec said, shaking his head. "How to make her want to stay."

"Have you really tried?" Mrs. Tattlewell asked.

"I don't know how I can make her feel like she belongs here?" Alec asked. "She's convinced herself she'll never fit in in Forest Hill."

Mrs. Tattlewell leaned forward in her chair. "Just tell her how you feel," she said. "And the rest will work itself out."

Alec said nothing. Only minutes before, he'd been ready to let her go, but was he being foolish? He was in love with her; he was certain of that, but was love enough? Was he enough? He really wasn't sure.

"Thank you for the supper," Alec said, getting up from the table.

Mrs. Tattlewell pursed her lips and nodded as Alec turned and left the kitchen, pausing at the back door. All of a sudden he knew what he had to do.

"Mrs. Tattlewell?" he said, turning around.

She looked across at him expectantly.

"Can you stay a bit longer and watch the children?"

Mrs. Tattlewell smiled. "You'd better hurry," she said. "The train will be leaving soon."

Alec nodded as he raced to the stables to saddle his horse and a short while later he was riding out of the gate.

He rode the five miles like lightning but as he jumped down from his horse, he heard the train's whistle as white-gray smoke billowed into the sky above the station.

"No," Alec said to himself as he raced towards it.

Just as he reached the entrance, he saw the train pulling away. He ran towards it but a porter blocked his path.

"Get out of my way," Alec insisted.

"The train has left the station," the porter announced. "You'll have to get the next one."

Alec stared at the train as the last carriage disappeared down the tracks and his heart sank to his stomach. He'd waited and now it was too late, Emily was gone.

Chapter Twenty-Five

Emily sat across from the headmistress, her stomach in knots as the older woman peered at her over the top of her spectacles.

"I appreciate you coming here today, Emily," she said.

"I needed you to know the truth," Emily replied. "So that you know I did nothing untoward or unbefitting of my position. Yes, I did stay with Mr. Kincaid, but it was only to be close to the children, and we thought it safer than me staying at Riverbend alone."

Mrs. Lockhart nodded. "And I believe you, Emily," she said.

Emily exhaled shakily. "I am so glad to hear that, Mrs. Lockhart," she said. "I was devastated when I thought that I'd disappointed you."

"I will admit, the letter did come as quite a shock," Headmistress Lockhart confessed. "Briarwood's reputation is of the utmost importance, and any kind of scandal could set us back."

"I understand," Emily said, nodding solemnly. "And I would never ask you to risk the reputation of the school."

Headmistress Lockhart nodded as she leaned forward. "That being said, I have made inquiries about this concerned citizen, and it appears his reach does not extend as far as he thinks."

The knots in Emily's stomach loosened a little.

"So, I have decided to put the matter to rest," she continued. "And to tell you that you still have a place here at Briarwood if you would like to return to teach in the fall."

Emily's heart caught in her throat. "Truly?" she asked.

The headmistress nodded with a smile, and it took every ounce of self-control for Emily not to throw herself over the desk and embrace her.

"Thank you, Headmistress," Emily said.

"We will see you next week then," she said, still smiling.

"Thank you again," Emily said, getting up from her seat.

Emily left Briarwood feeling lighter for the first time in days. As she made her way back home, she thought how strange it was that she'd walked this same path twice every day for months, and yet something about it felt unfamiliar. She knew she was going the right way, so why was her gut telling her otherwise?

"Emily!"

Emily was pulled from her thoughts by the young, tall, and very handsome man who was now running up to her.

"You're back!" Matteo said, grinning.

"I only got back yesterday," Emily said.

"And how was it?" Matteo asked. "Did you get to wrangle a longhorn?"

"Something like that," Emily said. "How are you?"

"Well," Matteo said. "Better for seeing you."

Emily smiled, shaking her head. He hadn't changed one bit.

"Where are the children?" Matteo asked.

Emily sighed. "They are staying in Texas," she said. "But they will be coming to visit at Christmas."

Matteo nodded and for a moment neither of them spoke.

"What are you doing now?" Matteo asked. "Please tell me you can come for dinner? It's my little sorella's birthday and my mama is making all her favorites."

Despite her reservations, Emily found herself agreeing to go.

"Alright. Why not?"

Matteo grinned. "Come on," he said. As they made their way through the neighborhood to Matteo's home, he peppered her with questions about her time in Texas, and as Emily spoke, she felt a strange pang of longing in her stomach.

"In almost every direction, the prairie stretches as far as the eye can see," she explained. "And in the late afternoon, when the sun is just right and the breeze is blowing, the grass ripples out like a brilliant golden tide."

"It sounds beautiful," Matteo said.

"It is," Emily agreed. "And after the sun sets, the stars begin to appear, slowly at first and then all at once, and when you look again, the prairie is covered in a sparkling blanket."

Emily glanced at Matteo; he was smiling.

"Sorry," she said. "I am talking too much."

"No," Matteo said. "I am glad you enjoyed your visit."

"I am glad to be home, though," Emily said hastily. "There's no place like New York."

As the words left her mouth, she wondered who she was trying to convince, Matteo or herself?

"So, you said the children were staying in Texas?" Matteo asked.

"Mm hmm," Emily said, nodding. "My sister wanted them to stay in Forest Hill with Alec."

"Alec?"

"Alec Kincaid," Emily explained. "The children's guardian."

Matteo nodded, and then, just in front of them, Emily spotted a tall man wearing a beige-colored Stetson, and her heart skipped a beat.

"Alec?" she said frowning,

Without thinking, she hurried over to him and put a hand on his shoulder. "What are you—"

But as the man turned around, Emily's heart sank.

"Sorry," she apologized. "I thought you were someone else."

The man tipped his hat and turned back around.

"Are you alright?" Matteo asked, stepping up beside her.

"I'm fine," Emily lied.

Perhaps it was because she'd just been talking about him or maybe it was because ever since arriving back in New York, part of her had hoped Alec would appear.

"Here we are," Matteo announced, gesturing to a modest wooden house on their right. "Home sweet home."

It was dark when Emily stepped back out of the Greco house and onto the street. She pulled her shawl around her shoulders against the chill in the air as Matteo stepped out after her.

"Well," he said, smiling. "I can confidently say that my whole family loves you."

Emily smiled. "You have a lovely family, Matteo," she said. "And I can't remember the last time I ate so well. I think I must have tried every dish."

"I think that's part of the reason Mamma was so impressed," Matteo chuckled.

Emily smiled. It had been a nice evening, but she'd struggled to fully enjoy it. Being around the table with Matteo's family had just reminded her of the dinners around the table in Alec's house with Mrs. Tattlewell, the Joneses, and all the children.

Matteo walked Emily back home, and they talked about the weather and the fishing. As they got to the front of Mrs. Bird's boarding house, they stopped.

"Well, goodnight," Emily said.

Matteo reached for her hand and held it in his. His skin was warm and rough. "Will you come again for dinner?" he asked.

Emily looked down at their hands for a long moment and sighed. His was not the hand she wanted to hold.

"I am sorry, Matteo," she said, gently pulling her hand from his. "But I can't."

"So you did go and fall in love with a cowboy?" Matteo said, smiling sadly.

"Something like that," Emily agreed.

Matteo took a step back, unable to mask the disappointment on his face, and Emily felt racked with guilt.

"I should never have agreed to come to dinner tonight."

"But I'm glad you did," Matteo said.

"You are?" Emily asked in surprise.

Matteo nodded. "We can still be friends, can't we?"

Emily felt awash with relief. "I'd like that very much," she said.

Matteo nodded. "Good," he said. "I'll be seeing you then."

"Goodnight," Emily said.

Matteo tipped his cap to her before he turned and headed back down the street. Emily watched him for a moment and then turned towards the boarding house. She walked through the small garden, across the porch and inside.

As Emily got ready for bed, she looked out the window at the rows of houses and felt that familiar ache in the pit of her stomach again. How could she long so much for something she hardly knew? This city had been her home all her life, so how did it suddenly not feel like it? She didn't understand.

That night, Emily dreamed of Forest Hill. She, Alec, and the children were camping by the river. They'd gone for a walk and, in the heat of the day, lost themselves among the branches of the weeping willow. She found herself all alone as a cloud passed over, blocking out the sun and turning the world gray.

She cried out, but there was no reply, and her heart began to race. Then, he was there, his arms wrapped around her waist as he rested his chin on her shoulder. She could feel his warmth and breathe in the sweet sharpness of his skin.

She closed her eyes, melting into him, and he whispered into her ear, and then, all too suddenly, she was awake and all alone in a city of over two million people.

Emily spent the next week trying to focus on the upcoming school term. She'd done barely any prep work while she was in Texas and had much to catch up on. Yet, no matter how hard Emily tried to focus on her work and forget about Alec, the children and Forest Hill, she couldn't. They kept sneaking into her head, and before she knew it, she was miles away, daydreaming.

Emily hoped that when school started, her mind would be better occupied. Yet even books and teaching didn't seem to help her mind from wandering back to Texas at the first chance it got. Then, shortly after the fall semester began, she was called into Headmistress Lockhart's office, and she knew it was because the girls were behind on all their lessons.

"Is something the matter, Emily?" the headmistress asked, a look of concern on her face.

"I am so sorry, headmistress," Emily apologized. "I know I've been a bit distracted, but I will get on top of the work and make sure my class catches up."

"I am of course concerned about the girls studies, but I am also concerned about you," the headmistress said.

"Me?" Emily asked, frowning. "But I am fine."

"Emily," the headmistress kindly remarked. "I know we do not know each other all that well, but I like to think you know you can trust me if there is anything the matter."

Emily sighed. "It's silly," she said. "And I can't rationalize it one bit, but ever since coming back to New York, I've been unable to forget Forest Hill."

Headmistress Lockhart paused as she waited for Emily to continue.

"I've only ever lived here," Emily said. "New York is my home, yet it doesn't feel like that anymore. Something about this place has changed, but I can't figure out what.'

Mrs. Lockhart took off her glasses and put them down on her desk.

"Have you considered the possibility that it's not the city that has changed, but you my dear?" she asked.

Emily remained silent for a long moment. Was the headmistress right? Had she changed over the summer, in such a short space of time? Yet, with everything that had happened and everything she'd been through, how could she be the same person she was before?

"Perhaps you are right," Emily said. "Perhaps this summer has changed me, but how do I go back to before?"

"You don't," Headmistress Lockhart replied. "There is no going back, Emily. Throughout our lives, circumstances and choices shape us into different versions of who we were, and we cannot go back."

"But what if this version of me can never be happy here?" Emily asked, feeling panicked.

"Would that be such a terrible thing?" Mrs. Lockhart asked in reply.

Emily paused. "My whole life, I've dreamed of teaching in a place like Briarwood."

"And you have," the headmistress kindly reminded her. "But maybe you are too afraid to admit that there are other things in your life now, too, other than teaching here."

Emily felt a lump form in her throat. "I don't want you to be disappointed in me," she confessed.

"Disappointed?" Headmistress Lockhart said in surprise. "Emily, I admire you. It's no easy thing to admit that you are unhappy, nor is it an easy to change it."

Headmistress Lockhart smiled just then, the corners of her eyes wrinkling.

"When you came to my office after returning from Texas, I could tell there was something different about you," she smiled.

"Different, how?" Emily asked.

"You were brighter, somehow," Mrs. Lockhart replied. "As if someone had turned on a light behind your eyes."

Emily said nothing for a moment as the headmistress leaned forward.

"Remember Emily, a house is just that until you fill it with people, only then does it become a home."

Mrs. Lockhart was right. New York had been home once, when it was filled with the people Emily loved, her father, mother, and beloved sister. But they were gone, and now she saw it as plain as day. New York wasn't her happy place anymore; it hadn't been for a long, long time.

Chapter Twenty-Six

Alec ran his hand through his thick, dark hair and sighed. Despite the fact that fall had arrived, it was still hotter than a blister bug in a pepper patch.

"We are going to need another roll of wire," Mark said. "I'll go and fetch one."

Alec nodded as Mark turned to go.

The past month had been an absolute nightmare. Alec had thought of little else but Emily and how she was getting on in New York. He'd thought about writing to her, but every time he tried, he couldn't think of the right thing to say. T

he only distraction had been Riverbend Ranch, which was under a siege of mighty bad luck. Every day, something new was awry, and Alec was beginning to think there was something behind all this bad luck, or rather, someone.

Alec walked over to his saddlebag and took out the metal water canteen. He unscrewed the top and took a long sip, the cool water soothing his parched throat. As he replaced the cap, he heard the clopping of hooves and frowned; Mark couldn't be back already. He turned to see a rider coming up the road from town. Even from where he was standing, he could make out the man's broad shoulders and wide-brimmed straw hat; it was Leonard.

Alec slipped the canteen back into the saddle bag and walked towards the boundary fence. As he did, his heart caught in his throat; seated behind Leonard was Emily.

"Good day, Mr. Kincaid," Leonard said, bringing the horse to a stop.

"Leonard," Alec said, unable to take his eyes off her.

What was she doing back here?"

Leonard climbed down off the horse and then helped Emily do the same. As he did, Alec crouched under the barbed wire fence. Cobalt, who'd been napping in the shade, came racing through the fence, his tail wagging as he jumped up on Emily and she scratched his head.

"Hello, boy," she said. "I've missed you."

Cobalt jumped down, his tail still wagging as he sniffed her skirts. Emily turned back to Leonard.

"Thank you," Emily said. "For coming to my aid once again."

"You're welcome, Miss Emily," he said, tipping his hat. "And welcome back."

Without another word, Leonard slipped his foot back into the stirrup and pulled himself up. He tipped his hat to them both before taking the reins and turning the horse back towards town.

Alec still hadn't taken his eyes off her. How many times over the past couple of weeks had he pictured Emily's face? The delicate curves of her lips and the arch of her neck. He'd gone over every detail of her, again and again, hoping that in time, his memories would fade and he'd forget. Yet, here she was, standing right in front of him again.

Without thinking, Alec stepped forward. As he did, Emily did the same, and then they both stopped. Emily was so close to Alec that he could feel her warm breath against his skin and he could count the golden flecks in her eyes as she looked up at him.

"What are you doing here?" he asked, his voice just above a whisper.

297

Emily said nothing as she reached up, cupping Alec's face in the palm of her hand, and he closed his eyes for a moment, savoring the warmth of her skin. He was so happy to see her, but he had to know why.

"Emily," Alec said, opening his eyes as he took a step back. "Why did you come back?"

Emily exhaled shakily. "All my life, I've known who I am," she said. "And then I spent one summer here, and I find myself questioning everything I thought I wanted."

Alec said nothing, his heart racing.

"I went back to New York," Emily continued. "Back to Briarwood, only to realize that the place I really wanted to be was here, with you and the children."

Alec took a step forward again.

"Do you mean that?" he asked, searching her face.

"I do," Emily said, reaching for his hands.

Alec's face cracked into a smile as he leaned in and kissed her, softly at first and then harder, pressing his body into hers as she ran her hands through his hair.

They were so lost in one another that Alec did not realize Mark had returned until the man cleared his throat.

Alec pulled away from Emily and turned to face Mark, who was kicking at the dirt with the toes of his boot, a roll of wire under his arm.

"Sorry," Mark apologized.

Alec caught Emily's eyes, and she smiled, bending her head.

"It's good to see you again, Emily," Mark said.

"And you," Emily agreed, meeting his eye briefly.

They all fell silent for a moment.

"Well, I'd better get on with the fences," Mark said.

"I'll be right with you," Alec said.

"Take your time," Mark said, a hint of amusement in his voice.

Alec and Emily waited until Mark was out of earshot and they turned to one another, Alec grinning and taking Emily's hand.

"I am so happy to see you," he said.

Emily looked up at him, her blue eyes shining. "You know I promised myself that I wasn't going to fall in love with a cowboy."

"Well, that was a very foolish promise to make," Alec remarked, smiling as he leaned down to kiss her again.

Emily giggled as Alec pulled away, staring into her eyes.

"You'd better get back to work," Emily said.

"I'd rather stay here with you," Alec replied.

Emily smiled at him, reaching up on her tippy toes to kiss his nose. "I'll see you back at the house," she said.

Alec smiled. "I like the sound of that."

Emily stepped back, and suddenly, she frowned.

"What is it?" Alec asked, his brow furrowing.

SALLY M. ROSS

"Didn't you and Mark already replace all these fences?" Emily asked, looking around.

Alec exhaled. "Somehow, they all came down in the night," he said.

"A storm?" Emily asked.

Alec shook his head as Emily's frown deepened.

"Then what?" she asked.

Alec clenched his jaw. "The last couple of weeks, Riverbend's been having a spell of bad luck," he said.

"Oh?" Emily asked. "What else has happened?"

Alec said nothing for a moment. He did not want to worry her, not after everything.

"It's nothing we can't handle," he said. "Why don't you get home and get some rest? I won't be long."

Emily hesitated a moment and nodded.

"Alright," she agreed, picking up her bag off the ground. "I'll see you back home."

She turned to go, but as she did, Alec caught her hand and pulled her into his arms, kissing her again.

"I love you," he said.

Emily looked up at him and smiled. "I love you too."

Alec waited for Emily to disappear down the road before he turned and walked back to Mark.

"So Emily's back?" Mark asked.

"Looks that way," Alec replied, unable to stop from smiling.

300

"I am happy for you," Mark said. "For you both."

Alec was happy, too. In fact, he was so buoyant that his feet felt like they might leave the ground at any moment. For the last two weeks, Alec had wrestled with the idea of going to New York and trying to convince Emily to return, but one thing had stopped him. He didn't want her to give anything up to be with them. He didn't want to persuade her to leave New York and Briarwood and have her come to resent him for it. It was always going to have to be her choice, and she'd chosen to come back to them.

As he returned home, Alec could hear the laughter from all the way down the road, and when he stepped into the kitchen, he found Emily, Mrs. Tattlewell, and the children all seated. They were crowded around a board in the center of the table.

"Alec!" Thomas shouted, turning to him in excitement. "Come see what Aunty Emily bought Lily for her birthday."

Alec crossed the kitchen and stood behind the children, catching Emily's eye.

"It's called Dominoes," Thomas explained. "And I've won twice."

"I've won twice, too," Lily added.

"Will you play with us, Alec?" Thomas asked.

"After supper," Alec promised. "Now, why don't you two go and play outside and get out from under Mrs. Tattlewell's feet."

Thomas took Lily's hand, and the two children skipped out of the kitchen together, leaving the adults alone.

'Well, I'll get started on the supper," Mrs. Tattlewell said as she smiled at Emily. "It's good to have you home."

"It's good to be home," Emily said.

Mrs. Tattlewell reached over and patted her hand before she got up from the table and walked over to the stove.

"Fancy a walk?" Alec asked.

Emily nodded as she got up and left the kitchen with him. The children were playing by the chicken coop as they walked past the barn.

"So what happens now?" Emily asked, her fingers brushing against his.

"I suppose we get married," Alec said, turning to face her. "That's if you can see yourself being stuck with me for the rest of your life?"

Emily tilted her head and smiled. "I suppose there are worse people to be stuck with," she smiled, her eyes shining playfully.

Alec chuckled as he reached for her hands and pulled her into him, kissing her softly. How was it possible that everything had come right in the space of a single afternoon? That he was being given a second chance at having a family and of being a father? His heart was just about fit to burst.

Chapter Twenty-Seven

Emily stared at her reflection in the bedroom window and sighed. Whoever would have believed that she'd be standing in a bedroom in Texas, all dressed up in white, about to walk down the aisle? Sometimes, Emily still couldn't believe it. A few months ago, she'd have laughed at such an idea, yet now she wanted nothing more.

The last few weeks had passed by in a blur. Mrs. Tattlewell and Kara had volunteered to take on all the wedding plans, much to Emily's delight. Being free from having to plan the wedding had allowed her time to get settled back into Forest Hill. While all her things had not yet arrived from New York, she'd made do with what she had. Emily had moved into Riverbend with the Jones's to avoid any more scandal before the wedding but was looking forward to being back home with Alec and the children.

"Look at you," Mrs. Tattlewell said, a note of pride in her voice.

Emily turned to see the older woman standing in the doorway, beaming.

"You look beautiful," she said.

"Do I?' Emily said nervously.

Mrs. Tattlewell walked across the room and gently pushed the tulle veil away from Emily's face.

"Miss Taylor really outdid herself," Mrs. Tattlewell said, looking Emily up and down.

Emily ran her hands down the tightly fitted silk and lace bodice, which fanned out at the hips into a full, bell-shaped skirt made of the most beautiful white satin. The leg-ofmutton sleeves were fuller at the shoulders and tapered towards the wrists. The high neckline was trimmed with cream-colored lace, and at the back, the skirts extended into a detachable train.

"Your sister would be so happy to see you here," Mrs. Tattlewell said, smiling. "To see you so happy."

Emily smiled, a lump in her throat. She would do anything to have Marie standing beside her right now.

"She wouldn't believe it," Emily said, laughing. "If she could see me standing here, all dressed up."

Mrs. Tattlewell chuckled as Lily appeared in the doorway in a red dress, her bonnet decorated in velvet, cream-colored ribbons.

"Lily," Emily said, smiling as she stretched her arms out to her. "You look as pretty as a picture."

Lily smiled as she walked across the room and into Emily's embrace. She hugged the little girl tightly before letting her go.

"Where's your brother?" Mrs. Tattlewell asked.

"Downstairs," Lily said.

"Well, we'd better get going. I've had a hard enough time keeping the children clean for this long."

Emily turned and glanced at her reflection once more before she took Lily's hand, and they all walked downstairs together.

"Thomas," Emily said, smiling. "Don't you look handsome."

Thomas beamed. He wore a pair of green knee trousers and a crisp white shirt under a rich-wool jacket in a darker shade of green. Emily looked between the two children, glad that the clothes Miss Taylor had made for them were getting some use.

As Emily approached him, Thomas crooked his elbow and offered his arm to Emily. She slipped hers through his, and they made their way outside together.

The buggy, which stood against the side of the barn was decorated in aster flowers of various shades of lavender, pink, and white. Beside the buggy stood Jeremiah, dressed in his Sunday best. As Emily and the children approached, he took off his cap and bowed his head.

"The buggy looks wonderful, Jeremiah," Emily said. "Did you decorate it?"

"I sure did, Miss Emily," Jeremiah beamed. "The youngins helped, too."

"Well, it looks marvelous," Emily remarked.

Suddenly, Cobalt barked, and Emily looked up to find him sitting on the front seat of the buggy, his collar decorated in flowers too.

"Goodness, Cobalt," Emily chuckled. "Don't you look darling."

The dog wagged his tail as Jeremiah offered Emily his hand and she climbed up onto the buggy. Mrs. Tattlewell and the children were seated in the back.

A short while later they were bumping down the road towards the church. As they got closer, the butterflies in Emily's tummy fluttered faster.

"You ready?" Mrs. Tattlewell said, as Jeremiah brought the buggy to a stop.

Emily nodded.

Jeremiah helped Emily down, and when her feet touched the ground, she smoothed out her satin skirts, and took a deep breath.

"Come along, dears," Mrs. Tattlewell said.

Emily took Thomas and Lily by the hands and allowed Mrs. Tattlewell to escort them across the road, through the small wrought-iron gates and along the wonky paving stones that led up to the church doors.

As she stepped inside, the congregation turned to look at her. Despite the rumors of her and Alec's impropriety, most of the town had come to the ceremony. Emily suspected it was Mrs. Tattlewell's doing. Yet, despite all the eyes on her, Emily hardly noticed. How could she?

Standing at the front of the center aisle, dressed in a dark gray suit with tails at the back, was Alec.

In the weeks leading up to the wedding, Alec had threatened on more than one occasion to show up to the church in his dirty jeans and ranch boots. But the truth was, Emily wouldn't have cared. He'd look handsome in any old thing, and she'd love him no matter what.

Just then, the organ began playing, and Emily walked slowly down the aisle with Mrs. Tattlewell by her side. Thomas and Lily walked in front of them, hand in hand.

As they did, Emily turned and smiled at Mrs. Tattlewell who squeezed her arm gently. She'd become a mother to Emily and Alec, and in truth, Emily wouldn't know what to do without her.

At the end of the aisle, Mrs. Tattlewell let go of her hand and smiled encouragingly. She shepherded the children to the front bench alongside the Jones's. Emily exhaled slowly before she walked up to Alec and stood by his side.

"You look beautiful," Alec whispered, his eyes shining.

Emily beamed at him as the organ music faded out, and the reverend stepped forward, clearing his throat.

"Dearly beloved," he began. "We are gathered here in the sight of God and in the presence of these witnesses to join together this man and this woman in holy matrimony. It is a solemn and joyous occasion as they embark on the journey of life together, seeking the blessings of God and the support of their community."

Emily caught Alec's eyes, and he smiled at her. Since leaving New York, she expected to have doubts, to wonder if she'd made the right choice, but she hadn't. Whenever she caught Alec's eye or heard the children giggling upstairs, she knew she'd chosen the right path.

"Marriage is a sacred institution, ordained by God from the beginning of time," the reverend continued. "It is a union not to be entered into lightly but reverently, advisedly, and in God's graces. In the spirit of this commitment, let us begin with a prayer."

Alec held tightly onto Emily's hand as they walked down the aisle together. Outside, the congregation had formed two lines with a gap in the middle, and as Alec and Emily passed through it, they rained flower petals down upon their heads, cheering and clapping.

Emily looked up at Alec, whose green eyes were shining.

"I love you," she mouthed.

"I love you," he whispered, leaning over, and kissing her.

The crowd cheered again as Emily turned her head, and for the briefest moment, she eyed a figure standing at the church gate, dressed in a plain blue dress, her hair in a bun. Emily's heart caught in her throat as the young woman smiled at her, and when Emily looked again, she was gone.

"Emily?" Alec said. "Are you alright?"

Emily nodded, blinking back tears. Marie had worn the very same blue dress the day she left New York, the last time Emily had ever seen her alive.

Alec slid an arm around her waist as Emily glanced at the spot where she'd seen her standing only moments before. She did not know if it was her mind playing tricks on her or if Marie had come to see her get married. In truth, it didn't matter.

Emily stood on the front porch, her head leaning against the wooden pole. Below her in the front garden, people were lounging lazily on blankets on the grass, having abandoned their chairs around the long table. It was the perfect afternoon for a wedding party, probably the last of the good weather before winter arrived.

"There you are, Mrs. Kincaid," Alec said, wrapping his arms around her waist. "I was wondering where you'd got to."

Emily smiled, pressing her back against his body. "It's a wonderful party, isn't it," she said.

"Indeed it is," Alec agreed. "I think we'll have a hard time getting everyone to go home. The whole town turned out to celebrate. Then again, no one in Forest Hill ever turned down a good party."

Emily chuckled. "Well, it's still early," she said. "And we haven't cut the cake yet."

Alec groaned softly, and Emily chuckled again. Mrs. Tattlewell had prepared such a wonderful feast that she also wasn't sure she'd be able to eat another bite.

"I think I had three servings of that mashed sweet potato," Alec said. "And two helpings of stuffing."

Emily turned around and looked up at him, her blue eyes twinkling.

"Well, we both know Mrs. Tattlewell isn't going to let us skip cake," Emily said. "So, you best just grin and bear it, cowboy."

Alec raised his eyebrows in amusement.

"Look at you," he said. "Sounding like a real Texas lady."

"Well, if you can't beat 'em," Emily said.

Alec laughed as he leaned in and kissed her. Just then, however, Emily felt a tug at her skirts and turned to find Lily.

"What is it, honey?" she asked.

"Lily said nothing as she pointed at Thomas and Sarah, pouting.

Emily sighed as she looked at Alec.

"I'll go and speak with them," Alec said.

Just then, however, Emily caught sight of a rider coming up the driveway, and she inhaled sharply.

"Who is it?" Alec asked.

"Mr. Caldwell," Emily said.

Alec turned and sighed. "What the heck does he want?"

Emily kept silent.

"Wait here," he said.

Alec turned and headed towards the driveway and Emily took Lily's hand and followed him, stopping just behind Alec.

Randall Caldwell brought his horse to a halt beside the barn, and Cobalt raced forward, barking and snarling.

"Cobalt," Alec called. "Heel."

The dog turned and came back to his master, sitting at Alec's feet, his hackles raised.

"I take it my invitation got lost in the mail," Randall Caldwell said dryly.

Lily, who was standing beside Emily, suddenly ducked behind her skirts, peering around at Randall, her eyes wide.

"What do you want, Caldwell?" Alec asked.

"Well, I've been hearing how much trouble you are having at Riverbend," Randall said. "But I suppose that's to be expected when you hire a city slicker to be your foreman."

Alec stepped forward, clenching his fists, and Emily caught his arm. Alec had told her his suspicions about Randall. He was convinced that he was behind all the problems at Riverbend. Alec reckoned that if Caldwell caused enough trouble, they'd give up and sell or that he'd cause enough damage that they'd go broke trying to repair it all.

"You know as well as I do that Mark has nothing to do with any of it," he spat.

Randall said nothing, his mouth twisting into a sneer.

"I don't know exactly what you're implying, Kincaid, but I can't say I like your tone."

"Well, I can't say I care what you like and don't like," Alec remarked. "But this is my property, and you'd do well to turn around and ride right out that gate before I set the dog on you."

Randall inhaled and his gaze turned to Emily.

"I hear that prestigious school in New York threw you out," Randall said, his eyes brightening. "Can't say I blame them."

"Actually, they didn't," Emily corrected him. "Apparently, the word of Randall Caldwell doesn't mean much in a place like New York."

Randall's cheeks flushed, and Emily could not help but feel a flicker of satisfaction in the pit of her stomach.

"Well," he said. "Let's hope you don't go the same way as your sister."

"What is that supposed to mean?" Emily snarled, her face blotching.

"You better not be threatening my bride, Caldwell?" Alec added, stepping forward.

"I was merely making an observation," Randall said. "The prairie can be an unforgiving place, especially for outsiders."

The muscles in Alec's jaw tightened as Cobalt growled.

"Get off my ranch, Caldwell," Alec spat. "Now."

Randall glared at both of them as he turned his horse and left. As he did, Emily looked down at Lily who was clutching so tightly to her skirts that her knuckles were white.

"Lily?" Emily said, kneeling down. "What is it?"

Lily said nothing; her face was pale.

"Lily?" Alec asked, crouching beside Emily. "It's okay, you can tell us."

Lily's bottom lip quivered. "That man, he was there."

"Where?" Emily asked as she glanced across at Alec.

"When ma and pa..."

Emily's blood ran cold as she stared at Lily. Was she saying that Randall Caldwell was one of the men who murdered her sister and Bill?

"Lily," Alec said. "Was that man one of the men who attacked the buggy?"

Lily hesitated and then shook her head. "No, but he was there," she said. "I saw him on his horse."

Emily looked at Alec, her heart racing.

"Lily," Alec said. "Why don't you go and see if you can help Mrs. Tattlewell with the cake, alright?"

Lily nodded before she turned and ran towards the house.

"Alec—"

"I know," Alec said, running his hand through his hair. "I know."

"But is it possible?" Emily asked.

"I don't know," Alec said. "But Lily is no liar."

"But if what she is saying is true, then Randall could have been involved in the murders," Emily realized.

As the words left her mouth, her stomach turned. Randall Kincaid was a bad man, no doubt about that, but what she hadn't realized was that he could in fact be a murderer.

Chapter Twenty-Eight

Alec and Emily sat in the sheriff's office in town. Sheriff Rourke was seated across from them, his face unreadable.

"Come on, sheriff," Alec insisted. "You and I both know what Caldwell is capable of."

Sheriff Rourke sighed as he sat forward in his chair.

"You just don't have enough proof," he said.

"We have an eyewitness," Alec insisted. "Lily saw him there."

Sheriff Rourke sucked his teeth. "She's just not a reliable witness," he said.

"Why not?" Alec challenged. "Because she's a child?"

Sheriff Rourke said nothing.

"Or is it because everyone thinks she's simple? Alec argued. "Because she's not, and if anyone in this town dares to say that to my face—

"Alec," Emily soothed. "It's alright."

"It's not alright," Alec said, his voice rising. "Lily saw Randall there as plain as day."

"What about the boy?" Sheriff Rourke said. "Did he see him too?"

Alec glanced at Emily and shook his head.

"He doesn't remember. He was running, pulling Lily behind him. She looked back; he didn't."

"That's a pity," he said. "He's older…"

Alec glanced at Emily, who was biting her bottom lip.

"You said so yourself that the highway robbery was strange," Alec reminded him. "It took place in broad daylight, and the Donnelly's were carrying nothing of value."

Sheriff Rourke nodded, but Alec could tell by the furrow in his brow that he wouldn't help them, despite having an eyewitness.

"I did find the whole situation quite unusual," Rourke agreed. "But it wouldn't be the first time I've seen something strange in these parts."

Alec sighed.

"Look, I can talk with Caldwell," the sheriff offered, shrugging his shoulders. "But that's as much as I can do."

"No, don't," Alec said. "If he finds out there's a witness, Lily could be in danger."

Sheriff Rourke nodded, although he pressed his lips into a hard line, suggesting he believed the whole story very unlikely.

"I'm sorry, Alec," Sheriff Rourke said. "But if you can't find more evidence or another witness, I can't help."

"And what about the trouble at Riverbend?" Alec asked.

"The Deputy hasn't found anyone suspicious," Sheriff Rourke said.

"Mark Jones had to put out three fires last night," Alec reminded him. "Three, sheriff."

Sheriff Rourke sighed.

"It's too late for wildfires," Alec insisted. "Randall's behind it. I can feel it in my gut."

"Then you need to find me proof, Alec," Sheriff Rourke insisted.

Alec stepped out onto the road and sighed in frustration. He'd always liked the sheriff, but the man was hesitant to challenge Randall Caldwell, like most people in Forest Hill.

"So what do we do now?" Emily asked.

"I don't know," Alec replied, shaking his head. "But we can't keep going on like this."

Emily sighed as she walked up to him and put her arms around his waist, and Alec wrapped his around her back, resting his chin on her head.

"I'm going to camp out at Riverbend again this evening," Alec said. "See if I can catch whoever is responsible."

Alec had stayed out several nights over the past few weeks but hadn't seen anyone.

"Take Mark with you?" Emily said. "Just in case."

Alec nodded. "I will."

So, that evening, he and Mark set up camp in the small stretch of trees on the eastern boundary of Riverbend Ranch. It was a clear night, and the moon sat high and bright in the sky.

"You head south," Alec said. "I'll head north and meet you on the western boundary."

Mark nodded as he mounted his horse.

"Watch your back," Alec warned him.

Mark tipped his hat as he turned and headed south while Alec turned north. He rode for about an hour when suddenly he caught a movement out of the corner of his eye. Alec pulled on the horse's reins, coming to a complete stop. He slowly dismounted, fastening the reins over a low-hanging branch as he walked slowly and quietly toward the boundary fence. As Alec crept forward, he heard the figure muttering to himself under his breath. In the bright moonlight, the metal hand-cutters in the man's hands glinted.

Alec watched as he hunched over the fence post and cut the first piece of wire. Alec took a step, and another, but as he did, a twig snapped under his boot, and the man froze. He turned slowly to face Alec; however, his identity was hidden by the brim of his hat. Yet there was something familiar about him.

"Stop right there," Alec warned.

But the man turned and ran, and Alec set off after him. They'd only gone a few hundred feet when the man's boot caught on something, and he fell forward, sprawling out against the hard ground. Alec jumped on top of him, rolling the man over on his back as he grabbed him by the scruff of his shirt.

He shook the man roughly, and as he did, his hat fell, revealing his face. "Jeremiah?"

Alec let go of him as he stood up, shifting his heels in the dirt. It couldn't be him.

"Mr. Kincaid—"

Alec continued to stare at the young ranch hand in disbelief.

"I am so sorry—"

"You?" Alec whispered. "It's been you all along?"

"I am so very sorry," Jeremiah repeated, shaking his head.

"But why?" Alec asked. "Why, after everything that we've done for you? "

"I-I I didn't want to," Jeremiah stuttered. "I swear."

Alec stood silent and continued to stare at him in confusion.

"I don't understand," Alex said, shaking his head.

"I-I didn't have a choice," Jeremiah said. "He threatened my sister."

"Who threatened your sister?" Alec asked,

"Mr. Caldwell," Jeremiah replied. "Just after Miss Emily left town, he came by our house. I got home, and he was there. I don't know what he said to Martha, she wouldn't say, but he made it clear that if I didn't do what he said, he'd take everything we have and run us out of town."

Jeremiah's words were sincere. He was telling the truth and the knowledge that Caldwell had targeted Jeremiah and his disabled sister only made Alec hate the man more.

"Why didn't you come to me?" Alec asked.

Jeremiah exhaled shakily. "I wanted to," he said. "But if I did, Mr. Caldwell would just find someone else to do his dirty work. I thought, at least if it were me, I could control the damage, make sure it didn't go too far."

That was smart, Alec thought, although he did not say it out loud.

"And I've been working overtime to repair the damage I've done," Jeremiah added.

That was true, too. Jeremiah started work first every morning and ended last every evening. Alec had just thought he was enthusiastic, but now he realized he was trying to right his wrongs.

"I understand what you were trying to do, Jeremiah," Alec said. "But I still wish you had come and spoken with me."

"I am sorry," Jeremiah apologized again. "I promise I'll stop—"

"No," Alec said.

Jeremiah frowned.

"If you stop, Caldwell will want to know why," Alec explained. "And who knows what he will do next or who he will send in your place."

"So what are we going to do?" Jeremiah asked.

Alec paused in thought. Sheriff Rourke told them that they needed evidence against Caldwell before he could take their allegations seriously, and Jeremiah was in a position to acquire that evidence.

"Jeremiah," Alec said. "You need to keep doing what you're doing."

"But you said yourself the ranch can't take much more of this," Jeremiah said.

"I know," Alec agreed. "Which is why I need your help. I need you to get as close to Caldwell as you can, and when the opportunity presents itself, I need you to look for evidence."

"What kind of evidence?" Jeremiah asked.

"Lily saw Caldwell the day Bill and Marie were attacked," Alec explained.

"He was there?" Jeremiah said in disbelief and horror.

Alec nodded. "But the sheriff doesn't think Lily is a reliable witness, and without any evidence, he can't do anything."

"So, you want me to try to find something that ties Mr. Caldwell to the murders?" Jeremiah asked.

"Yes," Alec replied. "And once you find what we need, we can take that to the sheriff, and you can tell him about Caldwell's threats against you and your sister."

Jeremiah stayed quiet, his face growing pale.

"I know it's asking a lot," Alec said.

"No," Jeremiah said, shaking his head. "I want to help."

Alec smiled sympathetically as he reached over and patted him on the shoulder.

"We are going to get him," Alec said. "The sooner Forest Hill is rid of Randall Caldwell, the better for everyone."

***

"Jeremiah?" Emily said, her voice rising in shock.

They were standing in the kitchen; it was just before dawn. Alec had sent Jeremiah home before he'd met up with Mark and explained everything that had happened. Afterwards, they'd both returned home.

"Caldwell got to him," Alec explained. "Threatened to hurt Martha and run them out of town."

Emily shook her head in disbelief. "That man is a monster," she said.

"He is," Alec agreed.

Emily walked over to him and slipped her arms around his waist.

"Well, at least it's over now," she said. "What time will we take Jeremiah to speak with Sheriff Rourke and give a statement?"

Alec said nothing as Emily looked up at him.

"Alec?" she prompted.

Alec sighed. "We're not taking him to the sheriff just yet," he answered. "Jeremiah's agreed to try and find the evidence we need."

"What?" Emily said, stepping back. "But Alec, he'll be putting himself in danger. If Randall catches him, he'll have his head, and surely Jeremiah's statement will be enough to get Randall arrested?"

"It may be," Alec said. "But it won't be enough to keep him there."

"What do you mean?" Emily asked.

"Men like Randall get a slap on the wrist for something like this," he said. "We need to find evidence that he was involved in Bill and Marie's murders. We need to get him arrested for something more serious than vandalism."

"But won't we be putting Jeremiah in danger?" Emily asked.

"Jeremiah's a clever boy," Alec said. "He won't get caught."

Emily frowned, pursing her lips, and Alec put his arms around her.

"It'll be fine," he assured her.

Emily sighed as Alec held her close, and as the first rays of dawn began to creep in through the gap under the door, Alec sent out a prayer that he was right.

Chapter Twenty-Nine

Emily stood on the edge of the porch, staring out at the distant hills. She had a light-colored shawl wrapped around her shoulders, but the weather here in Forest Hill was much milder than in New York.

As she rested her elbows on the wooden railing, she spotted Jeremiah in the distance. He was pushing a wheelbarrow. She'd not stopped thinking about the young man since Alec told her their plan. She was worried about him and what would happen if Randall caught him. In these parts, no one would bat an eyelid if you shot someone trespassing in your home.

"Penny for your thoughts?"

Emily turned to find Alec standing in the doorway. He wore a dark green cotton shirt and a pair of old denim jeans. He walked over to Emily and kissed her.

"You okay?" he asked, leaning on the railing beside her. "You looked a million miles away."

"I was just thinking about Jeremiah," Emily said.

Alec sighed. "I know you think it's a bad idea. But it's the only way we can prove that Randall was involved in your sister's murder."

"I know," Emily agreed. "But I just wish there was a way we could guarantee Jeremiah's safety."

Alec looked thoughtful.

"What are you thinking?" Emily asked.

"Maybe there's a way we can do exactly that," Alec said.

"How?" Emily asked.

"We are going to get Mrs. Tattlewell to invite Randall to tea."

Emily frowned, but before she had a chance to ask him any more about his plan, he was already disappearing back inside.

***

"Carry the basket carefully," Emily called after them. "Mrs. Tattlewell will have your hides if you break any eggs."

The children slowed down, not wanting to invoke the wrath of Mrs. Tattlewell. As they headed back towards the house, Emily looked around for Jeremiah, but he was nowhere to be found. She made a mental note to tell him that the latch on the chicken coop was coming loose and needed a new screw.

Emily followed the children in through the back door, and as she did, she stopped dead in her tracks. Seated at the table were Mr. Caldwell and Alec. Mrs. Tattlewell was standing by the stove, making tea.

"Children, go upstairs, please," Emily said. "I'll be up to check on you in a bit."

They put the basket of eggs down on the floor, and Thomas took Lily's hand, and left the kitchen.

"So nice of you to join us, Mrs. Kincaid," Randall said with a smile. "Your husband was just telling me all about Riverbend's new foreman and what a disappointment he's turning out to be."

Emily caught Alec's eye and he lifted his eyebrows just a fraction.

"Yes," Emily agreed. "Such a terrible disappointment, and we do so like the Jones's."

Randall scoffed. "I could have told you not to hire a city slicker, Kincaid," he remarked. "But it looks like your wife wears the pants around here."

Alec gritted his teeth but remained calm.

Mrs. Tattlewell carried the tea tray to the table and set it down before turning to Emily.

"I'll go and check on the children," she said. "I am sure you have a lot to talk about."

Emily gave her a tight-lipped smile, and Mrs. Tattlewell turned and left. Emily hesitated a moment before she joined Alec and Randall at the table.

"So, tell me," Randall said, helping himself to a finger of shortbread. "Why did you lure me here?"

Emily glanced at Alec.

"I know it wasn't because you know how much I love Mrs. Tattlewell's shortbread," Randall said, waving the biscuit in the air. "And given our history, I would have thought I was the last person you'd invite over for afternoon tea. So, why am I here?"

"Well," Emily said, leaning forward. "Alec and I thought it was time to bury the hatchet. We are neighbors, after all."

Randall took a bite of his shortbread and leaned back in his chair, his eyes moving between them suspiciously.

"You wish to bury the hatchet?" he repeated.

"Yes," Emily said as she glanced at Alec, who nodded.

"And as a show of good faith, we wanted to offer you the option of renting grazing land first," Alec said. "On Riverbend."

Randall picked at his teeth with his tongue before lifting his cup and taking a sip.

"Well, I must say that is mighty generous of you," Randall sarcastically replied. "Especially considering that if you hadn't broken your contract, all the grazing land on Riverbend would be mine."

Emily glanced at Alec.

"Yes, well," Alec said. "My wife is quickly coming to terms with the way things are done around here, so we can assure you that such a misunderstanding will not take place again."

"No," Randall agreed as he reached for a second finger of shortbread. "It most certainly won't."

"So, what do you say?" Alec asked. "Can we leave the past in the past?"

Randall took another sip of his tea, as he sat back in his chair.

"You two are good," Randall said. "Better than good in fact."

Alec frowned.

"What do you mean?" Emily asked.

Randall sat forward, resting his elbows on the table, his eyes hard. "Do you think I got to where I am today by being a fool?" he asked. "Do you honestly think I believe that either of you would spit in my direction if I was dying of thirst?"

"Mr. Caldwell—"

"I don't know what game you two are playing," he continued, his voice now dangerously low. "But I will find out, and when I do, well, let's just say we won't be discussing it over afternoon tea."

Randall sat back again as he drained his cup. Then he stood, helping himself to a third piece of shortbread before he turned and left the kitchen without a word.

Emily waited a few moments and then got up and walked over to the window, to make sure Randall was gone. When she was sure he'd left, she turned to Alec.

"Alec!" Emily hissed. "What was that all about?"

Alec sat back in his chair, smiling. "I think that should have bought Jeremiah enough time."

Emily's eyes widened. "Jeremiah is at Caldwell's ranch?" she exclaimed.

"He should be on his way home by now," Alec said. "I told him we could only buy him the time it took for Randall to drink a cup of tea."

Emily stared at him, the corners of her lips turning up. "You could have warned me," she teased.

"You tend to overthink things," Alec shrugged.

"I do not," Emily protested.

Alec got up from his seat and walked over to her, putting his hands on her shoulders. "Don't worry," he said. "It's one of the things I love about you."

Emily looked up at him and he leaned down and kissed her. And as he did, Jeremiah strode in through the backdoor, his face flushed.

"So?" Alec asked urgently. "Did you find anything?"

Without a word, Jeremiah crossed the length of the kitchen. He reached into his pockets and removed a small leather-bound book and several letters.

"Is this all evidence?" Emily asked.

"I think so," Jeremiah said. "I found it in a hidden compartment in Mr. Caldwell's desk, so I knew it had to be important."

"A hidden compartment?" Alec asked. "How did you find it?"

"Well, I was just searching for documents when I noticed a slight dent at the back of one of the drawers; a seam that didn't align with the rest of the wood, and when I reached in to touch it, the panel was loose."

"You're a regular Sherlock Holmes," Emily said, her tone impressed.

Alec reached over, picking up the small leather-bound book, and began to page through it.

"Sherlock who?" Jeremiah asked.

"This is a ledger," Alec interjected. "And look, two payments were made to the same person days before Bill and Marie's murder and one just days after."

"Who to?" Emily asked, peering at the ledger pages.

"There are just two initials, J.R.," Alec said.

As Alec continued to read, Emily picked up one of the letters, unfolding it. " This letter is from Bill," she said in surprise, looking up at Alec.

"Well, what does it say?" Alec asked.

"Randall," Emily read. *"I said I would repay my outstanding debts, but I need more time. I'll get you your money before the end of the fortnight."*

Emily looked up at Alec, frowning.

"Is it dated?" Alec asked.

"Emily shook her head. "Did you know anything about this?" she asked.

Alec grimaced. "I heard rumors he was a gambler," he said. "Although I never discussed it with Marie, she had enough to worry about."

Emily reached for another letter.

"Here's another one," she said.

"Randall," Emily read. *"Please stop sending men to the house; Marie is getting suspicious."*

Emily looked up at Alec again, her stomach in knots. Was Randall sending people to Riverbend? To do what? Collect Bill's gambling debts?

"There's one other letter from Bill," Jeremiah said.

"You read it, Alec," Emily said.

Alec picked up the letter and began. *"Randall,"* he said. *"Jesse Ringo and his men came by the ranch again today to deliver your message. I am a proud man, and so I do not write this letter easily, but please think about Marie and the children.."*

Alec lowered the note as Emily shakily exhaled.

"So, Randall was threatening Bill," she said. "But who is Jesse Ringo?"

"A known bandit," Alec explained. "He has quite a reputation around here."

"A boy I went to school with joined his gang," Jeremiah said. "But one day he got cold feet and ran. Jesse and his men caught up with him and, well, I can't say what happened to him in front of a lady, but it wasn't pretty."

Emily grimaced.

"That must be his initials in the ledger," Jeremiah said suddenly. "J.R."

"You're right," Alec said, picking up the ledger again. "So, Randall must have hired Jesse and his men to threaten Bill."

The knots in Emily's stomach tightened as she picked up the last letter Bill had sent. His words were desperate and afraid.

"Do you think Randall hired Jesse Ringo to attack Bill, Marie and the children?" Emily whispered.

Alec remained silent in thought, and then he nodded. Emily put down the letter, blinking back tears. So, it was Bill who got Marie killed in the end.

"Hey," Alec said, wrapping his arms around her. "We'll get Randall for this. We'll get justice."

Emily nodded as she wiped a tear away with her sleeve.

"Why do you think Mr. Caldwell kept these letters?" Jeremiah asked.

"Arrogance," Alec replied.

Emily looked down at the papers. Jeremiah had done it; he'd got them the evidence they needed to take down Randall Caldwell once and for all.

Chapter Thirty

Sheriff Rourke put down the ledger and sat back in his chair.

"Do I even want to know where you found these?" he asked, his eyes narrowed.

Alec glanced at Emily. "Probably not," Alec admitted. "But is it enough to prove that Caldwell is involved? To take the matter further?"

Sheriff Rourke sighed as he nodded.

"We also have Jeremiah's statement as well as his sister's," Emily added. "Although, I wish to clarify from the offset that I do not wish to press charges against him."

Sheriff Rourke looked over at Jeremiah, standing sheepishly by the door.

"What say you, boy?" Sheriff Rourke asked.

Jeremiah took a step forward, his hands folded in front of him. "I am the one responsible for the troubles at Riverbend," he admitted. "The cut fences, the fires, and the missing cattle."

Sheriff Rourke frowned, but said nothing as he waited for Jeremiah to continue.

"I only did it because Mr. Caldwell threatened me," Jeremiah continued. "He also threatened my sister, Martha."

"And what exactly was this threat?" the sheriff asked.

"He said that he would burn down our house and run us out of town," Jeremiah replied.

"So, why didn't you report this?" Sheriff Rourke asked.

Jeremiah glanced at Alec nervously.

"Come on, sheriff," Alec interjected. "Do you really expect a boy to take on Randall Caldwell and win?"

Sheriff Rourke exhaled slowly but remained quiet.

"Alright," he said. "So Mr. Caldwell told you to cut wires, light fires, and steal livestock?" he asked.

"Well, he told me to cause problems," Jeremiah said. "To make the Jones's lives miserable and to make sure they had to spend money to fix what had been broken and to replace what had been stolen."

Sheriff Rourke nodded.

"But of course, I don't want to press any charges against Jeremiah," Emily repeated. "Only against Mr. Caldwell."

"So, let me get this straight," he said. "You think Caldwell was responsible for the damage done to Riverbend and for the murders of Bill and Marie Donnelly?"

"That's right," Alec said. "And you can't deny the evidence, the statements or the fact it all comes down to one thing, Caldwell wants Riverbend and will stop at nothing to get it."

Sheriff Rourke said nothing for a long moment before he leaned forward in his chair. "I'm expecting my deputy back shortly. Once he's here, we'll go to Caldwell's ranch and make the arrest."

***

Alec closed the stable doors, securing them tightly. Despite it being early November, a storm was blowing in from the west; large black and purple clouds were bulging over the horizon. It was just past mid-afternoon, but it looked later.

Alec turned and headed to the barn with Cobalt at his side. As he did, he wondered if Sheriff Rourke had already made the arrest .

"Alec," Thomas shouted, running towards him. "Do you need some help?"

"Sure," Alec replied. "Where's your sister?"

"Helping Aunt Emily with supper," Thomas replied. "She sent Mrs. Tattlewell home before the storm hits."

Alec nodded. He'd sent Jeremiah home a short while ago too.

"Come on," Alec said, putting a hand on Thomas's shoulder.

They headed into the barn, and Alec showed Thomas how to feed the cows and refill the water troughs. But as he did, he heard a horse whinny and Cobalt raced out of the barn, barking. Alec followed the dog outside to find Sheriff Rourke, his face set in a grim expression.

"Sheriff," Alec greeted him, tipping his hat.

Sheriff Rourke dismounted, removing his hat. "You're not going to like what I have to tell you," he sighed.

"What is it?"

"When we went to arrest Caldwell, he was gone," Sheriff Rourke announced.

"What do you mean gone?" Alec said, frowning.

"I mean, vanished," Sheriff Rourke repeated. "The ranch and the house are abandoned."

"So, he knew you were coming?"

"Best guess is your little tea party yesterday made him more than a little suspicious," the sheriff replied. "Chances are, he went straight home and to his study, and when he opened that little secret compartment to find everything gone, I'd say he high tailed it out of there."

"But you have to find him," Alec insisted.

"We will," Sheriff Rourke said. "Not much can be done until the storm blows over, though."

As the words left his mouth, a deep rumble of thunder shook the ground beneath them.

"Look." Sheriff Rourke warned. "It's probably best if you and the Mrs. lay low until then. Chances are he's madder than a wet hen."

Alec sighed. "Keep me updated, sheriff."

"Will do," the sheriff said, putting his hat back on as he looked around. "Where's the boy, Jeremiah?"

"Sent him home," Alec replied.

The sheriff nodded.

Alec waited as he mounted his horse and rode off down the drive before returning to the barn. Thomas was standing beside the stalls where he'd left him.

"You hear that then?' Alec asked.

Thomas nodded.

"Best not to mention it to your sister or your aunt," Alec said. "No point in worrying them."

Thomas nodded.

"You finished filling the water troughs?"

"Yes, sir," Thomas replied.

"Good, then go and check on the chickens. Make sure they have enough food and water."

Thomas turned and left the barn. When he was gone, Alec kicked the empty silver pail, sending it rolling the length of the barn floor. Then he ran a hand through his hair, exhaling in frustration. He'd thought they were so smart, that they were one step ahead of Randall, but they weren't.

Alec left the barn, securing the doors as he'd done with the stables. The first drops of rain were starting to fall as he turned towards the chicken coop.

"Thomas," he shouted, his voice carrying on the wind.

The little boy did not hear him, so Alec ran over to find Thomas struggling to secure the door. Cobalt was at his heels.

"What's the problem?" Alec asked.

"The latch is loose," Thomas explained. "It'll blow open in the wind."

'Right," Alec said, nodding. "You go on inside, and I'll secure the door. Take Colby with you."

Thomas nodded as Alec turned and headed back to the barn. He didn't have a light to search with, so it took him a while to locate the screws, and when he left the barn again, the rain was lashing against the side of the building.

Alec ran over to the coop, but the rain was falling so hard and fast that he could barely see in front of him. His fingers were so slippery that he dropped one of the screws, which disappeared immediately in the mud at his feet.

"Rats," Alec muttered to himself as he searched the ground.

Then, he spotted a couple of large logs beside the woodpile. He ran over to them and rolled one over to the coop, securing it against the door. Then he fetched another and rolled it next to the first.

Alec turned and ran back to the house, almost slipping in a puddle as he ran and as he approached the back door, Emily pulled it open wide.

"Goodness, Alec," she said, turning to fetch a towel from the chair in front of the stove. "You're soaked right through."

"I couldn't fix the latch on the chicken coop," Alec said, taking the towel from her. "But I managed to secure it with two logs. It should hold."

"It's my fault," Emily said. "I saw it earlier today and meant to tell Jeremiah but with everything that's been going on..."

"Don't worry about it," Alec said, leaning over and kissing her on the cheek. "Where are the children?"

"Upstairs, playing Dominos," Emily replied.

Alec nodded as he looked out the window to see lightning lashing across the sky, and a rumble of thunder shook the glass in their panes. Cobalt was lying under the kitchen table, panting. Ever since he was a puppy he had never liked the storms.

"Do you need any help with supper?" Alec volunteered.

"No, thanks," Emily said, smiling. "The shepherd's pie is already baking in the oven."

"It smells delicious," Alec remarked, kissing her on the cheek.

"Go and change," Emily ordered, swatting him playfully with the damp towel. "Before the whole kitchen becomes a puddle."

Alec chuckled as he headed upstairs. He changed out of his wet clothes, buttoning up his shirt in front of the window. The rain was falling harder now; it was as if nature had pulled its own curtain shut around the farm, obscuring the rest of the world from view.

Alec turned away from the window and left the room, stopping outside the children's to watch them play for a few moments. Lily was beating Thomas, and the smile on her face filled Alec with happiness and relief. She was finally finding her way back to the joyful little girl he'd known before. It had taken time, but she was slowly healing.

"That's the third time Lily's won," Thomas shouted, shaking his head in disbelief.

"Well, it would be no fun if you always did," Alec reminded him.

"Do you want to play, Alec?" Thomas asked.

Alec opened his mouth to answer, but as he did, there was a loud banging downstairs. At first, he thought it was the storm, the wind blowing around the old rocker on the front porch. But then he heard it again, and this time louder.

"What is that?" he said, frowning.

"It sounds like someone banging on the front door," Lily said.

Alec turned and headed downstairs with the children on his heels. Emily was coming towards them from the kitchen with Cobalt running in front of her, barking. Alec glanced at her before there was another loud thud on the front door, and he reached for the doorknob. However, Sheriff Rourke's words echoed in his head, warning him to stay safe.

"Alec?" Emily said. "Open the door."

"I don't think we should," Alec hesitated.

Emily frowned, and without giving him time to explain, she walked forward and pulled open the door. Standing on the porch, soaked through to the bone, was the Jones family.

"What on earth are you doing here?' Emily asked.

"Riverbend's on fire," Kara said, trying to catch her breath. "Caldwell and his men, they set everything on fire."

"Caldwell?" Emily said, frowning.

"There's no time to explain," Mark interrupted. "Caldwell and his men are on their way here—"

Just then, there was a loud crack, and a tree branch came crashing down through the porch roof. Alec grabbed Emily and the children as she pulled them back inside and Kara screamed just before a booming rumble of thunder drowned her out.

Chapter Thirty-One

"Kara!" Emily shouted, shaking the woman by the shoulders. "Kara, stop screaming."

It was as if Emily's words had broken some spell and Kara went silent as tears rolled down her face.

"I can't look," she whispered. "I can't bear to look."

Emily glanced over Kara's shoulder to see Alec carefully helping Mark up off the ground. Thomas was there, too, trying to get Sarah and Ben out from under all the debris from the porch roof. Lily was standing beside her, clutching her skirts.

"Everyone is alive," Emily said. "It's okay, everyone is all right."

Kara turned around, and as she did, she whimpered. Alec was supporting Mark's weight; his leg was broken, the bone visible through a tear in his denim jeans.

"Sarah! Ben!" Kara said, rushing up to them. "Are you hurt?"

The children shook their heads, their faces pale. Kara pulled them into a tight hug.

"Everyone inside now," Alec commanded.

Emily stepped aside as Alec helped Mark through the doorway. Mark's breathing was ragged and his face was contorted in pain. Once Alec had him inside, Kara and the children walked in behind them, followed by Thomas.

"Emily," Alec said, turning back to her. "We need to lock all the doors and latch all the windows."

Emily nodded as she crouched down and looked into Lily's pale face.

"Kara,' Emily said. "Can you help me? Can you go upstairs and latch the windows."

Kara nodded as she turned and headed upstairs

"Is the bad man coming?" Lily asked, her eyes wide.

"I don't know," Emily said. "But just in case we need you to go upstairs and hide under your bed, okay?

Lily nodded.

Just then, Emily glanced down the hallway to see Alec helping Mark into the kitchen while Sarah and Ben followed them.

"Thomas," Emily said, still kneeling as she orientated herself towards him. "What I am going to tell you now is very important and I need you to promise me that you'll do exactly as I say."

Thomas nodded.

"Good," Emily said. "If something happens and I tell you to take your sister and run, do you promise me that you'll do as I ask?"

Thomas hesitated.

"I need you to promise me, Thomas," Emily insisted.

"I promise," Thomas said.

"Good boy," she said. "Now take your sister and go into upstairs with the others."

Emily went around the first floor, into the sitting room and then the dining room, latching all the windows as the storm continued to rage outside. As Emily stared outside, her stomach muscles contracted in fear. Randall had set Riverbend ablaze? But he was supposed to be in the sheriff's custody? What was going on? Just then, she felt a gentle hand on the small of her back and she turned to find Alec. His face was lined with worry.

"Alec," Emily said, looking up at him. "What's going on?"

Alex sighed, shaking his head. "Sheriff Rourke came by earlier," Alec confessed.

"What did he say?" Emily asked.

"That he went to arrest Caldwell and found the place deserted," Alec replied. "Caldwell was nowhere in sight."

"What?" Emily said, the knots in her stomach tightening. "Why didn't you tell me?"

"I didn't want to worry you," Alec said. "Sheriff Rourke said that there was nothing that could be done until after the storm's passed and even then, Forest Hill doesn't exactly have a robust policing department. Randall could have been miles from Forest Hill by now—"

"But he's not," Emily said, her voice wavering. "He's next door burning down Riverbend."

Alec exhaled shakily as he pulled her into a tight embrace.

"What are we going to do, Alec?"

Alec said nothing for a long moment before letting her go.

"Come on," he said, taking her hand.

Emily allowed him to lead her into the kitchen where everyone was seated at the table, including all the children.

Mark had his broken leg outstretched in front of him, his face ghostly white.

"Children," Emily said. "It's time for you all to go upstairs for a bit, okay? Go play a game of Dominos."

Sarah and Ben turned and looked up at their mother.

"It's okay," she assured them. "Do as Aunt Emily asked."

The children got up and ran upstairs while Emily and Alec took their seats at the table.

"Mark, Kara," Alec said. "We need you to tell us exactly what happened."

Mark closed his eyes, wincing, and Kara put a gentle hand on his shoulder.

"We were just sitting down to dinner when we heard horses," Mark explained, his voice wavering. "The rain was just beginning to fall."

"We looked out the kitchen window and saw Randall Caldwell. He was with a group of four other men. They rode up to the barn first. They had cans with them, full of paraffin."

"After the barn, it was the stables," Mark said. "And we knew we needed to get out."

"We used the bulkhead doors in the basement," Kara continued. "Then we cut through the ranch around the back so that we wouldn't be seen."

"Thank goodness for that," Emily said.

Mark glanced up at Kara, his mouth turned down.

"There's more?" Emily asked.

Mark exhaled deeply as he looked from Emily to Alec. "Jeremiah was with them," he said.

Emily's stomach sank to the floor.

"What?" Alec said.

"He was tied to the back of one of the men's horses," Mark explained. "He looked pretty beat up."

Bile rose in Emily's throat as she got up and rushed over to the sink. Alec was by her side a moment later, his hand on her back.

"It's going to be okay," he soothed.

"How do you know?" Emily said, turning to face him. "This is our fault, Alec."

Alec said nothing, but Emily could see he felt as responsible as she did.

"We are going to get him back," Alec said firmly.

After a few moments, Emily and Alec turned to face the others again.

"You said Caldwell and his men were coming here?" Alec asked. "How can you be certain?"

"When we were leaving via the bulkhead doors we had to pass behind the old woodshed," Mark explained. "I heard Caldwell shouting to his men to hurry up, that they had another ranch to visit."

Emily tensed. "Surely they wouldn't be foolish enough to ride in this?" she asked, as another rumble of thunder shook the walls.

"No," Alec agreed. "Randall's sense preservation is too high."

Mark pressed his lips into a hard line as he shook his head. "Randall looked different this time," he said.

"How so?" Alec asked, frowning.

"He looked unhinged," Mark said, wincing in pain again.

"Mark's right," Kara agreed. "If we hadn't got out in time, he would have burned the house down with us inside. I wouldn't put anything past that man."

Emily glanced up at Alec, his jaw clenching.

"What are we going to do?" Kara asked.

"It's too dangerous to go out in this," Emily reasoned. "We need to wait until the storm lets up some and then get the children out."

"Can we really afford to wait?" Alec asked. "If Mark and Kara are right, then Randall could be breaking down that door at any moment."

Emily exhaled slowly. "We can't send the children out in this."

"If it's a choice between waiting here for Randall, like sitting ducks, or taking our chances out there, well I'd rather face the darkness and the rain," Alec said.

"Well, I don't think I am in any state to go rushing off into the storm," Mark said.

"And I won't leave him behind," Kara added.

"Of course not," Emily agreed. "No one is getting left behind. After all, it's our fault that you are in this mess."

The room fell silent for a few moments, everyone lost in their own thoughts.

"Do you hear that?" Alec asked.

"Hear what?" Emily asked.

"I don't hear anything," Kara said, frowning.

"Exactly," Alec said. "The rain's stopped."

Emily looked up at Alec, her heart racing. Somewhere along the way, while they'd been debating the best plan forward, the rain had stopped, and now they were racing against the clock.

"I'll get the buggy hitched," Alec said, jumping into action. 'We'll ride straight to the sheriff's office."

"I'll get the children," Kara said.

"And I can help Mark," Emily volunteered.

Alec rushed to the back door and pulled it open while Kara disappeared upstairs to fetch the children. Emily walked over to Mark; his face was even paler than it had been just moments ago.

"Put your weight on me," Emily instructed.

With a bit of a struggle, Emily managed to get Mark onto his feet. It was evident from his shallow breathing that he was in a serious amount of pain.

"We are going to get you to a doctor real soon," Emily promised him.

Carrying as much of Mark's weight as she could manage, Emily got him across the kitchen and out of the back door. The ground was sodden, and they struggled across to the barn. Alec was already nearly done hitching the horse, his hand's working expertly as he looped and tucked.

As they got to the buggy, Alec finished with the last buckle and hurried over to them, putting his shoulder under Mark's arm.

"You going to be able to climb up?" Alec asked.

Mark nodded, although his eyes were full of uncertainty.

"We'll help you," Emily said.

However, just as they were about to help Mark into the buggy, Emily caught a movement out of the corner of her eye and turned to find Randall coming up the drive, followed by four others.

Suddenly, Emily spotted Jeremiah at the back, his wrists were bound together and he was being pulled behind the last rider.

"Jeremiah!" Emily cried, rushing forward.

Alec caught her by the wrist and she turned towards him.

"Let me go," she insisted.

"He'll kill you," Alec said, his voice barely above a whisper. "We need to be smart about this."

Emily opened her mouth and then closed it again.

"You need to trust me, okay?" Alec insisted.

Emily nodded. "Okay."

Alec let go of her wrist and she turned to face the group of riders again. As they got closer, Emily saw that Randall was soaked through, his dark hair sopping and his clothes stuck to his body. He didn't seem to notice, and his eyes were fixed on hers, dark, and full of malice.

Chapter Thirty-Two

"Emily," Alec said, doing his best to keep his voice even. "Get Mark back inside, fast."

Emily did not move, her eyes fixed on Randall.

"Emily," Alec repeated. "We need to get Mark back inside now."

Emily nodded as Alec shifted Mark's weight onto her.

"Go," he whispered. "Quickly."

Emily turned towards the house with Mark as Alec turned to face Randall and the other men fast approaching. As he did, his heart was beating so fiercely that he thought it might beat right out of his chest.

"What are you doing here, Caldwell?" Alec asked as the horses stopped in front of him.

Randall said nothing as his eyes darted from Alec across to Emily and Mark as she got closer to the house. He and Kara had been right; there was something different about Randall today; less composed. His eyes lingered on Alec for only a few moments before he turned his attention to Emily again.

"Emily," Randall shouted, a playful edge to his voice. "Where do you think you two are going?"

Alec turned to see Emily stop dead in her tracks and turn back to face him.

"Let Mark go," Alec said. "He has nothing to do with this."

Randall smiled, but there was no warmth or humor in it. It was as cold and dead as his eyes.

349

"On the contrary," Randall said. "I've been very much hoping for an audience with Mark Jones ever since he took over stewardship of Riverbend."

From where he was standing, Alec saw Mark tense up.

"I must say, I am very disappointed to see that you and your family abandoned the ranch, " Randall said, pouting slightly. "Like rats escaping a sinking ship. That being said, I shouldn't have expected anything else from city folk; all cowards, the lot of you."

"Mr. Caldwell," Emily said, her voice wavering. "Just let me take Mark back inside, please."

"Oh, I think you can call me Randall," he said. "After all, I've been in your home, and you've been in mine."

Alec glanced at Jeremiah. His long hair hung limply around his face like a curtain; where the rope was tied around his wrists, the skin was red and raw.

"Caldwell," Alec said, turning to look at him again. "We've both made some mistakes, but you don't have to do this—"

"Oh, I think I do," Randall interrupted, raising his hand.

Before Alec had time to react, the man directly behind Randall pulled out a pistol and pointed it at Mark. He pulled the trigger and Mark fell to the floor with a loud thud as the gunshot echoed against the buildings.

"No!" Emily cried, falling down beside him.

"Well, that's one problem taken care of," Randall said "Now, for the next one."

The same shooter turned his gun on Emily, but this time Alec had foreseen it and run towards her, jumping and shielding Emily with his body.

"How sweet," Randall sneered.

The man's finger slid over the trigger, and Alec closed his eyes. A second gunshot pierced the air and Alec braced himself, waiting for the pain and the darkness, but they never came.

He opened his eyes to see Randall hunched over feeling his chest, a bullet hole in the tree stump beside him. Who had fired the gun? Alec turned towards the house to see Kara standing at the bedroom window on the second floor. She had Alec's rifle in her hand, and her face was pale. Just then, she lifted the gun again and fired another shot. It missed again and the bullet ricocheted off the metal of one of the men's stirrups. The horse reared up and the rider almost slid off the back causing quite a commotion.

"Emily," Alec shouted, seeing their chance. " Get into the house, now!"

"What about Jeremiah?" Emily cried. "And Mark?"

Alec glanced down at Mark but he wasn't moving and there was no way they could get to Jeremiah without being shot. "We have to go," Alec said, grabbing Emily by the other shoulder. "Come on."

Alec and Emily raced the last few feet to the back door, evading several bullets as they rushed into the kitchen, the door swinging shut behind them.

"It's no use hiding," Randall shouted after them.

Alec turned to Emily. "Are you alright?" he asked. "Are you hurt?"

Emily shook her head, trying to catch her breath.

Just then Kara appeared in the doorway. "He shot him" she said, her voice trembling as tears streamed down her face. "He just shot him. Mark is dead."

'Oh, Kara," Emily said, walking up to her. "I am so sorry."

"We don't know that," Alec said. "Don't lose hope."

Kara nodded but said nothing as Alec met her eye. "What do we do now?" she asked.

Alec was speechless. He had no plan. They had to get the children out; that was the most important thing, and they needed to do it before Randall decided to set the place on fire.

"We need to get the children to safety," Alec said, looking between Emily and Kara. "I'll keep Randall and his men distracted out back, while you two take the children and go out the front."

"I am not leaving you," Emily said, her jaw set in determination.

"Emily," Alec reasoned.

"I can take the children on my own," Kara said. 'If Emily wants to stay."

Alec opened his mouth to argue when a bullet came piercing through the window, shards of glass flying across the kitchen floor. Alec, Emily, and Kara all ducked.

"There is no time to argue," Alec insisted. "Kara, can you get to the children ?"

Kara nodded.

"Good, then go," he said. "And take Cobalt, he'll help."

"Promise me you won't leave without checking on Mark." Kara pleaded.

"We won't leave him behind," Alec said. "You have my word."

Kara nodded and without another word, she bent low and hurried out of the kitchen, disappearing down the hall. Emily turned to Alec, who exhaled shakily.

"You ready?" he said.

Emily nodded as she shuffled closer. He slipped his hand into hers as he pulled open the back door, raising their arms into the air and stepping outside. Randall and his men had dismounted now and were standing in a line facing the door, guns in their hands. Alec glanced over at the horses and saw that Jeremiah was still tied to the saddle, his head resting on the hind of the horse.

"Well, this is a surprise," Randall said. "I was sure we'd have to set fire to the place."

Alec glanced at Mark's body unmoving on the ground. It was impossible to tell from where they were standing if he was still breathing.

"We want to negotiate," Alec said.

"Negotiate?" Randall laughed. "You are staring down the barrels of four guns. I think we are long past negotiating."

"I'll sell Riverbend to you," Emily said. "If you leave right now."

"You'll sell Riverbend to me?" Randall asked, his dark eyes gleaming.

"Yes," Emily said firmly. "I will sell the property to you; you have my word."

"Your word?" Randall said, his tone mocking. "We'll be neighbors?" Randall said. "Will we walk to church together on Sundays and borrow cups of sugar on occasion?"

The men chortled as Emily's cheeks flushed.

Alec said nothing, glancing at Emily. He knew they were running out of time, but they had to keep Randall talking. Luckily for them, the man loved the sound of his own voice.

"So, what's your plan then?" Alec asked.

"It's simple, Randall said. "Once you're all loaded with lead, we drag you inside and set the house on fire."

Emily tensed.

"There's something to be said about simplicity," Randall smiled.

"And once we're gone, the bank will foreclose on Riverbend, and the property will go to auction," Alec said, filling in the details.

"Exactly," Randall grinned triumphantly. "And I can finally right the wrongs done to my family all those years ago."

Alec and Emily kept still as Randall took a step closer.

"Boys," he said. "I think it's time for a family reunion. Go inside and bring out the rest of them."

The four men walked past Emily and Alec into the kitchen.

"I am sure you're wishing that you stayed in New York." Randall said, his eyes fixed on Emily. "But instead, you came back and made the same foolish mistake your sister did."

"You're a monster," Emily spat.

"Maybe," Randall agreed. "But if it's any consolation, I actually liked Marie."

"You killed her," Emily cried.

"She got herself killed by marrying a man like Bill Donnelly," Randall argued.

"And you think you are any better?" Alec challenged. "You two are cut from the same cloth—"

In an instant, Randall was beside him, his gun pointed under Alec's chin. Blood rushed to his ears as beads of perspiration ran down his back.

"Don't you dare compare me to that man," Randall hissed.

"Why not?" Alec said. "He was a bully, just like you."

Randall's hand was trembling.

"Randall, please don't do this," Emily begged.

Just then, there was the sound of heavy boots behind them, and Randall lowered the gun, his brow creasing.

"Where are they?"

"Gone," said the tall man with the handle brush mustache. "We searched the entire house. "

"Gone?" Randall cried; his face beet red as he turned his attention back to Alec . "Where are they?" he demanded.

"I don't know," Alec answered honestly.

Randall stared at him for a long moment before he exhaled in frustration. "Well, don't just stand there," he yelled. "Go and find them; they can't have gotten far."

The men turned and left, grumbling under their breath as they did.

"Get inside," Randall ordered. "Now."

Alec and Emily turned and walked back into the kitchen.

"Sit down."

Emily and Alec walked over to the kitchen table and sat down. Randall still had his gun pointed at Alec, but he was distracted, muttering to himself. He had not anticipated losing Kara and the children."

"Randall," Alec said. "You can stop this; it's not too late."

Randall sighed, shaking his head. "It sure is. .Granted, things could have gone different if your wife hadn't gone back on her word, but it's far too late now."

"Do you truly believe that Riverbend is worth so many lives?" Alec challenged. "Innocent people's lives?"

"The price of Riverbend has always been steep," Randall said. "Ever since the day of the auction all those many, many years ago when my great-great grandfather was so fixated on acquiring that property that he didn't even notice his own son floating face down in the pond at the bottom of their garden."

"But it doesn't have to be this way," Alec said. "All this death, all this pain."

"Doesn't it?" Randall contradicted. "Bill could have sold me the property in lieu of his debts, but he was too proud, so he gave his life, and Marie's, for that ranch."

"Then, everything you're saying shows that Riverbend has cost people too much already," Alec argued.

"It's too late, Alec," Randall repeated.

"It's not," Emily insisted. "Take the ranch. If it's caused so much death and pain, then we don't want it anyway. Take it."

Randall shook his head. "It's bigger than that now." "When you make deals with the devil, you can't go back on them."

Alec could not help but hear a note of regret in Randall's tone.

"Who did you make a deal with?" Alec asked.

"He wants this ranch once you're gone," Randall said, ignoring the question. "And I've agreed to purchase it for him."

Alec glanced at Emily, and he could tell she was thinking the same thing he was . They'd spent the better part of the last half an hour trying to talk Randall out of something that was beyond his control. Not even Randall Caldwell would be foolish enough to break an agreement with Jesse Ringo.

"You could tell him we escaped," Alec said, clutching at straws.

Just then, they heard someone yelling. It was Kara.

"Let me go," she cried as the men carried her through the door.

"Put her in that chair," Randall instructed.

The men carried Kara to an empty seat and shoved her down. Her face was flushed, but otherwise, she was unharmed.

"Where are the children?" he snarled.

"I don't know," Kara said, panting. "I told them to run, and they ran."

Randall sighed, gritting his teeth.

"What are you still doing here?" he barked at the men. "Go and find them."

"We don't take orders from you," the tall man said.

"Tonight, you do," Randall said. "Now go!"

The men threw Randall threatening looks as they turned and left the room. Randall leaned against the kitchen dresser, sweating.

Kara turned to Alec, her face pale.

"I'm so sorry, Alec," she whispered. "Cobalt, he attacked one of the men and got hurt."

Alec nodded, his stomach sinking. "He'll be alright. He's a fighter."

Kara nodded as Emily reached over and squeezed Alec's hand tightly.

The room fell silent for a moment. Randall kept his gun pointed at them, but he was lost in thought.

"What are you waiting for, Randall?" Alec said after a while.

Randall hesitated, glancing down at the gun in his hand, and Alec noticed there was no love lost between the man and his weapon.

"You've never shot anyone, have you?" Alec asked.

"Of course I have," Randall said a little too quickly.

"It's nothing to be ashamed of. I've never shot a man either."

"Do you think I need your approval?" Randall asked.

"I don't think care what I think, but you can't argue that we've known each other a long time, Randall, our entire lives, in fact. Does that not count for something?"

Randall went quiet for a moment. "Maybe it did," he said. "But not anymore.

"Do you really mean that?" Alec asked.

"I used to envy you," Randall confessed. "I'd sit in church and watch you and Olivia, your baby on the way. I used to think that you were the richest man around, but then she died, and your child with her, and I was glad, glad that I didn't have what you had – I didn't have a family to mourn."

Alec said nothing, taken aback by Randall's confession.

"You'd have thought you'd learned your lesson the first time," Randall continued. "But now you've gone and done it again."

The room fell silent again. Alec kept waiting for the right moment, a lapse in concentration when he could throw himself across the room and wrestle the gun from Randall's hands. But the man was nothing if not vigilant.

The storm clouds had since disappeared, and outside, the first stars appeared in the night sky. Suddenly, the silence outside was disturbed by low voices growing closer. Alec turned his head, catching Emily's eye, directing everything he was feeling into that look; how much he loved her, how much he wanted to protect her, and how she'd saved him in all the ways a person could be saved.

"Finally," Randall said as he walked over to the door.

Alec turned just as the men stepped back inside. The children were not with them, much to Alec's relief. But they were joined by a fifth man. He was tall, so tall in fact that he had to bend not to knock his head on the doorframe. He had long, brown hair that he wore in a plait down his back and a scar across his left eye.

"M- Mr. Ringo," Randall said, stuttering slightly as his face paled. "What are you doing here?"

Chapter Thirty-Three

Emily had never seen someone like Jesse Ringo in all her life. Of course, she'd heard the stories of the bandits of the Wild West, but she had never thought she'd be in a room with one.

"Caldwell," Jesse said. "Where are the children?"

"They ran off," Randall said, a crease between his brows. "But we've been looking for them."

"By we, you mean my men?" Jesse said, his voice dripping with displeasure. "They ain't your ranch hands."

"I-I know," Randall said nervously.

Jesse stepped towards Randall, paying Alec, Emily, and Kara no mind.

"You said this was going to be an easy job, Caldwell," his voice now dangerously low. "In and out, you said."

"I thought it would be," Randall confessed, beads of perspiration forming between his furrowed brows. "But then the children—"

Jesse inhaled deeply. "This isn't the first time you've let the children get away," he said. "Tell me, Randall Caldwell, do you take me for a fool?"

"O-of course not," Randall stammered.

"Then why are the men I sent to do this job running around in the night chasing shadows?" Jesse asked.

"We'll find them," Randall replied, a note of desperation in his voice. "We just have to keep looking."

Jesse silently turned around and sat at the kitchen table, orienting himself to face Randall.

"I am calling the deal off, Caldwell," Jesse said, leaning back and folding his arms across his chest as he stretched out his long legs.

"W-what?" Randall stuttered. "But you can't."

"Of course, I can," Jesse said. "After the mess up with the Donnelly's, I gave you another shot, but you're just embarrassing me now, Caldwell."

"I am sorry," Randall apologized. "I didn't mean to—"

"Of course you didn't," Jesse said. "But you're a weak man. If you had any guts in that belly of yours, this lot would be full of holes by now."

Randall said nothing as Jesse caught Emily's eye for a brief moment.

"I know you wanted the Donnelly's' ranch," Jesse said. "But it's probably best that you let it go."

"If you call off this deal, you won't get this place," Randall reminded him, suddenly finding his voice.

"You're right," Jesse said, frowning for a moment. "I suppose I'd have to find another ranch to purchase."

"There aren't any," Randall said. "At least not any good ones."

"There's yours," Jesse said, tilting his head.

Randall frowned. "B-but my ranch isn't for sale."

"It will be when you're dead."

In an instant, Jesse fired the gun from his holster directly into Randall's chest, and he dropped like a stone. A strangled scream caught in Emily's throat as she stared at his motionless body on the kitchen floor. Alec was on his feet and Kara had almost fallen off of her chair, now on her knees trembling with her head tucked under the table.

Jesse turned to them.

"You folks have a good night now," Jesse said.

Then without another word, he got up off his seat and left the room. The other four men stared at Randall's body, satisfied looks on their faces, before they followed Jesse Ringo out into the night.

For a long moment, no one moved, scared that they would be back at any moment; however, as the sound of hooves disappeared into the night, Emily could breathe again. She couldn't believe it, they were alive. She'd been so sure that they wouldn't live to see another dawn, yet they'd been spared, but not all of them.

"Alec—"

But Emily did not need to say anything; Alec was already rushing across the kitchen to Randall's side. He knelt down and put his head to the man's chest.

"He's alive," Alec said. "But barely. We need to try and get control over the bleeding."

Emily hurried over to the sink and fetched a dish towel, which she handed to him. Alec pressed it firmly onto the wound. As he did, he pulled Randall closer to the center of the room.

"We need more light in here," Alec said. "It looks like the bullet went right through, so I think I'm going to have to cauterize the wound."

Emily turned to Kara, who was still curled up by the table.

"Kara, I need you to get up and light the lamps."

Kara didn't move; she was staring at Randall with a mixture of anger and disgust.

"Why are you helping him?" she seethed. "It's his fault Mark is dead, that your sister and brother-in-law are dead."

Emily looked at Alec.

"We know, Kara," Alec said. "But letting him die isn't going to change what he did."

"It would make me feel better," Kara retorted.

"Kara," Emily said. "Randall has done us all a lot of harm, but Alec is right; his death will not bring anyone back."

Kara sighed as she turned to Emily. "I suppose you're right," she said. "Death would be a kindness. He should live to stand trial so justice can be served."

Without another word, Kara turned and fetched the small paraffin lamp from the hook by the window. She proceeded to light it while Emily walked over to Alec and knelt beside him. His hands were stained red with Randall's blood.

"What do you need me to do?" Emily asked.

"The bleeding is slowing," Alec said. "I need you to fetch my knife; it's upstairs."

Emily nodded as she turned and left the kitchen. She headed upstairs and fetched Alec's knife from on top of the dresser. The children were under strict instructions never to touch it, but Alec always kept it out of their reach just in case.

As she turned to leave the bedroom, she glanced out of the window. Where were the children? She hated to think of them out there all alone, cold, and afraid.

Emily returned to the kitchen and found Alec where she had left him. Kara was standing beside the open door, shivering as she peered out into the darkness.

"He's gone," she said.

"Whose gone?" Emily asked, confused.

"Mark, he's gone."

Both women turned to each other and smiled with relief. They knew that meant Mark was alive and must have gone for help. Now, all they could do was deal with their current situation and wait for any news.

"Heat the blade on the coal stove," Alec instructed. "Until it is white."

Emily did as she was told, and when the blade turned from red to white, she wrapped the handle in a kitchen towel and carried it over to Alec. He took it from her, and Emily turned away as Alec pressed the blade into the wound, which sizzled.

"Again," Alec said. "For the other side."

Emily took the knife from him, her stomach churning as she carried it to the stove again.

A short while later, Alec had cauterized the wounds, and the bleeding had stopped. Much to everyone's relief, Randall had not woken up.

"His heartbeat is stronger," Alec said.

"So what now?" Kara asked, turning away from the door.

"We need to get Randall into town," Alec said. "He needs to be seen by a doctor."

"And we need to find the children," Emily said.

"Can you two help me carry him out to the buggy?" Alec asked.

Emily and Kara nodded as they walked over to Randall. Alec took him by the shoulders while Emily and Kara each took one of his legs.

They were all panting by the time they got Randall's body out of the house.

"The buggy is gone," Alec said, frowning.

Emily turned to the spot where they'd left the buggy to see that Alec was right. "Do you think Jesse Ringo and his men took it?" she asked.

"I don't know," Alec said, frowning.

"So now what?" Kara asked, dropping Randall's leg. "We can't carry him into town."

Just then, Emily heard wheels coming up the drive. She dropped Randall's other leg and rushed towards the sound to see the buggy emerging from the darkness. In the driver's seat was Jeremiah, and seated in the buggy behind him were the children. Alec, who was still holding Randall's shoulders, put him down on the ground.

"I don't believe it," Alec said, shaking his head in disbelief. "Jeremiah?"

Jeremiah brought the buggy to a stop, and the children began to climb down. His face was bruised, and his nose was crooked, probably broken.

"Sarah! Ben!" Kara cried, rushing towards them. "Are you alright?"

She clutched them tightly, sobbing.

Emily turned to Thomas and Lily climbing down, and she and Alec grabbed them.

'Are you okay?' Emily asked, kneeling down.

Thomas and Lily nodded as Emily pulled them into a tight hug, and Alec wrapped his arms around them. After a few moments, Emily got up and turned to face Jeremiah.

"Thank you," she said, hugging him tightly. "Thank you."

Jeremiah hugged her back.

"Are you alright?" Alec asked, coming over to him and putting a hand on his shoulder.

Jeremiah nodded.

"How are you here?" Emily asked. "How did you find the children?"

Jeremiah opened his mouth to respond just as the sheriff appeared on horseback; however he was not alone. Behind him on the horse was none other than Mrs. Tattlewell.

"Well, this here's a real tumbleweed of a mess," she said as the sheriff helped her off the horse.

Mrs. Tattlewell's eyes fell on Randall who was lying on the ground, now conscious but in shock.

"I'd best get Caldwell into town," Sheriff Rourke sighed. "But once he's locked up, I'll be back to hear what happened."

"He needs to see a doctor," Alec said. "We tended to the bullet wound as best as we could but it'll need a professional."

Sheriff Rourke walked over to Randall and knelt down. He peered at the wound on his chest and shrugged. "He looks alright to me."

Alec helped the sheriff get Randall onto the back of his horse, his hands cuffed behind him and everyone stood and watched as they rode down the road, disappearing into the darkness.

"You all look like you could use a strong cup of tea," Mrs. Tattlewell said.

Emily caught Alec's eye and smiled as he wrapped an arm around her shoulders. Together, each holding one of the children's hands, they turned and headed back into the house.

Chapter Thirty-Four

A short while later, they were all seated around the kitchen table. Mrs. Tattlewell had put on the kettle before quickly mopping up the blood on the floor. She'd made a strong pot of tea, which she brought through before bustling back to the dresser to fetch some mugs. Mrs. Tattlewell was unflappable. Alec had always suspected as much, but now, she really proved it to be true.

"So tell us everything, Jeremiah," Alec said. "How did you get away?"

Jeremiah put his mug down as he looked around the table.

"Well," he said, clearing his throat. "I have Mrs. Jones to thank for that."

Kara looked at him in surprise.

"When her gun fired and the horse reared up, a knife slipped out of the saddle bag and landed at my feet," Jeremiah explained. "I waited until no one was watching, then picked it up and cut through the ropes. As soon as I was free, I ran over to Mr. Jones," Jeremiah continued, turning his gaze towards Kara.

"Is my husband alright? Kara asked expectantly.

"Yes ma'am, he sure is. The bullet only hit him in the arm. He's one lucky son of a gun. I got him onto the buggy and high-tailed through to town."

"And how did you find the children?" Emily asked.

"They were on the back road," Jeremiah said. "Heading into town."

"We were going to fetch the sheriff," Thomas said.

"You were?" Alec asked in surprise.

Lily nodded. "We didn't want the bad man to get you," she said.

"We all rode into town," Jeremiah explained. "We went straight to the hospital and once Mr. Jones was in good hands, we headed to the sheriff's office."

"And Mrs. Tattlewell?" Alec asked. "Where do you fit into all this?"

"Well, I was leaving the town committee meeting at the church when I saw Jeremiah and all the children filing into the sheriff's office," Mrs. Tattlewell explained. "I thought my eyes were playing tricks on me."

Alec looked at Emily and smiled. They were all safe. Mark was recovering in the hospital and Jeremiah was alive. Despite the odds, everyone was okay, and Alec did not have the words to describe his relief in that moment.

"I think it's time to get the children into bed," Emily said.

"But we're not tired yet," Thomas argued.

"Your aunt is right," Alec said. "It's been an eventful night, and you could all use some shuteye."

"But I won't be able to sleep without Coby outside the bedroom door," Lily said, her bottom lip trembling.

"Don't worry about him," Alec assured her. "He'll find his way home soon enough."

"Is it alright if Sarah and Ben stay over?" Kara said. "I'd like to go and see Mark."

"Of course," Emily agreed.

"We want to come and see father, too" Sarah said.

"First thing in the morning," Kara replied. "Right now, you both need to get some sleep."

"Come on," Mrs. Tattlewell said. "Bedtime."

The children reluctantly got up from their seats as Mrs. Tattlewell shepherded them out of the kitchen and upstairs.

"You should rest too, Jeremiah," Alec said. "And I am sure your sister wants you home. Let me drop you, and then I'll take Kara to see Mark."

"Are you sure?" Kara asked. "The sheriff said he was going to come back."

Alec turned to Emily.

"It's fine," Emily said. "If the sheriff comes back while you all are gone, I will tell him where you are."

Alec leaned over and kissed her on the cheek. "I won't be long," he promised.

As the buggy bumped down the dark road, Alec told Jeremiah what had happened in the kitchen with Jesse Ringo and Randall.

"I heard Ringo's men grumbling about Mr. Caldwell," Jeremiah said. "They didn't respect him. They thought he should be getting his own hands dirty, taking risks, and they certainly didn't like taking orders from him."

Alec nodded. He'd seen how disgruntled the men were and suspected that was why Jesse shot Randall. He would have wanted to prove that they were more than just hired hands, that his men were more important to him than the money Randall was offering. At the end of the day, no matter how important Jesse Ringo thought he was, he was worth nothing without his men.

"Do you think he will try something again?" Kara asked. "When he finds out that Caldwell's not dead?"

"I don't know," Alec said. "But I doubt it. I think he proved his point. He cut ties with Randall and that appeased his men."

Kara looked slightly disappointed. As Alec steered the horse toward Jeremiah's house, the lights in the window were still burning bright.

"Take a few days' rest," Alec said as Jeremiah climbed from the buggy.

"Are you going to take a few days off, Mr. Kincaid?" Jeremiah asked.

Alec hesitated.

"I'll see you in the morning," Jeremiah said with a smile.

He turned and headed into the house, and as Alec watched him go, his heart swelled with pride. Jeremiah was not only a resilient young man but also kind and resourceful. He was the kind of man who would have your back no matter what, and Alec respected him for it.

They set off back out of town, and not long afterward, they arrived at the hospital and found Mark lying comfortably in a bed.

"Oh, Mark," Kara cried as she hurried over to him and took his hand. 'Are you alright?"

"I've been better," Mark replied.

Kara half laughed, and half sobbed as she pressed her forehead against his chest. "I thought I'd lost you," she whispered.

"You ain't getting rid of me that easily," Mark teased.

Alec was standing by the door as a doctor approached. His name was Max Locke.

"How is he?" Alec asked.

"Lucky," the doctor said. "The break in his leg was worse, but, I managed to set it, although he is likely to have a limp."

Alec nodded. "Well, we're very grateful," he said.

"He's a tough cookie, that one," Dr Locke said. "I think he'll make one hell of a cowboy."

"He will," Alec agreed. "Although I am not sure there will be much of a ranch for him to go back to."

"I heard," the doctor said. "But things can be rebuilt."

"That is true," Alec agreed.

Alec turned suddenly as he heard Kara's footsteps behind him.

"Would you like to stay the night?' Dr Locke enquired. "We can set up a chair for you."

"I would," Kara replied. "Thank you."

"I'll be back in the morning," Alec said. "To see how Mark is getting on."

A short while later, Alec turned into the ranch gates and as he did, he spotted something running up the drive toward the house.

"Colby?" he said.

He brought the buggy to a halt and jumped down.

"Cobalt!" he called. "Here, boy!"

The dog, wet and dirty, stopped and turned around. He looked at Alec for a moment before running down the road towards him. Alec crouched down as the dog raced into his arms, licking his face.

"I knew you'd find your way back," Alec said.

He picked him up and put him on the buggy seat, climbing back up beside him. Minutes later, they stepped into the kitchen and found Emily and Mrs. Tattlewell seated at the table with Sheriff Rourke.

"Look who I found coming up the drive," Alec announced.

Cobalt ran straight to Emily, jumping up into her lap and she laughed, scratching him behind the ears.

"Well, that's a relief," Mrs. Tattlewell said.

Cobalt walked across to her and she patted his head, the only sign of his tussle a small graze on his right cheek. Then with another wag of the tail he turned, leaving the kitchen He was going upstairs to sleep on the mat outside the children's bedroom door.

"How's Mark?" Emily asked.

"Dr Locke did a good job," Alec said.

"Where is Kara?" Mrs. Tattlewell said.

"She's staying overnight at the hospital," Alec replied.

Mrs. Tattlewell nodded.

"Well, thank you for your time," Sheriff Rourke said, getting up. "I'd best be getting back to town."

Sheriff Rourke tipped his hat before he walked across the kitchen to the back door where Alec was standing.

"Alec," he said, nodding his head.

"I'll walk you out, sheriff."

As they strolled back to the barn where Sheriff Rourke had left his horse, neither of the men spoke.

"Sheriff," Alec said as they reached their destination. "I need your word you are not going to let Caldwell get away."

"From what Mrs. Kincaid tells me, Randall never directly killed anyone," Sheriff Rourke said.

"Not directly," Alec agreed. "But surely paying for the bullets is as bad as firing them?"

Sheriff Rourke sighed, shaking his head. "It's a mess, Alec," he said, his voice tired. "Caldwell employs more than half of the men in this town, and he's invested in both the general and the farm supply stores, not to mention the revenue generated from his property taxes."

"I know Caldwell keeps this town going," Alec agreed. "I know this town would struggle without him."

"Struggle?" Sheriff Rourke said. "It would go belly up."

"But don't you see, that's what Caldwell is relying on," Alec said. "He considers himself untouchable because he has this town and you in his pocket."

Sheriff Rourke gritted his teeth.

"I am sorry," Alec apologized. "But it's true. Randall said as much himself, but he's hurt people, sheriff. He's destroyed lives."

Sheriff Rourke sighed again. "I know," he said.

"We can survive without him," Alec said. "We can keep this town going. We'll all pull together and think of something."

Sheriff Rourke looked doubtful, but he nodded. "Alright, Kincaid," he said. "We'll do it your way."

"It's the right thing to do," Alec assured him.

Sheriff Rourke nodded, but he still looked unconvinced. It was no easy thing when the biggest employer and investor in your town was also a criminal.

Sheriff Rourke slipped his boot into the stirrup and pulled himself up into the saddle. He tipped his hat to Alec as he clicked his tongue and set off back to town. Alec watched him go before turning towards the house.

"How did it go?" Emily asked.

Alec sighed. "He said he won't let him go," he said. "But locking up Caldwell might cost us this town."

Emily walked across to him and slipped her arms around his waist.

"How do you feel about that?" she asked. "After all, this is your home."

Alec sighed. "This is our home," he agreed. "And Randall shouldn't be able to hold it to ransom."

Emily nodded. "So what happens now?" she asked.

Alec exhaled slowly as he rested his chin on the top of her head.

"We rebuild," he said.

Epilogue

Forest Hill, Texas, 1903

Five years had passed since the night of the late summer storm, as it came to be known. Since then, Forest Hill had fallen on the hardest times the town had ever known. After Randall Caldwell's arrest and trial, he was sent to Huntsville to the Texas State Penitentiary, and all of his property and assets were forfeited to the state.

The men who'd worked for him lost their jobs, and the stores in town suffered great losses. What Sheriff Rourke predicted would happen if Randall Caldwell was sent to prison did. Yet, the town did not disappear. In fact, several things happened that changed the face of Forest Hill.

The first was that the railroad was rebuilt. This was due to a wealth of minerals discovered some fifteen miles North of Forest Hill, which brought many new settlers from all across America. Many came with families and chose to settle down in Forest Hill as it brought them the peace and quiet of a small town while still allowing them to commute to their jobs in the mines.

The men who'd lost their jobs when Randall was sentenced worked at the mine, and the town began to recover, grow, and thrive.

Mrs. Kincaid picked up the heavy brass school bell and rang it loudly, calling the children in from their play. They all came into the brightly lit classroom, laughing and chatting.

"All right, children," Emily said. "Settle down, please."

It was a hot, sticky day in late July, and this would be the last day of school before they closed for the summer. The children shifted uncomfortably in their seats, and Emily knew they were counting down the minutes before they could go swimming down at the watering hole.

Emily turned to the large chalkboard behind her, and as she did, the children began giggling under their breath.

"Alright," Emily sighed, turning around to face the class. "I suppose the lessons can wait until the fall."

Cheers erupted around the classroom and Emily smiled.

"Be good this summer," she said. "And keep up on your reading."

"We will, Mrs. Kincaid," the class echoed.

"Alright, then class dismissed," Emily said.

There was the usual commotion as the children filed out, the girls with their heads together sharing secrets and the boys running ahead.

"Thomas? Lily? Sarah? Ben?" Emily called over the noise. "A word, please."

The children turned, dragging their feet.

"What is it?" Thomas sighed. "Alec said it was fine if I went to the watering hole with my friends."

He was thirteen now and the spitting image of his mother with his thick, blonde hair and hazel eyes. He was a tall boy, tanned from working at the ranch after school, and he was kind, but the years had not robbed him of his wild imagination.

"And I am not trying to stop you," Emily said. "I just wanted to tell you to keep an eye on your sister."

"I am not a child anymore," nine-year-old Lily argued, folding her arms.

"Of course, you aren't," Emily said. "You are practically a grown woman."

Lily pouted as Emily smiled at her. She was always telling Lily not to grow up too fast.

"Thomas?" she prompted.

"Of course, I'll keep an eye on Lil," Thomas said. "I always do."

That was true. Thomas and Lily were as close as they'd been the first time Emily had met them. Sometimes, Emily thought it was impossible for two to have shared such a traumatic experience and not to be irrevocably bonded by it.

"Sarah, Ben," Emily said, turning to them. "Does your mother know you are going to the watering hole?"

Sarah nodded. She was a sweet girl, gentle and quiet. "Yes, Mrs. Kincaid," she said. "And I'll keep an eye on Ben."

"I am only a year younger than you," Ben argued.

"Alright," Emily said. "Have fun."

The children turned and left the classroom, and Emily walked over to the window and watched them go. They'd stayed such close friends these past five years. Emily and Kara liked to joke that Thomas and Sarah would get married one day, and they'd all be related. Of course, Thomas and Sarah appeared disgusted by the idea, but then again stranger things had happened.

When the children had disappeared over the grassy knoll, Emily turned back to the classroom. She fetched a damp cloth and cleaned the board; then she straightened the benches and desks before fetching the broom and sweeping the floor. Once she'd finished sweeping, she sorted out her desk, putting her books and lunch pail to the side. Once that was done, she closed all the windows.

Emily stepped out of the school doors with her lunch pail in her hand and her books tucked into the crook of her other arm. She turned and closed the door, locking it behind her. Then she set off home. She'd only gone a few feet when Alec appeared over the hill where the children had disappeared. Even now, all these years later, the sight of him still made Emily swoon. While his dark hair was a little grayer and the creases a little deeper, he was still the most handsome man Emily had ever seen.

She caught Alec's eye, and he smiled at her. He had their four-year-old Beth by the hand and was carrying their two-year-old Jo in his other. As soon as Beth saw Emily, she broke into a run.

"Darling," Emily said, picking her up and hugging her tightly. "How are you?"

Beth said nothing as she squeezed Emily's face between her palms and giggled.

Emily laughed as she put Beth down and turned to Alec. Jo put out her plump arms, and Emily took her, kissing her on the brow.

"What are you doing here?" she asked.

"We came to walk you home," Alec replied.

"But how did you know I'd finish early?" Emily asked.

Alec smiled. "Because I know you," he said, leaning forward as he kissed her lips.

Emily smiled as he pulled away.

"Let me take those," Alec said, reaching for her books and lunch pail.

Emily handed them to him as she swung Jo onto her hip, and they set off back towards home.

"Where's Amy?" Emily asked.

"With Mrs. Tattlewell," Alec said. "She was sleeping so I didn't want to wake her."

"Good thinking," Emily said.

Out of their three daughters, one-year-old Amy was the fussiest sleeper. She woke up five or six times a night, so they had quickly learned that when Amy was asleep, to let her be.

"Another letter came," Alec said. "I stopped at the post office on the way to the school."

Emily nodded. For the past few months, Randall and Alec have been corresponding. It was undoubtedly the most unexpected outcome, considering everything that happened between them. Yet, Alec believed that Randall was trying to change. He regretted what he'd done and was full of remorse.

He'd found God and was searching for redemption. Most of his correspondence with Alec was about farming and ranch life. He had ample opportunity in prison to read and liked to write about the latest farming technology and advancements. In turn, Alec would write to him about the ranch and Forest Hill, what had changed, and what had stayed the same.

It was Alec's compassion that had allowed him to bring pen to paper, and she admired him for it. He could understand what it must be like for a man of the land to be locked up, unable to feel the dirt under his fingernails or the sun on his face.

By the time they got back to the ranch, the girls were complaining about being thirsty and so Emily sent them straight inside to Mrs. Tattlewell.

"Mark," Alec said, smiling. "What brings you here?"

Mark limped over to them, smiling. "I was hoping I could borrow Jeremiah for the afternoon? I need some advice about the cattle."

"Sure," Alec said. "I think he's in the stables."

"Much appreciated," Mark said. "And we'll see you for dinner?"

"Yes," Emily said. "I told Kara I would bring something for dessert."

Mark nodded as he set off towards the barn.

"I am quite looking forward to seeing the place again," Emily said. "It feels like ages since we've been to Riverbend."

"It has been quite a while," Alec agreed.

After the fire all those years ago, the house, barn, and stables were destroyed. There was no money to rebuild, so the Jones's moved back in with Mrs. Tattlewell. However, together, they'd managed to get the ranch back up and running, and over time, they'd begun to rebuild.

First the stables, then the barn, and finally the house. It had been a long and hard road, but the house was finally finished. Kara and Mark had wanted to surprise them and so they'd been banned from going to Riverbend until the grand reveal.

Emily and Alec headed into the house for lunch. Amy was awake now and sitting on Mrs. Tattlewell's lap.

"Hello," the older woman said brightly. "Beth and Jo are upstairs."

"I'll go and check on them," Alec said as he crossed the kitchen floor.

"Hello, darling," Emily said, walking over to the little girl.

She cooed happily as Mrs. Tattlewell handed her to Emily and got up.

"I'll get lunch on the table," she said, bustling over to the pantry.

"I worry we keep you too busy, Mrs. Tattlewell," Emily called after her. "What with the children and the cooking."

"Don't be silly," Mrs. Tattlewell said. "I've never been one for idle hands and have no intention of starting now."

Emily smiled as she kissed the top of Amy's head, breathing in her sweet scent. The truth was that they would all be lost without Mrs. Tattlewell.

A short while later, they all sat down to lunch together. It was quiet without the older children around.

"I hope they are alright," Emily said.

"They're fine," Alec said. "But for your peace of mind, I'll swing by there after lunch and check on them."

Emily looked across at him and smiled gratefully.

So, after lunch, Alec went to the watering hole to check on the children, and Emily went to the nursery to put Beth and

Jo down for their afternoon naps. While Mrs. Tattlewell took Amy for a walk in her carriage.

Emily must have fallen asleep with the children, for when she woke, it was late afternoon. Beth and Jo were still sleeping, so she quietly crept out of the nursery and went downstairs. She found Mrs. Tattlewell on the front porch in a rocking chair, Amy playing with wooden blocks at her feet.

"Are Alec and the children home?" Emily asked.

"Not yet," Mrs. Tattlewell said.

Emily frowned. They should be back by now. However, before she had time to worry, they came walking up the driveaway. Alec, like the children, with wet hair.

"Where have you been?' Emily asked.

"Sorry," Alec said, grinning sheepishly. "I might have been convinced to take a swim."

"No one had to convince you," Thomas said.

Emily sighed, shaking her head. Sometimes Alec was just a big child.

"Well, we are going to be late for dinner," Emily said. 'So everyone go and get ready quickly, please."

Alec and the children disappeared inside with Emily on their heels.

A short while later, they arrived at Riverbend. Thomas and Emily had run ahead with the girls, so it was just Emily and Alec on the path. He had his arm wrapped around her shoulders as the house came into view. It was modest compared to the house that had stood there before, but it was charming; made of red stone with a corrugated iron roof painted a rust color to match. A single-story house with a wraparound porch.

"So?" Alec asked. "What do you think?"

"I think you were right," Emily said. "After everything that's happened, we rebuilt our lives, and although some things may be smaller and simpler, they are so much bigger in all the ways that count."

Alec leaned over and kissed her, and a moment later, Mark, Kara, and all the children emerged from the house.

"Come on, slow pokes," Mark called. "Dinner is getting cold."

"Oh, goodness," Emily cried suddenly. "I forgot to bring the dessert!"

"Don't worry, Emily," Kara called, reading her expression. 'My aunt sent the dessert over earlier with Jeremiah."

Emily smiled, shaking her head as she and Alec walked toward the house to join the others. As they did, Emily thought about how different this life was from the one she might have had in New York, and she'd never regretted a thing. Although Marie wasn't there anymore, parts of her still were; in her children, in Alec, and in her love for Forest Hill. She was all around.

Just as Emily was about to step up onto the porch, she caught sight of the first star in the sky, but she didn't need to make a wish because all her dreams had already come true.

THE END

Also by Sally M. Ross

Thank you for reading "**Finding Family in the Rugged Mountain Man's Embrace**"!

I hope you enjoyed it! If you did, here are some of my other books!

Also, if you liked this book, you can also check out **my full Amazon Book Catalogue at:**
https://go.sallymross.com/bc-authorpage

Thank you for allowing me to keep doing what I love! ❤

Printed in Great Britain
by Amazon

36423221R00215